THE PRINCESS MUZZI

THE TRIBULATIONS
OF A PRINCESS

With Portraits from Photographs

BY THE AUTHOR OF

"THE MARTYRDOM OF
AN EMPRESS"

1901
HARPER & BROTHERS PUBLISHERS
NEW YORK AND LONDON

TO

MY BOY

FROM

HIS FOND MOTHER

" Ce livre est toute ma jeunesse ;
   Je l'ai fait sans presque y songer ;
Il y paraît, je le confesse,
   Et j'aurais pu le corriger."

" Mais...........................
   Au passé pourquoi rien changer ?
Va-t'en, pauvre oiseau passager ;
   Que Dieu te mène à ton adresse !"

ILLUSTRATIONS

THE TRIBULATIONS OF A PRINCESS

CHAPTER I

"A much-discerning public hold,
    The singer generally sings
    Of personal and private things,
And prints and sells his past for gold.

"Whatever I may here disclaim,
    The very clever folk I sing to
    Will most indubitably cling to
Their pet delusion, just the same."

"I DON'T say but what you are not a good little gentleman when you've a mind to, but his lordship he is uncommon particular about this 'ere eagle, and, if you don't leave it alone, I'll carry you away before you can so much as say Davy Jones, my little lord."

Thus spoke Mr. Jinks, the English stud-groom and general factotum of my father, laying a gentle but firm hand on my velveteen-clad shoulder, and drawing me away from the stout wooden enclosure inside of which a gigantic male eagle circled round and round at the end of a long, slender chain of steel that was securely clasped about its horny left leg.

This eagle, which my father had winged on one of our frequent expeditions along the rugged, precipitous cliffs that formed part of the boundary of our old family estate, was a source of continual delight and admiration

A   I

to me. I had begged hard for its life when it dropped at our feet, with one of its enormous pinions broken by my father's unerring shot, and from that moment I felt that I had a very positive claim on this magnificent bird—the emblem to me of power, strength, and imperial beauty.

"Let me go, Jinks," I cried, excitedly, slipping from the man's grasp. "That bird is as good as mine. Why do you meddle? I only want to give it some raw meat which I got from the *chef* on purpose for him."

"All right; throw it to the brute, then, while I'm a-watchin' of you; but you please stay at a respectable distance, for that 'ere chap is dangerous, and would peck out your bonny eyes, or tear you to pieces with its ugly, big claws, as quick as it would look at you; and, what's more, my lord he says to me, says he, 'Look to it, Jinks, that the youngster he don't go too near to that bird'; and I answers, 'You can trust me, sir, he won't.' So you see, my little lord, I'm bound to obey horders, and so are you, for the matter of that! It's not many noblemen as is to be compared with your daddy; never grudgin' a servant his privileges, never wrongly out of temper, with always a kind word ready, and a free hand with the tips. Oh, he is a thoro'bred, every inch of him, he is! A real gentleman, and no mistake; not one of them blessed *parvenouse* as don't know one end of a 'orse from t'other, and who gives themselves hairs just the same; but a true-born haristocrat. And as for me, I'll be damned if I care what I do for him."

With which peroration Jinks took the now empty meat-basket from my hand and marched me through the shrubbery into the saddle-room, which was one of my favorite haunts.

This little incident took place a great many years

2

ago—more, indeed, than I care to count; and yet it is still as vivid in my mind as if it had occurred yesterday, doubtless because it did not end with this admonition from my father's faithful retainer, but indeed came pretty near to costing me my life.

Childlike, I took but scanty notice of Jinks's warning, and morning after morning I stole Indian fashion from bush to bush to visit my friend the eagle. I invariably spoke to it as I would have spoken to a human being, and as if it were thoroughly able to comprehend my every word. I fed it with choice morsels coaxed from the *chef*, who was the arch-enemy of Mr. Jinks, and who was delighted to aid and abet me in my disregard of that worthy's injunctions. Indeed, so great was my affection for the superb bird that I gave him the grandiloquent name of "*Fulvius*," probably because my tutor, an erudite and distinguished priest, told me that it was a remarkable specimen of the *Aquila Fulva*. Bolder and bolder did I become, till at last I decided to waive all precaution and to climb into the eagle's sanded domain, in order to meet it, as it were, on an equal footing. Wasted chivalry, indeed!

So eager was I to put this brilliant plan into execution, and to avoid discovery, that I selected for my escapade the moment when I knew that my father was changing his riding-dress for a shooting-coat, and Jinks superintending the rubbing-down of the horse and pony from which we had just dismounted. Carefully and secretly I approached my goal, and, after propitiating "*Fulvius*" with a bit of raw steak—which, I am sorry to confess, had been brought thither in the pocket of my knickerbockers—I vaulted over the railing and walked fearlessly towards the great bird.

To my amazement the eagle dropped his prize and hurled himself at me with ruffled plumes, snapping

3

beak, and clutching talons, while his yellow eyes turned a fierce red. An unconscious instinct of self-preservation made me cover my face with my arms and drop flat upon the ground; but as I did so it flashed through my little, active mind that I was done for, and that it served me jolly well right, too!

The report of a gun, followed by a soft, choking weight of warm flesh and feathers that covered me from head to foot, was the last I knew. When I awoke from what must have been a swoon, I lay trembling on my father's breast; and looking up into his blanched face with a sense of confusion that made my head dizzy, I murmured, feebly:

"What is it?"

There was no reply, except a tightening of the strong arms that held me. Then the whole scene came back to me with a shock, and the consequences of my disobedience brought such a feeling of shame that I burst into tears, and, clinging to my father's neck, sobbed piteously:

"Oh, pardon me, papa! I did not mean to pain you so much! Please, please pardon me!"

"Hush! Don't cry, Pierrot! You must not be a baby. It is not like you to give way so. Let us forget all about it. You are sufficiently punished now, and we can let the matter drop."

It was just like my father—this little speech—just like his usual kindness and generosity, for now, as always, he tried to spare my budding pride, and therefore I felt better at once. When he put me on my feet again, my luckless encounter with " *Fulvius* " seemed to drift away like a bad dream, but yet my whole mind was filled with remorse at the thought that I had caused the death of my beautiful eagle.

No words can describe my admiration and gratitude

4

when I learned that my really miraculous rescue was due to my father. It appeared that from his dressing-room window he had seen me climb over the forbidden rails, and, seizing a gun from a table near by, he had shot the bird in the very nick of time. The range was so long, the aim so accurate, that this feat of arms became proverbial throughout the country. My young imagination was ablaze with a sort of adoring respect, and more than ever now I compared this dear father of mine to the heroes of chivalry whom I was ever so eager to read or to hear about.

I do not think that there ever was a closer relationship between a man and a little child than that which existed between my father and me. Our affection was an uncommon one, for I became his constant companion as soon as I could walk. At three years of age I was put on a pony. At five I thought nothing of following the hounds, or of tramping for hours together through the salt-marshes which line the Brittany coast, trying my skill, with a diminutive rifle, on sea-fowls, or on the rock-rabbits and hare that dwelt in the gorse and heather.

My little cot nestled close to my father's huge baldaquined bed, for, though my own room opened into his, I begged so hard not to be forced to sleep there that I gained my point, and morning after morning my first glance was for him, my first idea to plan out the day's excursions and rambles with him.

From where I lay I could look through *portières* into my little sanctum, which had been furnished by his orders in imitation of a Brittany peasant's room.

The bed, shaped like a cupboard, was of heavy, carved, pear-tree wood, with the heads of cherubs and of chubby smiling angels shining forth from the dark, primitive, sculptured panels. The draw-curtains attached thereto were of white serge lined with crimson cloth, and, like the coverlet, were embroidered in multicolored silks and golden threads, as the fête-clothes of the *paludier*— the workers of our salt-marshes—are to this day. At the head of this curious couch stood a little, ponderously carved praying-stool surmounted by a wooden image of the Blessed Virgin, whose outstretched arms always seemed to offer comfort to my strange and impulsive little soul. The walls were wainscoted, and the draperies of the windows and doors were of white embroidered serge, while my toys, books, and other most treasured possessions were enclosed in tall *bahuts*— those capacious presses, which are the pride of all Breton housekeepers.

It was a severe style of decoration for a child's apartment, yet it did not seem so to me, because I was brought up in a somewhat Spartan way, without any mollycoddling—to use a familiar expression—and because the severity of the apartment was relieved by the most superb view which I have ever seen in my life, framed by two deeply niched windows. The tossing mass of great Atlantic rollers, encircled on each side by high cliffs of bluish granite, against which they broke in prismatic spray, were a never-ending source of delight to me.

The dear old ancestral castle, all ivy-grown, with its turrets and battlements, stands up grimly, like the ever-vigilant sentinel of these wild regions, for it is wholly unhurt by six hundred years of storms and tempests, and is still firm at its post on the very edge of the precipice. Its balconies, sculptured by the hands of dead-and-gone artists, overhang one hundred and eighty feet of sheer rock, that form a natural buttress for the waves and shelter the pebbly beach, where at low tide I delighted to fish for crabs, prawns, and all the other mar-

6

vellous beasts and shells left behind by the retreating water in deep translucent pools.

My only trials in those happy days were my school-room hours, though they were made as pleasant as possible by my tutor, who was the kindest and most saintly of priests. He acted as chaplain, too, and every morning at six o'clock said mass in the private chapel of the castle, with that impressive simplicity which rises from a pure and faithful heart. How often have I in later life regretted my attempts at shirking his gentle teachings in those school-hours! But I was ever a sad truant, and often appealed to my father for freedom, especially during the hunting season.

"William of the Long Sword could not write or read, papa, and in those splendid days knights and nobles never learned anything," I said to him once, wistfully.

"You little scamp," he replied, laughing, "is this what you use your so arduously obtained knowledge for, to quote history with embarrassing *àpropos*. Now let me tell you, my boy, that King Ethelstane of England, who lived at the same period as did this precious William of yours, insisted upon all his nobles being taught to read and write, and Foulques le Bon once wrote to the then King of France, "*Apprenez, Monseigneur, qu'un Roy sans lettres est un Ane couronne!*"

With true Breton stubbornness I made up my mind, nevertheless, not to heed the wise remarks of Foulques le Bon, and I gave no credit to a king who, like Ethelstane of England, tortured his brave nobles with learning. But to please my father—and for that reason only—I did try to be more attentive and to behave myself in a way befitting a knightly youth, when Monsieur l'Abbé took up his daily duties as my instructor and mentor.

Jinks thought exactly as I did on the subject of science, and many were the long discussions we had in the sanctity of the saddle-room concerning this sore trial.

"You're a lad o' wax, my little lord," the stud-groom would say. "Strike me a loser if you ain't in the right to hate these 'ere lessons. Why they should all be a-tryin' to bother your sleek little 'ead with grammar and all that sort of stuff, when what you need to know is only 'ow to sit your 'orse straight and 'andle your gun proper in the open or under cover is what beats me. Why, bless you, my lovely, there's no need of learnin' for the like of you, for there's a deal in blood, and you've got that, and no mistake. Heducation is bosh for them as is not school-teachers, and in my mind is more 'armful than henviable."

Such was Mr. Jinks's philosophy, and I might as well confess at once that it met with my unalloyed approval. Jinks was, in my opinion, the very pink of perfection, for he was a splendid fellow on horseback and a great four-in-hand whip. And then he was so very amusing when, as we sat together in the saddle-room, he would blow the froth off his pewter and tell me long yarns about the fine times he had when he was a boy and rode race-horses on the Downs for his master, a celebrated horse-breeder

I have not as yet spoken of my mother, which may seem strange, but the fact is that this beautiful woman, of a graceful, dark, Spanish type of loveliness—although she is by birth a Russian—was to me throughout my childhood a remote Deity, unapproachable on the familiar, tender, and affectionate plane upon which my father stood. I admired her deeply à *distance*, and used to be very proud when I heard complimentary remarks made about the perfection of her tea-rose skin, her flashing black eyes, and her long, raven hair, and I can well remember often amusing myself by lying down on the carpet of her dressing-room and watching her slender curved feet, which, when unshod, I used to think formed natural arches, like little bridges.

Talented, witty, with that sharp, caustic, merciless wit which often cuts like the lash of a whip, she was singularly entertaining and clever, and yet somehow I never felt easy when I was with her, and I avoided her as much as possible. She awed me sometimes; but, strange to say, she excited me to revolt against any authority save my father's.

Her Muscovite imperiousness, her slow, mocking smile, and her extraordinary severity repelled me; and I would as soon have thought of confiding my little troubles and joys to a marble statue than to this *élégante*, whom I had once overheard saying that I was a distressingly homely child, and by no means a credit to two families as famous for their good looks and splendid figures as her own and my father's are.

I was a mere baby then, barely five years old, I take it, but her words remained indelibly impressed on my brain, and I felt humiliated and terribly hurt. Was I a monster? Perhaps I was. I knew that I was very small for my age, very pale, and with big, changeful, gray eyes that seemed to eat up half of my tiny face.

When I heard this unfortunate sentence I was crouching behind a curtain in the central hall, playing with a bull-pup, one of my dearest possessions, and with a child's innate tact I kept perfectly quiet until my mother had drawn her trailing silks and laces up the staircase on her way to dress for dinner. Then, with a beating heart, I bounded across the floor and planted myself in front of a huge mirror that filled in an entire panel of the otherwise tapestried walls. Ruthlessly pushing aside the fronds of some tall ferns and palms which decorated the base of the mirror, I stood on tiptoe and

9

surveyed my reflection with the curiosity one feels when meeting an absolute stranger.

The fires of the great twin hearths at either end of the large apartment were leaping into bright rosy flames, and created a dancing, fitful but vivid glow that showed me my small self plainer than daylight could have done.

It chanced so that on that particular occasion I wore a white serge sailor suit, the wide, drooping collar of which was relieved by a deep band of sky-blue silk with little silver anchors. I could not, for the life of me, discover the motive or the reason that had caused my mother to speak so, for in my own humble inner consciousness I thought that I looked every inch a bright and active little sailor-boy, and a very well-dressed one at that.

What thoughts may have raced through my unformed brain I do not remember. Probably resentment against my mother had the upper hand, but soon my natural *insouciance* regained the mastery, and, shrugging my shoulders—a detestable habit, which drove my decorous maternal relative to desperation— I ran headlong up-stairs to my own room, whistling loudly as I went. There I consoled myself by thinking that a man, when all is told, is in no real need of physical beauty, and that by-and-by I would grow up to be as tall as my father, who was a regular giant, even if I could not hope to be as handsome as he, and then also, to tell the plain and unvarnished truth, I knew that he loved me just as I was, which was quite sufficient a reason to make me scorn anybody else's prejudices.

I was very strong, in spite of my delicate slenderness —"just as strong as a box-plant," papa would say; and then he would add: "You weary your mother with your restlessness. Come out on the moor with me, where exercise will quiet you down, if such a thing be possible!"

During the shooting season my indefatigable little legs would plough through the furze and broom and heather of the *landes* in a continuous effort to keep up with my father's big strides, and all the year round I was out-of-doors, wandering on the pebbly beach, on the heath, or about the gardens, shouting with glee when a plover or a gull rose screeching above the salt-marshes, yelling myself hoarse with delight when the tumultuous waves came thundering upon that portion of the shore which is honeycombed with deep, sonorous, mysterious caves ceaselessly echoing the voice of the ocean.

At other times I was content to lie on the top of the cliffs, looking down upon the salt-marshes stretched out in the sunlight below me, like great square panes of glass that reflected the dark or rose-hued clouds above. The conical heaps of salt, ready to be carted away, looked to my vivid imagination like the tents of a cavalry camp. And again and again I inhaled rapturously the breezes that having brushed over all that brine smelled of crushed violets and filled my lungs with health and vigor.

This happy existence lasted until I was eight years old, varied only by autumnal house-parties, which were limited usually to three series of guests. I detested these times, simply because my father would be with me less then. The state apartments were opened; the great dining-hall was used in preference to the octagonal room that overlooked the bay. My father and mother usually dined together in this cosey room, when we were alone. When the above-mentioned guests were present, I was brought in every evening at dessert, clad in a white velvet suit, with broad lace collar and cuffs, silk socks, and little white patent-leather court-pumps. I felt intensely savage on such occasions, and could not help disliking all these people, who disturbed, no doubt unconsciously, the even tenor of my life for the time being.

"An ungainly and ungracious child," my mother frequently declared, with one of her chilling little smiles; and, truly, looking back upon those far-off times, I can easily realize how galling it must have been to her, sitting at the head of her superbly appointed table— the embodiment of feminine elegance, *chic*, and beauty —to watch my quaint, silent ways, the contempt with which I repulsed all blandishments. Eh! even my indifference to bonbons and sweets—coldly, not to say disdainfully, refused when her fair lady friends tried to coax me to accept that dainty bait.

All I wanted to do, and all I enjoyed doing, was to climb upon my father's knee and there sit within the curve of his encircling arm, absolutely passing judgment upon those exquisitely dressed, idle women, whom I could not bring myself to admire. Often when he carried me up to bed I would burst into a flood of passionate tears, cling desperately to him, and beg him to send away all those bad, cruel people, who kept him from me. It seems to me as if I could still hear him saying, soothingly:

"But, my little one, what makes you feel so unhappy? Surely you know that I love you better than all the world put together, you foolish little kitten!"

"Then send them away, dear, dear papa. I want you all alone to myself, and I hate, hate, hate them!"

Sometimes he tried severity. At least, I presume he fancied that I would mistake for serious displeasure his assumed frown and his terrible threat of "going down-stairs" and leaving me all alone if I did not instantly stop so disgraceful and unseemly an outburst. But I was at no pains to see through all that; and it was only when he, as a last resort, ended by saying: "*Vous me faites de la peine, mon petit enfant*," that the hardness at my heart would melt like snow and that I would humbly beg him to pardon me, promising to behave better on the morrow. Unfortunately my love for him was so strong that, like all other intense loves, it bred bitter jealousy, and my promises were only kept as long as his hand held mine, and I was in his immediate presence.

A little before my eighth birthday I noticed that my mother, who was usually as strong as a steel blade in a velvet scabbard, began to grow singularly delicate in health. Her beautiful Irish mare, "Lady Jane," was no longer saddled for her use, but had to be exercised by the grooms. Instead of taking part in the numerous dinners and *fêtes* given that spring in the neighboring châteaux—neighborhood is an elastic word in Brittany, where the distances are abnormally long— this beautiful mother of mine lay frequently on the lounge in her boudoir. Often she failed to join us in the castle chapel at early mass, and I noticed also that my father devoted much more of his time to her, redoubling his ever-chivalrous care, attending to her slightest comforts and loading her with costly gifts.

This seemed very unreasonable to me, for she had never been so fretful or so difficult to please, and I speechlessly wondered at his long-suffering patience, for I knew how quick-tempered he was and how intolerant of languor and peevishness. Nevertheless, this was perhaps the happiest period of my life, for I was more than ever before his companion. Moreover, it was at that time that he presented me with a larger pony than my old pet—almost a cob, indeed—who rejoiced in the high-sounding name of "Rob Roy."

How I did enjoy the swift gallops over hill and dale,

across grass and forest-land and the jumping of ditches and hedges in the teeth of the cold wintry wind that tossed my cap over my nose! At such moments I laughed heartily, for my father said that I looked like a little blind beggar. Delightful, too, were the long rides home, when, tired out but thoroughly happy, I gazed up at the handsome face that looked down upon me so merrily from the dizzy heights of the big bay horse "Moonshine" or the glorious English mare "Ninette." Alas! the remembrance of those glorious days has been pregnant with bitter regrets through the long years that followed.

Far be it, however, from me to imitate Stendhal, and to make these reminiscences of my life a continuous and wearying anthem glorifying my own personality, as it were, like that eminently introspective man who thought his to be the central pivot of the universe. Alas, my personality is—now especially—too slender a one to be of general interest. But I cannot go on with my present task without, so to speak, making my unworthy self a little too prominent. And so, kind reader, have patience with me, and do not accuse me of egotism or vanity if I dwell at some length upon the days of my childhood; for they are the pedestal of the strange existence which has fallen to my lot, an existence wherein I have many times had reason to be thankful that I came from a race of reckless, merry soldiers and of high-handed seigneurs. For it is some heritancy of their courage and their energy which has helped me to carry life's heavier burdens at the sword's point, I might say. Inherited qualities are the only ones which one may be proud of. Like most sporting people, I am an implicit believer in hereditary influences, and I am glad to be able to bless mine instead of having to blush for them.

14

CHAPTER II

"Und es wallet und siedet, und brauset, und zischt
  Wie wenn Wasser mit Feuer sich mengt!
Bis zum Himmel spritzet der dampfende Gischt,
  Und Flut an Flut sich ohn' Ende drängt;
Und will sich nimmer erschöpfen und leeren
Als wollte das Meer noch ein Meer gebären."

NEW YEAR—or, as we call it, "Le Premier de l'An" —was always solemnized with much pomp at home. Such was my eagerness to reach this blissful day that, with childlike inconsequence, I slept uneasily for many nights before it dawned. I would lie for hours together, wide-eyed and restless, thinking of the great illuminated fir-tree which was always prepared for me on St. Sylvester's Eve, instead of at Christmas, as is done in England, Germany, Austria, and Russia, and would plot and plan about the gifts which it was my especial joy to shower upon all those about me.

I was always allowed to select these gifts myself, according to my own taste, and this was a pleasure to look forward to indeed. My dear old tutor, Monsieur l'Abbé, was my only companion on these shopping expeditions, and he frequently had cause to raise his eyebrows to the roots of his silvered hair, and to lift his dimpled, admirably kept hands in dismay towards an unkind Heaven, when my choice fell upon a more than ordinarily incongruous object.

The unfortunate Abbé's position as my *sage Mentor*, was no sinecure, for I was what is commonly called "a handful," and his ideas of the dignity with which

15

a young personage of my rank and race should comport himself were continually upset by my erratic behavior.

How clearly I remember that last happy New Year's Eve and the day preceding it! Clad in a costume of dark-green velvet and furs, copied with much freedom of invention from Cossack uniforms, I entered the brougham, where the delightful old Priest awaited me, in order to drive to the nearest town. It was twelve miles over a road that ran along the picturesque and capricious shores of the bay and then turned into a great wood of pines and cork-oaks—a lonely spot, where I looked about with delicious shivers of anticipation for a glimpse of some straying Kourrigan or Farfadet. Perhaps I half hoped to see the Fay Melusina herself, flitting about under the dense shadows cast by those evergreen trees. On that memorable day I remember that, in spite of my extremely poetical and romantic inclinations with regard to fairies and hobgoblins, I was holding my foot in my hand and singing, *mezzo voce*, a few choice bars of a song the sailors on my father's yacht *Ichtis* were wont to shout at the top of their leathern lungs:

> " C'est les trois Cancrelats
> Qu'on mis la patte au plat—
> Au plat du Capitaine—
> Dondaine—
> Au plat du Capitaine!"

"What on earth are you singing, Pierrot?" exclaimed Monsieur l'Abbé, in amazement. "That is hardly proper French for you, nor yet a proper sort of song, is it?"

Quite unabashed, I stopped singing, and, looking up into the kind blue eyes where I caught the suspicion of a smile, I said, quietly:

16

"Oh, that's a *chanson de Mathurin* (a fo'c's'le song), which sailors sing when they are very drunk."

"And may I inquire where you heard sailors singing when in that shocking condition?"

"Ah, well, sailors are always drunk when they are at sea," I replied, simply; and with renewed jubilation I intoned another song from my repertoire, which began:

> " U'n brise à faire plier l'pouce—
> Rigi, rigo, riguingo !
> Avec le cœur en gargousse—
> Rigi, rigo, riguingo !
> Oh, riguinguette !"

"That's very pretty indeed, and I am pleased to hear what exquisite melodies you learn. You apparently have more aptitude for them than you do for your lessons, and I will take care to mention this to your attendants and to prevent you from roaming about on the yacht."

"Oh, Monsieur l'Abbé, you wouldn't deprive me of my little amusements, would you?" I pleaded, with so much earnestness that the dear old man could not help laughing. "Why don't you show more clemency to me, like the chap in *Horace* which you make me study about. You know he says:

> "' . . . Je ferai justice;
> J'aime à la rendre à tous, à toute heure, en tout lieu !'"

"Why, Pierrot, you are becoming too pert, my child! It is not seemly that you—" But all further remonstrance was cut short by our entry into that quaint old Breton town which I have described elsewhere, and which is the most perfect little mediæval jewel of a city that one can imagine.

We soon reached the Place du Parvis, where the

ancient cathedral casts the checkered shade of its stone lace-work, blackened by season after season of exposure to wind and weather. All around the square the houses are turreted and gabled, and their high-pointed roofs of dark-blue slate, stained here and there with pale golden patches of lichen, are marvellously preserved. The dusky little shops on the ground-floor display in faded lettering over their narrow show-windows the names of the present owners, which for the matter of that are the same as those that stood there hundreds of years ago. One is conservative in Basse-Bretagne, and a son takes up his father's trade from generation to generation.

I pranced into the largest of these enticing empo-riums followed by the Abbé, and lost no time in doing my best to drive the unfortunate shop-keepers half crazy with my boundless demands upon their patience. Long I remained undecided, hesitating between antique Armorican jewels, relics, objects of piety, and more modern but less artistic tokens of nineteenth-century industry. Finally, I pounced upon a very gorgeous blue velvet pin-cushion adorned with sea-shells and provided with a mirror which had, alas, the curious propensity of distorting everything that it reflected, and in loud tones I declared that I would give it to my mother.

"But, Pierrot," whispered the Abbé, "please don't scream so, moreover, your lady mother would not for a moment dream of placing this extraordinary object upon any of her beautiful dressing-tables."

"Oh yes, she would; there's a mirror, you know— she does so like mirrors. And then, Monsieur l'Abbé, please remember that you are to let me buy just what I like. That's the bargain. I'm to be good, and so are you."

Against such rhetoric there was naturally no appeal, and Monsieur l'Abbé merely gave me a look which afforded me some food for reflection and bade the highly-amused clerk wrap up the ungainly pin-cushion and send it to the carriage.

"Have you chosen nothing for your father?" added Monsieur l'Abbé, considerately.

"Is it likely that I should ever forget papa?" I responded, hotly; and then, turning to the glass case where the antique jewels sparkled on a bed of faded white satin, I pointed to a delicately wrought Breton heart and crown of burnished gold, whereon the following sentence in Gaelic, "*Our hearts are one,*" was incrusted in small rubies.

This time Monsieur l'Abbé made no observation or comment, even when the very lofty price of the little jewel was mentioned, and I even fancied that his features perceptibly softened, and he certainly was exemplarily patient in listening during the long drive home to the "*Rigi, rigo, riguingo*" of my beloved sailor songs.

The New Year ceremonies in Brittany are very quaint and original. On St. Sylvester's Eve I went into ecstasies at the sight of my fir-tree, which was fifteen feet high. It glittered like some heavenly toy decorated by the angels with bits of sunlit clouds and streams of silver moon-rays, stars, planets, and constellations of all descriptions. It was hung also with Paradisaical fruits and flowers, and with presents which were really far too valuable to be placed in the hands of so young a child. The village lads stood outside in the Cour d'Honneur singing the habitual carol, which I give here just as it amused me to jot it down from memory on my blotting-pad a while ago!

19

To my huge delight I was permitted to stay up for the *réveillon*, a gorgeous supper of a very indigestible kind, which begins at eleven o'clock and lasts till one or two in the morning, with a view of starting the New Year on its way right merrily, glass in hand.

The Christmas *réveillon* and midnight mass were also occasions of the purest enjoyment to me, in spite of the fact that I felt very sleepy. For these nights were the only ones out of the three hundred and sixty-five when I was allowed to remain out of bed after eight o'clock.

I still always love to dwell in thought upon the customs which prevail along the shores of dear old Brittany! not so much where railroads have invaded the country and cast hosts of tourists upon the beaches, but in my own dear Basse-Bretagne, where the usages of bygone days have been preserved in all their purity and charming quaintness. Visitors are a rarity in the little villages, hamlets, and tiny fortified towns that surround my old home. Now and then an artist or so, perchance, happens upon the place during the heat of the summer months, but that is a very exceptional occasion, and even to them does the true life of the people remain absolutely unbeknown. This is rather a pity, for the ways of the Bas-Bretons are far from commonplace, *tant s'en faut;* and no doubt they would prove of considerable interest to those who like the piquancy of what diverges from the beaten track.

I, for instance, never can forget the queer, nay, the touching ceremonies, both religious and otherwise, which I witnessed so many a time on the stormy coast of the *Mer Sauvage*, that dusky, romantic promontory where my childhood was passed, and I often compare them very disfavorably with the senseless, fussy, expensive, and downright vulgar ways of celebrating popular *fêtes* in other parts of the world which I have since visited. When once one has crossed the boundary-line separating the last branch of the railroad from our true *Bretagne au coeur doré*, one must needs say good-bye to all modernism and finicky civilization, and one feels one's self suddenly transported into the far dimness of the Middle Ages.

Reading and writing are considered by our peasants as quite extraordinary accomplishments, enviable and awful in their mysterious grandeur, and almost unattainable for any save the *Curé, Monsieur le Maire,* and the *Seigneur* — an appellation still in use where the Lord of the Manor is concerned. The thatched-roofed houses of these strange peasantry are, as a rule, windowless, the door alone serving to admit light, through its upper pane of greenish thick glass. Their food is of the roughest, consisting of *soupe aux choux,* black bread, salt-pork, salt-fish, and sour milk. Yet these good people are happy, and they enjoy their rude, wholesome life far more than does many a Crœsus, gorged with millions and luxuries galore! The Breton's honesty of purpose, simplicity of mind, quiet courage, sturdy loyalty, and deep, unquestioning faith are to be met nowhere else in the world, and if they be sometimes a little superstitious, they should be forgiven, for their whole conduct indicates that they truly believe in the reward of their virtues and the punishment of their faults after death, which belief is in itself, one is bound to state, a grand and beautiful source of comfort and of consolation while here below.

Christmas in Brittany is a strictly religious feast. It includes the midnight mass, and after this even the humblest families enjoy a hearty supper, wonderfully cooked before the monumental hearth of granite, inside which are fastened benches reserved for *les vieux* (the old ones). But New Year is the time for pleasure —as I have already said—for dancing, for rejoicing, and also the occasion of rather weird doings. The Bretons are a rather mournful race. They have something

22

of the sadness of the ocean mixed with their nature. So, when I speak of their pleasures and rejoicings, I do not mean what most other nations would understand by these words. For even their dances in no way resemble the airy motions of the waltz, the polka, or the minuet. They are heavy and ponderous, and are carried out to the strains of a semi-barbaric music, consisting chiefly of the sounds made by *bignious* (bagpipes). The costumes of the peasants lend weight to the extraordinary deliberation of their motions. For the *tracht* has been preserved for hundreds of years in all its integrity; and what with the heavy woollen stuffs, thick bullion embroidery, and silk kerchiefs of the women, and the numerous vests and coats surmounting the wide, many-folded breeches of the men, the dancers have but little chance to disport themselves airily.

St. Sylvester's Eve! What an event these words bring back to mind!

On the night of this, the last of the three hundred and sixty-five days of weary travail and privation, many superstitions hold sway. Those I allude to are probably known only to such people as have been born and bred in the most secluded and untravelled portions of Brittany.

The old legends, which are still looked upon almost as *actes de foi*, are strangely pathetic and interesting. One in particular haunted my childhood with its glitter of gems and its possibilities of unlimited wealth. So dearly do I love a good yarn that I cannot resist the temptation of setting this one down here, as a sample of the pretty, mystical tales which rocked my early dreams.

My father's old nurse, who was then nearly seventy, and who looked, with her snowy *coiffe* and her dear wrinkled face, like the incarnate spirit of mediæval Armorica, used to tell it to me again and again at dusk, in a thrilling voice, pregnant with faith. She—poor old soul—believed it to be true in every detail, and so did I in those days.

"Ever so many years ago, when the angels had not as yet turned their faces quite away from the wickedness of the world, and when the land was not infested with as many devils as it is now, there lived in Finisterre a stalwart lad, handsome as daylight, who loved a lass, beautiful and true. But, alas! the girl's father was rich; for he owned four fields, an acre of salt-marshes, and a clump of cork-oaks, and of course he would not hear of giving his little daughter to a sailor-boy who earned but a mere pittance by risking his life day and night on the cruel sea in a cockle-shell of a fishing-boat. And so the lad and the maid were very unhappy and mourned their wretched lot when they met by stealth on the edge of the *landes*.

"It was Christmas Eve, and on his return from the midnight mass the lad, whose name was Marie-Pierre, went to the stable and threw himself wearily down on a bundle of straw in an empty stall. He found here a warm and comfortable spot where he could be alone with his sorrow, undisturbed by the noisy rejoicings of the *réveillon*.

"Fatigue, however, soon overpowered him, and he fell into a deep sleep.

"When he had slept a little while he was suddenly aroused by the sound of voices close beside him. The tones were strange, muffled, and unnatural, and filled him with a nameless terror, which he had never felt before, for he was no coward. For a few minutes he lay with closed eyes listening intently, and trying to find out who had spoken. Meanwhile he trembled sorely and searched mechanically for the rosary in his pocket, to preserve himself from malefices.

24

"An uncontrollable curiosity at last compelled him to raise his head cautiously and to look up. The barn was dimly lighted by a great horn lantern, but his sight was rendered so acute by fear that he could see almost as well as in broad daylight. Again and again he glanced into every nook and corner, but could discover no one in the stable. Only the cattle stood near by, knee-deep in thick litter, yet a voice came from a stall near by. The occupant of this stall was a very aged ox, kept on the place more in gratitude for his past services at the plough than with any idea of possible further use. Marie-Pierre peeped through a chink in the wooden partition separating him from the decrepit animal, and to his horror discovered that it was the old ox that was talking.

"For a few seconds he was paralyzed with amazement. Then like a flash the memory of an old legend, according to which animals are endowed with the power of speech on Christmas Eve, between midnight and daybreak, rushed through his mind, and, though a cold shudder shook him, he resolved to keep absolutely quiet, so as not to lose a particle of what was going on.

"When the ox had completed the sentence which had awakened Marie-Pierre, the thread of discourse was taken up by an equally antiquated donkey at the farther end of the stable.

"'Ah!' exclaimed the latter, 'how blind men are not to understand the true ways of nature! If they were, for instance, told that we are able, on Christmas Eve, to speak as well as they do themselves, they would only shrug their shoulders and laugh in scorn at so preposterous an idea.'

"'Men only care for us,' retorted the ox, sententiously, 'because we help them to earn money. Money is all they care for! Yes, yes! money alone, and—

25

aha! if they only knew it—I, old and feeble and despised as I am now, could tell the wisest of them where un-dreamed gold and riches are to be found in such abundance that—'

"'What on earth are you talking about, old friend?' interrupted the donkey. 'You must of a truth be get-ting on towards your dotage to tell such extravagant tales, or else the clover and Christmas oats have gone to your head.'

"'Laugh away,' exclaimed the ox, extremely nettled by the donkey's remarks. 'But, for all that, I can as-sure you that during the Vigil of St. Sylvester, once in every hundred years, at the stroke of midnight, the old Druidical stones of Plouhinec, a mile from here, leave the spot where they have stood during so many long and weary centuries and go down to the sea to drink their fill. Beneath the place which they leave vacant while thus doing are great pits filled to the brim with treasure, and I have been told long ago by my sire that the glitter of the stones which men call diamonds, the soft gleam of pearls, the fiery light of rubies, heaped up therein, make a halo around the spot equal to the brightest moonshine.'

"'Whew!' brayed the donkey, excitedly, 'that must forsooth be a grand sight! But how is this treasure to be reached?'

"'The treasure is unknown to humanity, for this secret has never been betrayed, and even if men knew about it they could not touch it, for the stones would rush back and crush the thieves like insects under their awful weight, unless the blood of a Christian be sacri-ficed to the spirits which animate these monuments of past and pagan ages.'

"As the ox pronounced these last words, a distant bell boomed forth the hour of daybreak. This was the end of the time allotted to the animals for speech, and with a deep-drawn sigh they relapsed into silence.

"More dead than alive, Marie-Pierre lay in a sort of trance, stunned by what he had heard. Could all this be true? Could it be within his reach to become one of the wealthiest men on earth, and thus to win the hand of his own true love? A cold, clammy perspiration gathered on his brow, and he shook in every limb at the mere thought of the great fortune which seemed almost within his grasp. Gradually, however, he grew more accustomed to the idea, and a firm resolve filled his heart, to make the attempt and to enrich himself by robbing the stones of some of their treasure, if human strength and courage were of any avail to accomplish so terrifying a deed.

"The light of dawn was stealing into the stable when he at last got up from the straw which had served him as a bed. All was still as he made his way to the door, but when he was about to open it he stopped transfixed with astonishment; for there, stretched before him, lay a human form. It was that of an old man, miserably clothed in rags, with long, unkempt locks of grizzly hair, falling in disorder about his emaciated face. Marie-Pierre drew nearer, and recognized him as an old beggar of evil repute, who was wont to wander about the country craving his daily bread from the peasants and fishermen. On the impulse of the moment he bent over him, caught him rudely by the shoulder, and called out:

"'What are you doing here, Kerrick, and who allowed you to enter a decent Christian barn?'

"The old man opened his glittering eyes, which shone strangely from his parchment-like countenance, like jewels in a charnel-house, and shaking the young man off, said, with an ugly grin:

27

"'Keep quiet, my lad. You and I had better be friends. There is much at stake if we can agree! Moreover, your master allowed me to take shelter in his stable last night, and I thank the spirits that he did so!'

"Marie-Pierre saw at once from these words that the aged wizard — for so he was generally held to be — had, like himself, heard the conversation of the animals, and he realized that he must submit to all that might be asked of him, even if it were necessary to share with Kerrick the treasures of Plouhinec. In this he was right. The old beggar proposed that they unite in the attempt, and after a heated discussion they finally decided to go together on the Vigil of St. Sylvester to the Bay of Plouhinec, and, if they really found the words of the ox to be true, to unite their efforts in taking away all the gold and precious stones they could carry.

" During the week which followed this eventful night, poor Marie-Pierre lived as one in a dream, and by the 31st of December he was almost sick with anxiety and feverish expectation. To while away the time— the weather being too stormy for him to go to sea— Marie-Pierre often visited the wild portion of the *landes* where stood the enormous granite memorials of paganism, from which he sanguinely hoped to gain limitless wealth. During this period of enforced idleness it came to pass that a sweet and pious thought entered his heart, so that he set to work with chisel and hammer, and carved a cross upon the gaunt side of the tallest stone, taking much trouble and great pains to perfect this symbol of Christianity, which his simple, faithful soul worshipped.

" At last the long and weary days came to an end, and by eleven o'clock on the Vigil of St. Sylvester he

and old Kerrick started for the treasure Bay of Plouhinec. The weather was very cold for Brittany, and
the waves were rolling heavily with a deep roar upon
the beach, eighty feet below them, as they walked along
the edge of the cliffs. All about them rose huge piles
of menhirs, dolmens, and cromlechs—the sacred Druidical stones of the time of the Gauls—looking ghostly
and weird and terrifying in the fitful rays of the moon,
that now and again glided behind banks of tempest-
laden, angry clouds. It was almost midnight when
the two trembling fortune-hunters reached the spot
where the gigantic bowlders known as the stones of
Plouhinec raise their rugged and hoary summits towards the blackness of the sky. Silently they crouched
behind a rock near a steep incline that led down to the
beach, and there they waited, gazing eagerly at the
apparently immovable masses of gray, storm-beaten
granite before them.

"The minutes seemed to drag like hours, but at last
the dim sound of a far-away church bell was wafted
towards the uneasy pair as it began to strike the midnight hour.

"One, two, three—a smothered cry escaped the parched lips of Marie-Pierre, for he could no longer doubt!
The stones were slowly oscillating on their bases.
They swayed to and fro, faster and faster, with a heavy,
sickening, swinging motion, till at the last stroke of
twelve they tore themselves from their heather-grown
sockets and rolled pell-mell down the incline on their
way to drink at the sea.

"For several minutes the old man and the lad remained spellbound, then they rushed towards the
places left vacant by the erratic stones of Plouhinec.

"Oh! what a sight met their eyes! In the cold
light of the moon shining brightly now, diamonds

sparkled amid heaps of gold bars and nuggets. Rubies, emeralds, and sapphires glittered and scintillated and twinkled like so many wicked eyes tempting them to enter the open flank of the earth.

"'Fill your pockets! Hurry! Hurry! Hurry!' roared Kerrick, scrambling into one of the yawning pits and filling with handful after handful of gems a capacious canvas bag which he had had the forethought to bring with him. Almost blindly Marie-Pierre obeyed these directions, groping for the precious stones and thrusting them into his pockets and the bosom of his shirt as quickly as his trembling hands would permit.

"Suddenly a fearful rumbling noise reached their ears.

"'The stones are coming back!' shrieked Kerrick, and as he spoke the great blocks hove in sight, rolling back towards them, up the steep incline, knocking against each other in their terrific haste to reach the post which they were to occupy for a century to come.

"'We are lost!' cried poor Marie-Pierre, despairingly, struggling to his feet.

"'You are—not I,' yelled the old beggar, throwing himself on him.

"At this frightful moment the wretched lad remembered the last words of the ox's revelation—namely, that the blood of a Christian could alone pacify the spirits which animated the stones. Kerrick, to save himself, was going to kill him, for there was the flash of a keen knife in his upraised hand.

"But Kerrick had reckoned without his host. He did not know that by Marie-Pierre's pious deed one of the stones had become a Christian monument, and just as the murderer was about to accomplish his foul purpose the foremost block of granite, on the gaunt side of which the Holy Cross had been carved, knocked the

30

beggar into eternity and placed itself like a sheltering guardian before Marie-Pierre, defending him from the onslaughts of its grim companions which tipsily took possession of their reconquered coign of vantage.

" A long and terrible shriek of agony rent the air, and then there reigned a silence profound like that of death.

"On the cliff near Plouhinec there stands a rugged line of gray and lichen-grown stones, which date as far back as the days of the Druidical cult — eh! and long before that time even, before the days when ϕnyòç was reverenced and when the Celtic people turned to their high-priests as if they were divine beings. On the largest and haughtiest of them all one may see to-day a rudely carved cross. The good people of that region call it *la croix miraculeuse de Marie-Pierre*, and the richest *maître-paludier* for many miles around, who owns great tracts of salt-marshes, fields, woods, and pastures, claims to be a lineal descendant of the young fisherman whose sudden and marvellous access to fortune brought him the desire of his heart—namely, the hand of the prettiest girl in Plouhinec."

Old Gaud—which is the Breton for Marguerite— always concluded her story by telling me: "Little do we know, little can we guess, all the strange things that once used to be."

And then, in her high, quavering voice, she would sing, to a dirge-like air:

> " Wisdom is wanted
> By him who travels widely;
> He who nothing knows
> And sits among the wise,
> Becomes a gazing-stock."

For she used to be full of old proverbs and ancient lays, and she considered that it was one of her most clearly defined duties to teach me the legends and lore of my country.

I owe it to her that, from earliest childhood, I have looked forward with a species of awed delight to the countless little practices which make up the bulk of a true Breton New Year—and for the celebration of which the four-leaved clover, the mistletoe, "the four herbs of St. John," and those transparent sea-shells called "angels' wings," are indispensable.

Many years later, not so very long ago, in fact, I risked life and limb to bow to one of these particular little superstitions which appealed especially to me, for it deals with flowers, which I have always loved dearly.

I was then spending a few weeks of the winter in Brittany, at an old castle belonging to friends of mine. And having been reminded by a casual mention of the *fleurs de la Sainte Vierge* that such a thing existed, I made up my mind to go in quest of the legendary blossom in the most orthodox and approved fashion—that is to say, on the first night of the full moon in the last month of the year. Telling no one of my project, excepting the men on my yacht, I started, after a late dinner, on my long sail towards the precipitous shores of the island of Houat, which faces the wild bay of Quiberon.

The moon was shedding its brilliant light upon the waves, and the capes of Quiberon and Thuys showed on either side of us almost as plainly as had it been broad daylight. Directly ahead of us Houat formed a dark bank of filmy smoke-hued buttresses on the horizon. As the wind was in our favor, it took us a comparatively short time to reach the base of the cliffs, and then, accompanied by two of my sailors, I went ashore with less difficulty than I had expected. When we reached the summit of the island, it seemed to me as if I were standing at the masthead of a ship, for the place is curiously small and the sea looks boundless indeed from so great and narrow an elevation. I did not stop to admire the fantastically shaped, silvered rocks that stretched at my feet, nor the waters swaying all around me, however, but began my search immediately. I had but scant success at first. Vexed and discouraged, I turned to the older of my two companions and asked whether he knew where the flower which I desired so greatly could possibly be found. Respectfully pulling his forelock, he replied, grimly:

"I know the haunts of the plant, but much has to be risked in order to get it." Then, bending down, he lay flat upon his stomach on the very edge of the cliff, I imitating his example with as good a grace as I could. I must confess that a slight shiver of something very much like awe, if not downright fear, ran through me as I looked down sixty yards beneath me into the funnel-shaped end of the cup-like crevice denting the island from top to bottom. The sea rushed into this with every coming wave, so violently that we could actually feel the rocky walls trembling. Now and then a column of seething, ferocious-looking green water rose into the air, and the freshness and bitterness of the spray beat upon our faces. The noise was deafening, and the spectacle under such circumstances was one that might well inspire terror even in the breast of one born in Brittany.

The rocky sides of this peculiar kind of *souffleur* were worn by the storms of centuries into a series of irregular and jagged steps. On one of these, some fifty feet beneath us, I saw, by the now wellnigh perpendicular rays shed by Dame Luna, a patch of what looked like flakes of carded wool. But the old sailor, tugging

C　　　　　33

at my sleeve, shrieked into my ear that this patch was composed of plant after plant of the famous and luck-bringing blossoms I had come so far to fetch.

"Will you come down with me, Yann?" I cried, in almost as loud a voice as his own, in order to make myself heard above all that raging turmoil. He nodded his assent, though the proposition did not seem to enchant him. As soon as we rose to our feet the wind pushed and worried us so that, had I not been brought up amid the dangerous cliffs of Brittany, and besides by that time a pretty fair all-round mountaineer, I would have given up any idea of attempting to follow Yann along such a perilous path. Even then it was only with the utmost difficulty that I managed to crawl down at a snail's pace, realizing the continual and imminent risk that at any moment I might be precipitated headlong into the frothing water below.

Upon arriving at last on the ledge where the flowerets grew, we were both more dead than alive. I snatched a handful of the peculiar growth—leaves, buds, flowers, and all—and then turned to reascend the precipitous cliff. How we ever succeeded in reaching the top I do not know, but whenever I look upon those faded blossoms hanging in a little silver frame above my bed, I cannot help thinking that, after all, they must have been endowed with great luck-bringing powers. For how else could we have overcome the dangers of the expedition which my reckless fancy made me undertake that night?

But here let me pause a minute to regain my mental breath, which this flight into the depths of the past has hastened and shaken almost as completely out of me as did the violent breezes of the Isle of Houat on the night of my risky expedition to its dangerous cliffs. It is an exquisite torture to thus retrace one's steps, to let one's pen and one's mind run smoothly backward, as it were, like a little frightened, green-coated crab, blinded by the incoming tide, and seeking rest and shelter from the noise and danger which it hopes to avoid. For years I have tried to forget—to wrap my home-sickened soul in oblivion of what once used to be, yet do I now, with the celebrated inconsequence of *l'Eternel Féminin*, ruthlessly reopen old wounds and court burning regret.

"What fools we mortals be!" This is not a very poetical citation, but it is a true one, and serves my purpose well, for I am in that mood just now which makes one look at one's self, so to speak, from a distance, and laugh with absolute sincerity, but nevertheless very bitterly, at one's own folly for having dared to attempt fighting against what was ordained. The Turks are our masters in such matters, as are all Orientals, for they are such delightfully convinced fatalists that when they have solemnly shrugged their shoulders, and sagely decreed that "What is to be will be," they are content, and take no thought of the morrow in any sense of the word.

I am far, I see, from having reached such a state of perfection as yet, and my disappointment thereat is great. I have schooled myself to conscientiously believe that by now my dead had buried their dead, and that the past had drifted away from me like a cast-off garment which fitted me no longer, but I have lately, somehow or other, discovered the foolhardiness and folly of this presumption, and I realize, to my deep mortification, that true cynicism and I are not always as good friends as I believed that we had become.

It is snowing hard as I sit writing by the waning afternoon light. The sparkling atoms are whirling in through the window which I opened when I came in a while ago to cool my throbbing head and my feverishness. The little drifts which they make upon the carpet remind me of similar occasions when I used to let Father Winter invade my quarters, out of sheer mischievousness, in days of long ago.

What jolly, devil-may-care times those were, and how long it does seem since I left many precious things behind me, cloaking my self-willed surrender of rank and honors and of future brilliant certainties under the mantle of a sort of superb and haughty stoicism, which, if I am to talk plainly, was not *très bon teint !*

On his desert island Crusoe was a sage, although before his shipwreck he had been looked upon as by no means an extraordinarily resigned or easy-going spirit. My desert island—the one for which I set sail—I have never quite reached. And if I had—ah! well, what matters it? what would then have happened there is no use in surmising. The only fact clear to me is that I am sometimes wretchedly grieved at my incapability of shaping things as they should be shaped, and that I fail only too frequently to follow out the existence which I had planned for myself, and to which, for the matter of that, I had thought that I had become perfectly reconciled.

Indeed, I am at heart content to be now one of the crowd, a mere unit among the masses, a plain cipher, working my way along a far more arduous road than the one upon which I started out. I often come well-nigh to fancying that I have forgotten the past, and if anybody addressed me suddenly, as of yore, I would not, I feel certain, take the words as being meant for me.

Well, as we make our bed, so we must lie. There is never any turning back save in thought. I am dead to my world. The days of palaces are dead, too. But what of that? At heart—I repeat it—I am really content, perchance far more so than I know myself. And, thanks to the mischievous spirit which is forever within me, a rush of unholy joy sometimes floods my heart and stings me like a million needles at the thought of how amazed those who are my friends and know me now would be if they knew; and what would be the surprise of those who knew me then could they see the present as it is! But imagination—*la folle du logis*, as they call it in France—is a curse, so let me close this lengthy and rather purposeless parenthesis and return to my Breton New Year, *car nous en sommes loin*. I fear that I am telling my story too much *à bâtons rompus*, and with not a vestige of that solemn and admirably dignified method so dear to celebrated writers and to Academicians.

What a delightful New Year that last one was!—I mean the last before my child-heart received its deepest and worst wound, so far.

During the whole month of December our rugged coast had been swept by storms of such unusual violence that I was forced, much against my will, to spend many hours within the castle walls. At five o'clock on New Year's Day I was standing at the end of the upper hall, looking out at the sea and the sky, when my father's steward happened to pass by. He stopped for a moment, and, patting my head gently, said, kindly:

"Well, how do you do, my little dear?"

He was an old retainer of our family, which he considered to be immeasurably above all others throughout the length and breadth of the land. He was, besides this, a wise and sagacious fellow, well informed as to his duties, fairly educated, and, what is better, a true and loyal Breton.

"I am very well, thank you, Kerradec," I replied; "but just look what a funny sky this is."

He glanced at the stormy, cloud-laden heavens, and, screwing up his white eyebrows, remarked: "So it is, so it is. I wouldn't be at sea to-night for a good deal. There is ugly weather coming, as sure as my name is Yvon Kerradec."

Truly the spectacle presented by the sunset sky must have been a remarkable one, for I remember it as clearly to-day as if it were still before me. A murky confusion of wind-torn clouds was rising from the west, clouds that had the color of dark copper, with black, metallic ridges like a crow's wing. The sun was sinking rapidly towards the horizon amid a heaped-up mass of blood-red vapors, tinged here and there with green blotches. The wind, which had been high all day, was now rising to a gale with an alarming shriek and beating the waters into froth. Even while we stood there watching the waves, they began to rise in that utterly confounding fashion that is so characteristic of our dangerous coast. They rolled in like high watery walls, crashing against the rocks on which the castle stands, with hungry, pitiless energy. Kerradec hurried towards my father's suite of rooms, and, lifting the heavy *portière*, called out to him that there was a blow coming on which would mean disaster to any ship running along the coast, and asking what the orders were for the coast-guardsmen with regard to signalling to the life-saving station two miles away. Instead of answering, my father, who was slipping on his dress coat, turned to his valet, an old soldier who had served under his orders when he was in the army, and bade him bring another suit of clothes and his oil-skin coat and sou'wester.

"Run to mamma, Pierrot, and tell her that I may be late for dinner. I am going down to the beach," he said, quietly.

I obeyed instantly. But as soon as I had delivered

38

the message I flew to my room, donned my own little storm-suit of oil-clothes with feverish rapidity, and then bounded down-stairs just as my father was emerging from his room.

"What, you rogue! You imagine that you can come with me in such weather?" he exclaimed; but I easily perceived that his indignation was only assumed, and that he liked to see me anxious to be always at the front. So I replied, demurely:

"Please take me along, dear papa! I hate to remain here without you, especially as it is New Year's Day!"

I am afraid that I was a very old-fashioned child in more than one respect. Which is perhaps explainable by the fact that I never played with children of my own age, but was either alone in the home park or in the company of grown-up people, whose language and phraseology I recklessly, and sometimes, no doubt, very amusingly, borrowed.

Clinging to my father's hand, I descended the narrow, spiral stone stairs which led directly from his study to the *cour d'honneur*, and then, to my huge delight at first, the wind began to buffet us. Its deep, sinister voice moaned all around. The clouds, blacker than ever, were blown about in a way that was bewildering. The hollow, hoarse voice of the tempest swelled to positive fury, and as we reached the bottom of our rocky fastness the spume torn from the white crests of the inrushing breakers nearly blinded us. My enthusiasm was oozing out of me, for streaks of cold rain were commencing to pelt us like sharp lances and, under the pressure of the wind, my breath almost failed me. But I would not for the world have confessed that I had been rash in insisting upon coming, and so I set my lips firmly together and said not a word, holding desperately to the strong hands of my two companions.

The dreadful turmoil increased with every passing minute. There were moments when the wind whistled sourly and stridently, as if it were in a paroxysm of anger, and then, grave, cavernous, and powerful, it sounded like the weird harmony of some immense cataclysm.

A sinister gloaming that!—showing the gigantic waves hurling themselves over each other, with a curtain of grim mists for a background.

We were almost abreast of the little life-saving station now, and, with a sort of hopeful yearning in my heart, I gazed upward at the jutting point of rock where the *semaphore* (marine signal-house) profiled its gibbet-like arms against the lowering sky. My father hailed the men on guard several times, but the snarl of the hurricane was so great that his voice seemed to have lost all sound. Finally, with a quick gesture, he picked me up, and began to climb the slippery steps leading to the platform half-way up the cliff, where the *guerite* of the *douaniers* clung to the granite wall.

" *Donnez la moi donc, je la porterai bien !*" shouted Kerradec, holding out his hands to take me from the comforting shelter of my father's arms. But unheeding this offer he hurried on, as if the nearly insurmountable difficulties of the ascent, in the gathering gloom which enveloped us as a shroud, and in the teeth of a storm such as is seldom seen even in Brittany, were a mere joke.

I hardly heard the orders he gave to insure the prompt rescue of any vessel unfortunate enough to be skirting our coast that night, for I was drowsily leaning against his shoulder, covered by the folds of his great-coat.

When we reached the sands once more we found that a few men, old sailors all of them, had gathered there and were looking at the grand and awful spectacle with that stolid watchfulness which denotes the mariner all the world over.

They uncovered their heads as my father approached, and fell back a little, watching his tall figure with affectionate pride. For they knew his undaunted courage, and his mere presence there was reassuring to these men, who thought of their boys far out at sea, now, as on every night in the year, drifting helplessly at the mercy of the elements.

The angry roar of the ocean was the *Dies Irae* these mariners had listened to from their boyhood, and the solemnity thereof lent to their natures much of the depth and melancholy to which I have already alluded. Thus had they no actual fear, for in the integrity of their faith they felt that the murderous waves were ruled by the will of Almighty God. But their hearts were filled with the solemn awe and dread of such a situation.

Ah, no! the Breton fisherman, whose time is employed, whose bread is earned, by old Father Ocean, is never smitten with a craven's fear. But he is aware of the boundless power to sustain or to take life which belongs to such forces, and realizes the dangers by which he is always surrounded. "*Il faut bien toujours en finir un jour ou l'autre,*" as a bereaved grandfather once said to me, after hearing of the loss at sea of the last grandson and sole bread-winner left him. Tears were weakly coursing down his weather-beaten cheeks, but a resignation of the finest and bravest kind kept his old lips from trembling. Men must die, and it does not matter so much, after all, how they do die—epidemics, wars, accidents, ah! even broken hearts—all carry out the laws of nature in that respect. And in the end what will it signify whether a thousand poor souls more or less take their flight towards heaven on a night like the one I am now speaking of, when the roaring sea gathers in its quarry?

The lightning flashed now again along the dense vault above us, where the clouds were riven by sudden sheets of lurid flame, and I slid from my father's grasp and clapped my hands, in my ignorant, childish glee. Alas! my joy was soon quenched. For the intense glare showed us two fishing-smacks standing out against its hellish glow, as they labored among the murderous rollers.

My father glanced over the distance between the boats and the beach, with grave care depicted on his handsome face. Then, lifting a whistle to his lips, he gave a well-known call, that pierced even that deafening clamor.

The two apparently doomed boats were exactly opposite to us, and if they were once caught by the current that runs at mill-race speed between the horn-shaped ramparts of the inner bay, they would be drawn undoubtedly into the breakers. Even I could see that! Would the life-boat come in time? That was the unspoken question depicted in every eye witnessing the coming horror.

Determinedly my father turned to the men, who, in their eagerness, now stood shoulder to shoulder with him.

"Get me a strong rope, quickly!"

Strangely enough I understood, and a new terror swept over me. To interfere or to implore never occurred to my mind, but I took his hand and kissed it passionately, clinging to him with a despairing strength that caused him to recollect my presence, and made him perhaps realize what his heroic endeavors for the sake of others would mean to his own little child should he perish.

Stooping down, he lifted me in his arms, and, whispering hastily in my ear a few words of comfort and of encouragement, he handed me to Kerradec, who was in vain expostulating with him. Trying the strength of a great coil of rope that had been brought, he began to throw off his heavy coat. When the lightning shone out again, one of the boats had disappeared, while the other could yet be plainly seen in that spectre light, as it flew on the top of a monstrous wave straight to its destruction.

"The life-boat is coming," yelled Jinks, who had joined us without my noticing it. "Wait, my lord, for nothing will live through this 'ere storm. For Gawd's sake, don't you go a-drowning of yourself, my lord!"

"Hush, Jinks! What words for Pierrot to hear!" he answered. "The life-boat will be too late; come, help me there!"

Jinks was silenced and seemingly abashed. With his own trembling hands he knotted the rope about his master's waist. A glance across the boiling sea showed all present that the urgency was great indeed, for the little brown-sailed, dismantled craft was heading with hideous and relentless rapidity towards the foremost scrap of the chain of rocks

A new sight to me, and one which I will never forget, was the iron resolve in the face which I loved best of all. It was that of a calm and resolute man, one accustomed to leadership and to the absolute responsibility of his actions. I seemed to feel that if I cried out or attracted his attention towards myself I would only be hindering the precautions which were being taken for his safety, so I clung tightly to Kerradec's bull-like neck and kept my eyes fixed on the superb figure, standing alone in front of the little crowd, with a rope round his body and another in his firm, strong hand.

There came a great thundering wave, and at the precise moment when it retired I saw my father dash in after it and disappear between the folds of black water, as if they were to hold him forever.

Another flash of lightning, and I saw his head above the livid foam.

"There he is, Kerradec. Oh! haul him in; don't let him go any farther!" I fairly yelled, unconsciously digging my nails in my helpless bearer's flesh.

"Quiet, my little one, quiet! He knows what he is about, and the saints will protect him! Be quiet, I say!"

I was quiet enough after this admonition; my heart beat to suffocation, but all my powers seemed to have passed into my straining eyes. Instinct told me that death was hovering over him, that the boldest daring was as a wisp of straw against the might of that infuriated mass of water. I bit my little clinched fist in my agony to repress the sobs that filled my heaving chest. I doubt whether I fathomed the boundlessness of my apprehension or the immensity of my enthusiasm; for, in spite of all, the feeling that I was witnessing the most magnificent thing on earth—an exhibition of flawless courage, a total abnegation of self in the cause of humanity, welled up in my heart. A few days before, my Abbé had given me a fine old engraving representing the gladiators before Cæsar, and I suddenly remembered the Latin inscription, " *Morituri te salutant.*" Was it not a fitting greeting for those doomed men on the wreck to give to their would-be rescuer? This thought may seem ridiculous, bred as it was from a small child's terrified fancy, but nevertheless, to this day, whenever I come across that short sentence in print, it carries me back with painful swiftness to that awful night on the Brittany coast when the first dawning

44

A RECOGNITION OF MY FATHER'S BRAVERY

of what life would be to me without my father filled me with despair.

Another and yet another sheet of lurid, ghastly lightning showed us the bold swimmer amid the churning waters steadily nearing the shattered bark. Then the unnatural glow died out, and impenetrable darkness lay over the bay. What happened during these indescribable moments of suspense I only heard later, for the limit of my childish emotions had been reached, and I realized nothing clearly again until I found myself kneeling beside him, where they had drawn him up on the wet sand, clinging passionately to his prostrate form, and listening, as in a dream, to the shouts of those about us who were proclaiming in wellnigh delirious tones that he had saved six lives.

"But he is dead! He is dead!" I cried, hoarsely. *" Saints anges du Paradis, rendez le moi."*

His eyes unclosed, faintly he drew me towards him, and as he did so he murmured:

" C'est fini ; ne pleure pas, mon petit enfant."

*   *   *   *   *   *   *

It is the privilege of dramatists and of novelists to shift their scenery with bewildering swiftness in order to suit their purpose. This is natural, since they wish to extort as much artificial emotion as possible from an ever-ready and sensation-loving public. The tantalizing asterisks which often divide interesting chapters, like neat but painful sword-cuts, have been invented by *littérateurs* for no other purpose than to ease up situations which have reached a towering climax, and to precipitate the earnest readers from a nerve-shaking situation into some sunlit, summer valley, where the rustle of foliage, stirred by fragrant breezes, the splashing of oars on the surface of azure lakes or rivers, is conjured up by the cunning of the writer, with the eminently praiseworthy object of soothing their deeply stirred and painfully excited imaginations.

I am, alas! not a novelist, far less a dramatist, and I cannot presume, therefore, to tamper greatly with the tricks of the trade, useful as they might prove to be to a humble chronicler of real life like myself. It is unfortunate, because the incidents of real life are so tame when compared with those of fiction that a ray or two of limelight, judiciously applied, as is done on the stage *aux grands moments*, would serve my turn admirably now. As it is, I can only utter a befitting *mea culpa*, and deplore my sad lack of ability, before proceeding with my unambitious recital of every-day events.

There was a suggestion of divine forgiveness in the air as we returned to the castle. The waves were tossed more gently upon the beach by the gradually relenting wind, and the sea-mews, whose peaceful slumbers had been disturbed by nature's ferocious orchestra, circled above our heads with much fluttering of their broad pinions. I was too tired and also too young to realize the pathos of this return to joy and calm, while so close to us in the depths of the cruel ocean the stiffening limbs and cadaverous faces of the drowned were settling to their eternal sleep. In spite of my high-strung nature, I was nearly asleep when I was borne into the hall that to my blinking eyes seemed a fairy palace worthy of any of my favorite heroes.

My mother's low, high-bred voice woke me from my torpor. She was remonstrating with my father, and so absolutely unbearable and cruel did her reproaches seem to me that I jumped from the fur-covered lounge near the fire where I had been put, and confronted her.

"I won't have it!" I cried, excitedly. "Oh, mother!

46

mother! How can you speak of yourself after what he has done to-night! How can you think of your anxiety and your pain when he is here all drenched and cold and worn-out, and when he has saved six lives from that black death out there! You are cruel, cruel! like a beautiful, bad fairy!" I concluded, in a passion of uncontrollable tears.

My haughty lady mother gazed at me in amazement, with the contempt which this outburst surely deserved.

"Recollect yourself!" she said, sternly. "Whom do you think you are talking to?" And then, turning towards my father, who was about to draw my shivering little figure to the shelter of his arms, she continued, in her own cold, disdainful way:

"Your system of education is not successful. The child is becoming unmanageable."

"Hush, Vera!" he murmured, softly. "Pierrot will beg your pardon later. Now we are both unfit for further parlance, and must beg you to excuse us." And suiting the action to the words, he lifted me from where I crouched at his feet, and carried me up the broad stairs to his rooms, while she stood as one transfixed watching us, her shining silken draperies and the frosty fires of her magnificent jewels clothing her in a glitter like that of an angry moonbeam.

That night, when the much-delayed ceremonious New Year's dinner was ended, I was brought down as usual to the banqueting-hall. All my fatigue and my sorrow had gone, and nothing but the intense pride of being the child of such a father as mine remained. How noble he looked, with his face still white and drawn, and with the dark, hollow circles under his eyes painted there by his recent struggle with death!

The country magnates who sat at his hospitable

board looked up at him with positive reverence, it seemed to me, and drank his health again and again, while outside the dull sound of the passing-bell which was being tolled for those *péri à la mer* mingled with the booming of the sea.

My mother, as radiant as ever, ignored me entirely. I knew that I had offended her as I never had before, and that the perfunctory forgiveness granted me at the urgent request of my father counted for nothing. I must make this confession complete, moreover, by adding that I was by no means in a contrite frame of mind. The events of that afternoon had awakened me from the white, dreamy sleep of infancy; and, sitting in angry and silent judgment on my mother, I unhesitatingly condemned her. May Almighty God forgive me for it! So deep was my resentment that I felt as if every vestige of filial affection for her was gone from my heart forever. Had she not blamed my father for proving himself a hero once more?

At midnight, when I knelt before my little wooden image of the Blessed Virgin, I deliberately omitted my mother's name from my prayers, and went to bed with a guilty conscience and a heavy heart.

CHAPTER III

" The coldness from my heart is gone
But still the weight is there,
And thoughts which I abhor will come
To tempt me to despair!"

THE salt breeze was blowing violently in my face and flapping the hood of my little mackintosh over my head as I walked rapidly along the narrow path crossing the dunes. I was in a fearful temper, angry with myself and all the world besides, and smarting under a sense of injustice which made me set my teeth hard and stamp my foot occasionally as I flew onward followed by a breathless groom who did his best to follow me.

The weather was in absolute keeping with my mood, for a storm amounting almost to a hurricane had been raging throughout the night, and even now in the late afternoon the leaden-hued sky hung above the tossing waves of the bay like a pall and threw a ghastly greenish light upon the beach strewn with torn-up sea-weed and tossed-up bowlders.

Worse and worse grew the weather. Huge black clouds seemed to close around me, and the wind bullied me so furiously that the much-alarmed groom was forced to hold me with both hands to prevent my being carried away by the overwhelming gusts. On, on, I sped, gasping for breath as fatigue began to give place to excitement, but fortunately the turreted roofs of the *Château de la Fée*, as my grandmother's residence was called, began to appear, dimly silhouetted against the angry sky, and in a few moments we came to a mullioned side

D   49

entrance, overhung with ivy and drooping creepers. I rang the bell with a violence that awoke echoes throughout the building. An old man - servant opened the door immediately, and stood bowing low, but with an expression in his honest blue eyes which brought me partly to my senses, and made me realize what my dishevelled appearance might be after my fight with the weather. Fortunately I cared little for what old Jean thought of me, one way or the other. He had known me since I was born, and was, besides this, one of the last specimens of a long-departed class—a devoted, respectful family retainer, who would never have permitted himself to judge *les maîtres*, however extravagantly they might act. Telling him that I must see my grandmother at once, I ran up the stone staircase, where huge tapestries and inlaid sets of armor added to the mediæval aspect of the place, and rushed into the apartment, half boudoir, half library, where I was certain to find my father's venerable mother.

The sight which met my eyes as I entered was of a nature to restore calm to the most rebellious spirit, and it acted upon me like a shower of cold water, making me instantly more rational in mind as well as in behavior. The room, which for many years to come was to be my one harbor of peace and rest, was large, and furnished in exquisite taste, though with a tendency towards the fashions of two hundred years ago. The Italian cabinets and tables were ponderous and massive. The hangings were sombre, and the walls were hung with many celebrated paintings and family portraits. Comfort of a more modern kind was not by any means excluded, however, and the whole aspect of this delightfully romantic chamber was brightened by quantities of flowering plants and palms that stood in heavy inlaid *jardinières*. Clusters of Bengal roses and heather, set in shallow bowls of ancient pottery, nearly always filled the air with their clean, faint perfume, and the tastes of the mistress of all these treasures were divulged by a grand piano, a harmonium, a spinet with a beautifully painted lid, an easel set by one of the windows, and a litter of books and music. There, too, near the monumental hearth of carved green marble, stood an embroidery frame, indicating that she was not an idler, but a woman who, in spite of her years, found pleasure in a well-occupied, busy life.

As I came in, she rose from a low chair which she had been occupying, while gazing at the vast panorama of land and sea stretching before the balcony windows at the other end of the room, and came towards me with outstretched arms. At nearly eighty, my grandmother was one of the prettiest old women I have ever known; she looked like a fairy godmother, and it is scarcely a wonder that the simple peasant folks should have called her lovely home *le Château de la Fée.*

Her hair was like spun silk, in its soft and silvery whiteness. Her pink-and-white complexion and her large, black-fringed, dark-blue eyes had retained all the dewy *éclat* of youth. Her figure was still straight and slender, while her tiny hands and feet were shaped like those of a Greek statue. Clothed in sweeping ivory-tinted laces, with a great Byzantine cross of emeralds, sapphires, and onyx hanging at her throat, amid her far-famed pearls—pearls which she wore day and night, according to a superstitious belief in their luck-bringing influence—she seemed to me at this moment especially the very embodiment of all that was sweet and dainty, delightful and comforting, and I felt suddenly ashamed of my tumbled locks and flushed face.

"What on earth is the matter, my dearest child?"

she said, gently, as with a gasping, exhausted sob I threw myself down before her on a cushion and buried my face in her lap.

"Everything is the matter," I gasped, clutching her dress, as a thoroughly frightened child is apt to do when in great distress of mind. "I—well, I wish I were dead!" With which last words I burst into a veritable agony of pent-up tears.

For a moment my grandmother said nothing. She quietly removed my bedraggled coat, smoothed my short, rebellious locks, and contented herself with some mute caresses, until the first paroxysm of my grief had spent itself. Then she drew me towards the bright fire of blazing logs, and in her calm, even, musical voice asked, softly:

"This is not at all like you, Pierrot. What has caused you to lose your self-control so completely, my dear?"

"Oh!" I exclaimed, wrathfully, "you are right, *grand-mère*. I know that I am unmanly and stupid, but I hate injustice, and when papa is not there I get nothing else—and—oh! it drives me wild!"

"Hush! Hush!" murmured the kind voice of my lovely granny; "do not speak like that. You are not yourself just now, my poor little one. You must have something to eat and a short rest, and then I will talk this matter over with you."

I gazed at her in surprise. What could she say that would have any influence upon a subject so excessively painful to me? But still there was something so sympathetic and persuasive in her tone that I suffered her to take me to her dressing-room, where the disorder of my costume was quickly repaired, before I went downstairs to have tea with her. At first I could not swallow a mouthful. But gradually the warmth and cosiness of my surroundings, the charmingly appointed little table, with its dainty china, brilliant silver, flowers, fruit, and cake, and, more than all, the loving care bestowed upon me, acted like a balm, and when we had finished our *goûter* I felt very much better. Then, drawing me down beside her in the depths of her capacious *bergère*, she gazed at me with a thoughtful expression, which I had often seen on her delicate features, but which to-night was tinged with a deep sadness that I had never noticed before.

Suddenly she bent forward and, crossing her white, slim hands, said, in a low, tender voice:

"My poor little Pierrot! You are too young to understand most things yet. But you are an unusually bright and clever child, and I am going to try the experiment of talking to you as if you were what you so picturesquely call a 'grown-up.'"

The big room was perfectly still. Alone the ticking of the huge Louis XIV. clock could be heard during the ensuing pause, for the storm had ceased and the red rays of the setting sun were breaking out between banks of gold-lined clouds, sending a ruddy glow in through the tall oriel windows. Granny sat in deep thought for a moment, as if she had momentarily forgotten my presence, her still so remarkably youthful eyes looking full into the rosy sunset, and I sat under a kind of strange spell, watching the gems sparkle on her fingers and the gleam of the pearls about her neck. My grievances came back to me as I did so with redoubled vigor, although I felt sorry to have brought so much perturbation into the crystal-like purity and exquisite refinement of the atmosphere which invariably surrounded my grandmother. Perchance she was right to say that I was too young to understand many things, but I am sure that I felt some of them acutely.

The cause of my present troubles was an innocent one enough, and one which I loved, for the beginning of this period of revolt and dissatisfaction had been brought about in the following fashion before the outset of the summer, when I literally lived in the park and gardens, taking my daily lessons there with my dear old Abbé, under the spreading boughs of flowering laburnums and lilac-trees. The gardens at home, sheltered from the ocean winds by enormous crenellated walls as ancient as the castle itself, were really a thing of beauty, and the pride of both my parents, from whom I have inherited my intense devotion to flowers. My own particular corner was one of my greatest preoccupations. I dug and planted and pruned and watered my plants, and was continually making inroads upon the superb *plattes-bandes* and hot-houses of the head gardener, who always threatened to disclose my numberless thefts to "The Great Powers," and yet never did so, poor old man, for he loved me dearly, and had been in my grandfather's service before my father was born.

One morning early that spring I was very busy with a plot of reseda and cockle-shells, which I was attempting to transplant. My Abbé, sitting on a garden bench near-by, was piously reading his breviary, and my dog Bataille was lying in the sun, occasionally catching a gnat with a snap of his big, lazy jaws. I was so absorbed in my work that I did not notice my father as he approached and stood close beside me. My name, softly pronounced, made me turn round, and then I saw him. His hands were behind his back, and on his face was a serious yet joyful expression, which struck me at once.

"Oh, papa, what is it?" I cried, throwing my spade with a crash upon the gravelled walk.

"Pierrot, what do you think? The blessed angels have brought you a little brother!"

I stared hard at him; then, with one of my unexpected, reckless bounds, I threw myself literally upon him.

"Have you got him behind your back? Show him to me, papa! Please show him to me!"

This was too much even for the Abbé's gravity, and he burst into a roar of laughter, in which my father joined heartily. When their merriment had subsided, and the worthy priest had been thanked for the congratulations which he poured forth from the depths of his honest soul, I was taken into the house to view the little stranger. I was a little offended at having been laughed at, but I did not like to say so, and when my father took me in his arms to carry me up-stairs, as was often his custom, I nestled against his shoulder and patted his cheek with my little hands, grimy from gardening though they were.

My mother's room was slightly darkened by rose-colored blinds, and she lay in bed, looking so lovely that she made me think of the little Madonna of Correggio which hung in my father's room. Beside her, on a lace-covered cushion, was a really magnificent, fat, rosy, blue-eyed baby, with tiny rings of golden hair, as fine as *fils de la Vierge*, on its soft, round head. I gazed speechlessly at this picture, listened mechanically to the twittering of a little bird bursting its tiny throat with gleeful melody in the garden below, and in my amazement took no notice of the hand extended to me by my mother.

"This is your little brother, Pierrot; won't you kiss him?" she said, in a weak voice, which did not sound like her own at all.

"Do not speak, my dearest! Do not tire yourself," whispered my father, and, pushing me forward, he continued, "Kiss your little brother, Pierrot, but go softly about it." Thus admonished I bent gently down and pressed my lips to the smooth forehead, but I did not like the feeling of that yielding, velvety flesh under my lips, and I drew back quickly.

"Are you afraid of him?" said the nurse, a tall, lean, white-capped woman whom I had not observed before. I shrugged my shoulders, and, in a voice loud enough to be heard at the farther end of the next room, I exclaimed that I was afraid of nothing, "*of nothing at all in the whole world!*" A queer smile lighted up my mother's pale face, and, turning her head a little towards me, she said, proudly:

"Is it not a beautiful baby, Pierrot—so big and plump and rosy?"

A singular feeling clutched at my heart for a second. "Ah, yes!" thought I, "a beautiful one, plump and big and rosy! Not small and pale and gray-eyed like me!" But as I was a rather good child, in spite of my many faults, I answered: "Yes, Matushka, it is very pretty —just like a wax doll," and then, hastily kissing my mother's hand, which she had let fall on the coverlet, I flew out of the room, pursued by the "Gently, gently, my child!" spoken somewhat angrily by the white-capped nurse.

My daily life was by no means altered by this addition to our family. I saw yet a little less of my mother than I had done before, for she was so wrapped up in her new and precious possession that she devoted her entire time to little Bertrand, and for some to me quite unexplainable reason she invariably called him the *Son and Heir*. This woman of the world, fond of pleasure and of amusement, became a model mamma with the advent of the baby, who from the first moment was treated by everybody excepting by my father, who never dislodged me from my estate in his affections, as the autocrat of the entire household before whom all were forced to bend the knee.

I loved this little brother dearly, but I would have loved him far more had I not been strictly forbidden to touch him or to approach him except by special permission. As it was, I soon learned to hold aloof, and continued to do so until the magnetic attraction radiating from him proved too strong to be resisted.

The summer with its customary series of out-door pleasures, the fishing in the shallow pools at the foot of the cliffs, the long hours of paddling in the wet sands or amid the big rocks made slippery by sea-weed, and among which I gathered mussels, small oysters, clams, and other treasures, including huge green crabs and jelly-fish, were enjoyed as heretofore. More than ever I adored the sea, and ran in and out of the water twenty times a day in hot weather, so much so, indeed, that my mother, enthroned on a cane arm-chair, sheltered by a colossal sun-shade on the sands, with the baby's nurse beside her and a novel on her lap, warned me languidly to be careful lest my feet should become webbed like unto those of a duck.

As time went on I realized more and more that strange times, indeed, had come to pass, and that I was in some way a source of continual irritation to my mother and to all those who formed her own *clique*, or miniature court. I was unceasingly reproved when my own dear daddy was out of hearing, and my childish heart began to swell with a sense of perpetual injustice which I was, however, too proud to confess to him.

This unenviable state of affairs reached its climax during a short trip which he was forced to undertake to Paris, and which the dangerously hot weather reported from there prevented me from sharing with him.

My mother was still a model parent to me in many ways. She was ever heedful of my needs, both of body and of brain. But I felt, as young children feel what they cannot explain—and in this case it was—that since my brother's advent into her life I had become an unimportant member of the household. When, by chance, I touched her, I felt numb and cold. Yet I was not at all jealous of that beautiful baby who was her idol. On the contrary, I loved him passionately, and soon displayed the same ruses which had once distinguished my secret intercourse with the eagle "*Fulvius*," in order to steal to the nursery when the little fellow was alone with his attendants.

How I did coax them to let me hold him for a minute, or to kiss his soft, little face, or his morsels of chubby hands, like crumpled apple-blossoms! He was beginning to know me, and often crowed with delight when I came in, much to my gratification. Moreover, there was a flavor of forbidden fruit in these stolen interviews, which made them a thousandfold more attractive to me, for I felt that I was doing a doughty deed and risking terrible consequences by thus infringing my mother's orders. Nor was I mistaken in this, as I was doomed to soon discover.

On the afternoon of my hurried flight to my grandmother's "*Fairy Castle*," when reaching home after a long ride with Jinks, I entered the house by a side door, and, cautiously threading my way through the long galleries and up the back staircase, I came at last to the day-nursery. Opening the door noiselessly, to my joy and surprise I found the baby lying on a thick rug, enclosed by a movable barrier of cushioned bamboo, and gazing with that peculiar vacant stare of the very young at the painted ceiling above. Evidently his nurses had left him there out of harm's way for a few moments, for I heard their voices in the adjoining *lingerie*, as they laughed and chatted.

Here was my opportunity. Very carefully I stepped over the low barrier and, sitting down, drew the little lace-shrouded bundle of soft, warm babyhood on my lap. I was shaking with excitement, and my joy was boundless when I discovered that the tiny autocrat did not resent my intrusion, but allowed me to fondle him as much as I pleased. Nay, I fancied that he actually winked his big blue eyes at me, just as if he entered into the spirit of this unusual spree. Again and again I kissed his round cheeks and clasped his wee fingers, which closed vigorously about mine, and I became so absorbed in this blissful pastime that I did not hear the light footsteps of small booted feet, nor notice that I was discovered in *flagranti-delicto* until a sudden shadow intercepted the light from the nearest window, and fell like a menacing cloud upon the baby's upturned, dimpled face.

"So this is how you obey me, is it?"

The voice was astonishingly cold and stern, almost cruelly metallic, and my mother, in her tight-fitting riding-habit, her slender hands clinched upon the handle of her whip, struck terror to my usually very dauntless little heart.

The slow, suffocating beating of my heart sounded loudly in my ears, like the regular strokes of a merciless sledge-hammer. I put the baby down on the rug with lingering tenderness, and then stood up, squared my shoulders, and forced myself to look my mother full in the eyes. All the imperiousness of a long line of ancestors who had been leaders of men and had known no rule but their own caprice rose in my entire being like a swiftly rushing tide. My fear vanished, and I determined to fight for what I considered my rights.

With a step my mother reached me and put her hand heavily on my shoulder.

"You young hawk! Lower those bold eyes when I speak to you," she said, harshly. "Do you think that you are master here? Not so, my haughty one! *Nous avons changé tout cela.* You dare to disobey your mother? Ask my forgiveness at once!"

I remained stubbornly and resolutely silent and obstinate.

"Do you hear me?" she continued, now evidently beside herself with fury, and scarcely measuring the value of her words. "You are robbing your brother of his father's love. You are more to him than even I am, and it is time that you should be put back where you belong, you little usurper!

> "O Venus! Schöne Frau meine;
> Ihr seid eine Teufelinne!"

An angry woman! Is there a fiercer thing on earth? Hardly, I think, especially when the woman is young and fair and high-bred, for then it is as if one witnessed the fall of an angel. "*Eine Teufelinne!*"

Those flashing black eyes, that marmorean skin, white with passion, the drawn crimson lips showing the pearly teeth clinched rigidly, gave one the impression of a fiend broken loose! And yet—this was my mother, the mother whom I had known in other moods, on whose knee I had sometimes rested my head, who had stooped over me in my childish dreams, whom I had always been so proud of in spite of all!

"You have no right to speak like that," I cried. "If papa was here you would not dare to! I've done no harm, and you are always cruel and unjust to me!"

I was so indignant, so deeply roused, that a red mist

seemed to fill the room, and I doubled my fists till my nails cut the flesh of my hands. Fleet was the retribution. I had never as yet been beaten, but now I tasted for the first time, in all its fulsomeness, the bitter humiliation of corporal punishment. Down came the supple leash of the hunting-whip upon my shoulders, not once, but twenty times at least, before I realized the horror of what was happening to me. Then, with a yell of rage, I snatched at the knout-like weapon, and with surprising force I hurled it out of the window, smashing the thick glass thereof to atoms. Gathering myself together, I ran like a pursued animal out of the room, down the broad stairs, and into the stable-yard, in search of dear, sympathetic old Jinks. There was nobody in sight save my own faithful little groom, a lad of fifteen, who was devoted to me, and who, seeing me dishevelled and shaken by dry, convulsive sobs, rushed towards me and laid hands on me.

I shook him off with as little difficulty as had he been a feather—such was my excitement—and ran on at full speed through the park with the lad following in my track.

The smallest details of this wretched chain of events were before me again as I now watched my grandmother, and yet I hesitated to tell even her, whom I loved so devotedly, what had happened. It had to be done, however, and so, with flaming cheeks and halting speech, I finally made a clean breast of the whole matter.

There was no doubt about her being greatly moved. When I came to the description of the ignominious thrashing that had been administered to me, the effect on her was far greater than I could have imagined. The high-bred face of the old aristocrat grew set and stern, her eyes flashed like live sapphires, and she drew herself up with what I saw was indignation, pure and simple.

Tears of mortification had risen to my eyes, and, encouraged by my grandmother's silence, I exclaimed, spitefully:

"We will see what papa says to this!"

Quick as lightning her fingers were placed on my lips, and, in a tone serious and solemn enough to frighten me thoroughly, she said, with much decision:

"Your father will say nothing, because I trust that through you at least he will never hear of this—this out—this unfortunate incident."

"Nothing?" I echoed, extremely perturbed.

"Certainly, nothing! Would you play the part of informer on your mother, and even in such a case could you see your way to justify your glaring disobedience, or your violence, not to call it by a harsher name?"

I hung my head.

"*Vous l'avez voulu, mon enfant! C'est la guerre!*" she added, sadly, "your mother will not forgive you this day's work, but I do not think that she will speak to your father about it."

"Of course she won't," I murmured. "She knows that he would not stand having me beaten like a dog—yes, like a dog, grandmamma—I the eldest son, who will some time be the head of the family."

"Hush, hush! I cannot allow you to say such things," and almost to herself she murmured, woefully, "*Voilà bien ce que j'attendais!*"

At this juncture a footman appeared at the door, and announced no less a personage than my mother. With a smothered exclamation I jumped to my feet and stood anxiously watching the meeting of these two thorough-paced women of the world, under whose exquisite court-liness and polish I had somehow or other instinctively guessed long ago that no great love was concealed.

I had never realized as completely as I did now the

inimitable grace, the languor, ease, and the absolute mastery of any situation, however difficult it might prove to be, which were such marked characteristics of my mother. She was, indeed, a perfect type of that most alarming of animals, a great *mondaine*, unhampered by the small scruples and the diffidence begotten by a tender heart.

I looked on with the fascination of a bird gazing at a snake, while she bent before her mother-in-law—the only being in the world of whom she stood in some awe, I believe—and raised the latter's hand to her lips. I had seen this form of homage repeated on every occasion when the two women had met in my presence. But to-day it impressed me with a sense of insincerity on one side and of bare toleration on the other, which left an unpleasant impression on my mind.

"I am sorry that this unruly child should have disturbed you, *ma mère*," said my mother, with gracious apology in her dulcet tones, "and I have come to send Pierrot home if you will permit it. His father will return in the morning, and, as you know, he would miss him sadly should he find him absent upon his arrival."

"You will have some tea, Vera, before thinking of going," replied my grandmother, and, turning to me, she bade me go and tell the butler to refill the samovar. "You need not come back, Pierrot, until I send for you, as you have had your *goûter* already; you can go to the gardener and ask him for some of your favorite carnations to take away with you."

I understood perfectly why I was thus sent away. And I was by no means displeased to avoid the impending explanation between my mother and grandmother. The carnations were, of course, a mere excuse, for I was not allowed, as a rule, to go near the wonderful collections of multi-colored blossoms which were the talk of the whole country-side. I thought, with a return of my eternal *insousiance*, that, after all, *à quelque chose malheur est bon*, as I walked towards the glass-houses, followed by Pirame, the great bloodhound, so gentle to his friends and so fierce to his foes, who shuffled along on his huge, noiseless pads, thrusting his damp nose in my hand, *en vieux camarade*.

Naturally, I was not informed of what took place during the memorable half-hour of my absence, but the result of the interview between the two *grandes puissances* was a surprising one. When I returned to the room, tenderly carrying a sheath of odorous carnations, given me by special command, the two women were to all appearances peacefully discussing the strange inclemency of the weather, and my mother's dark, slumberous eyes scanned me with a nonchalant indulgence to which I had not of late been accustomed.

"Your grandmother has been kind enough to plead your cause, and has been so successful," she murmured, with unwonted suavity, and with an amiable condescension which was marked by poignant irony and which I did not like—the melodious voice was so relentless in spite of the apparent kindliness of the words—"that I am ready to forgive your extraordinary behavior, provided you feel genuinely repentant."

Restive little beast that I was, I could not bring myself to reply in a proper fashion, indeed. I would have liked nothing better than to throw down my precious burden of flowers and run from the room, rather than face the necessity of expressing totally absent regrets, for my past ill conduct.

I had often gloried in my childish pride at the thought that my forefathers had died on the scaffold, in the grim slaughter of Quiberon, and at the time of the Crusades, that they had been loyal and plucky beyond all things always, that they had been incapable of uttering a lie to save themselves even from the most awful predicaments. I knew that their atmosphere had been one of fidelity, of courage, and of dignity. Why should I, then, their descendant, claim to be sorry when nothing was further from my mind. Furthermore, my mother would know perfectly well that I was merely cringing to avoid further chastisement, and this was bitter gall to me.

Fortunately, my grandmother came to the rescue. Drawing me towards her, she said, persuasively: "There is never any shame in confessing one's wrong-doings, Pierrot, or in asking pardon for an offence. It is the truest and noblest form of courage to do so."

Thus adjured, I looked up less dejectedly and said, in a low, shamed voice, hardly above a whisper:

"I beg your forgiveness, mother."

A slight frown drew her delicately pencilled brows together. Such an *amende honorable* did not satisfy her, evidently. The famous theory about *la voix du sang* is, I fear, a mere illusion, for it is by no means a spontaneous or an irresistible growth, and just then I felt acutely that whatever *amour maternel* my mother might have felt for me once was now obliterated by an all-engrossing passion for her last-born, and also by some other cause which I was quite unable to comprehend.

A cold shiver ran between my shoulders when I took her extended hand and brushed it with my lips. My heart was extraordinarily heavy, but I did not like to have this noticed, and so I withdrew to the window under pretence of admiring my flowers, taking but slight heed of the "*voilà qui est arrangé, mais ne recommençez plus,*" uttered by my parent, and which seemed

E

to me to be the promise of a mere truce instead of the
beginning of better things.

I looked forward with dread to the drive home which
I supposed I should have to take with her, for her horses
were just then curvetting and prancing beneath the
windows. Fortunately, I was spared this *mauvais quart
d'heure*. In my agitation I had not noticed that she was
already dressed for a dinner which she was to attend
at the château of the famous sporting Baron de la
H. J., whose skill when hunting boars and wolves in
his own immense woods was only equalled by his lordly
hospitality. A long, soft wrap of white Indian crêpe,
embroidered with silver threads, partly concealed her
primrose-hued gown, and the little hood which she now
carefully drew over her head framed her almost perfect
face in a halo of lace that enhanced its cameo-like
beauty. While slipping her bracelets and *porte-bon-
heurs* over her white Suède gloves, she said, in her ordinary cool, well-modulated voice:

"Your grandmother is kind enough to send you home
with Jean, and has asked me to let you take dinner
with her, Dushka. I am delighted to conform to her
wishes in the matter, and only hope that my leniency
will encourage you to behave better in the future than
you have in the past.

When my mother called me "Dushka"—which in
Russian means something like "my little soul"—she
reached the utmost limits of maternal tenderness, for
that was the only endearing name which she ever used
towards me. I was all the more astonished, therefore,
to hear her use it now, and could not help thinking, glee-
fully and rebelliously, that "*she had gotten it hot and
heavy*" indeed from granny, for else she would not
have gone so far out of her way to be kind to me after
my defiant attitude towards her.

66

If this was the case, I, at any rate, received no enlightenment on the subject, for when my Lady Mother had taken her departure I was treated to a little sermon, tenderly but firmly administered by the darling old woman whom I cherished with all my heart, and whose favorite grandchild I knew well that I was.

While she was talking to me I stood pensively on the balcony, one of the long windows having been thrown open to let in the balmy evening breeze, laden with the perfume of flowers and the freshness of the ocean, and watched the gulls flying lazily about in the purified atmosphere. I have always loved gulls, they are such irrepressible, noisy, silvery creatures; and *"Granny's Gulls,"* as I used to call them, were old friends of mine which I took the utmost pleasure in feeding whenever I came to see her. The instant I showed myself they used to wheel round and come rushing towards me with harsh, discordant cries meant no doubt for joyful greetings, but which on that special occasion grated on my nerves, for I was feeling very much bruised, both morally and physically.

Being very honest when in self-communion, even in those days I admitted to myself that my mother had good and just cause this time to be deeply angered, but yet, *la voix de la nature* said nothing to me, and I was simply humiliated to have placed myself absolutely *dans mon tort*.

Indeed, I felt somehow like a soldier who runs away before the enemy. Why had I not faced the music and taken my punishment, however hard it was, like a man, instead of flying for sanctuary. That thought hurt me deeply, and degraded me in my own eyes. Insubordination towards a superior officer! "I ought to have been shot," I muttered between my teeth, dispersing the importunate gulls with a wild wave of my outspread

arms and a vicious stamp upon the stone floor of the
balcony, which hurt my foot considerably.   The sea,
the rocks, the sand, the greenish-blue sky, and the gorgeous setting sun all went round me in that whirl of
wrath like spinning tops, and I suddenly felt like crying
out with sheer vexation of spirit.

At home I never was allowed to come down in the
evening before dessert was on the table, as I have already stated, but my grandmother treated me differently, and on the rare occasions when I remained with her
after tea-time I took my dinner in her company, proud
of the honor, and behaving as decorously as I could
in order to show my gratitude and appreciation of this
high favor.

On that particular night her old friend the Marquis
de l'A. arrived upon the scene and cheered us up
with his wittily told hunting stories.   A famous sportsman, the marquis was the glad possessor of an unrival-
led *équipage de chasse*.   His horses and hounds were
regarded by true connoisseurs as superior to all
others.   His castle contained a remarkable sporting museum, and in the library, among other countless treasures, was a hunting-book recording many
celebrated boar-hunts of the last century.   I was awfully fond of him, and never tired of hearing his delightful yarns about fur and feather; indeed, to be
noticed by the master of the white-liveried A. hunt
—the oldest in France—was a distinction which I fully
appreciated and greatly plumed myself upon.

That night I enjoyed a *fête complète*, for, instead of
being sent home at half-past seven, my grandmother
apparently forgot me, and I sat as quiet as a mouse on a
hassock between the two old friends, who discussed at
great length the chances of the coming hunting season.
Until recently my grandmother had still followed the

hounds, and her renunciation of this her dearest pleasure was by no means due to the infirmities of age, but, as she candidly confessed, to a sort of *fausse honte* and a quasi observance of conventionalities which are silly, indeed, when they condemn so hale and hearty a woman as she was to relinquish her distinguished place in the hunting-field, merely because she has attained the time when her less privileged sisters are prostrated by the weight of years.

"Ah, *mon ami*," she said, with a positively girlish laugh, "how much I do miss the cool, bracing mornings when we used to start bright and early at the tail of the pack—the dear doggies joyfully rushing out of the kennels while we were mounting our impatient and eager horses. I often catch myself humming the ever-welcome lines of the 'Sortie du Chenil.' You know—

> " 'Sortez du Chenil,
> Mes vaillants limiers.
> Il faut aujourd'hui faire belle chasse;
> Montrez, mes bons chiens,
> Montrez, votre race . . .
> Franchissez, buissons et halliers.' "

"That's right," laughed the marquis. "Why, you are as young as you were twenty years ago, and I call it a downright shame that you should have forsaken us. We miss you so often that I think it is mere selfishness on your part to lock yourself up here in your charmed castle like an angered fairy. You should have seen your grandmother, Pierrot, in those days! There was never a woman to touch her. Always splendidly mounted, and wearing habits that fitted like gloves, she was the picture of a horsewoman and of a huntress."

"Fie, my dear friend! Curb your enthusiasm! You are becoming quite lyrical. Pierrot has seen you in the saddle and you cannot help confessing *qu'après vous il faut tirer l'échelle.* My sons are superb on horse-back, especially this little chap's father. But you are *tout-à-fait de l'ancienne école; de la vieille roche!*—you are faultless!"

And thus did the two old "comrades" make me an excuse for bringing up a host of pleasant memories which filled my little sporting soul with delight, and made me more anxious than ever to keep up the traditions of my race, every member of which had apparently an unconquerable taste for trying to break his or her neck across country.

Later, just before I finally departed, accompanied by the faithful Jean, I had the pleasure of hearing the gallant marquis singing, accompanied by my grandmother's tender touch on the ancient spinnet, those inimitable strophes of De Musset, "La Nuit de Mai," which she had set to music herself. And as we drove rapidly along the moonlit road I warbled with praiseworthy impartiality mixtures of the "Sortie du Chenil," and of—

> " Poëte, prends ton luth et me donne un baiser;
>   La fleur de l'églantier sent ses bourgeons éclore.
>   Le printemps naît ce soir; les vents vont s'embraser,
>   Et la bergeronnette, en attendant l'aurore,
>   Aux premiers buissons verts commence à se poser.
>   Poëte, prends ton luth et me donne un baiser."

CHAPTER IV

> "À l'horizon court un nuage
>   Au flanc noir :
> Pitié, car nous aurons l'orage
>   Avant ce soir."

IT has always been a subject of painful surprise to me that Almighty God should ever permit the black wing of real, deep, despairing sorrow to touch the brow of the very young. I do not mean in saying this to be irreverent. Far be such a thing from my thoughts! But the agony of a childish mind is infinitely more terrible to witness than that of the already formed and tempered being, armed *cap-à-pie* to fight the battles of life. The white purity of youth should rightfully not be disturbed or tarnished by a blast from that destroying furnace which we must all enter sooner or later. Intense bitterness, intense anguish, intense loneliness of soul and of heart, are burdens far too great to be borne by the soft organism of a child, and when such a thing comes to pass, alas! the little spotless spirit is scarred forever with a mark which nothing can efface.

I speak strongly, for I know what such a wound means, and I have carried through life the shuddering remembrance of the hour when it was dealt to me. For a long time it left me no hope of any kind. Weak and giddy with horror, I wished a thousand times that I could die, wished it passionately, ceaselessly; for death seemed to me the only healing power, the only possible road out of my misery. The aged, strangely enough, fear *Pallida-Mors*, but for the young she has no terrors, and, indeed, often appears in the guise of a kind and soothing deity.

One morning I awoke to find the big bed alongside of my own empty. I stared curiously around me, with a vague impression of calamity. Had I overslept myself? No, for the broad metal face of the tall Louis XIV. clock, whereon the early sun's rays shone, told a different tale. Where could my father be? He never went out before breakfast without taking me with him, and, as the door of his dressing-room stood wide open, I felt sure that he was not taking his usual cold plunge. I sprang quickly from my cot, little knowing that I was nearing the turning-point of my existence. I wrapped a bath-robe around me, pulled on my slippers with violent haste, and ran out into the upper hall. Everything was quiet and sunny there. The tapestried walls seemed to open vistas of green forests around me—forests peopled by dwarfed hunters and horses, above which hovered doves twice as large as themselves. This quaint, primitive art had often made me laugh, for little did I know of the value of those splendid pieces of work, but I did not feel much like laughing just then. Rapidly, but noiselessly, I bounded down-stairs two steps at a time, forgetful of the fact that my costume was not everything that it should be. In the *Salle des Gardes*, I was met by Monsieur l'Abbé, who, catching me in his arms, checked my rapid flight.

"Go back to your room, Pierrot," whispered he. "Your father has a headache, and is lying down in his study; you must not disturb him."

"Papa a headache! Nonsense!" I cried, incredulously. "Why, papa is never ill. It cannot be true." Then with a sudden, overwhelming, panic-stricken burst of fear I relapsed into Gaelic, and, clutching the Abbé's arm with all my might, I fairly shrieked:

"Marw ĕo! Marw ĕo!" (He is dead! he is dead!)

"Holy Mother of God, what ails the child? Why, you silly little thing, it's nothing of the kind! He has a mere headache. Don't be a baby, Pierrot! I never saw you like this. Goodness gracious, you are as white as chalk!"

Kindly and gently the blessed old man carried me upstairs, for my trembling legs literally refused all service. Then I felt ashamed of myself. And yet the agony of those few moments still remained with me. My ears were buzzing as if my skull were full of water, and a myriad of infinitesimal sparks of light, forming themselves into dazzling stars, kept passing before my eyes in the most bewildering fashion.

As I sat in the great chair before the window, gazing dizzily into the morning mist called forth by the early sun-rays, and which, like folds on folds of pink gauze, covered both sea and shore, my heart stood still, and I choked down a sob that rose in my throat. Then I drew myself up slowly, and rang the bell to call my attendants. In the mean time Monsieur l'Abbé was vainly endeavoring to explain matters to me.

"Please say no more! Please don't speak to me!" I implored, forcing myself to be calm. "As soon as I have had my bath and am dressed I will ask you to take me to see papa, for I know that he is very ill."

"My child, it is not so. Do not grieve thus. Pray believe me. Your dear father is not in any danger. But why do you wish me to take you to him? Surely, if he be awake, you need no safe conduct to his presence."

I shook my head, but did not reply, for I would not tell my Abbé that the uppermost wish of my heart was to avoid one of my mother's adamantine edicts of banishment.

73

My strange presentiment, which at first had seemed out of all proportion and reason, was nevertheless but the beginning of a long spell of unutterable misery, for my father sickened with typhoid fever. All was done for him that could be done. Our old doctor, a learned and shrewd man in spite of his rough exterior, was unremitting in his care, and when the crisis approached he summoned the greatest and most celebrated physicians from Paris, who shook their heads, murmured some platitudes about the resources to be found in a strong and healthy constitution, consulted together in solemn conclave, and, after duly pocketing their enormous fees, disappeared from our horizon like extraordinarily brilliant but intensely awful and mysterious constellations.

And meanwhile he who was my all lay in the gloom and silence of his chamber, although outside the air was mild and fragrant, and Nature looked her best in her autumnal splendor of golden furze and bracken, murmuring seas, and many-hued sunsets. All the splendor of his life seemed snapped asunder in its prime and perfection. His great strength was gone from him. The poor, whom he had helped, and who came daily clamoring at the gates for news of him, were abandoned. Day and night white-capped Sisters of Mercy watched by him, and both my mother and his own were with him in turns from early morn till late evening. He was delirious most of the time, his superb gray eyes, enlarged and rendered intolerably bright by fever, roaming incessantly about him. Soon it became evident that he could only be soothed when I—poor little mite—was near him. He called for me in his delirium, and the physicians declared that he must have his way. How proud and happy this made me, in the midst of a sorrow so great that it aged me at once and carried

74

me without transition from childhood to adolescence. He was never contented except when I knelt at the side of his bed, or sat quite close to him, and held his burning hand in both of mine. Yet his mere presence was sweet to me, with a sweetness which bordered on anguish.

I did not realize this, of course, because my thoughts and my feelings were all confused and inarticulate, but I have done so since, and also the helpless sense of impotency to save him or even to be of real use which weighed like lead upon the warmth and usual self-reliance of my little soul.

I pause here, seeking words with which to render my meaning exactly, or to picture the plight I was in. Hardy, and loving all out-door sports and seafaring ways as I did, yet this temporary imprisonment in a sickroom was evoking in my whole being something at the same time mystical and restive which was utterly unlike my customary pluck—something, in fact, which, wherever it is found, presages woe. My relations with my mother, thanks to my grandmother's almost constant presence, were less strained than they had been since my brother's advent into the world, but nevertheless we made but poor progress—she and I—when left alone together *par hazard*. I disappointed her perhaps as much as she chilled me, although I attempted sometimes to please her by little attentions, taking the form of a few flowers gathered during the daily walks which, much to my distress, I was made to take with Monsieur l'Abbé, and which were brought to her diffidently by me; of a cushion placed behind her back or a footstool drawn forward to rest her slim and always beautifully shod feet upon. But unfortunately we do nothing well that we do half-heartedly, and in spite of my excellent intentions there must have been something forced in

75

these small advances of mine, and she either detected this, or else disliked the whole proceedings, for I always felt mean afterwards, and just as if I had made myself unbearably ridiculous.

My mother's anxiety and concern during my father's illness were genuine and sincere, and yet they did not soften her in the least. An *enfant gâtée* always, one who all her life had had everything her own way, she maintained a serene immunity from all disagreeable obligations, only breaking through her selfish habits when it suited her to do so, and then by singular fits and starts. She was like a self-indulged child who occasionally gives way to a generous impulse on the spur of the moment, and then feels inclined to yell its lungs out from sheer impotent regret at having done so.

She herself had a *santé de fer* in spite of her fragile appearance, but she dearly loved to act as if she were doomed to die soon. Yet she had no real sympathy for physical ailments — in others. Like all perfect comedians, she knew the difficult art *d'entrer dans la peau du bonhomme*, which, in French theatrical jargon, means identifying one's self wholly with one's part. I found out much later that she persuaded herself at times that she was really in a distinctly perilous state of health. This is a useful gift to possess when one likes to rule one's *entourage* with a sufficiently effective rod.

At last the terrible strain caused by my father's critical condition began to relax, for his medical men pronounced it to be their opinion that the patient was on the mend. The crisis was past, they said, and within a comparatively short time he would be entirely out of danger. The reaction was something indescribable to me, for I passed suddenly from the depths of despair, with all the elasticity of youth, to boundless joy and hope.

THE TRIBULATIONS OF A PRINCESS

It never occurred to me, for a minute, that the encouraging words of the doctors could be doubted, and even when my father recovered consciousness, and when the extraordinary weakness left by the departing fever made him look absolutely corpse-like, as he lay for hours together motionless and silent on his bed, my ecstasy remained unchecked, and I felt as if I could have continually shouted for sheer joy, so profound was my bliss at this unexpected convalescence.

Very slow, however, was the progress made by him, and it was only after many weeks that I once more had the intense gratification of driving out with him, accompanied by the young intern from a Parisian hospital who had, during his entire illness, remained in charge of him at the castle.

At last a day came when the imposing Parisian specialists swooped down once more upon us and decreed that only a season at Vichy would complete this marvellous cure, which they ascribed, of course, to their own profound science and unerring ability. For once my mother completely overruled my father's desires. She would not hear of my being one of the party, which left Brittany for the famous bathing-place without me, and she gained her point. With a sorely grieving heart, but by no means unhopeful of the future, I said what I believed a temporary good-bye to the father whom I was never to see again alive. It was our first long separation, and I took it very hard. Thanks to the absence of my imperious mother, however, I had things pretty well my own way at home. My aunt had been left in charge of the household, and she relaxed her surveillance to such an extent, her tastes being above all musical, and engrossing all her time, that, with the exception of my school-room duties, I was free to ride, drive, or roam about after my own sweet will. This

I did, sometimes with my Abbé, sometimes with Jinks, but usually by myself within the boundary walls of the immense park. When I say that the drive from the park gates up to the castle was six miles long, it will explain how it was that I did not feel very much like a prisoner. Even my bed-time hour had been left more or less open to question. Old Gaud, for some unexplained reason, hated to thwart me at that time, and her oft-repeated "poor little dear" and "poor little child" would have made me uneasy had I not been too young to realize that there must be some good cause for her veiled sympathy and pity.

One sultry night, that I shall remember all my life, I was kept awake for several hours by the exasperating sound of a vilely played violin rising from the open windows of the music-room directly beneath my own. My aunt had discovered that one of our young neighbors was what she called "a very promising musician," and had therefore undertaken the task of making him rehearse some old scores which she thought his talent was especially fitted for. My recollections of this much-vaunted genius are dreadful. Many years later I heard one of those jingling, mournful tunes he used to play on his cheap fiddle executed by the master hand of the great Sarasate himself, and I fled from the imperial concert-room where it was being so superbly rendered, for the sad memories the tune brought back to me made me faint, and so absolutely wretched that I was forced to seek solitude and fresh air, in order to avoid making a spectacle of myself.

My nerves were pretty well shaken up, too, on that hot night in Brittany, for three days before a curious thing had come to pass, one which the superstitious Bretons of my *entourage* had shaken their heads over in gloomy foreboding, though nobody ventured to utter aloud the dread which had filled every soul on the subject. Shortly before midnight on that occasion a loud crash came from my father's apartments and aroused the household. On entering the empty rooms it was found that not only had his heavy cavalry sword become detached from its fastenings above his desk, but that a large mirror, let into the opposite wall, at least thirty-five feet away, was split from end to end. I could not help giving considerable importance to this incident, even though it was carefully explained to me that the fracture was caused by atmospheric conditions — a ludicrous elucidation of the mystery that I was fortunately too young to scorn. What with the uncanny impression created upon me, however, by this accident, and the torturing music from below, I tossed and tumbled on my little cot, and finally climbed into the bed where I had been used to see my father, and to be greeted by his cheery "good-morning."

A flood of bright moonlight filled the lofty room, where every object was clearly distinguishable. Through the open windows a gentle murmur of the waves, and a strong perfume of reseda and heliotrope, mixed with the pungent smell of sea-weed and wet rocks, poured freely in. After a long time the music ceased, and I dropped into a sort of restless doze through which I heard, or seemed to hear, many strange noises, including the sound of hurrying footsteps. I was so tired, however, that I did not thoroughly awaken until I became instinctively conscious that somebody was looking at me. With a violent start I sat up. There, at the foot of the great bed across which I lay, stood a figure draped in lugubrious crêpe veils. It took me some moments to recognize my mother, for I had never seen her otherwise than marvellously gowned in light and brilliant colors. Her presence seemed to me so awful

79

at that moment, and so unexpected, that I could scarcely repress a shriek of terror, and it was only after a twice repeated struggle for speech that I at last gasped out:

"Is that you, mother? What is the matter?"

Without a gesture, without a single motion of her lithe body, she said, in a monotonous voice:

"Your father is dead!"

I have a vague remembrance of uttering one wild, piercing cry, and then heaven and earth seemed to pass away from me.

* * * * * * *

Try as I may, I cannot bring myself to describe the days, the weeks—almost the years that followed. Such a process would entail probing too deeply into a wound that has never healed completely as yet, although the scars of many others now add their pain to it.

Everything seemed to have to come to an end, so far as I was concerned. I saw the world through a black curtain, the thick folds of which allowed no ray of hope to brighten my unhappy lot. At first I resolved to let myself perish with hunger, and refused to take any food, so that I might at once rejoin my dead father. There is little doubt that I would have succeeded — for I have always been singularly stubborn and firm of purpose—had it not been for a young friend of my father's, a captain Comte d'A., who, pitying my despair, took the law into his own hands, and, by dint of clever coaxing, of pointing out to me what he whom I had lost would have wished me to do, led me back to something like reason. For, thanks, in a great measure, to the way in which this crushing blow had been dealt me, I certainly was partially insane for a time.

Petit Pierrot, in those gray eyes,
That gaze in such defiant wise
  Upon a hostile world, nor show
  A tremor in their steady glow—
What a rebellious mischief lies!

Innocence, pluck that never dies,
Hatred of wrong in every guise,
  Gleam there—how merry they can grow!
      Petit Pierrot!

But, ah! how many t'would surprise,
If they could even half surmise,
  The tenderness that lies below
  That bright, brave look, and faintly know,
The depths of love that you comprise,
      Petit Pierrot!

F. J. H. S.

The care and truly unequalled devotion displayed by the young cavalry officer towards a broken-hearted child will always remain with me as one of the redeeming features of the human race. Such exceptions are rare—at least I have found them to be so. But when they are met with they leave an indelible mark upon one's life, and change one's whole views about this poor world of ours. Perchance, however, it was a bad service which Charles d'A. rendered me; for if he had not saved me from myself, I would have long ago been at rest. It chanced that at that very time my little brother was attacked by some infantile ailment, and the whole establishment was in an uproar lest it should become serious. My mother sat up day and night with untiring self-forgetfulness, my kind Abbé had gone to attend a dying brother, and during that period, excepting for my one friend in need, I was alone. Old Gaud, too, completely shattered by the death of her beloved nursling—my Father—was so ill that grave doubts were entertained as to her recovery.

The captain and I wandered about, speaking seldom, but in thorough communion of thought and feeling. For he, too, had loved my father devotedly, and owed much to the superior ·officer who had constantly befriended him when he first entered the army. He was paying his debt of gratitude now, capital and tenfold interest, by what he did for his erstwhile chief's forlorn little child.

Ten years later, in the midst of a brilliant court reception, I was told suddenly that Comte d'A. had been killed during a skirmish with the Touaregs in far-off Africa. Special mention was made of him by the French ambassador, who was my informant, and also of the magnificent bravery with which he had sacrificed his life to save those of many others.

"Oh, God, this is Thy justice and his reward!" I muttered, unconsciously, while the old diplomat went on talking about the hero whose butchered body was being brought back to France, wrapped in the folds of the tricolor. My thoughts were echoed by His Excellency's words: " A fine death! The finest of all! *Celle d'un soldat pour sa patrie. C'était un brave!*"

"Oh yes! Brave and gentle! Loyal and true to the end!" I mused, and turned away blinded by tears, sickened with the gay scene surrounding me. I could not stay there, and so went to my own apartments, where I could at least mourn him in peace. How I realized then—

> " Le prix d'un cœur qui nous comprend,
> Le bien qu'on trouve à le connaître,
> Et ce qu'on souffre en le perdant."

CHAPTER V

"S'il est à vous, votre Rhin allemand,
  Lavez-y donc votre livrée;
  Mais parlez-en moins fièrement.
    Combien, au jour de la curée,
  Étiez-vous de corbeaux contre l'aigle expirant?"

I HAVE now come to the turning-point of my existence — an experience fraught with such amazement and chagrin that at the time it seemed to be the greatest possible humiliation, though I see now, as I look back after many years upon this amazing surprise, that it had a certain humorous aspect in spite of its bitterness. My father had now left us since several weeks, and I was still staggering under the blow that had fallen upon me with such unparalleled brutality when one morning my mother summoned me to her august presence. She was sitting—probably in order to add to the solemnity of the occasion—in my father's study, a room so sacred to me now that it seemed like desecration to see her occupying it. She had grown very thin and ethereal-looking of late, and as I glanced at her hands, stripped of all their great, glittering rings, I was struck by the transparency of her fingers. Her widow's weeds did not suit her at all, and they hardened her appearance. With a weary gesture she motioned me to take a seat opposite her, and in the same monotonous intonation which she had not shaken off since her husband's death, she said:

"I have sent for you because the time has come when you should be made aware of the true state of affairs, as far as you are concerned." She paused as if seeking for words, and I gazed helplessly at her, wondering what new calamity was about to overtake me. Was she going to send me to the convent, as she had often threatened to do whenever I had been particularly difficult to manage in the past? Leave Brittany? I never could do that! For there every nook and corner was pregnant with memories which were my only consolation now, and I resolved on the spur of the moment to shake myself together and make a stand against any such arbitrary measure, if she so much as hinted at it. Those few moments of suspense were simply terrible! and I felt little beads of perspiration start on my forehead as I awaited sentence.

"It was your father's desire that you should not be told what I am about to disclose to you until you reached your tenth anniversary, but circumstances have altered that, and I judge it to be my duty to tell you that you are not what you believe yourself to be, a boy, but merely a little girl."

That was funny! So funny, indeed, that, in spite of my sadness and lack of spirits, I burst into a strident, nervous laugh, thinking *à part moi* that my poor mother had become suddenly insane with grief, if she were not of a truth joking, which seemed possible, so ridiculous was her assertion. Very much shocked, she struck the top of the desk with her closed hand and exclaimed, angrily:

"Do you think that I am not serious? Or does your habitual heartlessness lead you to consider such an important question a laughing matter? and at such a moment, too! Now don't interrupt me, and I will tell you how, when you were born, your father's disappointment at your not being a son was so profound that he insisted on having you brought up as if you had been of the right sex. I tried my best to dissuade him from so doing, but my entreaties were vain. Even when your brother was born I was not allowed to tell you that you were occupying the position which rightfully belonged to him, probably because it might hurt your feelings."

A wild rage had been gradually stealing over me, and when my mother concluded this strange revelation I was absolutely beside myself with passion. My face must have revealed as much, for a restraining touch was put on my shoulder, and, in stern, low tones, my mother said, grimly:

"None of your mad pranks, if you please! Truth is truth, and it had to be told sooner or later. If I had had my way, it would have been sooner. You will be good enough in the future to adopt not only the garments, but also the manners, of the sex to which you belong. Moreover, should I by any chance hear or find out that you have failed to obey my orders, I will send you immediately to a convent, and you shall not leave it again until your marriage, which I intend to take place as soon as possible."

Her grasp relaxed, and without a word I rushed out of the room, down the stairs to the other end of the house, where my Abbé was comfortably ensconced in his private sitting-room, reading *The Lives of the Saints*, or some other such meritorious work not at any rate in keeping with the abrupt appearance of a youthful demon like myself.

The outward calm which I had managed to preserve while in my mother's presence now gave way, and for the first time in my life I was seized with violent hysterics. It was only later on, when the combined efforts of Gaud and Monsieur l'Abbé brought something like comparative peace to my mind, that I at last began to grasp and understand my mother's attitude towards

85

me since Bertrand's advent, and the resentment with which she looked upon the innocent interloper that I was. It took me longer to become even ever so slightly accustomed to my new estate, and I can describe my feelings during the following months as nothing short of a long-continued torture, which began when I woke up in the morning and was only terminated by sleep.

The long and short of it was that I felt ashamed and miserable beyond compare. All my dreams of heroic deeds in the future—of gay and reckless soldiering, of dashing sports, as well as many, many other hopes and ambitions—had been destroyed at one fell stroke. When I looked upon my puny little self in the severe mourning frocks which were so incongruous, when coupled with my short locks and boyish manner, I wept often savagely with disgust and fierce disappointment. Was ever child placed in such a predicament? I believe not; for a singularly manly spirit had been fostered in me by my father, and my unfortunate lack of affection for my mother had engendered in me so great a dislike for everything feminine that this sorry combination has to this day left its stamp upon my whole individuality and character. I am of an abnormally sensitive turn of mind. The idea of ridicule has always been exquisitely painful to me, and it was that perhaps which hurt me most, because I felt myself both ridiculous and in a way debased. The only title I could claim now was that of a regular tom-boy, for so intensely anxious was I not to show my humiliation and *déchéance* that I purposely—perhaps instinctively—avoided all elegance of dress or grace of behavior, and when my attendants tried to embellish my pale, washed-out little self with ribbons or trinkets I tore them off and stamped upon them ferociously. I need not mention that these misdeeds were scrupulously concealed from my mother, for it was well known by those who surrounded me that I need expect no mercy at her hands if she ever found them out or knew of the long hours of rebellion which I frequently gave way to.

My fits of rage were truly awful. Cruel tears would rise to my eyes, but they were not called forth by sorrow alone, and the fire of anger scorched them as they rose. I stamped my foot passionately, set my teeth as a terrier does when snarling, and in one word made a regular little beast of myself, lying flat on the ground and writhing there in agony, like some animal hurt to death.

I resumed most of my habits, however, concerning outdoor life and sports, for our old doctor declared to my mother that any attempt at cooping me up would result in a serious breaking-down of my health. I was therefore allowed, Heaven be praised, to ride, drive, and romp, as much as I pleased, and, as my dear Abbé still continued to superintend my education, I gradually became, if not reconciled, at least a little more accustomed to the radical changes which had taken place around me.

Soon, moreover, grave cares of another nature befell, not alone myself, but all the inmates of the castle, as well as the entire population of France, for the most Homeric war which has been fought in modern times was about to be begotten by the foolish ambition of a woman and the weakness of a man, who, broken by illness and disappointments without number, did not any longer possess even that brilliant audacity which had made it possible for him to ascend the throne of France. Every one knows how that culpable and imbecile war originated with the paltry excuse of a German prince's candidature to the throne of Spain, and ended in the most cruel and pathetic of disasters.

I well remember that during that fateful summer of

1870 our peasantry asserted that they had received from Heaven a sign of what was to come. We were called out from our little beds to witness this extraordinary manifestation, which took the form of a ruby-red aurora-borealis, filling with its scintillating waves the entire vault of the midnight sky. Wrapped up in cloaks, and held by our attendants on the great balcony which overhung the sea, we watched this surpassingly beautiful but also strangely awful spectacle. Little as he was, and unable to realize what he saw, Bertrand cried out with fear, and had to be swiftly borne away, while my mother coolly remarked that it was good for children to observe the phenomena of nature, whether they liked it or not.

At the outset of the campaign no one in the length and breadth of Brittany dreamed for an instant of the possibility of defeat. *"Ce que nous allons leur en ficher une raclée!"* was heard on all sides, and the belief that our ever-victorious army could be vanquished never even so much as entered into any one's calculations.

The Franco-Prussian conflict has been described so ably by great writers that it is not for my paltry pen to attempt anything of the kind. So I will content myself with weaving some of its incidents into the warp of my own history, just as I remember them, and without any desire whatsoever to follow in the footsteps of the official or non-official chroniclers of that period.

It is almost useless to say that all eyes were turned towards the Rhine, and that the general impression was that the abhorred Prussians would be reconducted by our proud and powerful armies to their own boundary-lines at once. The idea that these dark-uniformed, machine-made, beer-drinking cohorts could ever invade our territory, conquer our cities, and crush our spirit was too ridiculous to be considered. Our soldiers had been victorious at Castiglione, at Marengo, at Wagram, at Austerlitz, at Eylau, at Iéna, at Friedland, Lützen, Smolensk, La Moskowa, in Spain, in Africa—everywhere, in fact. Prussia, Austria, Russia, England—all had been forced to bend to our might sooner or later. Why, then, should we be defeated now? Preposterous! The old men who had fought with the First Napoleon grunted beneath their white mustaches, and, rubbing their palsied hands together, declared that *ces sales Prussiens* would regret forever and aye the day when they once again attempted to pit their negligible strength against our all-conquering power. With hurrahs and cries of triumph our soldiers departed, fancying themselves already covered with imaginary laurels, and waving above their heads the glorious old flags glittering with the names of the countless victories won in the present and the past by us.

The news of MacMahon's disaster at Fröschweiler, of Frossard's at Spickeren, was at first not only disbelieved wholly, but also ridiculed. MacMahon beaten! That could not be! Nobody seemed to take into consideration that his small corps had of a truth accomplished prodigies of valor, but had been, alas! overwhelmed by the brute force of an entire army. But when the Bretons finally comprehended and assimilated the fact that despised Prussia had scored, there was such an explosion of hatred against the victors and against the " Francs "—as the rest of the French population is designated by all true Bretons—those Francs who had allowed themselves to be thrashed and routed—that no pen can portray the state of frenzy into which the whole country-side was thrown. Execrations without number were launched at the heads of " incompetent chiefs," and every man, woman, and child swore that the shame must be avenged, and this indignity which had been put upon the grandest people in the world be washed away in oceans of blood before the children of France could again draw an honest breath.

When the Prussians crossed the Rhine, when at last it dawned upon the simple-hearted peasants and fisher-folks that the entire nation was hurrying towards total ruin, a sort of prostrated stupor replaced the rage of the first days, and Napoleon III., as well as his consort, became the scapegoats upon whom torrents of bitterest and rancorous abuse were poured.

The Breton is essentially monarchical in his beliefs, and the reign of the Third Napoleon never was kindly looked upon by them. Indeed, at the time of his marriage to Mlle. de Montijo, there was a universal outcry against so great a forfeiture, and when upon several occasions the sovereign put his foot on Breton soil his reception was of the coldest not to say of the most repellent nature. The stanch and faithful heart of this ancient people was centred on the King—*Le Roy*—as they designated Henri V., Comte de Chambord, the hermit of Froshdorff—the last of a long line of glorious monarchs.

Napoleon, the usurper, the perjurer, the adventurer, who, according to many, was not even distantly related to that greatest of modern generals, Napoleon I., filled them with disgust and with a feeling of distrust which nothing could appease. And if, during the eighteen years of his successful reign, he was an object of such dislike, it can readily be imagined what sentiments he inspired when he lost his crown, ruined his country, and surrendered his tarnished and useless sword to the King of Prussia, and was despatched with some of his innumerable fourgons and tinsel-coated retinue to the castle of Wilhelmshöhe, a disgraced and dishonored prisoner of war.

Bah! even now it makes me shudder to recall the sensation of positive nausea which overwhelmed my little childish being when I was told that the army in which my father had served, and his ancestors before him, had sustained a reverse so grim and so final that no effort—be it ever so magnificent—that no bravery—be it ever so complete—could ever quite efface the stain which darkened its 'scutcheon.

I will remember to my dying day that tragic winter—so cold, so severe—when even in our balmy seclusion, where roses, myrtles, and violets usually blossom from November to November, we felt the grip of frost and the bite of searching, snow-laden winds; while dun-hued fogs enshrouded the bay, and seemed to drop like a veil of mourning over both land and sea. How pitiful, how pathetic the long evenings were now! They began at five in the afternoon, and we sat huddled around blazing fires, with saddened countenances and sorrowful hearts. Descriptions of bloody battles were read aloud to us by the Abbé, who could scarcely repress his indignation and emotion. Had it not been for my sake, indeed, he would have joined the army as a chaplain long before that. My uncles, my cousins, all our masculine relatives and friends, were serving their country, and more than once their names appeared upon the list of those *morts au champ d'honneur*.

After, the incredible number of wounded which littered the gore-soaked soil of poor old France, and for whose accommodation the public and private field-hospitals hastily established everywhere were inadequate, were transported to the four corners of our dismantled country, and we too, thank God, received our share of this eagerly sought burden. The "*Orangerie*," the picture-gallery, and many a lofty salon and reception-room, were transformed into *ambulances militaires*, where rows of little white beds held wounded heroes, bruised, and battered, and maimed during the turmoil of battle. My mother, assisted by my grandmother, my aunts, and the numerous members of our household, nursed these fallen soldiers by day and by night with faithful devotion. There I served my apprenticeship as a nurse, and what little knowledge I may have then gathered of that most glorious of all sciences—namely, the relief of human suffering—has stood me in good stead later on. From the first I felt that I was in my element. Soft-footed and noiseless as a mouse, I crept between those dolorous couches without any feeling of repulsion at the horrors I daily witnessed. As a precautionary measure against contagion from the fever cases, I was clad in white linen, like a diminutive Sister of Mercy, and my hair, which, much to my despair, was beginning to grow long, was completely tucked away under a prim little cap shaped very much like that of a nun. This won for me the surname of *la Petite° Religieuse*, though I trust and sincerely hope that the sacred habit of a real religious never served as a blind to conceal so hot-headed, unruly a creature as I was then.

My ever turbulent and untamed nature absolutely writhed under the fearful humiliations suffered by my country. Extremely precocious, thanks to the awful events through which I had passed in rapid succession during the last months, I felt the shame of it all with as much acuteness as any grown-up person might have done—nay, as had I myself been a disarmed and disgraced soldier, and, in my fits of impotent fury, I went so far sometimes as to thank Almighty God for having recalled to him my dear father before this heart-breaking and supreme experience of boundless patriotic distress became his. Yet my faith in him was ever so great that I could not help feeling that had he lived matters would have been different. How he would have fought! Surely he would have known how to meet the supreme difficulties of such a situation. I used to picture him to myself rallying about him the demoralized troops, cheering and encouraging them by his own noble example, and flying with them at the very throat of the dismayed enemy.

The rendition of Sedan, that of Metz, the alleged treason of Marshal Bazaine, the siege of Paris, and that horror of horrors, the Commune; when drunk with blood and shame brother devoured brother, and Frenchman killed Frenchman, amid a blaze of murderous flames and the crash of historical monuments, followed upon each other like the varying and ever-growing terrors of a nightmare, leaving us palpitating with anguish and almost cursing the day when we were born.

Our villages were peopled now only by weeping, wailing, sable-clad women, who all had lost either a husband, a son, a father, or a brother. The crushing debt of five milliards owing to the Germans before they consented to evacuate our territory, was but yet another martyrdom inflicted upon us, and yet this amazing sum of money was paid, paid to the last sou, by a people fallen, it is true, from their once so high estate, but yet in a measure rehabilitated by their absolute surrender of all that which they could surrender, in order to liberate France.

The nobles and country magnates crippled themselves, sadly drawing to the uttermost limit upon their exchequers; the peasants mortgaged their fields and sold their harvests before they ripened; while the highest ladies of the land pawned their jewels and gave up all display of luxury, regretting only that they could do so little when they saw the humble peasant girls and the poor fishermen's wives cutting their luxuriant tresses as if they had suddenly been stricken by the plague, in order to add what little gold they thus obtained to the glittering treasures which the relentless Prussians so greedily demanded. So absolute and general was this feeling of utter devotion to a beloved country in its dire hour of need, so naturally did it come to us, that it was without a murmur that I saw the racing-stud which my father had so loved pass into the hands of English dealers, and his yacht, the beautiful, exquisitely graceful *Ichtis*, sold to a wealthy Spaniard, who looked to me as if he were made of chocolate, with his round, lustreless eyes, his swarthy skin, and his brown, curly beard—which as much as anything else made me detest him.

"*C'est pour la patrie, mon petit Enfant,*" whispered my grandmother, when she noticed that my eyes were brimful of tears, and that my chest was heaving with a sorrow almost too profound to be kept under restraint.

"*Pour la patrie*"—that explained and made everything possible at that moment. Every drop of our blood would we willingly have shed to efface the pity of it all, and to have known that France could once again hold up her head as in the proud and cloudless years when she had been *Reine et Maîtresse*.

Seven years later I reassumed temporarily the rôle of military nurse at the opposite extremity of Europe, and went through many days of terrible strain and fatigue in ambulance tents, where fresh blood was flowing and where the stricken men which we tended were carried from the battle-field still throbbing with life and enthusiasm under their torn, powder-smeared uniforms. What a different spectacle was that of the Castle "*Infirmerie*," permeated by the fever of old wounds, filled with the moaning of delirious patients, who often wept like little children in helpless despair at their own weakness and uselessness while the enemy yet remained unrepulsed and defiled our fairest provinces. Exhausted, almost collapsed, looking more like skeletons than like human beings, with their white, cadaverous visages and their sleepless eyes, they made up a picture of nerve-shaking misery in spite of the care with which they were surrounded, the freshly gathered flowers placed each day at their bed-heads, the snowy linen of their sheets and pillows, and the roaring, merry fires, kept up continuously, not only to warm but to purify the air which they breathed.

We were very proud of our different wards, especially of the one which had been organized in the " *Orangerie.*" The great big golden -fruited, white- blossomed trees, rising from huge square majolica tubs, sufficed in themselves to adorn the place and make it cheery and attractive to our patients. There were very few blossoms on these trees, so few, indeed, that their perfume could in no wise interfere with the salubrity of the place; therefore, much to my joy, they were not ordered to be removed by the attending physicians.

Before *l'année terrible* I had never seen death, and all painful spectacles had been spared me, so that my first experience in this respect was a deep and lasting shock. Fortunately the first time that I saw a spirit pass away in that luxurious little hospital of ours, it happened to be under the most favorable circumstances —if one may so express one's self—for it was that of a young and remarkably handsome soldier who died without a murmur, just as had he fallen asleep, and whose beautifully chiselled features immediately assumed that unutterable look of peace and supernatural content which is sometimes met with on the countenances of those who leave this sad world of ours before they have

had the occasion to empty to the dregs the bitterness of
its cup. Indeed, ever since that day death appeared to me
in the guise of an all-powerful soother, and of a friend,
much more than in that of an enemy. It served to make
me realize also that when my Abbé told me that my father
was now at rest and happier than he could ever have been
on earth, the worthy old man was speaking the truth.
There was consolation in that thought, although it was
tinged always with the regret that for once that dear
father of mine had been selfish in not allowing me to
share that grand, enviable peace, and had left me behind, unloved and misunderstood by those whose duty
it should, it seemed to me, have been to cherish me all
the more, since I had lost my all.

Such beings as was my father leave after them an
eternal remembrance and an ineffaceable impress upon
the existence of those who have loved them. Up to this
day, during a career of much variation of feeling and of
country, it has only been my fortune to meet with three
creatures who seemed to have been made by Almighty
God with a special care and for a special purpose, whose
qualities so far outnumbered their failings that the
latter entirely disappeared and gave merely the impression of those dainty transparent shadows which one
observes in Corot's finest pictures, a mere veil over yet
more beauty. Two of these *êtres d'élection* have
gone before: one was my father, the other my Empress. About the third I will be silent, excepting for the
fact of venturing to hope that during the many years
which, please God, will be his upon earth, he will realize
what boundless power a truly pure, earnest, and cour-
ageous spirit can wield over our ever-struggling, sin-
ning, and suffering humanity.

" J'ai vu sous le soleil tomber bien d'autres choses
Que les feuilles des bois et l'écume des eaux,

Bien d'autres s'en aller que le parfum des roses
Et le chant des oiseaux!

" Mes yeux ont contemplé des objets plus funèbres
Que Juliette morte au fond de son tombeau,
Plus affreux que le toast à l'ânge des ténèbres.
Porté par Romeo.

" La foudre maintenant peut tomber sur ma tête
Jamais ce souvenir ne peut m'être arraché;
Comme le matelot brisé par la tempête.
Je m'y tiens attaché."

CHAPTER VI

" I am sick of the hall and the hill, I am sick of the moor and the
    main!
Why should I stay? can a sweeter chance ever come to me here?
Oh, having the nerves of motion, as well as the nerves of pain,
Were it not wise if I fled from the place and the pit, and the fear?"

THIS Franco-Prussian campaign, upon which I have
lightly touched in the preceding chapter, was in a measure a welcome truce in my strained relations towards my
mother. Every mind was so taken up during that time
with the woes of France that personal matters dwindled
into nothingness; but, alas! as soon as our existence
regained its ordinary placid course, like a torrent temporarily imprisoned by ice and suddenly freed from all
restraint, the sad strife, so unfilial, in spite of the fact
that it was concealed by great outward marks of respect
on my side, and by apparent parental solicitude on hers,
broke out with renewed vigor.

" C'est fini, nous ne nous comprendrons jamais!" I
often mused. And although at that time if my mother
had softened towards me in the slightest degree I would
have eagerly responded to her advances, her constant severity, her perpetual nagging—a very trite
word, but there is no better to describe her ceaseless
fault-finding whenever I was in her presence—repelled
me more and more, and drove me often to positive desperation.

It is but seemly that I should here confess the fact—
if it be of any interest—that I was endued with an extraordinarily exasperating turn of mind myself, and

98

NO LONGER PIERROT, BUT MARGUERITE!

that the tact and patience required to tame such a nature as mine is hardly ever to be found on this earth, and can only be replaced by a deep and all-conquering love. When such qualities are united, as they were in my father, the result is strangely perfect, but otherwise a situation of this sort is liable to increase in difficulty as time goes on.

The very thought that I was now expected to behave like a little girl, decorously and in a perfectly maidenly fashion, was more than sufficient to goad me on to the most execrable displays of boyish daring. How I escaped with my life is really amazing, for I was never so entirely happy as when climbing the most dangerous portions of the cliffs, going out alone in stormy weather in my cockle-shell of a sailing-boat — which, I must say, I managed quite ably—or riding barebacked those of the horses that had not been thoroughly exercised, and consequently most resented my attempts at curbing their will.

Once a rather typical incident occurred, under the following circumstances: Shortly before his death, my father had given me a very pretty *jardinière* of Roman pottery, containing a beautiful double camellia, the faintly pink, velvety blossoms of which were a delight to me. This *jardinière* stood on the broad ledge of my bedroom window, and I treasured it almost above all other things in my possession. One morning the woman who was in charge of the sweeping in my part of the castle unfortunately knocked it down with her broom-handle, smashing both pot and plant into pieces on the tessellated floor. I happened upon the scene at that very moment, and so great was my rage that, although I was invariably polite, nay, even affectionate, to all those faithful old servants of ours, I flew at the culprit, whose name was La Cognate,

99

and, shaking her violently, showered upon her a volley of epithets the only merit of which was their extreme expressiveness and pointed application. Terror-stricken, the poor little peasant-woman entreated me to forgive her, but I raved on with such passion that she might as well have been talking to the wall for all the effect which she produced. In the midst of this pleasant little colloquy my mother entered the room, and stood for a few seconds literally rooted to the spot in the extremity of her surprise.

As she declared afterwards, she could not believe her eyes when she saw a child of hers demean itself in so shameless a way, and she instantly demanded that I should go down on my knees before the weeping Bretonne and crave her pardon. I need not state—for I am sure by this time that it is useless to explain what manner of a devil frequently raved within me—that I flatly refused to obey, even when I was given the ultimatum of complying with my mother's request or of being locked up in my room on a delectable diet of bread and water until I "came to my senses."

Had somebody at that minute been shrewd enough to point out to me the odium of my conduct and the injustice thereof, all would have yet gone well, but, instead of that, fuel was added to the flames, when my mother contemptuously ordered La Cognate to throw away the remnants of my treasure—bruised leaves, buds, pottery, and all "rubbish," she called them, just as I was snatching them from the ground, with the idea of preserving them like relics. This was too much!

I set my teeth, clinched my fists, and remained stonily obdurate to all objurgations, until at last, after going, when left to myself, through a period of absolutely disproportionate despair—when compared to the misfortune to which I had been subjected—I lay panting on the floor, sobbing piteously, with a vague intention rising in my mind of putting an end to everything by jumping out of the window on to the rocks below.

Slowly and wearily the hours dragged along. I tried to read and to look at pictures, but I could not fix my attention, and when at six o'clock my mother herself brought me my pittance, and commanded me to go to bed, I was reduced for the first time in my life to downright sullenness.

Tired out with weeping, I finally fell asleep, but woke up when the moon, then at its full, flooded the room with its bright rays. It was past two o'clock in the morning, and my misery returned to me with such a rush of indignant feeling that I decided, on the spur of the moment, to display the contempt which I felt for the treatment I had received. Suiting the action to the thought, I dressed myself quickly and silently, and, throwing open the casement of one of my windows, I looked down the sheer ivy-covered wall which overhung the pleasure-ground by some sixty feet. The ivy was so ancient that its trunk was thicker than my arm and as strong as a steel cable. Hastily I resolved to make good my escape by means of it. I stuffed the pockets of my reefer-jacket with the bread brought for my dinner, and which had remained untouched on the table, then I proceeded to pack a small haversack with a suit of boy's clothes and different other things I greatly prized. When this was done I stole on tip-toe into the room which had been my father's, and, standing on a long divan, I detached from the wall a broad-bladed hunting-knife, which I buckled around my waist.

Strange to say, all these preparations cheered me wonderfully, my despair and sadness had flown as if by magic, and as I went about them I began to hum softly to myself some snatches of the "Complainte de Saumur," which my father had often sung in the dear, merry days of yore.

> "Un jour de cuite
>   Et de pituite
> Tupin, là-haut, était tout attristé,
>   Car dans l'Olympe,
>   Quand on y grimpe,
> On n'trouve pas toujours de la gaîté!"

The sound of a creaking wainscoting made me pause, and I looked about, praying in my heart that no one should hear me. All was silent again, so silent that I distinctly perceived the rustling of the night wind in the great ivy. I jumped from the divan to the floor, and began to lace my tall gaiter-like boots, resuming my song as if nothing out of the way was on my mind. I rattled, in a subdued tone, through the eleven couplets, and when I reached the last—

> "Prends mon aumône,
>   Car je m'abonne,
> Et veux agir en vrai sous-officier,
>   Hippologie!
>   Viens, ma chérie!
> Avec Vénus je vais t'étudier!"

At last I was ready to go, but unfortunately the familiar words of the "Complainte" had once more changed my mood. I had so often laughed heartily at this queer ditty, although I did not understand the sense of it all, that my present desolation and horrible loneliness contrasted cruelly with the fun and frolic that had disappeared forever from my life.

The huge room was bathed in moonlight, the toilet-table, with its glitter of gold and of silver, its large mirror, and the famous blue-velvet Christmas pin-cushion (which, rejected by my fastidious mother, had been annexed by my father, who told me subsequently that he liked it because I had selected it) stood out from the dark wall as clearly as had it been midday.

Suddenly I caught sight of a life-size portrait of my father, painted when still in the army, and at that time a dashing young officer. The soft, silvery effulgence pouring in through the casements enfolded the superb work of art in such a way that the tall, soldierly figure, the handsome face, so perfectly modelled, the long mustaches, and especially the glorious eyes, gave me the impression of absolute reality. Step by step I drew nearer, gazing passionately and with rapt adoration at the picture.

Why did he not speak to me? Why was he so immovable, so distant?

"Papa," I murmured, in an awe-struck whisper, "dear, dear papa, speak to me! *C'est Pierrot qui est là, et à qui vous manquez tant! Pierrot, qui vous adore et qui ne peut pas vivre sans vous!*"

But the calm, determined face remained motionless, the eyes, supernaturally brilliant and large, did not smile at me, and, with a sob of unutterable anguish rising in my throat, I fled from the room as if I had been pursued by furies.

He did not answer me! He was gone forever from his own little boy, so why should I remain in that place, which knew him no more? In an instant, however, I collected my wits, and, securely fastening my knapsack to my back, after mechanically crossing myself—a soldier cannot pray very long when the trumpet calls—I clambered over the window-sill, and, clutching the ivy with fingers and knees, I began my perilous descent. I never glanced to right or to left, and, skilled in cliff-climbing, I especially avoided looking downwards, for the sight of the void beneath would, I knew, render the task a more difficult one yet.

It seemed as though I was very close to the dark-blue sky, where the stars sparkled brightly. One false move, and then there would be a headlong rush, and silence forever! Who would care? I thought, excepting dear little Bertrand, who was yet too little to sorrow deeply at the loss of his clandestine playfellow, and my old Abbé, who often said:

"La mort n'est pas une porte qui se ferme, c'est une porte qui s'ouvre.
    La vie présente est éclairée par la vie future."

Such thoughts travel swiftly at similar moments, and, while clinging like a swallow to my slender hold upon the grim old wall, I reflected that he would think me happier dead than alive, and as to Gaud—well, she was so near the Great Gates herself she would not mourn for long. A flight of pigeons, disturbed by the shaking of the venerable ivy, flew upward with a startling whirl of silky wings, and circled bewilderingly above my head, frightened and distressed. My foot slipped; a second more and I would have been precipitated from the yet dizzy height—for I was barely half-way down—but I recovered myself with the promptitude of a sailor, or a squirrel, and before I had even realized the greatness of the danger I was standing firmly on the turf, safe and sound, without as much as a scratch or a bruise.

Cautiously I made my way towards the stables; the two watch-dogs, Romulus and Remus, who prowled about all night, came bounding towards me over the grass, but they had scented me, and did not make a sound. Their joy at this unexpected meeting took the form of enormous leaps and jumps, then they followed me like two gigantic tame lions, until I came to the iron railing enclosing the paddock. To enter the main stable was quite out of the question, for this would have aroused the men, but in a small, separate building—an old tower—in fact—Bucéphale, "*the pink horse,*" as we called him, lived in solitary state. He was immensely large and unusually powerful, cream in color, with a faint suggestion of strawberry about his coat, mane, and tail—*un cheval à crins lavés,* as they say in France. The head was large, heavy, with broad but tapering ears, moreover he was well ribbed-up, had fine shoulders and an immense girth and loins. But he was ungainly to a degree courting ridicule, and so he remained in durance vile, nearly always out of sight, except when the under-gardeners needed his enormous strength to drag their ponderous carts about or to haul timber or stones. Moreover, Bucéphale's temper was not an easy or an agreeable one; perhaps the consciousness of his own homeliness made him restive; but, be this as it may, certainly he inspired all who approached him with boundless distrust. I alone had a sort of sneaking affection for him, and often brought him carrots and apples in his solitary prison, climbing into the manger to put myself on easier equality with him.

Fleet as an antelope, I now ran to the old tower, actuated to speed by a fury of resistless goading. Swiftly as a swallow darts, I rushed into the dark stable, unloosed the horse's halter, climbed upon his broad back, and in another five minutes, having walked him noiselessly over the sward, I was off at full gallop, scattering shreds of the early morning mist, as I went on my breathless way, to right and left. I rode straight through the park, keeping to the grassy borders of the paths, for fear of being heard. It was a good thing for me that I had been tossed upon a horse from my earliest years, for

Bucéphale, going *ventre à terre*, was not an easy mount to stick to, but I never swerved, and clung to him like a monkey. Soon I passed out of the park through a gap in the most ancient portion of the mediæval walls —a sort of dismantled postern, draping its worn sides under cascades of luxuriant ivy and honeysuckle— and swept on to the weird, deserted *Landes*, heading towards the left side of the promontory on which the castle is built. I saw nothing as I dashed onward, except that Bucéphale was reeking with smoke and foam, and that I must speedily check him or else founder him. The rapidity of my flight was telling on me, too; my brain, shaken up like a bowlful of porridge, had no sense; my hands, sore and lacerated, pained me, and a sound of bells and general confusion was in my ears. Yet I remembered my object in riding forth, and now guided my horse to a break in the cliffs, where I knew that I could reach the rugged shore and hide myself in a deep, dark cave, vaulted like a cathedral, and which bore the rather creepy name of "*La Grotte du Diable.*"

At the beginning of the abrupt descent of this rocky crevice I paused and jumped to the ground. The water looked especially treacherous, and was of that peculiar opaque green which betokens storms or very high tides, and the rising wind carried with it a strong, bitter flavor of brine and sea-weed. For a moment I stood undecided, holding the halter of Bucéphale, who was snorting at my side, and shaking his huge bulk as the cool breeze struck his steaming sides. The path I had to descend, ordinarily used by coast-guards, was very steep and difficult, but I was past heeding such trifling obstacles, and, dragging my exhausted horse behind me, I began my downward course. The loose stones and sand preceded us in noisy cataracts as we advanced cautiously, and both of us stumbled and recovered our footing many a time.

How lonely it was on that incline, facing the restless ocean, which grew more and more menacing! The weather was becoming decidedly bad. A low cloud smote me with a short-lived torrent of rain-drops, sharp like needles, and I instinctively rubbed my disengaged hand across my eyes. The sun was quite hidden now, and a weird, livid light lent a leaden color to the southern horizon. The sea grew heavier and heavier, foam like white powder covered every rock, and there was a raw, hard, unseasonable feeling in the air, while my friends the mews whirled above my head, screaming dismally.

At last I reached the beach, and managed to steer Bucéphale into the cave. Poor old chap! what with the rain and his own previous drenched condition he was in a sorry plight. I led him to the upper end of the grotto, where the sand was fine and dry, and, standing on a bowlder, I rubbed him down as best I could with a piece torn from his stable blanket, which I had left on him when I abducted him from his tower.

The equine giant looked at me intelligently, and I thought a little pitifully, as I thus exerted myself on his behalf, and he completed my work by rolling luxuriously in the dry sand above mentioned.

I was so tired that I, too, lay down at full length and closed my eyes wearily. A wave splashing me slightly made me sit up with a start, and I perceived that the tide had made me a prisoner. An instantaneous certainty that I was lost came over me, and I gazed helplessly at the water, which now, like a wall, arose before the opening of "La Grotte du Diable" and rapidly gained ground. Scum and little pebbles were hurled in my face, and Bucéphale whinnied and sought refuge higher up, pawing the ground impatiently. The flicker of noon through clouds was hardly perceptible, and I could see but dimly, for all around me hung a gray mist of spray, which the wild winds drove furiously inward. I sighed and joined the horse, who looked like an indistinct and shapeless mass, without hardly any form or color to distinguish it from the brooding gloom and slaty walls of the cave.

"*Mon pauvre vieux, nous sommes fichus tous les deux,*" I said, leaning against him and speaking more emphatically than politely. The old chap grunted and turned his ungainly head towards the incoming water with a sniff of contempt.

"*Tu n'as pas peur?*" I continued, and, as I was beginning to feel pangs of hunger, I took out what little food I had brought with me, and shared it with him, *en frères.*

Little by little, however, my thoughts returned to my grievances, and my only wish was to lie down quietly and to die there in solitude. A sob shook me, for there seemed to be no hope now of ever emerging alive from that awful trap.

"Am I a coward or an utter brute, or both?" I asked myself. "I came here to escape; well, my escape will be for good and all. What of that?" The idea cheered me, and I waited in calm indifference for the end. I had not realized that this would be one of the high tides of the year, or else I would not have sought refuge in my present impregnable fortress—impregnable, except by the ocean itself. My eyes swept over the remorseless breakers, and then I suddenly thought of Bertrand. "How could I leave him?" I cried aloud, wrathfully. "How could I?"

The hours passed. The violence of the storm and of the waves abated a little, and still I sat motionless, for I had lost almost all consciousness, all memory, save of that beloved little brother, who would possibly cry bitterly when he was told of my death. It seemed to me that the solitude around me and the dangers with which I was beset were not more desolate than my own fate. Numbed and stupefied, wet, cold, and faint, I asked myself why I had run away, and what good I had hoped to achieve by this mad freak. I patted from time to time the big horse, who stood patiently waiting by me, turning his docile eyes with a wondering sadness towards the narrow outlet across which the setting sun was now casting a blinding glow through a rift in the purple clouds.

After a while I noticed that the tide was receding, and little by little it dawned on me that we were saved. Reeling slightly, I rose and stretched myself, and watched the ruddy rays fade, the sky turn to a sickly blue, the water noiselessly drain itself out of my cave, and at last the stars peep forth far, oh, so far above me; and then it was that I heard a faint echo of shouting human voices. Ah, yes! a searching-party, I thought. I would see Bertrand again, after all! But the odd stupor that comes from long exposure and hunger was stealing over me. My feet and hands tingled, and I gazed dizzily to the ocean vapor below me and the granite roof above my head. My heart stood still in my breast, and there was no strength left in me to shout back. I saw the light of a lanthorn cast its red glare into the cave, and then I must have swooned.

All that day the faithful people of my dead father's household had been looking for me. Ever since the moment when it was discovered that my bed was empty, my clothes and knapsack gone, and Bucéphale away from his stable, they had scoured the land.

At last they traced the horse's footprints and followed them near to the cave. But the tide prevented even these brave men from coming to me sooner, and their distress was great when they realized that I would of a certainty be washed out to sea.

They, however, by a last scruple of conscience, determined to visit the grotto as soon as the passage leading to its narrow inlet became free, and there, to their intense amazement, they found me, saved as by a miracle.

It would be useless to describe my return home; I myself do not clearly remember it. But one thing will stand out in my memory ever—the frantic joy of Bertrand when we met again. My mother had been too thoroughly frightened to be severe. She said but little, and what she did say concerned merely creature comforts of which I stood in sore need.

The tenderness of my tiny brother made me repent greatly for what I had done, and unsolicited I promised my mother never to act again in so reprehensible a way. Tears came like dew on my parched little heart. I laid my soul bare before Almighty God, and tried to pluck my pride and stubbornness and impatience from their bleeding roots. That night my resolve was taken; I decided to conquer myself, and I hoped to succeed; yet I often faltered upon my way and mused—

> "The darkness over my road doth creep—
> Of a guide I am bereft;
> Which path leads from this lonely deep,
> Is it to right or left?"

CHAPTER VII

"The rosebud shakes because
A bird on its twig flew,
My own soul shakes because
I think, my dear, of you;
I think, my dear, of you;
My darling, charming maid,
Thou art the richest gem
My God has ever made!"

MY uncle's castle! Is there any place in the universe where the traditions and customs of the past have been so extraordinarily preserved? And my uncle himself— haughtiest of the haughty, and a trifle narrow-minded old aristocrat, who would never abate one jot of the magnificence which he considered due to the name he bore! His stud was faultless. His cook was an artist in his line. A retinue of admirably trained servants filled the vast halls, the stables, and the gardens. The banqueting-room, the picture-gallery, the *enfilades* of *salons*, were worthy the gallant old family tree which was his pride. Pride of race, not of rank, was his most marked characteristic. It showed in the erect carriage of his head, in the flash of his dark falcon eyes, and in his whole bearing. He was the type of a chivalrous *Seigneur*, better fitted for the days of knighthood than for our degenerate period. He hated everything modern with a cruel and a savage hatred which he failed to conceal or to temper, and which strongly colored all his actions, as it soured and wounded those who did not think and feel as he did. But he was, nevertheless, too much

111

of a thoroughbred by nature to ever follow or accept the vulgar indecorum of our time, which makes it possible to state one's opinion at every turn—be it ever so harsh —and *à tous risques*.

To him discourtesy was worse than the breaking of the commandments. Hence he did not associate with people of whom he did not approve.

His hatred of the *bourgeoisie* was as deep and ingrained as the hatred of game-birds for a red dog; but he loved his peasants—his vassals, he called them— and was kind and paternal to them in the extreme. He had never married, and his noble old house was kept by *la vieille Catherine*, a dragon of virtue, who bristled with good qualities. She was a stately person, with hair as white as silver, dark robes, and a "Henin"- shaped cap, that gave her the appearance of a figure taken from some old missal. I irreverently called her *la vieille Catherine*, although every one else addressed her as "*Dame Catherine*."

The castle was a great Gothic pile, which in days of yore had been blasted with petronels and riddled with arrows and bullets. Yet it still possessed a solemn beauty, given to it in ancient times by those masterly hands that built for the pure love of art, and with the intent of erecting imperishable records of their toil. It stood on the top of a high hill, surrounded by deep, secluded valleys, dense forest lands, sheltering an abundance of game in their dusky recesses. A semi-royal palace, silent and solitary and impressive, only a few miles from the eternally moaning ocean, but far from the roar and filth of steam and the vandalism of progress.

I used to spend some weeks of every year there, but my mother seldom accepted the courtly but cold invitations sent to her as in duty bound by her brother-in-law.

These two detested each other—no weaker term will do. The grave, severe, somewhat suspicious character of my uncle made a striking contrast to my mother's self-indulgent, capricious and unreasonable nature. When she brought her restless spirit, her marvellous gowns, and her mundane fragrance to the stately old place, he shuddered at the discordance which she produced therewith, and his grim, stern smile of disapproval must have cut her at times like a whip.

To me he was always good and indulgent. *"Tu es de la vieille roche, toi, petit Crapaud!"* he often said. *"Tu ressembles à ton père et à nous tous!"*—a compliment which pleased and gratified me beyond measure.

"And you," I retorted one day, "are like Parsifal, or Perceforest, riding away to find the emerald cup of legend."

He laughed his low, grave laugh. "An *old* Perceforest, then," he muttered, "on whose head much snow has fallen."

We were riding across the home woods, and the slanting beams of the setting sun pierced through the closely packed dark stems of the glorious trees he loved so much.

"How old are you, Marguerite?" he suddenly asked, turning in his saddle to look at me, as if an unexpected idea had just occurred to him.

"I will be fifteen next August, *mon oncle*," I replied, proudly.

"Fifteen next August," he repeated, musingly, "which means that, as we are in November, you are only fourteen and three months. *Par ma foi, petite fille,* you look much older than that—almost a woman, in fact. You are like a white rosebud about to burst into bloom, my dear. Forgive your old uncle if he tells you so."

"Why, you dear old darling, how poetical you are!" and with my usual impetuosity I threw myself almost off my horse and hugged my uncle as a young bear would its sire. I was not accustomed to hear nice things about myself, and his words delighted me.

The dying sunlight played among the leaves, turning them to gold, and suddenly a shadow fell athwart a venturesome scarlet ray, thrown like a broad and dazzling arrow a little ahead of us.

With this weird glow shining full upon him was a boy, mounted on a superb hunter—a boy but little over twenty—tall, lithe, and broad-shouldered, with a thoroughly beautiful, fearless face, large hazel eyes, and tawny, short-cropped curls.

"Alban!" exclaimed my uncle, "where do you drop from?"

The lad started a little, and looked at us with a glad smile.

"I have ridden with the hounds all day, hoping to find you at the meet, or during the run."

In the half-laughing words there was an inflection of pain and regret that struck my ear with a vague sense of sorrow. His eyes looked earnestly, almost beseechingly, at me; his lips, under his light, silky mustache, were tremulous. Then he laughed the soft, merry laugh of his still lingering boyhood.

"Thank God, I have found you now!" he said, simply.

My uncle turned his head towards him, and a warmth and gentleness overspread his grim features, such as I had seldom if ever seen there.

"Good boy!" he murmured, as we broke into a trot, all three abreast, under the rapidly deepening forest shadows. "Come home with us and share our dinner. Marguerite is *mattresse de maison* just now, and, if you get naught else, you may feed on flowers, for she has taken the decoration of the table in hand, and turns it into a fairy bower at every meal."

Alban was my uncle's godchild, and the apple of his eye. For he was also the son of his dearest friend, the Marquis d'A. The young man had just entered the army, and was on a short furlough before the departure of his regiment, the —th Dragoons, for the south of France. A singularly rare and interesting type was this manly lad, capable of the maddest follies, when roused, but shy and almost timid in his every-day bearing. He enjoyed risking life and limb in reckless rides, for he was terribly in earnest in whatever he undertook to do. I had not seen him very often, for he had joined his regiment immediately after leaving the cavalry school at Saumur. But during this last visit to my uncle's we had ridden and driven and walked a great deal together, with my dear avuncular relative for a chaperon.

Alban was a young dare-devil, who had played with death more than once, but to me he was extraordinarily gentle. And even young and guileless and quaintly childish as I still was, I could see that he liked me well in spite of all the reserve which the old French etiquette imposed upon our slightest actions. I had never been a moment alone with him. Such possibilities do not exist even between cousins and near relatives in our world. Yet, *l'amour est enfant de Bohème, et pardessus le marché un petit espiègle*, who laughs at etiquette and makes his meaning plain in spite of all imaginable obstacles. I began to think in those autumn days that Alban was a veritable hero—and so he finally proved to be, poor, dear boy! His frank, clear eyes, so soft at times, so trustful, his handsome features, with their sunny candor, his daring and grit and inimitable *chic*, made up a *tout-ensemble* that filled my youthful mind with wonder and admiration. I was a small noddy-bird, with no knowledge of life and no experience. But

I was certain that my father would have been pleased with Alban, and that was enough to make me glory in my drawing affection for him.

Now I look back upon myself as I was then with the grimness of a veteran, hearing those who have never been wounded jest at scars, but still the bloom of that first love has never been rubbed off, nor has its memory faded.

As we rode over the smooth sward of the stately gardens, a tall, commanding figure came out from the deep shadow of the celebrated royal elms that sheltered the front terraces.

It was Alban's father, who declared to us that he had come to claim his old friend's hospitality for dinner. The marquis was a *gentilhomme de race*, if ever there was one. He possessed a supreme and easy grace, full of dignity and many martial and virile qualities, wonderfully blended together, and there was no effort or assumption in his courtly manners. He was a stately personage, with iron-gray hair and long, sweeping mustaches like those of a Pandour—a man of iron courage and strong constitution—was this old-fashioned *grand-seigneur*, and my heart went out towards him as he lifted me from my saddle and before setting me down on the sanded drive kissed my cheek as if I had been his own little daughter.

It was seven o'clock when we assembled in the great dining-hall, where our four covers were laid at the upper end of the long board, loaded with plate, and, as my uncle had promised, with flowers and fruit that I had arranged. Below the salt sat my uncle's chaplain, his secretary, his chief steward, and his equerry; for such was the ancient rule he invariably followed. The moon was rising, and the nightingales were singing outside, and through one of the open casements long flower-laden tendrils of clematis and jessamine were swung gently inwards by the light night wind.

Instead of going up to my room immediately after dinner, as usual, I lingered on the terrace, where the three men were smoking. Finally I wandered off to where a climbing Rose de Dijon, covered with hundreds of blossoms, cast a shadow checkered by moonbeams upon the stone flooring, and sat down on the elaborately carved balustrade. I could not have explained why, but my whole soul was filled with a sort of awe and trembled within me as if I had reached the supreme moment of my fate.

Suddenly Alban detached himself from the group and joined me. His face was pale and grave, but his eyes had a suppressed, and to me a surprising, light in their depths. I felt as if the dark woods, the sleeping *parterres*, were wheeling around me. We were both mute, and he no longer looked at me, but at the star-studded sky above us, beseechingly, it seemed almost.

"Marguerite," he said at last, tremulously, "I am a man of few protestations—hardly a man, even as yet —but I know my own mind, and I am steadfast and true. I love you, my dear, with all my heart, with all my soul, with all my strength! You are too young as yet to hear and understand such words, but I am going away so soon, that I could not bear to part from you without telling you that I am yours, and will be yours always!"

I looked straight up at him, and without a word I placed both my hands into his. I heard the quick indrawing of his breath, as he knelt at my feet and rested his curly head against my knee.

"Marguerite! My *Marguerite des Marguerites!*" he murmured, softly, "my pearl of pearls! my treasure, you are the richest gem that God has ever made!"

With tears in my eyes, I rose, trembling a little. How deliciously all this sounded! Alas! poor little me!

"My father and my godfather know that I love you, Marguerite," he continued, "and they are glad that it should be so. In a year I will come back and claim you as my own, my little, beloved girl!"

We were now standing side by side, and he drew me gently towards him. Suddenly I was filled with a palpitating, intoxicating hope. I felt intuitively that the old, fearless, high-handed, single-hearted love which had inspired great deeds to long-vanished knights and ladies was within our grasp, that it was not dead, but lived again in all its poetry and romance, and little as I suspected or knew of love, my instinct told me that Alban was a lover such as any maiden might be proud of—might esteem, respect, and adore. With him I would be free forever from tyranny and injustice. We would live a wonderful life, *tissée d'or et de soie*, like unto a continuous fairy tale. All these wild, joyous thoughts whirled through my brain as my head rested confidently on his shoulder and his hand softly caressed my hair.

"I will love you forever, Marguerite, with a love that is a religion—a love so sacred, so holy, so pure, that you will learn to give me such a love in return."

The night wind shook the rose-leaves upon us, and the nightingales in the thickets stopped their singing, as if they purposely hushed their melodies in order to listen to that other *alleluia d'amour* uttered so near to them.

A little later we came hand-in-hand to where the sponsors of our love still sat, lazily smoking.

"It is wise sometimes to listen to one's heart," said my uncle, stretching his hands in solemn benediction towards us.

What a peerless evening this was! *C'était le ciel!*
But when the time came to separate a swift, painful
thought made all my joy turn to bitterness. For my
uncle said that on the morrow he would write to tell
my mother of what had happened, and ask her for her
consent to a conditional engagement. I had forgotten
her, I am sorry to confess, as completely as if she had
never existed. Would she approve? or would she take
me away and separate me from my newly found happiness? Alas! she adopted the latter course. I might
have known from the first that she would. My uncle's
letter brought her to us as rapidly as her posters could
draw her carriage there.

She stood in too much awe of her brother-in-law—
who was also my guardian and my brother's—to openly oppose his wishes in this matter, but she adopted
the anxious, plaintive mien of a doting parent, eager
to insure her beloved child's welfare. After shedding
many tears, which did not lessen in any way her exceeding loveliness—she knew the art of weeping grace-
fully—she implored " her dear brother " to let her take
her "precious little girl" away for a while. Of course
she argued that she had nothing against Alban, *en
principe*. He was all that could be desired; perhaps
not very wealthy, but, to be sure, what did that matter?
Dear little Marguerite had enough and to spare. But
time was needed to prove the sincerity of such an affection, besides which she would never permit her
daughter to marry before she had reached her eigh-
teenth year, etc., etc., etc.

My guardian uncle, who acted also as my guardian
angel, just then was forced to confess that there was
truth in what she said, and he brought me round to a
comparatively reasonable state of mind. The upshot
of it all was that a few days later I started with my

mother, Bertrand, my Abbé, and a few indispensable members of our household, for the Riviera, which, so my "doting parent" claimed, was the only place where she could recover from so many nerve-shattering emotions.

My last interview with Alban was heart-breaking. We were so young that the separation was all the more severe. Such sorrows are healed quicker than one thinks, but yet they leave a scar that other blows are apt to open again. *C'est la vie, et elle n'est pas gaie!* We plighted our troth, and the dear boy, with tears in his eyes, slipped on my finger his mother's own "*bague de fiançailles*," a grand, translucent emerald, in an old-fashioned setting of dead gold and diamonds. It was a rare and a very valuable jewel, at which my mother looked askance; but my uncle was present when I timidly showed it to her, and so I was allowed to retain it. My first ring! That deep-hued gem, just like the color of the forest trees beneath which I had met Alban on that momentous afternoon I have described earlier.

Brittany was to know us no more for a long time; but I was not aware of this, then, or else I would have felt still more wretched than I did. From the Riviera we wandered, in the spring, to the Italian lakes, and then to Tyrol. In August we went to Baden, which was as crowded as it always is, and overflowing with foreign hordes: Russians, Austrians, Englishmen—foremost among them the "dear prince"—Englishwomen of high rank, who had come thither to bask in the sunshine of "His Presence"; South-Americans, clothed as brilliantly and chattering as loudly as a cage full of parrots; North-Americans, who were "doing" Europe with scrupulous care and attention; Greeks and Turks and even Egyptians, whose long, dark coats and red tarbouches gave them a ludicrous resemblance to so many bottles of scarlet - sealed claret — in one word, the usual fashionable gathering, idling, laughing, promenading, gossiping, and listening to the music all day long in the parks, or at their respective hotels.

I hated the whole thing, and longed for Brittany. Bertrand and I spent all our time with the Abbé, on the outskirts of the parks, in the woods, or at the chalet which we had taken for the season. It was a pretty, carved toy, overrun with wistaria and honeysuckle, and surrounded by comparatively large grounds all a - bloom with gorgeous, mundane-looking, frivolous flowers, with which I could not make friends. German soil, I reflected, could not bring forth anything that I might in honor admire.

The houses in Baden all had a lively expression, with their bright green shutters and gayly striped awnings, and the people were entirely too dashing, too noisy, too fond of pleasure for my taste. Of Alban I heard rarely—short, stiff little letters, sent under cover of my mother, which, under the circumstances, could not be other than *froides et guindées*. But I did not make allowances for that, and when compared with his impassioned words, they struck my heart with an ever-increasing chill. He was still with his regiment in the South, and mentioned the numerous *fêtes* to which he and his brother officers were bidden. But of his love for me he never spoke. The *Toujours fidèlement à vous* at the end of each of these naturally trivial documents, and the *Chère petite mienne* at the beginning, was all the tenderness they contained. I was as yet too unformed, too primitive, to read the deep feeling between the lines, or to realize that this young suitor of mine, this *enfant gâté de la vie*, was true and loyal to his promises and to his love.

I have thought since that my mother's little comments were the triumph of artfulness: *"Alban s'amuse"; "Alban est à l'âge où tout invite au plaisir"; "Charmant garçon, on doit se le disputer,"* etc., etc. Every little laughingly spoken, double-barbed sentence made me wince, for it never occurred to me that they were the first telling shots of a carefully and shrewdly planned campaign in which I should be the loser. Of course, our semi-engagement had been kept a profound secret, and not even my dear Abbé knew a word about it.

One morning Bertrand and I started bright and early for a distant forest glen, accompanied by my maid and by the boy's *valet de chambre*, the same old soldier who had acted in a like capacity for my father. The stillness of the dense woods was disturbed only by the sound of rushing waters and the calls and trills of countless birds. We walked slowly over the moss and short, dense green grass. The calm was something beautiful beneath the verdant vault which shut off the ardent rays of the sun, and my dear little brother and I laughed and chattered light-heartedly as we went along. At the top of our voices we sang snatches of our favorite Breton songs, two of which I roughly transcribe here as I have already done in the case of the dear old New Year's carol, simply because I love the sound— nay, the very look—of them, for the sake of "Auld Lang Syne." I was still a child, with all a child's love for mirth and fun, so that we were soon scampering among the lichen-grown rocks, like two merry squirrels playing at hide-and-seek, and pelting each other with clusters of flowerets and buds made into fragrant balls.

Bertrand was growing every day dearer to me. This handsome little lad of seven, with his wonderful gray eyes, his golden curls, active little body, and his delicate coloring and slender, muscular frame, was the only playmate I ever cared for. When with him I was once more a romping, agile boy myself, and as my Lady Mother had long since repealed her veto against our being together, we simply adored each other, and spent all our leisure hours in close companionship, riding,

driving, and walking, or playing *à la petite guerre* with a wonderful collection of leaden soldiers, our favorite toy.

At last we reached a small gorge, enclosed by fern-covered rocks, where exquisite flowers blossomed in profusion, and forthwith we set to work to gather cyclamens, violets, and blue gentians. A tall bunch of foxgloves on the top of a dangerously steep bank so took my fancy that with my usual recklessness I started to climb the almost perpendicular incline like a regular monkey. Unfortunately I stepped on a loose stone, and, unable to recover my footing, I tumbled to the bottom of the miniature precipice, where, much disgusted with myself, I lay on a patch of moss. The worst of it was that Bertrand and the servants were quite out of hearing, he having just run back to get our flask of cold tea from the waiting carriage. My ankle was badly twisted, and I was perfectly incapable of getting up without assistance. Twice I tried to struggle to my feet, but at last I gave up the attempt, and, sitting resolutely down on the now wofully crushed moss, I began to halloo lustily, in hopes of attracting attention. No such luck was in store for me, however, and I was growing disgusted with myself for my carelessness, when a tall figure came running towards me from the direction opposite. to that which Bertrand had taken. The unknown was a handsome man, with clear blue eyes and extremely long, silky, fair mustaches. His Norfolk jacket, knickerbockers, and untanned leather gaiters did not prevent him from looking every inch a typical aristocrat. Taking off his soft felt hat, and bowing with a grace which even in my ridiculous position I could not help noticing, he asked whether he could be of any assistance to me. I replied to this singularly well-timed offer by asking him to aid me to regain my footing. This was a difficult task, for my ankle was so sore that walking was out of the question. For a moment we looked at each other in some dismay, and then, struck suddenly by the ludicrous side of the affair,

I burst into uncontrollable laughter. He speedily followed my example, though in a quieter and more dignified manner. Then I asked this interesting unknown to be so very kind as to step down to the road in order to summon my servants, adding that my brother's valet was a strong fellow who would carry me easily to the victoria waiting for us on the high-road. To my great surprise an expression of vexation spread over my new acquaintance's clean-cut features.

"If you will allow me, mademoiselle," he said, quickly, and with some bitterness, "I think I can fulfil that office as well as a servant. It will save time, and I will endeavor to make the transit as little disagreeable to you as I can."

Observing that a refusal on my part would most certainly hurt his feelings, I thanked him, and, apologizing for the trouble I was giving him, allowed him to lift me from the ground. He carried me as easily and comfortably as if I had been a baby, to the spot where my servants and Bertrand greeted me with intense astonishment. I explained to them what had occurred, and I was soon helped into the carriage. Turning to the *bel inconnu*, I thanked him again for his kindness, for I thought that indeed he was a real trump.

"It is I who thank you, mademoiselle," he replied, "for having granted me the privilege of being of service to you." Then, he added, somewhat hesitatingly, "I hope that this is not the last time that I shall be honored by seeing you. An acquaintance so romantically begun should not end abruptly."

My faithful maid, Marie, who took her duties as duenna very seriously to heart, intervened here, murmuring something about "monsieur's kindness," and stating the necessity of taking me home at once, in case our prolonged absence should cause anxiety.

And then we drove off, leaving him standing bare-headed on the edge of the road, his blue eyes following me lingeringly, while naughty Bertrand, under the flapping brim of his large sailor hat, made faces at him —*la nique*, as we used to call it.

For a few days I suffered a good deal from that sprained ankle, but I soon recovered, and forgot all about the handsome stranger who had come to my rescue so opportunely.

I was very much taken up just then with the idea of appearing at my first party, and only hoped that the accident would in no way interfere with this great event.

Grand - Duchess V., who was spending the season at Baden, had announced that she would give a *bal blanc*—a novelty in those days. None of the dancers would be over twenty, but it was not to be, strictly speaking, a children's ball, for the venerable age of twelve was to be a *conditio sine qua non* in order to receive an invitation. Poor Bertrand felt very bitter, since he was thus ranked among the infants who were not invited.

On the eventful evening I drove with my mother to the grand-ducal villa, feeling very much pleased with myself. She was an artist in her way, and my plain white *voile* frock, made *à la Niobé*, with the skirt clearing the ground by several inches, and the clasp of fresh white marguerites barreting my long, hanging braids, were a poem of their kind.

I had been told so often I was an ugly little thing that vanity had no share in my elation and delight, but I have never been shy, and I looked forward to the evening's amusement with eager anticipation. Nor was I disappointed. The dear, kind - hearted grand-duchess whispered here and there that this was my first little social treat, and everybody was most attentive to me. The grand-duke insisted upon dancing the open-

ing quadrille with me, in spite of the adamantine edict
which prohibited all grown-up people from joining us
young disciples of Terpsichore.

Suddenly, at the end of the ballroom, I saw my mysterious rescuer. He was leaning against the wall,
and was literally devouring me with his eyes.

Just as the orchestra struck up the "Blue Danube"
waltz, he crossed the floor, and, bowing low before me,
said, in French, with a slight but very pretty foreign
accent, " *Voulez-vous, mademoiselle, me faire la grâce de
valser avec moi ?*"

From her seat under a group of palms my mother
signalled to me most peremptorily to accept, and I did so
at once.

What a waltz that was! I had never imagined anything like it, the gliding, easy, equal motion, the delightful sense of security while the strong arm was encircling me, the intoxicating music, the perfect floor. It
was a dream.

A marguerite fell from my hair as we at last stopped,
and he furtively slipped it within his glove. I looked at
him with some surprise, but he drew my arm within his
and led me towards the lamp-lit terrace as if he had just
done the most natural thing in the world.

The lovely spectacle presented by the illuminated
gardens pleased me immensely, and, if I am to tell the
truth, I was flattered by the evident devotion of my tall,
good-looking companion, who, now that I saw him in
glittering full-dress uniform, attracted me very much
by his soldierly splendor.

I stood beside him, quiet as a mouse, the sweet music
of the orchestra throbbing in the air about us, the flower-
laden balcony in front of us wrapped in a golden mist.
I had not the faintest idea who he was, for he had taken,
evidently, the law into his own hands, and had asked

nobody to introduce him to me. But my mother's gesture of unmistakable command showed that she was perfectly informed as to the rank and status of the man I had looked upon as a *Robin des Bois*. He must certainly be a great personage of some kind, or she would not have silently bidden me accept so unceremonious an invitation. He plucked a half-blown white rose from a vase near by and fastened it deftly in my hair, whence the marguerite had dropped.

" *Du bist wie eine Blume*," he whispered, under his breath, and then, with the suspicion of a laugh, he said, aloud:

"One good turn deserves another. Will you reserve the cotillion for me?"

"If mamma lets me stay for it, yes," I replied; "but she does not like me to keep late hours." He laughed outright this time.

"Why, you are a little woman already. Surely you are not still confined to the school-room and to the constant care of your governesses?"

"I have no governesses—at least, I mean, no governess in chief. I have been brought up by an abbé."

"Dear me, what a lucky abbé! But his task is now surely accomplished. One cannot perfect perfection."

It was my turn to laugh. "I wish mamma could hear you," I exclaimed. "She thinks me very far from perfection, I promise you."

How wonderful all this seemed to me. But wonders were not at an end, for my usually so severe and fault-finding parent not only permitted me to dance the cotillion, but when we drove home she actually praised me—a thing she had never done before—patted my head, and declared that I was quite a credit to her. She also made me acquainted with the identity of *Robin des Bois*. It was a revelation which made my sleepy eyes open very wide with an astonishment not unmixed with a queer little thrill of pride at what my mother called my most amazing conquest. Sometimes earthly things have their importance and their weight, especially when one is very young and very inexperienced, which certainly was very much the case with me.

> " Ah, be content with earthly things,
>   Nor seek the mystic's vain desire,
> Though life into the darkness wings.
>
> "See how the red sun lowly swings,
>   Tipping the yellow corn with fire,
> And be content with earthly things.
>
> " The bee upon the blossom clings,
>   The birds of summer's sweetness choir,
> Though life into the darkness wings.
>
> " The wind that through the starlight sings
>   Is full of peace : then why aspire?
> Ah, be content with earthly things.
>
> " Content with what the morrow brings,
>   Forgetful of the far-off pyre,
> Though life into the darkness wings.
>
> " Sweet are its chequered happenings,
>   Its little loves, its petty ire.
> Ah, be content with earthly things,
> Though life into the darkness wings.'

CHAPTER VIII

" Quinze ans !—l'âge céleste où l'arbre de la vie,
Sous la tiède oasis du desert ambaumé,
Baigne ses fruits dorés de myrrhe et d'ambroisie,
Et pour féconder l'air comme un palmier d'Asie,
N'a qu'à jeter au vent son voile parfumé !
Quinze ans—l'âge où la femme, au jour de sa naissance,
Sortit des mains de Dieu, si blanche d'innocence,
Si riche de beauté, que son père immortel
De ses phalanges d'or en fit l'âge éternel !"

HALCYON days! The little girl, always thrust in
the background, always found fault with, humiliated,
scolded, repressed, was suddenly a petted creature to
whom everything was permitted, and whose every wish
was gratified almost before it was uttered! What was
the meaning of it all? I could not understand. Bertrand used to put his arms around my neck and hug
me delightedly, saying again and again: "Oh, you
poor dear old Margot, I am so glad to see you treated
as well at last as I have always been myself!"

Dear little chap! There was not a tinge of meanness
or of jealousy in his nature, and I loved him for it.

Robin des Bois was everlastingly with us, and a very
pleasant companion he was. For he organized excursions, sent my mother quantities of flowers, danced
attendance upon me under her benignant eye—wonder
of wonders—and made himself so indispensable that
even I looked forward to his daily appearance upon the
scene with unfeigned pleasure.

I did not realize that he was the magician who had
thus transformed my existence for me, and although

I sometimes imitated blunt little Bertrand and saucily called him Karl *tout court* (which, by the way, seemed to enchant him), I considered him quite a venerable person, in spite of his good looks and surprisingly youthful appearance. For was he not twenty-one years my senior? *Presque un ancêtre, enfin!*

One evening he brought me a great cluster of forget-me-nots as blue as his eyes, and asked me to wear them for his sake. Something in the tone of his voice grated upon me, and I laid the flowers on the table, saying, coldly, that I did not like forget-me-nots, and that they were silly flowers. An angry look from my mother left me absolutely unmoved. I was beginning indeed to pay but scant attention to her opinion, for her sudden change of front with regard to me had bred a singular carelessness in my attitude towards her which was not unmixed with a tinge of contempt. Cold, cruel, sometimes fierce, but always dignified and sarcastic, she was a being created to inspire awe. But when she was sweet and affectionate she became extremely insincere, and failed to impress me with anything but distrust.

Karl seemed much hurt at my rejection of his insipid flowers, and after dinner he withdrew with my mother to her own sanctum, where they were closeted together until long after I had retired.

On the next day I was summoned early to my mother's dressing-room. She was sitting near one of the windows looking out upon endless geranium-beds, scarlet, pink, and cherry-colored, showing dazzlingly bright in the sun-glare, her delicate profile lighted *à la Rembrandt* by the conflict of brightness and shade fighting for mastery beneath the downspread awning.

"Karl, my dearest," she began, in her softest and most dulcet tones, "has done you a great honor. He wishes you to be his wife."

Had the ceiling fallen upon my head I could not have been more surprised. Incredulously I gazed at my lovely mother with a sort of fascination, watching the gentle rise and fall of the lace flounces above her graceful breast.

"Why, Matushka," I said at last, with an irrepressible laugh, "you are making fun of me. Karl is old enough to be my father; surely you mean that he has asked *you* to marry him. He cannot fancy that I love him! How very, very foolish!"

A truly imperial frown contracted her dark eyebrows.

"Old? What ridiculous nonsense!" she exclaimed. "Why, he is barely thirty-six! And as to your loving him or not, you can be no judge of such a matter. What should you know about love? Love is an idea, a fancy —it does not last. What is needed in a union which endures through life is solid esteem. You must learn to understand the prose of existence, my child. Life is far from being all poetry, as you seem to think. God forbid that I should advise you any kind of worldliness, but still truth compels me to speak to you as I do. Remember that as Karl's wife you will have it in your power to do much good, and that your marriage may be made subservient to God's own service. This is a very grand offer, Dushka. Your position will be one of almost unequalled magnificence. And this alliance, moreover, suits me absolutely. You know that I am not easily dissuaded from anything I wish, so do not expect me to yield to any girlish gush, silliness, and fallacies. Marry Karl—I can assert that you will."

I began to be seriously alarmed, for I knew that my mother's will was of iron and her tactics so clever that she generally carried her point on all occasions.

And what about Alban? I instinctively avoided

speaking his name, feeling that it should be kept in reserve as a final and decisive argument.

"Why are you so anxious to get rid of me, mother?" I said, gently. "Are you tired of having me with you?"

"What idea is this, Marguerite? Pray recollect yourself; your manners leave much room for improvement. I insist upon your telling me now what your objection is to marrying Karl."

"I think that he is a great deal too old for me and that he is also not a man I could either trust or ever care for."

"My dear, what do you know about men? How can you venture to form an opinion, and how dare you assert such a thing of a person whom I consider a most suitable husband for you? I am surprised at you. Karl has behaved most charmingly towards you, and you are very ungrateful. But enough of this. You are my daughter and must do as I wish in this as in all other respects."

For a moment we confronted one another. I was seriously alarmed, for I felt that any further resistance on my part would not avail. I had been so often bowed down by my mother's inflexible decisions that I knew to my cost, alas! that she never yielded when once her mind was made up. Moreover, I was still too much of a child not to be in a measure dazzled by the brilliant prospect of becoming, at an age when most girls are still in the school-room, one of the greatest ladies at the most superb court of Europe. It did, in fact, at one moment flash through my mind that my mother's words and point of view were not so surprising, after all, perchance.

Had it not been for Alban I am not sure that I might not have yielded at once, for she became suddenly very winning and persuasive. God forgive her, she knew only too well what she was doing. She was fully aware that Karl was a *roué* and a *débauché*, that his intrigues had been countless, and that he had never attempted to curb his passions, being burdened by but few principles and entirely devoid of morality.

He was for the time being madly in love with me, but this particular brand of sentiment was not of a nature to attract a similar feeling in the very pure and guileless heart of an innocent girl. My mother could not help knowing that a few hours would suffice to open my eyes to the future that lay before me, that though I was barely fifteen, yet my girlhood would soon be crushed like a spring blossom torn by a ruthless hand. She knew decidedly and *à n'en pas doûter* what I would bind myself to, and she could not fail to see that Karl's offer of marriage was the result of a fiery and unworthy passion—a means to an end—the only means to obtain the prize he coveted.

I hardly heard her finishing sentences, although the last words thereof aroused me from the deep reverie into which I had allowed myself to fall. "To-night you will greet Karl as your fiancé," she said, as she rose from her chair, indicating by this that the interview was brought to a close and the case dismissed.

"I am sorry, Matushka," I said, with sudden decision, "but this is impossible; I am engaged to Alban, I love him, and I do not love Karl."

Oh! the look of boundless scorn which she gave me, and the laugh that followed—low, melodious, a silvery ripple of long-drawn-out irony—making me tremble as if I had unexpectedly been struck a perfidious blow between the shoulders.

"Alban!" The word contained yet more insidious mockery than the burst of mirthless laughter. "Well, my girl, if you are going to sacrifice such a man as

Karl to a worthless boy admirer who has by this time not only tired of you, but of the very thought of you, I cannot say much for your powers of intellect."

"Tired of me!" I repeated in dismay.

"So much so," she continued, still laughing, "that he is going to marry another heiress, an English beauty whom he met and fell in love with just as rapidly as he did with you. *Que voulez-vous? Ce sont les hommes qui sont volages; et bien fol est qui s'y fie!*"

It was much later only that it struck me as strange that my mother should have been able to lay her hand with such convenient *à propos* upon the slip of newspaper which she held out to me at that instant, saying, in the same little sneering way, "Here is your proof, if proof there need be."

For a moment the printed lines danced before my eyes, blurred by a queer, misty, shifting twinkle. Then they grew plainer and seemed to burn before me as if they had been written with blood.

"*On annonce le très prochain mariage de Lady Z. la ravissante fille du célèbre Diplomate Anglais Lord X. avec le fils du Marquis d'A. Les jeunes gens se sont rencontrés cet été dans le Midi où l'heureux fiancé est en garnison, et ont reçu le fameux coup de foudre tant vanté des romanciers,*" etc. The trivial, nauseating journalistic prose proved too much for me, and I allowed the paper to flutter from my nerveless hand to the floor.

Poor, stupid, easily misled child! It never occurred to me that this was a case of mistaken identity, that the "superiorly informed" journalist meant Alban's brother, who had been visiting him, although I was not aware of this, and that my boy was true to me, true as steel, while my mother had joyfully pounced upon this *pièce à conviction* which made it possible for her to attain at a bound the completion of her so cleverly laid plans. What she would have done without it, I cannot say. But probably, being given the many resources of her brilliant imagination, she would no doubt have found other roads to success.

At any rate, she must have thought her victory an easy one, and might have said with the great Napoleon, *Rien ne réussit comme un succès*, for with blazing eyes, undimmed by the faintest suspicion of tears, I looked unflinchingly at her, and in a voice so absolutely discordant that it sounded as if it belonged to some strange and unknown being, I said, haughtily:

"You are quite right, Matushka, I have been very sentimental and ridiculous. I am ready to marry Karl whenever you like, to marry him or any other man whom you select for me, so long as I can marry at once, and put an end to all this—this—" here that queer new voice broke a little, and I shuddered—"this outrage!" I finally pronounced, and at a run I escaped from the room, never stopping in my terrified flight until I reached a secluded thicket at the end of the garden, where I flung myself brutally down upon the ground.

Of the hour that followed I have no clear remembrance. It was not a pleasant one. Torn by conflicting emotions, I heaped bitter reproaches upon my mother at one moment for having separated me from Alban and thus brought about the wreck of all my hopes, and the next I commended her for the foresight and prudence that had spared me the inconceivable bitterness of being jilted. "*Ah! mon bel ami*," thought I, "you are marrying a noble heiress—less noble and probably less of an heiress than I am myself — but I need not break my heart over such a trifle, for my reply to your *billet de faire part* will, by my own marriage announcement, bearing a name coupled with mine that will strike "*you*" with some astonishment. And then, suddenly, helpless, irresistible tears came in floods to my relief, making me look so unlike my usual self that when, at last, I crept home to dress for dinner and for the trying ordeal which was to come, my maid held up her hands in indignant horror and fell to weeping herself, out of sheer sympathy.

Before I went down-stairs—a transformed being, clad with exquisite care in white gauze—although I was still ghastly pale and preternaturally serious, every outward trace of what I had just been through was effaced. I had coldly and solemnly drawn Alban's emerald ring from my finger, and had carefully locked it away in a secret recess of my jewel-case. Hardly had I performed this cruelly painful little ceremony when a footman knocked at the door and placed in Marie's hands an enormous white bouquet and an oval package tied with snowy satin ribbons.

Without a single thrill of pleasure or curiosity I laid the flowers on the bed and pulled the parcel open. It contained a white velvet box wherein lay fifteen rows of matchless pearls, as big as hazel-nuts, and a card on which was written in French: "I send, with my tenderest gratitude and my eternal love and reverence, pearls to my priceless pearl. Wear them, for my sake, as a symbol of the chains that henceforth bind me to you.—KARL."

Poor Marie's eyes were distended with amazed admiration as she timidly touched these royal gems. "*Plus belles que celles de votre maman, cent fois plus belles, ma petite chérie,*" she murmured, rapturously, attempting to clasp them about my neck. I pushed her off, petulantly. "Drop these—chains!" I said, somewhat incoherently. "I will wear them on my wedding-day, for I am going to be married very soon. Aren't you pleased?"

Marie looked at me with stupefaction. "Married?" she echoed; "my little white lamb, are you joking? Married, and to whom? To Monsieur Alban? Is he coming here?"

"Monsieur Alban, forsooth! how little you know me, *ma bonne fille*. No, not to a brainless, heartless baby like him."

"Surely," she whispered, her face blanching and her hand grasping my arm almost violently—"surely you are not going to marry—that—that—"

"Hush, Marie!" I interrupted, severely, and with a firmness which had never as yet been mine. "I am engaged, and I will soon be married, as I tell you, and I will be ever so mighty a personage, and if you behave very nicely I will take you away with me to live in my palaces and castles and villas, and on my yachts, too."

" *Bon Dieu! Sainte Vierge Marie, ma bonne patronne! Prenez-nous en pitié, ma petite fille est devenue folle!*" muttered the astounded woman, crossing herself devoutly to keep away the evil spirits which in her opinion had taken up their abode in my brain.

I shrugged my shoulders, irritated at her astonishment; but, suddenly seized with remorse, I flung my arms about her, roughly kissed her on both cheeks, and fled down-stairs without waiting to hear more.

I paused to recover my breath in the central hall, which wore a very festive appearance and was gayly decorated with flowering plants. " *Ça commence bien,*" I thought, bitterly. " *Allons y gaiement!*" and then I made my way to the drawing-room, which was filled with an admirably selected gathering of guests — *Le dessus du panier! la crême de la crême! la fleur des pois!* in one word. There was a murmur of congratulation as I entered, and the pride which was second nature to me stood me in good stead and held me upright and

smiling, while I was receiving compliments and fe-
licitations.

Karl was at my side, but said not a word. For the
first time I saw him looking serious, and this gravity
pleased me far better than could have any protestations
or effusiveness. The dinner seemed interminable. I
was silent during its whole wearisome length, and ate
nothing. Karl had the supreme tact to say very little
to me. Once only he bent his handsome head and murmured so that nobody else could hear what he whispered:

"You have made me supremely happy, Marguerite.
The devotion of a lifetime will be as nothing to repay
you for your generous consent to my heart's greatest
desire." I gave him a rapid, beseeching glance, and
he immediately turned to his neighbor, Grand-Duchess
A., and entered into a lively conversation with her.

When all the guests had taken their departure save
Karl he clasped both my hands within his own and
kissed them passionately.

"I thank you," he murmured with evident emotion.
"I told you the simple truth when I said that you had
made me supremely happy. I wish you to be happy,
too, Marguerite, to enjoy life while you can, and to leave
grave thoughts and grave cares for older years. You
look very serious, my little child. But you are tired
now. Go and shut your pretty eyes and sleep the sleep
of youth and of love!"

My mother, resplendent in pearl-hued velvet, *point de
Venise*, and sapphires, smiled a little triumphantly as
she heard him. She had landed her big fish, and it
pleased her to see it glitter at the end of the hook.

"Have I your permission to give your daughter her
engagement ring?" he asked her, with one of his inimitable bows.

"*Faites donc, mon cher,*" she replied; "*c'est votre droit, vous pouvez même l'embrasser, si vous y tenez.*"

Involuntarily I drew back. My mother's flippancy and slight, mocking smile enraged me, and Karl's calm and courtly answer made him rise at once surpassingly in my esteem.

"*J'y tiens, madame, croyez-le, mais pas comme cela, à son heure.*"

I hardly noticed the scintillating half-hoop of marvellous diamonds which he slipped on my finger, for "*in petto*" I was thinking, "I can surely be as generous as he," and unhesitatingly I lifted my face to his! A deep flush spread over his features, his arms encircled me, and he closed my eyes with his lips.

"*Vous êtes un petit amour, ma chérie,*" he whispered, as he released me.

Of the six weeks that followed there is little to say. I felt sometimes like a child who stands in the bewilderment of too many New Year's presents, for wedding-gifts were pouring in upon me from every corner of Europe; splendid, sparkling, magnificent, undeniably welcome presents, for I cannot deny that I loved jewels, and my days were a perpetual round of *fêtes*. We had left Baden, and were in Paris at our solemn old residence in the Faubourg. Lengthy councils with famous *couturiers* took up a great deal of my time. Soon I would journey to my fiancé's own land, where our marriage was to take place, and my mother declared that it was impossible for us to go back to Brittany before that early date. I had not heard from Alban again. His emerald still lay in the secret drawer of my *coffret à bijoux*, for, with a feeling of jealousy and vindictiveness quite unusual to me, I would not for a moment entertain the idea of returning it to him. The "English beauty and heiress" had, I thought, long ere this been provided with another gem taken from the collection of the long dead Marquise. This ring was mine. And though I would now never wear it, neither should anybody else. I had my hours of discouragement—many of them—when I silently but bitterly reproached my mother for taking me away from Alban, as she had done. "Poor boy," I would then think, "he grew tired of waiting." For it seemed to me, indeed, that years, instead of months, had elapsed since that glorious autumn night when he had told me of his love. At those moments the very touch of my mother's hand, her smile, her voice, her every gesture, maddened me, and I looked at her so strangely and hostilely that she would fall into her old habit of scolding me, and used to tell me that I was *farouche, une enfant terrible*, etc., etc., etc.

I knew very well that I did not love Karl. I was touched and flattered by his countless and unceasing attentions, and often taxed myself with ingratitude for giving him so little in return. He was an ideal fiancé, always in a sunny mood, always ready to say or do a graceful thing; but the divine spark was missing from our intercourse, and instinctively I felt this.

One day, when we were stepping from the carriage in the Rue de la Paix, before a famous jeweller's, we came face to face with Alban's father. I felt myself growing as pale as a ghost, while my mother, on the contrary, and much to my surprise, flushed scarlet. The stately old man raised his hat in profound salutation, and, in spite of her obvious desire to avoid talking to him, she could not do otherwise than speak a few words of greeting.

With an audacious and dazzling smile, she remarked hurriedly:

"I must congratulate you on your son's approaching wedding; I hear that he is very happy."

The Marquis bowed stiffly. "I may, I presume, offer my own congratulations in return," he said, coldly. "Marguerite is certainly fulfilling your highest ambitions."

The stern, slightly contemptuous look in his eyes galled me. What did he mean by speaking like that, when it was he who should have felt both ashamed and uncomfortable? This utterly confounded me.

"Marguerite is a good child," drawled my mother, placing a caressing hand on my shoulder.

"And a very happy one," I interrupted boldly, although there was a big lump in my throat and an agonizing sensation at my heart.

Again he bowed in the same uncompromising, icy fashion. "Your assurance thereof is very pleasing to hear, but—" Here my mother interrupted him with a rudeness which I had never known her to render herself guilty of before:

"Marguerite, we must not keep the Marquis standing thus bareheaded in this keen wind," and with a regal inclination of her lovely head she drew me abruptly into the great and superb shop, the door of which had during this colloquy been patiently held open by her footman.

What would have occurred had the Marquis been allowed to finish his sentence? I have often thought of that. The misunderstanding would have been cleared up, no doubt, and my faith in Alban would have been restored, but was it not too late to break off my marriage, and, even if this had been possible, would my mother—nay, even my guardian, enraged though he was at the present state of affairs—have faced the scandal of such a rupture?

Who shall probe the mystery of the past, who shall say "this should have been"? Wiser heads than mine, at any rate. For even to - day, when most veils have been torn asunder, when I know that my mother willingly misdirected and ruined my life, and became as surely Alban's murderess as if she had killed him with her own hand, I do not feel that I am in a position to judge.

A year later I was present at a state ball in the *Salle des Palmiers* in St. Petersburg. Never before had I felt so burdened with uneasiness and forebodings. Yet no night had ever quite equalled this one for me, as far as social triumphs are concerned. Outside the world was white, for it was the beginning of the cruel Northern winter. Across one-half the heavens there was outspread the glory of the aurora borealis. And as we sat at supper in a veritable bower of flowers and verdure the rosy glow of this choicest and most fairy-like of all nature's phenomena shimmered through the lace of the window curtains. I shall never forget that night, for it was then that I heard of his death—a death met on the battle-field in the burning sand of the Algerian desert, just like the one dealt to that other man so dear to me, Charles, Comte d'A.

I received one letter from his father—only one, thank God! A harsh, bitter, unrelenting letter, and cruelly unjust, too. But he did not know, poor broken-hearted man, that my share in all this was only one of inexperience and ignorance.

"Alban is dead. He died, as they tell me, the death of a soldier," wrote the relentless father; "but I know better than that! Before the world you may be wholly blameless, but yet it is you who killed him. Indirectly, even directly in a manner, you were the cause of his leaving country, family, home, to seek release from the pain which he was not brave enough to live down. I feel that his blood is upon your hands. He sought death and he found it from an enemy's sword—or otherwise, on your account !"

Exaggerated as this accusation was, it hurt me as much as if it had all been true, but I never tried to clear myself in the eyes of the bereaved, hard old man, *à quoi bon !*

Who deserved most pity, I thought at times—Alban or I?

> " Oh! no, that is not death which death we call
> When on the coffin clods of earth do fall;
> That is not death, when o'er us shadows creep
> And, mouldering, we are laid in endless sleep,
> Nor call that death, when for us others shed
> True tears or false, over our narrow beds.
> Ah! that is death, and that is death alone,
> When we our own existence do bemoan!"

CHAPTER IX

" Flower, white daughter of the day-spring fair,
      The dew's sweet pensioner, ere rise of sun
      By some rude hand and careless, all fordone—
   Flung bruised and broken in the highway there!"

" YOU are a stranger child than even I thought. You have no adaptability, no *monde*. You look scornful and unsympathetic excepting where animals and beggars are concerned. You make me ashamed of you —you are such a dreamer, such an idealist, and so very illogical withal! *Je désespéré de vous complètement, ma chère! Vous êtes stupide, et vous le faites exprès!*"

My mother yawned daintily, rose from her chair, and glided towards a long side-table upon which were heaped numberless wedding-gifts which she gazed at approvingly.

" You are neither gracious nor graceful. Sometimes you are, I might say, downright ungainly. Yet grace is what a woman needs most of all. It is one of the few qualities I pride myself upon possessing, but, alas ! one cannot say of us, *Mater pulchra, filia pulchrior !*"

I glanced at my mother, at her queenly figure, with grace noticeable in every movement, and yet a sort of disgust filled my heart. "Honor thy father and thy mother"—the old, old law. How easy it had been, and was still, and how natural to honor my father, to whom honor of the highest kind was always due! But my mother—!

146

A shudder ran through me, and involuntarily I thought that she was selfish and cruel beyond words.

Her merciless, melodious voice broke upon the silence.

"There is a *lacune* somewhere about you, Marguerite. I really have little reason for being proud of you. I had hoped that the result of my teachings, actions and example, would have a different effect. I have secured a magnificent position for you—my first duty as a mother—and if you are not content you are positively offending Heaven."

"I am sorry to be so great a disappointment to you," I interrupted, unable to bear this any longer. "You know perfectly well that I am not like other girls, that I am like nobody else in fact. And if there be a *lacune* in my nature, it is none of my own making. When you separated me from Alban I think you destroyed all my chances of real happiness and of true womanliness. I loved him dearly, tenderly, absolutely—" She fairly stamped her foot. "Hold your tongue," she exclaimed, harshly; "are you mad? A baby like you, to talk of love! Really, you are too ridiculous! Your heroics do not become a great lady! Alban, forsooth! What next, indeed? A lad of twenty-one, with a miserable pittance of a couple of hundred thousand francs' income to sustain the glory of his marquisate, when he inherits it, and who now is a subaltern in a cavalry regiment with a hale and hearty father, and an elder brother who will very probably outlive him and have many children, just as in the fairy stories. So this insane idea is still in your head, *Madame la Vicomtesse!* You little idiot, mooning about with your Romeo from garrison to garrison, *ce traîneur de sabre*, possessed of a face like a cameo and of an allowance of ten thousand francs to cut a figure with—*Tous mes compliments!*"

"That is enough, mother!" I said, with rising passion

in my voice, and, without giving her time to retaliate, I ran out of her boudoir.

I went to my own room and locked the door. Then throwing myself on the bed, I lay there for a long time, face downwards, struggling with my feelings, which were not enviable or pleasant.

A few hours later my maid came to dress me for the dinner and *soirée de contrat*. I was to wear my first long dress that night, a cloud of pale-pink moire silk and gauze, with showers of apple-blossoms nestling everywhere.

A sense of unreality had come upon me. My nerves were tingling curiously, and my usually colorless face was slightly flushed. Marie's eyes were red and swollen with weeping, and this irritated me beyond measure. Why should she cry over me? I disliked always to be pitied. And why also should she pity me? Why? Why? Why? As she braided my long hair she hurt me once or twice, for her hands were trembling. Nervous and exasperated, I cried, "Be more careful, Marie; you are positively idiotic to-night!" The words were hardly out of my mouth when a stinging slap marked my cheek with four slender white bars. My mother had entered unnoticed. She was clad in all the glory of full court dress, and sparkled with jewels from her head to the tips of her satin-shod feet.

"Be good enough to beg Marie's pardon," she said, calmly. "To-morrow you will be your own mistress, but to-day you are still under my control, and I cannot permit my servants to be treated like dogs."

Tears of mortification welled up in my eyes. I was awfully fond of Marie and of all the other members of the household. And though the indignity of the punishment was perhaps greater than the offence, still I felt that it was deserved, and, moreover, my mother's striking—if I may be forgiven so execrable a pun—reproofs were nothing new to me. Poor Marie, in her dismay, burst into a fresh flood of tears, when I threw my arms about her neck and kissed her, humbly begging her to overlook my fortunately unusual and unseemly behavior. It was evident that she was filled with indignation at being the involuntary cause of my humiliation, and when my irate parent had taken herself and her gorgeousness away, the faithful soul went down on her knees and kissed my hands, wetting them with her tears, and calling me *Un pauvre petite ange maltraité, une petite sainte,* and goodness only knows what other names of endearment which I was sorry I deserved so little.

I sat through the banquet that night like one in a dream, feeling all eyes upon me, but quite indifferent even to the remarks made about my extreme pallor. Karl was very attentive, yet he acted during the whole trying ordeal with the tact and dignity which, when he chose, he knew so well how to assume.

Tired out and still dazed by so much novelty, I finally retired, was undressed, and went to bed with a sigh of pleasure at being left alone at last. It was midnight, and I was very sleepy. But as soon as I touched the cool pillows I grew strangely wide-awake and lay watching the moonbeams filtering through the tall stained-glass windows, and pondering over Marie's last words before leaving my room. "*Mon pauvre petité ange, c'est votre dernière nuit de tranquilité. Que Dieu vous prenne en pitié,*" she had said while arranging the coverlet over me.

Why should God, too, take pity on me? "*Ma pauvre vieille Brétonne,*" I mused, "she is so very mysterious.

We all are in Brittany. Dear Brittany, I wish I were there now!"

And then I lay quite still, my eyes fixed on the tinted moonbeams, my hands clasped, and my mind wandering in a maze of future pleasures, including the possession of all that position and wealth could bring —superb horses, great jewels, and acres of glass-houses filled with millions of flowers. I thought of Karl, too, a great deal. He was singularly handsome; of that there could be no doubt. And he was very fond of me; at least he seemed to take a peculiar delight in being near me, and his eyes followed me everywhere with a persistent, glittering, hungry look which must be, I thought, the sign of a great love. Alban had never looked at me like that. His gaze was soft and tender and melting, but, of course, he was so much younger —a mere boy. And now I must forget him, so my mother had said. I *must;* and I could never, never see him again. A little dry sob rose in my throat. I turned violently over, buried my face in my unbound hair, and after a long time went to sleep — the deep, dreamless sleep of childhood.

On the next night our marriage was celebrated with all the pomp and splendor that a brilliant court could lend to such nuptials. The weight of my cloth-of-silver *manteau de cour* and of my jewels made me feel faint. The myriads of lights, the overpowering perfume of exotics, the solemn roll of the organ, gave me a sensation of dizziness to which I had never before been subject. From beneath the drooping folds of my bridal veil I glanced once or twice at Karl kneeling beside me on his velvet *prie-dieu*. He looked strangely to his advantage in his brilliant uniform. His face was unlike any I had ever seen. To me it was full of mystery, and I was always attracted by mystery. Ah! had I but known!

He interested me, moreover, with that subtlest of flatteries, the appearance of an all-absorbing adoration, extremely gratifying to a little thing who had been so oft humiliated as myself.

Immediately after the ceremony we left for Italy, stopping on the way at a wonderful castle built in the middle of a clear blue lake—a lake which was flooded with moonlight when we arrived, and looked like a huge mirror, where the encircling trees and plants cast lace-like shadows disturbed now and again by the stately motions of some grand and imposing-looking snow-white swans gliding easily and with singular dignity on the calm bosom of the water. The whole picture was like fairy-land.

The profound peace and serenity of that early autumn night seemed to fall upon me like a mantle, and I gazed at the glistening lake rapturously, at the carved and ivy-grown walls of the beautiful building whence a subdued light of a soft roseate tint shone through rows of mullioned casements. The pinnacles and towers and the high steep roofs gleamed as if some magician's cunning hand had modelled them from purest silver. This was a place indeed where lovers could live out a dream such as all lovers long to dream. But, alas for poor *Amorino*, what a disappointment ! What sore distress ! What pathetic and rough awakening was to be his portion, if he were really slumbering while awaiting us under those verdure-wreathed eaves ! He was to be rudely shaken, sent forever on a hurried, terrified flight—as far as I was concerned at least—his tender eyes ruefully filled with bitter tears.

As we passed through the ranks of bowing servants, no foreboding of coming evil overshadowed my mind. To me, marriage was nothing but a mystic union, and I went to encounter my fate with as innocent a faith as if

I had merely undertaken a long pleasure trip around a new world, with a delightfully devoted and affectionate companion.

If any human creature made of flesh and blood can ever be absolutely pure, I was then as pure as the untrodden snow of a mountain summit, in my absolute ignorance of the dark passions of life and of their terrible realities which *le commun des mortels* endeavor to glorify by lending to them the very misleading denomination of love.

There had not as yet been enough in Karl's caresses to enlighten me as to the demands of this so-called love. He had been to me a Prince Charming, courtly and deferential to the utmost degree. He had treated me like some fragile and precious statuette which the slightest touch might break and destroy. Figuratively speaking, as well as otherwise, he had knelt at my feet, and the sensation was a very charming and novel one to me, *où je ne voyais pas malice!*

When we were left alone he kissed my hands with as much ceremony as if twenty people had been present. I smiled up at him and then at the great room where we stood. The latter had preserved in all its integrity the charm and splendor of by-gone days, with its cedar walls and ceiling, embossed and gilded and painted, its pale satin hangings and deeply embayed windows. Masses of camellias, azaleas, and orange blossoms had been brought there to make the whole place bloom like an Oriental garden, and on the porphyry hearth a fire burned gayly, adding its warmth and brilliancy to the whole perfect *mise en scène*. On a small table lay a dainty supper, the dishes and plates and flagons nestling among marguerites and faintly tinted roses.

"Are you hungry, my lady love?" said Karl, half seriously, half mockingly, snatching up a napkin and tucking it under his arm in regulation-waiter fashion. "I am but the humblest of your servants, and would fain serve you even as a slave does his august and revered mistress. It is for you to command, for me to obey."

I laughed, a merry, careless laugh, crinkling up my eyes in sheer fun, and making a little mischievous grimace. "*C'est bien, monseigneur,*" I rejoined, "*mettons-nous à table, esclave et maîtresse, dans une touchante égalité ; venez.*"

He bent his blue eyes upon me, perplexed, no doubt, and vaguely astonished at such unconquerable guile-lessness and stupidity on my part. Then his regard acquired an eloquence both fiery and impatient; it became dull and fierce and sullen, and suddenly the feeling came over me that some horrible and unexpected abyss yawned at my feet. My pulses fluttered strange-ly, and I drew instinctively back with a sensation of unnerving fear and terror, of which I was instantly ashamed.

With much contrition, I laid my hand on his arm and murmured, "Are you angry? What have I done to vex you?"

"Nothing," he replied, nervously, plucking at his long, fair mustache. "Nothing, my dear; how could *you* anger me?"

The chilly sensation increased; I turned from the table and looked abstractedly into the leaping flames.

"You are tired," murmured Karl, "I will call your women. *Au revoir !*" and brusquely he left me.

I seemed turned to stone. I did not heed the rapid process of being undressed. My customary cold bath revived me a little, but I thrilled through all my nerves and looked about me as if the great chamber where my attendants left me alone was haunted.

As on the previous night, the moonbeams streamed in through lofty painted casements. The pink light of a night-lamp fell on my snowy bridal bouquet, and I felt lost in the immense bed, with its heavy brocade canopy, its perfumed sheets and lace-covered pillows.

I sat up, my long batiste garment fastened at the throat by a knot of orange buds, falling around me like a shroud. I pushed my braids back by a familiar gesture and listened. The waters of the lake below the windows lazily lapping the base of the castle, the murmur of the gentle breeze in the foliage—that was all I heard. Then the door was softly pushed open and Karl entered.

"What is it?" I cried—"what has happened?"

He smiled a reassuring smile and quietly came towards me.

"I have come to bid you good-night, my little wife," he said, in a queer, vibrating voice that was new to me. "I am your husband now. I have a right to love you, and to tell you so."

I remained mute. My heart was beating to suffocation, and I would have given everything I possessed to run away.

"I do love you, and you are mine!" he exclaimed, and, with a savage gesture of triumph, he took me in his arms.

Marriages are made in heaven! Marriage is a sacred institution, a holy bond. God save the mark!

And what about a childhood perished in a night? What of an innocence killed and buried forevermore? Is that also heaven made, preordered, praiseworthy?

The sin of my mother against me rankled in my heart. Why had she not warned me? why had she allowed me to be thus sold in bondage, blindly and not knowing what I did?

154

Too proud to complain, too astounded, too debased in my own eyes to seek even the comfort of religion, I fought alone and silently, with my repulsion, my disgust, my unvanquishable fear, my pain, and my disillusion, looking back wistfully to the past, looking forward hopelessly to the future. My heart had surely turned to marble, and yet there was life enough left in it for me to hate Karl with a furious, all-absorbing hatred—to despise all men and to abhor all women. And, God of mercy! I was as yet but fifteen and three months! I had a horror of myself, too, yet I could not escape from myself. Amid the to me loathsome magnificence that surrounded me I yearned for the peaceful, hazy shores of Brittany, for the fresh, pure, clean existence which was lost to me forever now. I never wept nor wailed; but the violent coloring, the penetrating perfumes, the noble sights of Italy nauseated me, and the whole world seemed to have become a shameful Inferno. I was a child no more! I had become an embittered, sorrowing woman, and, like Mignon, I longed for my lost childhood and my own land.

> "Ah! commes les vieux airs qu'on chantait a douze ans
> Frappent droit dans le cœur aux heures de souffrance!
> Comme ils dévorent tout, comme on se sent loin d'eux!
> Comme on baisse la tête en les trouvant si vieux!
> Sont-ce là tes soupirs, noir esprit des ruines?
> Ange des souvenirs, sont-ce là tes sanglots?
> Ah! comme ils voltigeaient, frais et légers oiseaux
> Sur le palais doré des amours enfantines!
> Comme ils savent rouvrir les fleurs des temps passés,
> Et nous ensevelir, eux qui nous ont bercés!"

CHAPTER X

"Des Lebens Mai blüht einmal und nicht wieder;
  Mir hat er abgeblüht.
Der stille Gott—O weinet, meine Brüder—
Der stille Gott taucht meine Fackel nieder,
  Und die Erscheinung flieht."

"Auch ich war in Arkadien geboren,
  Doch Thränen gab der kurze Lenz mir nur."

A GIRL of sixteen, on an uncommonly hot-looking thoroughbred, struggling violently and flinging his dainty, lean head about viciously, in emphatic protest. A large green lawn, velvety and smooth, exhibiting a number of high and well-made jumps, hurdles, doubles, banks, and a couple of forbidding stone walls. A frosty autumnal sky, blue like a dead turquoise, and in the middle distance a belt of russet and gold-hued trees, with here and there a blotch of scarlet-leaved bushes.

Six months before, that slender, pale-faced rider had thought life a very acceptable thing; now life was of no more interest to her than had she been a hundred! A repugnance and a depression which nothing could allay weighed her down, and she only felt at ease when out in the open with her dogs and horses. This girl-rider had once been merry little Pierrot, then happy-go-lucky Marguerite, and now she was *Muzzi*, for so all her world called her, by a sweet-sounding foreign corruption of her flower-name, a *sobriquet* invented by her new friends, her new family, her new country!

MUZZI IN HER FAVORITE GARB

To myself I seemed so changed that in *Muzzi* nothing of my old self subsisted. My existence had become a ceaseless pageant, a continual round of pleasures, but the main-spring thereof was broken.

The steeple-chaser I was riding that morning gave me much trouble. He snatched and tore at his bit and moved round and round, and up and down, as if he were stepping on burning coals during the pauses between jumping. A treacherous fellow was "The Chief," and one of the stone walls in particular he absolutely objected to. I wheeled him sharply about, and, bending forward, gave him a slap with my open, ungloved hand on the side of the head. Quick as lightning he tore across the grass, but just in front of the detested obstacle he stopped dead short, and slewed around at the very instant when he should have jumped.

"Ah, ha! Is that the way with you, you devil?" I exclaimed, thoroughly out of temper now, and trotting him back into the middle of the lawn. I seldom lost patience with my horses, but "The Chief's" behavior was sometimes outrageous, and I was determined to give him a lesson and reduce him to terms. Again the supple, recalcitrant steeple-chaser avoided the leap with extraordinary agility, and it seemed a miracle to me that I did not go over his head. "You want a first-class thrashing, my lad!" I muttered, savagely, and for the first time I prepared to use the short, heavy whip I carried. As I brought it down upon the bay's shining flank he stood still for a second or two, trembling with amazement; then he reared straight on end, in a manner that was horrible to feel, twisted himself around, and bolted.

Away and away up the grass-covered ground he sped like a demon, the wind whistling past my ears and taking my breath away.

"He has too much spirit to stand being thrashed like a mule," I thought to myself, and, in spite of my annoyance, I was proud of the beautiful, untamed creature I rode. But obey he must, so I soon succeeded in stopping him, and brought him back to the stone wall. I settled my reins, squared myself, and triumphantly landed "The Chief" on the other side.

"Well done, little girlie, well done, that was masterly, and *Ertek en ahhoz!*" (I am a judge of it).

I looked up, wondering, and found that the clear, silvery voice was that of the Empress, who, having ridden up noiselessly on the turf, had witnessed, unbeknown to myself, the last part of my fight with "The Chief."

"*Ez nagyon tuzer lò*" (this is a very high-spirited horse), I said, laughing a little, well pleased with such praise, "but he is not really bad. *Nezze csak, hogy hegyezi fuleit*" (just look how he pricks up his ears); "he understands every word one says."

It was her turn to laugh. "Get off, little one. I am going to have a try myself," she added, slipping from her saddle with that inimitable and exquisite grace of movement which was all her own.

"Oh, don't, please," I cried, impulsively; "he is dangerous sometimes, and what a thousand shames it would be if he were to mangle you!"

"How about yourself, then, Muzzi? Would it not be a shame, too?" she remarked, tentatively, laying her narrow, slightly tanned hand on "The Chief's" mane.

"I would be glad if he did," I said, impulsively.

The Empress looked at me, wistfully, but she said nothing, and with a shrug of my shoulders I jumped down, and held out my hand for the reins of the superb hunter from which she had just dismounted.

A boundless and solid affection had arisen between

my sovereign and myself, despite the difference in our years. We were friends *à la vie et à la mort*, as was proved, after all is said and done. She alone had guessed, although I had never spoken a word to her, or to any one else, of course, about the matter, that my marriage was a failure in the full sense of the word.

While our two horses amicably rubbed noses, we stood side by side between them. Suddenly, with an impulse of tenderness, the Empress looked into my eyes, and murmured softly:

"*Chère, ne dites pas cela*—you have a fond, tender heart; do not misrepresent yourself; all will come right sooner or later."

Her eyes were dim, and her hand pressed mine with a genuine sympathy which hurt me sorely, for my heart-wound could not bear probing. I turned petulantly away, gazing at the morning mist which still veiled the landscape. "You are so piteously young to feel as you do," she continued; "you will live to be consoled."

"Perhaps I am wicked," I replied, almost angrily, "but I would sooner not wish to hear you speak like that *Megszolitàs*—forgive me if I am rude." She gave a little weary sigh, and, with a quick bound, launched herself upon "The Chief's" back.

The bay gave one wild leap forward, like a stag, and was off. Frightened at the danger she ran, although I knew her to be the finest and most perfect horsewoman that ever was, I lengthened the left stirrup of her horse, vaulted in the saddle, and followed her. With admirable ease she set him going, and flew a big double as if horse and rider were sustained by wings. But when the bay came to the stone wall, thoroughly realizing that he had changed hands, he resumed his former defences and prowesses, and a singularly pretty piece of horsewomanship ensued, which, nevertheless, kept my heart in my throat all the time.

At last the twice-conquered animal was brought to the wall by the Empress at a steady, sensible canter. Gradually increasing his pace, he soared over the solid, perilous mass and performed this feat to a close without a sign of revolt; only a slight shiver of his satin skin betrayed the fact that he was irritated and ashamed at having yielded.

I could not help gazing admiringly at my companion, as we rode off together, followed by our grooms, who had been waiting at the entrance to the lawn. How young she looked! There was an unwonted color in her cheek and a triumphant light in her eyes. How imperially she held her slender figure; what an expression of matchless refinement and dignity sat upon those perfectly chiselled features, and what a contrast she was to all other women! Those beautiful eyes, how rarely they smiled, but how well a smile became them! What an interesting personality was hers! Never before, never since have I met anybody like her. Oh, my Empress, my darling, why did I ever lose you? After many years this same bitter, unutterably bitter, question rises to my lips. I cannot resist looking back with anguish unfathomable to those days which will never fade from my mental vision. In all my life I have cared for very few; I could count them on the fingers of both hands and leave out the thumbs; but she I adored for her goodness, her pluck, her purity, her nobility of thought and of deed, and beyond the grave I adore her still. My patron-saint—for a saint she always was—now and forever!

> " Félicité passée,
> Qui ne peut revenir,
> Tourment de ma pensée,
> Que n'ay-je, en te perdant, perdu le souvenir."

I was constantly with her, in person or in thought. She moulded me, strengthened my whole nature, cultivated the little good that there was in me. Her sorrows were my sorrows; her few joys my greatest raptures. Devoted as I was, heart and soul to her, I would have scorned the very idea of doing anything of which she might disapprove. The standard she set me was a high one, but just because she set it, I tried with the highest incentive in the world to attain it, although I never quite succeeded in so doing, and am still striving in vain

We both loved the sea, the mountains, and the country, and were never content when in towns, however enviable our dwelling-places might be. Even the Riviera was too *alambiquée*, too cloyed with sweetness, too thickly populated, and too artificial to suit us. Corfu, with its terraced rocks, luxuriant and picturesque, planted all over with flowering trees and silvery olives, was, on the other hand, a paradise we both enjoyed to the uttermost. It was delightful to follow the narrow, zig-zag paths winding up through the endless orchards of orange, lemon, and almond trees, starred all over with their white and pink blossoms; to mount the rocky roads lined with moss-grown stones, in the crevices of which tiny flowerets grew in generous profusion; to push our way through the labyrinth of interlaced branches, followed by our dogs, and carrying our sketching materials. Often there were ledges of rock which had to be jumped over, but we were both too athletic to let such obstacles trouble us, and were well rewarded when, reaching the summit, we gazed upon the indefinite hazy horizon, the deep blue sea, studded with reddish-brown sails, and the far-away coast stretching into endless realms of sparkling light and violet shadows.

We were interested in everything and everybody;

in the boat-builders, the fisher-folk, the flower-venders, the orange-growers, and the very, very poor, who roosted high up on the rose-hued, mica-crusted rocks, in tiny wooden cabins, overshadowed by pale cactus-spikes, and surrounded by waves of fragrant sea-pinks.

The red-hot light of the African sun, the orange sands of the desert, the white, sloping town of Algiers, backed by the dark-needled Italian pines, piercing the transparent air with their sharp, shaggy heads, were also favorites of ours. The distant scarps of the brown Kabyl Mountains were as familiar to us as the Alps, the Pyrénées, or the proud Tyrolean ranges. For we were wanderers whenever we could shake ourselves free from court etiquette and court glitter, and we thanked fate ardently when it became possible for us to leave everything behind in our unhampered flights from civilization.

Well versed in all the ins and outs of Oriental life, the Empress undertook to initiate me to the mysteries of the East, and she acquitted herself admirably of her self-imposed task. Midnight rides in the desert, visits to old palaces hidden away in narrow, dusky streets, and hunting - parties on the reed - grown shores of the gulf, were only a few of the excursions which she planned out for my benefit. She was indeed an invaluable guide for any one who, like myself, was anxious to penetrate beneath the surface of what is commonly called *La poésie de l'Orient*—a romantic glamour which any tourist well provided with money can enjoy. No; her knowledge went far deeper than that, for she had made a very careful and extensive study of the land which once was the home of Hannibal, and I enthusiastically followed her wherever she chose to lead me.

The Orient! How much is contained in those two

TO MANY A SPHYNX !

words! What tragedy, what poetry, what secret and potent charm they reveal! When once assimilated it must always haunt the mind. It prostrates one with wonder and awe. Like the call of the crested hopoe, or the "*Ah-ah! Ay-ah!*" of the Egyptian donkey-boy, it seems to ring forever in one's ears. In spite of all that may be said to the contrary, in spite of European rule, in spite of the persistent efforts of modernists to invade it, the East is still the East, and will always remain so—a wonderful land, rich in beauty, in interest, and, alas! in many sombre, shameful deeds. How painfully surprised I was when I discovered the depth of human suffering and torture concealed beneath the fair exterior of this grand continent—luminous, romantic Africa!

I shudder when I remember one incident recounted to me on a gala night at Gezireh, when the Khedive of Egypt threw open his marvellous palace to hundreds of guests.

The lace-like structure of the snowy buildings was a veritable glimpse into fairy-land. They stood among groves of feathery palms, bamboos, mimosa, and banana plants, the immense green leaves of which towered above a majestic sweep of shaven imported turf adorned by tall *jets d'eau*, gorgeous masses of tropical plants, parterres flaming with all the hues of the rainbow, and borders of incomparably fine gloxinias, dwarf gardenias, and crimson *pourpier*.

Gigantic ferns clustered beneath the deep shade of some scaly Himalayan pines, while from the carved porticos garlands of passion - flowers and tea - roses drooped in graceful festoons.

The Khedive could assume, when he considered it worth his while to do so, the aspect of a perfect *Grand Seigneur*, and he certainly possessed the difficult art of knowing how to receive. Taste and money combined to make those celebrated Gezireh receptions an enchant-ment: the music was perfect, the refreshments delicious, and the suppers of Lucullan magnificence, while the gay uniforms and jewelled toilettes of the viceroy's nu-merous *invités* completed a *mise en scène* of unimpeach-able splendid Oriental magnificence.

The night to which I refer was one of star-and-moon-lit beauty. No pen could ever hope to describe or brush to reproduce the royal blue of the skies—not the dark-black hue we are accustomed to in Europe, but a lumi-nous transparency unequalled for its soft brilliance. The rapid waters of the Nile murmured and gurgled musically beneath the flower-laden balustrades of the marble terraces, and the splash of the fountains fell melodiously upon the ears. I had just been dancing, and, tempted by the cool, dusky gardens, I accepted the arm of a celebrated diplomat, who begged me to go for a short stroll before the beginning of the cotillion.

For a few moments we stood on the steps of the palace, gazing back at the wonderful pageant presented by the ballroom. The walls were concealed by silken draper-ies, embroidered in gold, silver, and seed pearls, and the groups of dancers looked almost unreal and like personages in a dream picture.

"Why does Mustapha Pacha F. always wear a glove on his right hand? It is contrary to etiquette here, is it not?" I asked of my escort.

"If he were to remove it," replied his Excellency, "you would perceive an ugly semicircular scar on the back of his hand. Let us go into the gardens, and I will tell you under what peculiar circumstances he received this wound, the traces of which he is so anxious to hide."

Filled with curiosity, I wandered out into the fresh night air with my old friend, and listened with eager interest to the following tale of sinister and grim cruelty:

THE TRIBULATIONS OF A PRINCESS

. "In 1876," began the ambassador, "the English government, alarmed at the Khedive's terrible extravagance and repeated appeals to the European money markets, sent out to Egypt a special commission, consisting of the Right Honorable Sir S. C., and several others, to inquire into the financial status of the country. These gentlemen, although received with flattering hospitality and courtesy, experienced the greatest difficulty in obtaining the information they desired. In the short space of ten years over £100,000,-000 sterling had been borrowed by the Egyptian government, and of this immense sum only a ridiculously small portion had found its way into the state treasury. What had become of the balance? Two people alone could tell. One of these was the Khedive himself, and the other his Minister of Finance, Mustapha Pacha S., the most powerful man in Egypt. It is impossible to conceive the enormous wealth of the latter. Large tracts of country belonged to him, and he had the right of coining money in his own name. His splendor and magnificence were unequalled in the East. His harem of over three thousand women occupied the immense palaces in which all the government offices are now located, and he had a special body-guard in his seraglio of over four hundred superb Amazons, who, on state occasions, donned armor and helmets of pure silver. A member of almost every European order of knighthood, he was on terms of intimate acquaintance with all the principal statesmen in Paris, London, Berlin, and Vienna. The English envoys accordingly devoted all their energies to win him over from the then Khedive in order that they might be able at last to sound the puzzling depths of Egyptian finance. It seems that they were about to succeed, when, late one Thursday night in the month of June, a carriage stopped at one of the

side entrances of Abdeen Palace. A short, stout gentleman, with a very pronounced Jewish type of countenance, jumped out, and, limping rapidly up the stairs,
demanded to see his Highness at once. The Khedive,
on being informed that his visitor was Mr. Julius B.'s
confidential secretary and factotum of the Minister of
Finance, ordered him to be admitted immediately.
After kissing the hem of the monarch's coat in the customary fashion, the secretary informed the Khedive
that the minister had been won over by the English
envoys, and in order to save his own position had determined to turn king's evidence, and to reveal to them
on the following Saturday the whole of his Highness's
financial transactions. The latter, fully aware that
such disclosures would inevitably result in his depo-
sition, determined at once to prevent at all costs their
being divulged. The next day was Friday, the Mo-
hammedan Sabbath. After performing his devotions
at the mosque with exemplary piety, the Khedive proceeded in an open victoria to the palace of Mustapha
Pacha S., and invited that minister to accompany
him during his usual afternoon drive. As this was
by no means the first occasion on which his Highness
had thus honored him, the minister had no reason to
be surprised, and, pleasantly chatting together, the
Khedive and Mustapha Pacha S. drove to this very
palace of Gezireh where we are now. On alighting at
the door, the Khedive, turning to his minister, invited
him to supper on board the vice-regal yacht, which
lay moored in midstream, and suggested that Mustapha
Pacha S. should go on board immediately with the
Princes Hussein and Hassan, saying that he himself
would follow as soon as he had taken a bath.

"The minister, therefore, accompanied by the Khedive's sons, embarked at these very steps you see here

at your feet, and was rowed off to the yacht. A merry evening was spent on board, the whole ship being illuminated, and occasional snatches of music and laughter were wafted over to the shore. At about eleven o'clock the Khedive and both princes returned alone, leaving on board the minister with the two vice-regal chamberlains, Mustapha Bey F. and Sami Bey B. Shortly afterwards the noise of a brief scuffle on deck was heard by the people on the bank of the river, and then all was quiet and the lights were extinguished on board. Soon after midnight the yacht cast loose from her moorings, and noiselessly glided up the stream towards the first cataract.

"Nothing more was ever seen in this world of Mustapha Pacha S.

"On the next day a decree was issued stating that the Khedive had banished his Minister of Finance to Upper Egypt, for having dared to oppress his much-beloved subjects, etc. Four days later the yacht returned to her moorings off Gezireh Palace, and when the two chamberlains resumed their service it was noticed that Sami Bey wore a handkerchief round his throat as if to hide some wound on his neck, and that Mustapha Bey F. had his right hand in a sling. Nothing, however, can long be kept a secret in the East, and it soon oozed out that Sami's throat had been lacerated by the nails, and Mustapha's hand had been bitten through by the teeth, of the unfortunate Minister of Finance, when they strangled him with their own hands on the night of the supper. Both Sami and Mustapha were rewarded for their services by being made pachas. Sami, who became Prime Minister at the time of Arabi's insurrection, was later on sent to Ceylon, while his companion, Mustapha, after being engaged to an English lady, who broke off the marriage when she heard the history of his hand, became a cabinet minister. Julius B., the private secretary, a German Jew who betrayed his benefactor and master, was naturally also rewarded by being made a pacha, and by becoming Under-Secretary of State in the department of which Mustapha was minister."

After listening to this narration, I returned to the salons, a sadder and a wiser woman. The wondrous charm of the evening had been broken by what I had just heard, and I soon took my departure from the place which had witnessed so grewsome a deed, and probably many others of the same distasteful nature. I did not feel like dancing any more, for the sweet strains of the music could not prevent me from fancying that I heard on the night breezes the agonized cries of poor Mustapha Pacha.

CHAPTER XI

"Now are the autumn days. The sunrise is less bright;
Far from their nests the birds have taken flight;
Happy is he who flies with loved ones dear;
But one is sorrowful, left lonely here,
All lonely here!"

IN September Karl was ordered to take charge of a brigade of cavalry, as honorary commander, during the great autumn manœuvres on the northern frontier, and *"my chum"* Rudi soon joined us in his character of honorary colonel of the regiment of lancers garrisoned there. Our friends said good-bye as if we were marching off to the field of battle, and I took a sad farewell from my beloved Empress before abandoning my comfortable and beautiful home.

A few days later we reached our station on the border of the great plains. There the country is flat and melancholy, with now and again a cluster of stunted willow or birch trees, some great forests, and many a stream of running water bubbling through the tall grasses. No one, however, who has ever seen it can deny the grandeur of those boundless vistas of prairies, with the undulating range of the mountains in the dim distance, and the little villages, with their blue and pink cottages dotting the landscape with many bright spots. But in winter the desolation of the place is really heartrending, and to remain for six months in the snow, badly protected from the elements as we were, was far from being a cheerful prospect. The nearest railway station was nine hours distant, and the greatest diversions we had were hunting, driving, and riding.

There are few places about which the world at large knows as little as of that far eastern portion of Europe, with its startling contrasts between the abject poverty of the peasantry on the one hand, and on the other a wealth in which barbaric and mediæval magnificence are often strangely blended with the quintessence of nineteenth century civilization and refinement. It is out of the beaten track of the tourist, and is unknown, save to the guests who throng the castles of the great nobles during the hunting season, and to the officers of the army.

To the latter in particular it is a spot of more than ordinary interest, for it has long been recognized by military authorities as certain to become, one day or other, the principal field of operations in the event of war between three empires. Large bodies of troops are continually maintained in the surrounding districts by these three great powers, for frontiers are close at hand, and, indeed, there is one spot where the outposts of the three countries are all within sight and hail of one another, being only separated by wooden barriers painted in the colors of each respective nation.

Frontier duty is regarded by officers as being one of the most disagreeable features of the service, and thus do the majority of officers' wives decide to remain behind in the gay capital, at any rate, until the winter is over. Princess T., the wife of Major Prince T., of the —th Lancers, and myself, were the only two women who happened to be, therefore, as we called it flippantly, "on active service."

Our station was a small and miserable village, a few miles distant from the foot of the mountain ranges, and lay in one of the most desolate parts of a desolate country, with hamlets few and far between, surrounded by swamps of reedy wilderness and great sandy stretches dotted with meagre trees. It was a colorless and mournful place, and when we arrived the first touch of cold weather was making the distant forests bare, and covering the plains with a continual shiver of breeze among dying grasses and fading heather.

The distance was a nine-hours' drive, as I have just remarked, and over execrable roads, from the nearest railway station, to the little village which appeared to us to be on the very confines of the earth. To make things worse, the wretched place did not possess a single decent inn, and the cavalry barracks were in so neglected a condition that it was impossible to take up our quarters there.

We hired a long, low, rambling kind of wooden structure, which could hardly be called a house, so primitive was the fashion in which it was built. It contained twenty large, bare rooms, with crumbling pine walls, provided with narrow windows, and doors which would neither open nor shut. The flooring was rude in the extreme, for it consisted of nothing more than beaten earth, damp, evil-smelling, and cold.

A chill like that of the catacombs fell upon me when I first entered this dismal abode, and a feeling almost akin to discouragement crept into my heart when I thought of my many beautiful residences with all their treasures of art, and their numberless conveniences. Nevertheless, I quickly realized that faint-heartedness would not help me much, and summoning a force of regimental carpenters to my assistance, I was soon hard at work making the place habitable. I must confess that it took me a long time to accomplish this, but three weeks later, notwithstanding, nobody would have known it for the original dwelling. The rough floor was covered with deal boards over which thick carpets were spread, Eastern hangings hid the dingy walls from view, and many good pictures, bric-à-brac, and trophies of arms brightened the rooms, while Egyptian divans, piled with softly tinted cushions, gave a homelike appearance to this house which on our arrival was so graceless and barnlike.

When the absorbing excitement of arranging, unpacking, hanging pictures, nailing draperies, and procuring palms, ferns, and flowering plants, as an indispensable adjunct, had subsided, I began to see what a lonely spot it was that we were doomed to inhabit for a comparatively long space of time; an absolute solitude, with an unchanging melancholy about it. The estates of the nobles were, of course, a great resource, but the distances seemed interminable, and made it difficult for us to be on very neighborly terms, especially after the winter set in in good earnest, when the nights became terribly wild, and the howl of the hurricane and of the hungry wolves combined to make up a really horrible concert.

How very much out of place did the delicate, elegant, and frail Princess T. look in this rough, uncivilized spot, and yet without her sweet presence it would have been a thousand times more unbearable. Her charming ways and her blond beauty seemed to bring light and cheer to everybody, and the young officers, who were, of course, deprived even of the questionable amusements to be found at a military casino, grew in the habit of coming to see either the princess or myself every evening, when we would play whist, or sit and chat around a bright fire of fragrant pine logs, often listening to some dreamy melody of Chopin, played by Captain Count G., who was a wonderful musician.

My childhood training now stood me in good stead

and service, for I enjoyed out-door pleasures more than ever, and feared neither wind nor weather.

In my leisure hours I took particular pleasure in training a young pig which I had bought from a peasant. The animal was very intelligent, and I taught him not only all the tricks of the circus, but also to smoke a pipe and play dominoes. He was a great source of amusement to us, and was ushered into the dining-room by my butler every evening after dinner, with huge bows of blue ribbon tied around his neck and tail. It is needless to add that he was always politely invited to partake of cake and fruit, which he invariably did with a very good grace. Indeed, I was still enough of a child then to enjoy such fun immensely.

Moreover, I had a great many quixotic ideas of my own concerning the welfare of the people about me. Their more than rudimentary ideas of cleanliness and hygiene—nay, of common morals and decency—called for a serious looking after. The conditions were appalling; the people were poor, of a poverty which wrings the heart, and reminds one of *"the abomination of desolation"* spoken of by the prophet Daniel! Their very life's blood was sucked out vampire-like by the Hebrew usurers: men with gaunt visages and shambling gait, wrapped in long greasy kaftans reaching down to their feet, and with mangy, fur-bordered caps upon their filthy hair, which curled in twin corkscrews or *peiches* drooping over their bloodless ears.

The village inns, low drinking places at best, were invariably kept by Jews of this class, who enticed the peasants by all the means in their power to consume as much *wodka* as possible. When once they succeeded in making their wretched victims run into debt, they pounced like vultures upon them, forced them to mortgage their land, and little by little obtained such a hold on the poor devils that the latter became mere tools in their hands, cowed by the perpetual fear of seeing their fields go to the hammer.

I tried my best to make my way into the homes and the hearts of these miserable people, but found the undertaking almost impossible, so suspicious and disaffected had they become. They seemed hard and thankless, stupefied by drink, want of proper food and fair treatment, and yet if once one gained their confidence they were sometimes susceptible of showing genuine feeling and even gratitude.

One day I got myself into a grand scrape, which very nearly ended most disagreeably for me. I had gone off alone on one of my riding expeditions, intending to have a gallop before luncheon. The weather was unusually mild, and as I rode over the flat grass-land, enjoying the crisp, bright air, I was quite unconscious of the fact that unawares I had wandered over the frontier, a thing which any of us had been strictly forbidden to do. Before I noticed my mistake I was miles away from home and far into foreign territory. I was just in the act of retracing my steps when I heard the rapid patter of horses' hoofs and the blood-curdling whoops of the Cossacks ringing on the frosty breeze. Looking up, I espied a party of about fifty of these terrible *gardes-frontière* galloping towards me, with their lances glittering in the sun, and their little horses' long, shaggy manes fluttering in the wind.

Very much put out, I dug my spurs into the flanks of my English hunter, "Will-o'-the-Wisp," and, wheeling him around, I sped away at a break-neck pace, pursued by the Cossacks in full cry. By this time I had been long enough on the frontier to know what awaited me should I be caught by this lawless tribe of half-savage men, who were capable of any imaginable misconduct in a case like this particular one. I urged my horse forward with a touch of the spur that the noble beast hardly needed, for he clearly seemed to understand that for once he was being chased instead of chasing, and covered the ground with the swiftness of a hunted deer.

Meanwhile one of the Cossacks, evidently better mounted than the others, was coming closer and closer upon me; with a few desperate strides his pony was beside me, his hand was on my bridle rein, and "Will-o'-the-Wisp" reared on his hind-legs, making frantic efforts to shake him off. Fortunately, I carried a heavy, silver-headed hunting-crop, and, swiftly raising my arm, I gave him a blow across the eyes which sent him reeling from his saddle to the ground.

Without looking behind me, I started off again, with the now infuriated men at my heels, and I was just on the point of being caught a second time when I saw the river sparkling like a band of silver a hundred yards in front of me. Then I knew that I was saved. My hunter, excited as he was by this mad race, could clear at a bound, I felt certain, the twenty-eight feet or so of deep water which separated me from our own territory, for at this place the boundary-line between the two countries is formed by this stream. I also knew that the Cossack ponies, although active, were in no condition to accomplish such a feat as this leap was.

This narrow river, at best, was a dangerous obstacle, but the take-off was sound, springy pasture; the landing was more or less boggy, and very slippery. I settled my reins and squared myself in a thorough business-like way for the leap. I felt that it would be touch and go, but at that instant I could have ridden the head off the "Old One" himself. "Will-o'-the-Wisp" approached the water at a thundering pace, rose like a bird over the steep bank and rushing water, and landed on the other side as lightly as a feather. While in the air, a sudden sensation of doubt assailed me— would I succeed? would we clear the yawning gap? The feeling of relief and exhilarating triumph which followed the success of this supreme effort are inexpressible. As I jumped from my saddle and allowed my nervously shivering horse to stand at rest, I heard a yell of disappointment from my pursuers. I could not help even at that moment laughing aloud at their discomfiture, as they stood completely baffled on the opposite margin of the river.

I need not add that when I reached home I was soundly berated for my so-called imprudence and recklessness.

The owners of the nearest castles, although the financial circumstances of many of them were much impaired, were very hospitable. They bombarded us with invitations to dinner, to luncheon, to supper, to hunts, and to dances, with untiring constancy, and they really did all within their power to make us comfortable and merry while under their roofs. Comfort, however, is seldom met with in those once so luxurious, now often sadly impoverished country - seats — huge, rambling structures, half fortress, half palace, where many remnants of past grandeur accentuate the painful and pathetic aspect of the present decay.

When you are invited to dinner there, you are treated to costly wines and to all sorts of *primeurs*. Venison, game, flesh, and fowl, weigh down the festive board, which literally groans beneath its load of antique plate and of rare Sèvres and Dresden china. But should you arrive at the château unawares, you might find the family sitting before a tureen of *barsch*-soup (a mixture of beet-roots and sour milk) and a dish of sausages and red cabbage, for such is mainly their daily fare. Whenever I chanced to stay over night at one of these residences I was conducted with great ceremony to the state apartment, usually hung with moth-eaten tapestries, and furnished in a gorgeous and lavish if much tarnished splendor, the sole reminder of by-gone centuries. But, alas, the sheets and pillow-cases were worn thread-bare, and the towels on the toilet table ready for use consisted of a lamentable collection of holes and of a great embroidered crest and coronet in one of the remaining corners.

Far from seeming ashamed of this melancholy state of affairs, the lady of the house would smilingly tell me that servants are not to be trusted, and that she had been so preoccupied by her numerous social duties that she had not been able to spare the necessary time to examine her linen stores.

The negligence and carelessness of these great ladies are almost past comprehension. More indolent than any harem woman, they take their household duties easily, carelessly, and consequently everything goes wrong. They will dress magnificently when the occasion requires it, but often go without the simplest necessaries of life.

Princess X., a celebrated beauty, used, quietly and quite openly, to take her diamonds out of pawn before the beginning of the *Fasching* (carnival season), and send them back there with equal *insouciance* on the first day of Lent. Everything is sacrificed in that quaint region to the ambition of preserving ancient racial traditions, and many, indeed, are the members of this old aristocracy who willingly deprive themselves of every delicacy and comfort during eight months out of the year, in order to cut a figure befitting their rank during the season.

M   177

The striking contrast between this gilded misery and the truly princely abodes and status of some of the great nobles, who have retained their pristine glory and wealth, is full of pathos.

Among the most perfect residences in the whole of Europe is Count Maurice P.'s magnificent castle, from which we were only a few miles distant. It was built by a long-dead French architect of immense talent; its sculptured walls are mirrored in the transparent waters of a lake, while the snow-capped mountains rise behind dense woods at the back of its Versailles-like gardens. It is one of the grandest places at which it has been my happy lot to stay. It has acres of palm and glass houses. In the stables one hundred and twenty horses of the purest breeds of England, France, Austria, and the Ukraine were lodged in marble loose-boxes, the straw of their bedding was plaited like a Japanese matting, and the count's coat-of-arms used to be designed in colored sands every morning by the grooms upon the unique mosaic floor. In the centre of the stable silvery jets of water played on masses of arums and of lilies blossoming in the shell-shaped basin of a fountain, and in the adjoining hall the horses could enjoy their daily hot or cold baths like the daintiest of coquettes.

There is a theatre between the banqueting-hall and the winter garden, with a stage as large as that of the *Comèdie Française*, and hundreds of halls and chambers cluster around monumental staircases, up which twenty-five men might walk abreast. Every nook and corner of this magnificent house is filled with treasures of art of priceless value, and the luxury displayed in each detail of the service during my old friend's lifetime was absolutely unequalled in its completeness and grandeur.

THE TRIBULATIONS OF A PRINCESS

At a dinner given by the Count and Countess in our honor, during Rudi's sojourn with us, the flowers in the banqueting-hall alone represented a value of over £6000 sterling. The table-cloth, of old Venetian point, was entirely covered with white camellias, forming an indescribably lovely velvety mass, while the plates of jewelled Sèvres were each of them surrounded by a fragrant circle of pale-pink roses. The middle and side pieces of the surtout represented a stag-hunt, sumptuously wrought and chased in pure gold. Long garlands of camellias and rose-hued lilies drooped from the ceiling, forming a sort of quaintly ideal tent over the table, and a tall hedge of white and crimson azaleas raised their silky blossoms against the diapered gold of the walls. Sixty footmen with powdered heads, in white plush liveries worked with silver, served the thirty guests under the direction of three butlers and a major-domo. All the women present were in court-dress with gemmed stomachers, tiaras, and diamond-encrusted orders glittering beneath their fair shoulders. The men either wore gala uniforms or the national costume of costly velvet, fur, and jewels.

This dinner took place a few days after my adventure with the Cossacks, and the general officer in command of the various detachments of that corps on that portion of the frontier was one of the guests of the evening. At dessert he spoke of this ridiculous incident, not dreaming, of course, that the heroine thereof was sitting across the table from him. He concluded his recital by saying, with a hearty laugh: "My men were quite staggered when they saw that pretty she-devil fly across the river as if both herself and her marvellous steed were endowed with wings. Had their wounded comrade not shown sorry proofs of her tangibility, I believe that to their dying day they would think they had pursued a spirit. I myself would give much to know who this little imp of Satan was."

Impelled by Heaven knows what unconquerable love of mischief, I said, calmly and with becoming modesty: "I was that imp, general!"

He stared helplessly at me, for my young face and small, slender form were not in keeping with his preconceived idea of a daring Amazon, galloping alone on forbidden ground, and felling worthy Cossacks to the earth with a blow from her mighty arm. Everybody laughed until they cried, excepting Karl, who looked daggers at me, and the poor general, who remained silent and ill at ease for the rest of the evening, in spite of my sincere and eager attempts to cheer him up, and to make him forget his involuntary *faux-pas* and my deviltry in placing him in so awkward a position

In the vast forests surrounding Count Maurice's enormous domain, the bear, the wolf, and the wild boar are hunted with all the splendor of royal hunts, and the moon and torch-lit *curées* in the great *cour d'honneur* at night are a sight not often seen in our commonplace and prosaic times.

During the months I spent out there I was able to thoroughly appreciate the startling contrast between the rough daring life of the soldier, the misery of the peasant, and of the impoverished aristocrat, the sordidness and villany of the Jews, and the quasi-barbaric luxury displayed by those nobles who, as I said already, still possess immense fortunes. An interesting one at any rate is this life on the frontier; and I finally grew to like it, the bracing and violent exercises, the long rides and drives, the hunts, and also the *fêtes* at the many châteaux, where we were so cordially and eagerly welcomed.

During the whole of October and November we hunted

four times a week, and I was pleased at being nearly always the first in at the death, and of obtaining the foot or brush, although I was fast becoming a trifle *blasée* on that score.

Many were the golden pheasants, red partridges, and spotted snipes that fell victims to my gun, and in my youthful exuberance I began to pride myself on what I audaciously called my unerring aim.

In December we went wolf-hunting. One generally waits to begin this fascinating kind of sport until the season is sufficiently advanced to render the animals furious with hunger and emboldened to give battle. We used to start at ten or eleven o'clock on moonlit nights. Four of our swiftest horses were put to the sleigh, the management of which was confided to a remarkably able driver. All depends on this personage during these expeditions; if he lose his head or his grip on the ribbons, and allows the frightened horses to run away during the chase, one stands an excellent chance of being thrown off the low vehicle and devoured by the ravenous wolves. A bundle of straw is tied behind the sleigh and allowed to drag in the snow as a bait. A sucking-pig wrapped in a strong canvas bag is taken along, and occasionally the poor little brute is pinched, so that his dismal squeaks may attract the attention of the wolves and make them start in hot pursuit on the chance of a hearty supper.

When once started at full speed on the smooth white hardened plain, one soon comes in sight of whole squadrons of wolves, their long, crouching gallop falling noiselessly on the frozen snow, their emerald-green eyes lighting up the silvery dusk of the night like myriads of supernatural glow-lamps, their low, growling bay sounding like distant subdued thunder of a peculiarly sinister kind. As soon as they are near enough, one pegs away at them with ball cartridges, and it is not unusual to kill from one hundred to three hundred animals in one night. I know of no excitement compared to this, as one's life is continually hanging on a thread, and the swiftness of the motion, coupled with the delight of success when the fierce, ungainly beasts fall one by one, victims to one's skill, is enough to stir up the tamest blood.

The most passionate lovers of wolf-hunting whom I have ever met were Count and Countess C. and Count and Countess W.-D. Both these families possess fortunes of royal proportions, and belong to the noblest stock in Russia. Indeed, of all the members of the then Czar's court, the C.'s were the only ones accepted by the sovereigns as personal friends and relatives, and allowed the enjoyment of absolute freedom from all etiquette when in the imperial presence. Such personages have nothing to gain either financially or in rank from the monarch's favor, and their utter and whole-souled devotion to the crown is of a most beautiful and disinterested nature.

Another *enragé* on the subject of wolf-hunting was in those days Prince S., later Duke of B. This amiable personage was an original, if ever there was one, and the most litigious of all noblemen in the length and breadth of the universe, for at one period of his extraordinary career he managed to entangle himself in an inextricable net of over sixty different lawsuits! Indeed, if gratitude were a sentiment of which lawyers were capable, the legal fraternity should long ere this have erected a magnificent *statue de reconnaissance* to him, for he has proved an absolute and inexhaustible gold-mine to the profession.

But all this is quite beside the question, and I render myself culpable of idle gossip, so I would far rather return to our chases and hunts out there in the wilds, during that, to me, memorable autumn and winter.

> " As fleet-winged birds flit round from bough to bough,
> So do my restless thoughts flit backward now;
> As sweets are gathered by the honey-bees,
> So do my musings call glad memories!"

" *Térjünk vissza a mi ügyünkre!* " as the good old saying goes.   (Let us return to the business in hand!)

CHAPTER XII

" These are the Four that are never content, that have never been
    filled since the Dews began :
  Jacala's mouth, and the glut of the Kite, and the hands of the
    Ape, and the greed of Man!"

"WELL, if you think you can ride the horses *she* does,
you have a pretty good conceit of yourself, that's all
I've got to say, my lad!"

The words struck my ear, while my hunter sidled and
backed here and there, flinging his delicate head impatiently about, and tossing snowy flakes of foam over
my faultless habit. Try as I might, I could not help
laughing at the discomfiture of the imperial heir-pre-
sumptive and the dumfounded expression which came
over his peaked, sallow features, this Prince whom
the portly keeper of the "Stag-Hound Inn" had mistaken for an ordinary mortal, a mere unit among the
largest meet of the season.

I turned my restless horse away, fearing, in my mischievous delight, that I might be tempted to set the Boniface right regarding the lofty status of his august interlocutor. But as I did so I caught the Prince's amazed
protest, as well as the reply thereto, which must have
been hard to swallow, for I heard myself referred to as a
" spirited, plucky, fearless, fine madam, worth a dozen
brace of washed-out dudes!"

This finished me up, and I fled across a field, putting
my hands down upon the withers of my excited thoroughbred to steady him. . I was literally choking with
laughter, and the flat, melancholy country-side, with its

MY FAVORITE HUNTER "GOLDEN ARROW"

cover of clustering wind - torn trees, its many sullen-looking streams, running at mill-race speed through the tall grasses of the plain, seemed transformed *pro tempo* into a land of enchantment for me.

I had no great liking for this arrogant, bumptious, imperial princelet—now a great and mighty emperor. Besides, I was so young and ardent a sportswoman that even so strange a compliment as that just mentioned went straight to my heart.

I gazed with rapture at the boundless vistas of green prairie and russet and tawny colored trees, and at the undulating range of the distant mountains, showing faintly in the dim distance, as I swept rapidly over the magnificent park and grounds of our M. S. H. Count Maurice P., whom I have already mentioned in the preceding chapter, and at whose gates we awaited the departure of the hunt.

I was recalled to the business on hand by the eagerly expected notes of the horn, sounding the "Depart."

went the sweet, shrill, somewhat *rauque* harmony, so dear to all true-born followers of Nimrod and of Diana. The music of the horn was followed by lusty cheers; the hounds wheeled round and began to work in an almost mathematically straight line of waving tails and glossy backs after a glorious red stag, who at once gave us a taste of his power by leaping, with one admirable, clean jump, across the bubbling waters of the little river which gleamed amid tall reeds and rushes.

Indeed, the stag started off on his long journey as superbly as ever did hunted animal, his pursuers sailing away at the tail of the pack, none more forward, I may humbly add, than myself and my darling sorrel stallion, "Golden Arrow."

We crossed a broad, sandy road, the hounds streaming before us, and the master hallooing like mad and uncurling the long, supple lash of his whip with exuberant energy. The *animal de chasse* was by now but a distant speck, bounding on the elastic turf.

Ah! but this was galloping! I bent my head down, closing my lips tightly to prevent the swishing breeze from parching my mouth and throat, but my soul was quivering with joy, and I envied the master his stentorian voice, for I, too, would have loved to shout and cheer and give vent to my uncontrollable enthusiasm.

Soon our course lay through tangled, dangerous grass-fields, over huge hedges and yawners, which emptied several saddles, without, however, slackening our thundering pace until the stag lost himself momentarily in the depths of a pine wood.

This short check was timely, for both horses and riders were beginning to feel the strain on their muscles and lungs. But soon we were off again; the hounds rushed into a thicket, picked up the scent, and the race began once more.

Doggedly and stubbornly did we now gallop, for the deer just viewed had cleared, with apparently quite unimpaired strength, a blackthorn hedge nearly seven feet high. A fearful scramble among the hounds ensued, and the huntsmen whipped them off, cursing savagely under their breath at the delay, although the poor brutes' eagerness was well worthy of praise after this exhausting run. We had now reached a wild and very rugged portion of the country; dusk was falling, and a cold wind, blowing through the rustling needles of the pines, chilled us to the bone.

Truly the situation was becoming interesting. Nowhere was there a sign of life, save when a plover rose suddenly with a whistling shriek from the rush-fringed edge of a water-course, and of all those who had started so gayly, there were only seven riding with the pack—the master, his son, who was then a brilliant young officer of *Chasseurs*, two huntsmen, the imperial Prince, Rudi, and myself.

"Golden Arrow's" heart was thumping furiously under his dark-green girths, and these frantic beats seemed but an echo of my own breathless gasps. I glanced at the tiny watch set in the handle of my whip, and was amazed to find that the run had lasted two hours and fifty-five minutes, including that one blissful check.

At that moment the stag, who very probably felt satisfied with the excellent dance he had led us, rushed into a marshy, slimy pool, sheltered by a semicircle of jagged, moss-grown rocks, where he stood at bay, looking as fresh as if he had but just been started.

My hunter pricked up his dainty ears, sniffed the air, and twitched with passionate impatience at his snaffle; his blood was up, his soft eyes danced with ardor and flashed with excitement. No wonder, for that headlong rush through the bracing air was positively pregnant with mirth and mischief, which that neck-or-nothing chase could alone have produced upon horse and rider; and the hunting-fire was in "Golden Arrow," as it was in myself. Across the hilly rise of the turf, through the brushwood, 'twixt the gnarled boles of trunks blackening in the fast-gathering shadows, the hounds rushed up pell-mell, and, splashing with frenzy through the shallow pool, threw themselves upon the grand animal who had nearly saved his foot, but who was killed with the customary *"who-whoop"* ringing far and wide to the very peaks of the mountains. As loud a shout, I should say, as was ever echoed by the ringing cheers of any hunt in the world.

"After him, my beauties—my beauties—tally-ho! Hark forward!" I fairly shrieked, quite as wild by this time as "Golden Arrow," who curvetted and danced madly under me. But the *"death"* cooled me off, for I never have been able to witness without a shudder this sudden collapse of a royal-courageous beast, whose pluck and endurance have been all in vain, and who sinks butchered beneath the blow of a cruel knife, a blow dealt savagely, ruthlessly, and with a sort of ghastly, inane joy.

"Oh, Lord!" I whispered, "I wish I were a better huntress."

"*Nèkem vgy latszik, hogy, önnek nines szuksege ta nitora*" (meseems you don't need a teacher), replied Rudi; but I exclaimed, impatiently, "Of course I do, but you know how the saying goes, '*Ki farkassal tart, annak vonitni kell*' (he that herds with wolves must learn to howl), and I will yet rid myself, some time or other, of this cursed weakness."

My comrade laughed again. "*Annal jobb*" (so much the better), he cried, "you little fool! Muzzi, Muzzi, confound it, when will you cease to be so damnably soft-hearted? You have so many manly qualities in your little tiny self, why on earth can't you carry matters further a bit, and give up feeling sorry for every man, woman, child, or beast in distress? It spoils the whole effect."

"Shut up! Rudi," I retorted; "you are more soft-hearted than I am. Don't pose, *please.*"

"Well, and supposing I am, what of it, you goose? It's absurd to pity any living creature whose death is as swift and painless as that stag's was; it is to linger that would be hellish."

Many years later these words of my comrade's recurred to me and made my agony of sorrow and regret for him less poignant.

In spite of my extreme fatigue, I was nevertheless sorry when the hunt was over. Whatever I might be elsewhere, my one ambition was to remain always the queen of the hunting-field When in the saddle, an unconquerable desire of being ever first behind the hounds took possession of me, and gave me the grit to urge my invariably difficult horses over gates and fences, springing deer-like on innumerable on-and-off doubles, in order to maintain a continual racing speed from which nothing but a fall could turn me.

I do not think that I had even then, in these the most buoyant days of my youth, a grain of vanity, but of my *quasi*-magical influence over horses I was inordinately proud. It had won for me the one affection I valued most, that of my Empress, and, even had it done naught else for me, I should have been well satisfied.

The "foot" was my prize on the day of the memorable run above described, and, although I had hunted long enough to have become a bit *blasée* with regard to such honors, yet I confess that I was sincerely delighted to see it dangling at the off side of my saddle.

"I trust that somebody will have the goodness to tell me where we are," panted Count Maurice, sliding from his wellnigh done-up horse. "I cannot remember leading such a steeple-chasing hunt as this one for many a long year, and, although I imagined that I knew the country well, yet do I now solemnly give myself up for lost."

His words were greeted by a merry ripple of laughter, which made us momentarily ignore our sad plight and the probable loss of our dinner, not to mention an interminable jogging towards home at the dead of night.

Stobo, the oldest of the two huntsmen, an undersized man of forty or thereabouts, with a hatchet face, cunning, greenish-blue eyes sunk in a much weather-beaten countenance, and a nose pointed like that of a ferret, approached, cap in hand. In a voice as foggy as if he had followed the sea as a profession from his earliest youth, he informed us that we were close to the mountains, and that a mile farther on we would find some sort of a village where perchance we might obtain bread and sour milk, or even *barsch*-soup, besides fodder for our tired-out mounts. A delectable outlook, indeed!

"Show the way!" growled the Count, to whom the prospect evidently did not appeal. "God send that we may drag ourselves there without being called upon to carry the horses."

I burst into irrepressible laughter, which *haut-fait* seemed to irritate our choleric master, for he paused with one foot in the stirrup, and, turning his keen eyes towards us, cried out, wrathfully:

"Wait until you are as old as I am, and doubled up with rheumatism — then see whether you'll laugh at the comforts of a situation like the present."

"You are not at all old," I replied, checking any sign of my unholy joy. "Prince William here is ten times more fagged out than you are, and Heaven knows that age or rheumatism cannot serve him as an excuse."

This unfortunate youngster glared at me furiously, while the Count, thoroughly pacified, vaulted into his saddle and began pounding down a muddy path, overhung with birch-trees, the drooping leaves of which showered damply upon our shoulders as we followed his burly form and the lean silhouette of Stobo, our attractive leader.

"Have a cigarette, Muzzi," exclaimed the irrepressible Rudi. "You and Willy join me in a calumet of peace."

"Why of peace?" I retorted, tentatively, looking up into the merry eyes of "my comrade Rudi"—this being the titular etiquette of our brotherly and sisterly affection.

He shamelessly stuck out his forefinger towards the Prince, who had by this time sunk to the gloomy depths of a *bona-fide* fit of sulks.

Poor Prince! His ordinarily pallid and somewhat volcanic complexion seemed to have faded to a putty hue, and we had the joke entirely to ourselves! Indeed, there was something warlike and almost defiant in the thin, sternly set lips and coldly glittering eyes of the lad.

Suddenly he jogged off at a sort of obstinate plodding trot, leaving us far behind in the fast-gathering gloom.

"Now we're alone," laughed Rudi. "Don't mind him, Muzzi; he'll be all right again after lunch."

"Mind him—you may be sure I don't, poor chap! but I am very sorry to have nagged him. He is an unfortunate sort of a boy, and it is a shame to make fun of him."

This wave of good sentiment was broken by our extremely opportune arrival at the little mountain village, which to us was the land of promise, but which geographical authorities have not honored with recognition, and is only to be found on the most minute and complete of staff maps.

As is invariably the case in those regions, the village was built entirely of wood, the Jewish houses being distinguishable from those of the peasants by an extra coating of harsh blue coloring on their thinly plastered walls. As we passed under the *shrank*, a gigantic and most dangerous-looking pine-wood post, painted in the national colors, which crosses all roads leading into villages, and bounds up in the air at a touch of the toll-gatherer in a most uncanny fashion, in order to let carriages or riders pass by, a crowd of natives came running out of their hovels to gaze at us with an admiration which our muddy and exhausted condition did not deserve or invite.

A thin, scraggy Jew, wearing a long kaftan and greasy *peiches*, or side curls, hurried out of a dirty little inn standing by the road-side and entreated us, with a most imploringly comical gesture of his grimy hands, to honor him with our visit.

I have seen many Jews during my life, alas! orthodox and unorthodox ones, but a frowzier, more uninviting-looking specimen of *"the chosen race"* it has never been my luck to encounter. Even the hounds seemed to recoil from him, and drew back snarling between the very legs of our horses.

"Il faut faire contre fortune bon coeur," sighed the Count, throwing the reins of his hunter over its neck, and descending heavily to the ground, which was a strange mixture of sharp pebbles, rotting vegetable matter, and dark-hued slime of a most offensive quality. We all followed his example and filed into the low-ceiled *Wein - Schenke*, where we were met and almost suffocated by an all-pervading stench of onions, stale cheese, sour beer, and, I am sorry to say, filth.

I noticed that Stobo, who had preceded us to parley with mine host in a strange patois which was unknown to me, looked at the villanous innkeeper with a stare of something more than the usual contempt and disgust which is the undisputed portion of any member of the Jewish race when addressed by a Christian out there.

Indeed, the tone of the conversation was so cutting and so terse on one side, and so cringing and obsequious on the other, that I was quite amazed that any human creature would permit himself, as this Jew did, to be thus addressed without showing so much as a sign of resentment or indignation.

After a few minutes of such pleasant palaver, Stobo came nearer and informed us that we could obtain bread and cheese and also some *rosoglio* and ale to wash down this enticing fare. A pitiable groan from the Count and a derisive chuckle from Rudi were all the answer given, and with praiseworthy resignation we sat down at a rickety table, innocent of any kind of napery, which was soon covered with foggy glasses, black bread, and that horror of all horrors, sheep-cheese, a whitish, glistening, moist substance, the rubber-like elasticity of which no teeth on earth can hope to reduce to anything digestible.

I have retained very clearly in my mind's eye the picture presented by this abominable little way-side eating-house, down to the most unimportant detail, and what a picture it was! Rembrandt mayhap would have delighted in the rich, dusky hue of the exceptionally unclean walls, and in the fitful gleams of ruddy glow thrown upon the even filthier and darker rafters overhead by a fire of pine cones and needles crackling in the stove. But what effect of light and shadow, be it never so artistic, could compensate the strong smell of sheep and garlic, and the abominable dirtiness of our surroundings, especially the painful assiduity of that awful, feline, soft-footed Jew, who hovered above us like a bird of ill-omen, casting glances of fear and of malignity from his little red-rimmed, bead-like eyes about him, as he nervously attended to our wants? So great was his apparent terror that one would have been justified in supposing that he believed us capable of having purposely come to sack and pillage his place and to put his family to the sword.

I could bear the whole thing no longer, and, jumping to my feet, I walked to the little window, which, in lieu of curtains, was garlanded with chaplets of onions and of black, pungent sausages.

"The moon is rising, Count Maurice," I cried, joyfully; "can't we start?" And then, catching sight of the village street, as my eyes slowly descended from the pure, star-studded heavens down to the earth, I exclaimed, "Oh, Lord! what is the matter; there is as big a crowd outside as if a wedding were going on or a murder had been committed."

I had been speaking in German, but when the word *Mord* (murder) left my lips the wretched Jewish innkeeper gave a squeal like that of a shot rabbit, and, turning on his heel, fled out of the room by a back door.

"Hullo, what's up with the creature?" exclaimed the Count, who stopped in the act of carrying to his lips a glass of thick, pink, syrupy *rosoglio*, and wellnigh dropped it in the extremity of his astonishment.

Stobo, who had until now stood silently behind Rudi's chair, took a step towards the master, and respectfully whispered something in his ear.

"Good heavens, you don't say so! Why in thunder did you not tell us before? Pay the beggar and let us be off. The nasty, contemptible brute! Hurry up, I beg! I'll thank you to see that the horses are brought round at once;" and with a revolting shrug of his broad shoulders Count P. seized me by the wrist and fairly dragged me out of the house.

Nothing can surely equal the ravenous curiosity of village populations, and it seemed as if we would never accomplish the task of mounting our horses, for, like a herd of cattle, stood the inhabitants of the place and possibly of all its neighboring regions, packed closer to each other than sardines in a box, leaning over one another's shoulders, peering beneath one another's arms—a jostling, struggling, swaying mass of humanity, seething about us in their endeavors to see "*the quality.*" It was by no means an easy job to extricate our horses and dogs, who disliked this demonstration as thoroughly as we did, from such a throng.

The Count was by this time as angry as a bear, and, regardless of his vassals' feelings, began to lay about him with his whip in no measured way, yelling the while at the top of his voice for them to fall back, which they did with such a will that they tumbled helplessly upon each other, quarrelling and growling in the most ludicrous manner.

Meanwhile Rudi, who had managed to bring his curvetting horse alongside of mine, whispered, laughingly:

"This is the day for exhibitions of some choice brands of tempers. Why, what between our dearest master, and friend Willy, we have had a rare chance of admiring the sweet side of human nature! By-the-bye, what made our revered and honored M. S. H. yank you so unceremoniously from the festive scene of our Lucullian supper?"

"Oh! do stop, Rudi," I said, impatiently; "you are always making fun of everything and everybody. That crowd meant kindly just now. I'm sorry they did not pull you off your horse in their enthusiasm, and as to the Count, why, he's tired and a wee bit sulky, that's all."

I deplore to state that at this juncture a volley of oaths met our ear, emanating from the dear old fellow whom I was in the act of defending against my comrade's accusations of ill-temper. This proved to be the last straw, and he gave vent to such a guffaw that Prince

William forgot his own grievances and rode up to us, inquiring what had happened. Rudi's peals of laughter rendering him unfit to reply, I answered for him, assuming a lofty tone, improvised on the spur of the moment, with a view of marking my disapproval of the imperial and imperious young man's previous shocking behavior. Dignity and I, however, have never trotted amicably in double harness, and my assumption of a manner so foreign to me had the result of making the Prince gaze at me with so comical an expression of stupefaction that my facial nerves quickly relaxed into a grin almost as broad as Rudi's.

By this time it was nearly eight o'clock, and we seemed to be riding in a sea of deep indigo, studded overhead by myriads of bright diamond points, and rendered transparent here and there by the cold light of a glittering, sharp-edged half-moon, which showed its mocking profile above the black scarps of some forest-covered mountains. The horses were too tired for us to dare attempt a trot on the uneven stone-strewn path we were following, and, although we had all donned our covert-coats, we formed a rather pathetic bunch of shivering riders, while the hounds dragged themselves painfully on their soft pads, looking ghostly in the fitful, shifting light.

Thoroughly fatigued, and somewhat bored, too, I suddenly turned to the master, who was almost immediately behind me, and asked him what had caused him to leave the inn so precipitately.

"I ought to have apologized already for ushering you so unceremoniously out, my dear child," he replied, gravely; "but, to tell you the truth, my disgust at discovering under whose roof we had been breaking bread made me forget what little manners I possess."

"There is no apology needed," I said, quickly, "but

will you not beguile this long retreat by telling us what sort of a discovery you made?"

"A very unpleasant one, I assure you. It is a long story, and by now almost a forgotten one, yet had I known who that beast of a Jew was I would have walk-ed home hungry and led my horse by the bridle, and yours as well, before I would have entered his filthy *Schenke*."

These words, of course, whetted our curiosity, and we clustered around him, entreating him to tell us the story. It proved to be one of those dramatic incidents one is supposed to encounter solely in novels, but which, in spite of this firmly grounded idea, abound in real life, especially on the border-lands of civilization.

I do not think that Count P. was what one might call a remarkable *raconteur;* yet the tale he told us that night created a most vivid and unforgettable impression on all our minds.

"Some years ago," he began, "this part of the world was even more desolate and wilder than it is to-day—which is saying a good deal," he added, waving the handle of his whip towards the gloomy plain which we were now traversing. "In the winter, especially, travel-ling was anything but pleasant, and gave one a fair idea of Siberian trips. Dear me! I remember well those endless sledge drives over a frozen world, the steel-color-ed sky above, glowing now and again towards the east with all the hues of the aurora borealis at night, and during the day the dazzle of snow and ice striking one almost blind. The poverty of the people was some-thing to be remembered; it is pretty bad now, but then it was past comprehension, and the crass ignorance, the dirt, the drunkenness—bah! it makes my stomach heave to think of it! You may be sure that at that time, even more than now, the cursed Jew-traders were responsible for a good third of this distressing state of affairs, for the peasants, as is their worthy habit, even to this day, in order to obtain *wodka*, mortgaged their harvests before they were sown, and would have sold their children, too, at so much a pound to the rascals, had it been possible to do so. Well, this *Schweinehund* (pig-dog) we had the bliss of seeing to-night appeared upon the scene some forty years ago, and opened a sort of road-house, at the side of the highway. He prospered, of course, as all his confounded tribe have a knack of doing, and finally succeeded in lording it over the whole village, which he practically owned. Finally he managed to force a small *Gutsbesitzer*, or land-owner, who was deeply in his debt, to give him his daughter in marriage. Such unions were very rare in those days, and this especial one aroused the deepest indignation for miles around. But the unfortunate girl, who was barely sixteen and a beauty, was coerced by her drunken scamp of a father to give her consent, and she left her comfortable home — comparatively speaking — to share the fortunes of the execrable usurer, who took her in payment of her father's indebtedness.

"Finally she died when giving birth to her second child, a little girl, the other one being as fine a specimen of a boy as was ever seen, at least so I have been told. Time passed on, and the usurer became more and more abhorred and feared, until finally his victims turned *en masse* against him, and his luck forsook him to such an extent that he was finally reduced to a state of relative poverty. Long before this occurred, however, his son had, as soon as he grew up to boyhood, fled the paternal house, no one knew whither; while the daughter was transformed into a sort of *fille d'auberge*, who bore no enviable reputation, and shared with her sire the hatred and contempt of the peasantry.

Finally, one fine day, or rather night, in the depths of winter, a little sleigh drew up before the wretched inn which we honored with our presence a while ago. On the threshold of the half-open door stood the attractive-looking daughter of the Jew, wearing the picturesque costume of our peasant women, and over her graceful head a flashy silken handkerchief to shield her from the intense cold. The traveller, a tall, broad-shouldered man, in the prime of youth, and wrapped in a costly fur pelisse, jumped out of the sleigh, and, bowing courteously to her, asked whether he could secure a night's lodging at the pot-house, of which she seemed to be the mistress. She answered that her father was from home, but that she herself would see to his comforts, and, bidding the driver carry his traps into an extremely dirty room, the door of which she threw wide open, he followed her inside the house, and sat down wearily on a low bench before the glowing stove.

"Without speaking, the young hostess stood by the clumsy table, curiously examining her handsome guest through two glinting slits of half-shut eyes. In spite of her undeniable beauty, there was something fierce and cruel in the expression of her brilliant, delicate face, and, on the only occasion when I saw her, her swift, stealthy movements reminded me involuntarily of a young leopard about to spring on its prey.

"While she was preparing a supper for him, which doubtless was as palatable and toothsome as the one we partook of with so much relish ourselves, she managed to question him so cleverly and adroitly that, although he must have been reluctant to answer, she learned that he was very well off and travelling for a great furrier. A little later she ushered him to a miserable room under the roof—I saw the place after the crime, and I assure you that it gave me a shock, so dark and dismal and mouldy did it look. She watched her guest as he unfastened the straps of his portmanteaus, and scattered upon the crazy-looking bed and unsteady table some magnificent fur rugs and other costly belongings; then, without apology or even a word of good-night, she left him, satisfied, no doubt, with what she had seen.

"Now, mind you, I'm telling you this story as it was told to me, and I do not vouch for details—it's a sort of piecing things together without much attempt at creating an effect; but, somehow, the whole affair, when I think of it, seems to paint itself upon my mental retina, and that is how the trick comes easy to me, perhaps, of making you see the dramatic situation just as it appears so often to my imagination. Moreover, the minute details of the incident leaked out during the inquest and trial, so that I need be no conjurer to place them vividly before you.

"Well, to return to our muttons, or rather to our amiable Hebrew friends. It appears that upon reaching the lower floor the girl carefully bolted the outside entrance; then, stretching herself upon the projecting ledge of the huge porcelain stove, which is, as you know, the bedstead of our peasantry in winter, she listened intently to the footsteps of her guest overhead. Soon these muffled sounds ceased, and the silence became absolute and intense, broken only by the crackling of the icicles on the roof.

"Two hours or thereabouts passed thus, and still the girl on the stove-ledge lay motionless, with wide-open eyes, which wandered uncannily from one dark corner to another. Suddenly she raised her small, dark head, and, after listening for a few seconds, jumped to her feet and unbolted the door. Outside stood a man, tall and thin, with stooping shoulders and the repulsive, lowering cast of countenance which you had the ill fortune to gaze upon to-night. He shook the snow from his long cloak as he entered he room, and strode towards the stove, where he proceeded to warm his half-frozen hands, while the girl hastened to place his supper upon the table.

"Then, approaching her father—for such was the late visitor—she whispered, pointing to the ceiling with her finger:

"'There is a gentleman asleep up there, a fine gentleman, who has lots and lots of money and fine clothes, and a fur coat fit for a king. He came late to-night and asked for supper and a bed, so I put him up as well as I could. I think that he is going away in the morning. He told me he was a fur-trader, although I do not believe it, and, of course, he cannot get anything to buy or sell in this place.'

"The Jew listened to this whispered report without raising his head from the coarse fare which he was greedily consuming, but, as she paused from sheer lack of breath, he said, musingly: 'A rich fur-trader, eh? Did he tell you that he had lots of money?'

"'No,' the girl replied, 'he did not tell me so, naturally; but when I took him to his room he opened a box full of gold things, and I saw his beautiful furs and velvets, and he wears a diamond on his finger, and Mitchka, who drove him here in his sleigh, told me that he had given him five rubles for himself—just think of it, five rubles above the usual price for driving him here. He must be very rich, for even *Their Nobilities*, when they hire a sleigh, never give but one ruble as a tip to the driver.'

"The Jew was probably foxy enough to pretend indifference concerning his pretty daughter's prattle, and merely asked her whom she had seen that day.

"Offended by this lack of interest displayed by her

worthy parent, she answered surlily that old Ephraim had called to see him, and had told her that if he did not send him some money by the end of the week he would make life a hell for him; that he had raved about the cruel way he had been treated, and added that he would show no mercy.

"This time the girl had no reason to complain of the effect created by her words, for the Jew was hit on a sore spot. All this noise was about a couple of hundred rubles, a sum that he had borrowed from Ephraim five years before, and which had since then been growing larger year by year, because that unnatural co-religionist only consented to renew the paper on condition that thieving interests should be added to the principal every time the sum became due.

"When the girl had retired to her own quarters, leaving the Jew alone with his unenviable thoughts, she heard him pacing slowly up and down the room, muttering blood-curdling curses and presumably calculating his chances of extricating himself successfully from the countless difficulties which hedged him in on all sides.

"It was by that time approaching the hour of dawn, snow was falling heavily, and the wind, which had risen, was rattling the window-frames and howling dismally around the corners of the rickety old wooden house. Stealthily and cautiously, as though he feared to awaken a slumbering infant, the Jew—as he explained later— lighted a tallow dip at the glowing embers of the stove, and, unfastening the drawer of a worm-eaten buffet in the corner, drew out a long-pointed, slender-bladed knife, which he kept well sharpened for the purpose of killing sheep in the season. (The picture which he must have presented while testing the razor-like blade on the end of his finger should, methinks, have been a peculiarly sinister one, with the flickering light of the spluttering candle throwing a succession of reddish shadows on his vile countenance.) When satisfied with the keenness of the murderous weapon, he blew out the candle, and, removing his shoes, returned to the stove. During a few moments he gazed abstractedly at it as if counting the bricks wherewith it was constructed; then, with another curse—possibly for luck this time—he crept to the staircase, which he ascended as if treading on eggs. These highly interesting details were furnished by himself to his lawyers before the trial, and he said also then that God had tempted him, if you please.

"In the room above all was perfectly still. The dim light from the dying fire was bright enough to show the handsome stranger lying stretched out at full length upon the bench-like lounge, his blond head pillowed on the rich blue velvet of his dressing-gown, one muscular white hand hanging to the floor, the other — on which sparkled the great diamond—thrown back above his head. Gently the broad chest heaved, and the slight creaking of the door did not even cause the young man to turn in his sleep. Softly and cautiously the beastly wretch drew nearer and nearer, until he touched the edge of the sofa; then, with one swift movement of his thin but powerful arm, he plunged the long knife into the side of his unfortunate guest. Truly did the blow go home. A short struggle, a gasp, a gurgle as of a pump filling with air, then silence again, broken only by the hurried breathing of the assassin bending over his victim. The knife, which stuck in the ghastly wound, prevented it from bleeding freely, but the great blue eyes of the dead man had opened in the death agony with a stare of boundless horror and of reproach. With a shudder the Jew shrank back, and slowly retreated from the room ' à reculon,' never once taking his eyes off the dead man's face.

"When he once more reached the lower floor, his first act was to unlock a closet where he kept his provision of spirits, and, filling a tea-cup to the brim with this dangerously fiery stuff, cheap *wodka*, he drained it to the last drop. Somewhat restored by this copious libation, he entered his daughter's room, and, shaking her by the shoulder, called to her to get up.

"Completely bewildered, as well she might be, the girl confronted her father with blanched lips and quivering limbs. 'What do you want, old man?' she screamed. 'Are you drunk? What is it you wish?'

"'I have killed your fine gentleman because I wanted his gold to pay Ephraim, and also to put an end to your eternal taunts, and I may as well tell you that if you do not come up-stairs to help me hide the corpse I will kill you, too.'

"With a groan of terror the girl covered her face with her clasped hands, and rocked herself to and fro, moaning piteously. At last, trembling from head to foot, she reluctantly followed him. She read in his eyes that there was no escape for her, and that she would share the traveller's doom were she to refuse to accomplish the gruesome task imposed upon her. Two hours later, accordingly, every trace of the awful tragedy had disappeared from view. The Jew, whose strength was proverbial for miles around—a rather remarkable quality for a Jew to possess, by-the-bye—had carried the rigid body into a small outhouse, where he concealed it under piles of fire-wood, while his daughter, who was gradually recovering her devil-may-care pertness, and whose mean little heart was very likely beating at the thought of all the pleasures which the gold of the murdered man would procure for her, busied herself diligently with hiding in various corners of the house all his covetable belongings. Hers was so wild, untamed, and naturally cruel a nature that, despite her first revolt against the bloody deed, she would doubtless have hesitated now, had it been within her power, to resuscitate the body of the young stranger, for fear of having to restore his treasures.

"At eight o'clock the first post-cart stopped on its way before the door. The Jewish innkeeper was on duty, as usual, and the dainty little mistress of the house stood on the threshold, glancing coquettishly at the driver, from under the silky folds of her flaring kerchief. Among the passengers was the owner of the St. Peter's inn, the best which our town boasts of. Big, burly, rubicund, and good-natured, Petrowski Ivanovitch was then the type of a really successful Boniface.

"He had served in the army, was a hard drinker, and never passed a *Schenke* without generously treating all his companions of the moment. That morning Petrowski seemed more jovial even than usual, and, jumping from the cart, he advanced, exclaiming:

"'Ha! ha! you old fox! you've had a splendid surprise, eh? Upon my word, I don't grudge it to you, although you are a mean old Jew, for you have had your share of bad luck; but still such a stroke of fortune will make many of your enemies curse you the more.'

"'What do you mean?' said the amazed innkeeper. 'I have had no stroke of luck that I know of.'

"'No stroke of luck!' repeated the other, with evident surprise. 'Why, had you no visitor from foreign parts last night? What's become of him, then?'

"The father and daughter exchanged looks which would have given a close observer food for reflection.

"'Well,' the Jew admitted, cautiously, 'my girl says that a stranger did stop for a bite of bread and cheese last evening, but he pursued his way at once.'

"'You must be joking; it isn't possible. I told him

yesterday when he left my house, where he had put up for the night, that his plan was a bad one. I, for one, hate practical jokes when they are carried too far; but still he cannot intend to wait any longer before showing himself in his true colors. Why, my esteemed friend, it's your own son who ran away from home fifteen years ago, come back from the Americas with a big fortune for you and that little girl there, who is going to be a great lady now.'

"'My son! My son! Oh, God of revenge! Is it my son, my first-born, that I have killed!'

"The words rang out dismally and re-echoed on the morning wind, while the assistants stood speechless with horror, unable as yet to realize the full sense conveyed by them. With a piercing shriek the girl fell face forward on the snow in a dead faint, while her father, tearing at his scanty locks, ran into the house, calling to those about him to come and see the body of his murdered son."

We all gasped with horror as the Count finished his thrilling story, and the silence remained unbroken for a few minutes, except for the regular beating of our horse's hoofs on the hard road. Presently the thin voice of Prince William piped forth:

"Tell me, Count, how is it that this eminently kind and righteous father should now be at large, instead of having long ago paid the penalty of his abominable crime?"

"Oh! that is only because his son's money, which he inherited in spite of all, more's the pity, served to pay some extremely clever lawyers and doctors who induced the jury to believe and declare that the old devil had committed this revolting deed in a fit of temporary insanity, brought about by financial troubles. The creature was detained in a lunatic asylum for some time, and when he came out of it he was as poor as ever, and his fine lady daughter had fled. She is, I have been told, plying a not altogether worthy trade in Berlin; or perhaps she is dead, which it would be far more satisfactory to believe."

Slowly and solemnly far-away church bells chimed out the Angelus, the muffled sounds echoing sullenly over the plain, which was broken here and there by clumps of dark fir-trees. Very melancholy did the landscape look in this northern twilight, where everything was gray and motionless, the moon glittering in the steel-hued sky and shining strongly on the broad track, framed on both sides by denuded birch-trees, which we were now following. Far away in the east glowed a faint suggestion of aurora borealis, and from this unnatural dream-like light the smallest objects, as well as the biggest ones, borrowed weird and ghostly shapes. A little cart, drawn by a shaggy pony, hove in sight, the noise made by the sharp hoofs of the rapidly trotting animal, coupled with the jingling bells attached to his collar, breaking merrily upon the solemn silence.

"How far are we from home now, I wonder?" inquired the Count. The driver of the cart, who was clothed in sheepskins and sat sideways on the dashboard of his clumsy vehicle, knew his Excellency at once, and called out:

"Less than a verst. Your nobility can see the lights of the village now;" then, shaking the pony's greasy reins and pointing with his whip as he spoke, he passed on and was soon lost to sight.

"How creepy you have made us all feel!" I said to the Count. "That was an awful story of yours."

He laughed his cheery, throaty laugh, and, with a shrug of his broad shoulders, exclaimed: "You are a very likely object for creepiness, are you not? A little woman who has remained locked up in a room at the dead of night with a murderous, ruffianly burglar, without betraying a trace of fear, cannot easily make me believe that my little yarn, ugly as it may be, has seriously unnerved her. By-the-bye, it's your turn now; tell the youngsters that little incident; it will help us all to forget how tired and weary we are, and make this confounded last mile or so endurable."

The request having been taken up by Rudi and Prince William, I was forced, *nolens volens*, to recount my experience with the burglar, an adventure which had taken place a few weeks previously :

"I had come home late on the eventful night when it happened. I could not have been asleep for a very long time, when I opened my eyes and gazed about me with that peculiar feeling which is begotten by the sensation of some strange presence near you. The large room, lighted by the warm glow of the fire and by an unusually large night-lamp, was, however, perfectly still, even the tiny Bengalis in their silver cage were huddled together like so many little balls of down, and had not stirred. Suddenly I saw a man of gigantic proportions stooping over a scintillating mass of jewels scattered before him. No, I was not dreaming, neither were my eyes deceiving me, for I could hear the sound of his quick breathing, hissing through the clenched teeth, shut with bull-dog tenacity upon the handle of a long, sharp-pointed *Kandjar*. The man's back was towards me, and his face, reflected by the large mirror in front of him, was one which one is not likely to forget, especially when seen under such peculiarly trying circumstances. The sunken eyes had a piercing, restless look, the complexion was dark to swarthiness, the jetty hair and beard framed the bullet-head with a tangle of matted curls, and the square shoulders and massive arms looked huge under his long-skirted *touloupe*. I lay perfectly still, watching him almost indifferently, while he coolly pocketed one after another the diamonds and rubies that I had worn that night at Princess C.'s hunt-dinner, and which my sleepy women had omitted to put away after undressing me. I mentally took note of his every movement, as if I were merely safely ensconced in a proscenium box, enjoying, with a thrill of interest, the villain's dark deeds on some theatrical stage. I even felt quite indignant at the ruffian's unpardonable lack of gentleness when he brutally snapped in twain a superb and favorite tiara of mine which was too bulky to enter even his capacious pocket.

"Gradually, however, a sense of the danger I was running began to dawn upon me, the spell was broken, and, with a slight shiver of apprehension, I slowly and noiselessly withdrew my right hand from beneath the bed covering, and yet more slowly and cautiously reached for the revolver which hung above my head among the drooping draperies of the canopy under which I had slept. My heart beat so loudly the while that I wondered why my nocturnal visitor did not hear it and pounce upon me with his terrible knife. At last I grasped the weapon, the cold, metallic touch of which magically restored to me my customary *présence d'esprit*. Carefully levelling it at the intruder, I stretched out my arm to its full length, and I said quietly:

"'Don't you think that your errand here is likely to lead you into trouble?'

"If the ceiling had dropped upon his head, or the Bengalis in the cage had flown into his face and attempted to peck out his eyes with their tiny beaks, the fellow could not have looked more abjectly terrified and amazed. With a hoarse execration, he not only dropped the handful of bracelets, rings, and pendants which he held, but also, relaxing his grip on his weapon, he allowed it to fall with a clatter at his feet.

"Dreading that he might gather himself together for a spring towards me, across the long room, I hurriedly added: 'I wouldn't approach nearer if I were you, for my bullets can reach you before you can stir, and if you move I will be under the painful necessity of killing you like a dog.'

"Never before nor since have I seen on a human countenance such a mixture of baffled rage, impotent fury, and sickly fear. He closed and unclosed his fists nervously, shooting ferocious glances at me from under his shaggy brows. But prudence was evidently to him the best part of valor, for he stood as if rooted to the spot, without uttering a word.

"'Now,' I continued, 'what business had you to enter my room at night in order to steal jewels, celebrated throughout Europe, and which nobody would ever have dreamed of buying from you? See how foolish you are, and how stupidly you have risked your precious life, not to mention the unpleasant hours you are going to spend here until I can see you delivered into the hands of the guard.'

"At this taunt he literally ground his teeth. 'Oh, yes,' I continued, undisturbed, 'you thought that even should I awake I would be a contemptible adversary, that I would cry and beg for mercy, and be only too happy to entreat you to accept those tempting trinkets yonder, so that you should spare me. You know, doubtlessly, that my servants sleep beyond reach of my call, and that my husband and his aide-de-camp are absent, so that I am completely unprotected. Well, now, you see what a mistake you have made. As you see, I am quite able to look after myself, and, what is more, I am not a bit afraid of you.'

"Why I thus rambled on I cannot tell, but I suppose that I must have felt a bit lonely in this big room, with that motionless figure towering in the corner, and that the sound of my own voice made matters a little less dreary. The situation was by no means so favorable as I attempted to depict it, for there was nothing to prevent my prisoner from springing upon me when I became overpowered by fatigue, and from putting an end to my galling remarks and to my slender hold on existence as well. But he apparently did not realize this, for suddenly throwing his hands before him—the movement intuitively causing me to tighten my pressure on the trigger — half entreatingly, half menacingly, he jerked out:

"'Let me go; I won't hurt you; but just let me go— let me go.'

"My outstretched arm was shaking badly, although I had changed the hand in which I held my weapon several times during the course of this interesting conversation, and I felt sorely tempted to grant the poor devil's pusillanimous request. But something within me seemed to forbid that, and, settling myself more comfortably on my pillows, so as to rest my elbow on my raised knee, I shook my head in emphatic denial, as if the proposal were too preposterous to be countenanced for an instant. Then, with an unexplainable feeling of compunction, I said, somewhat pityingly:

"'You must be tired of standing there so long; sit down on that pile of cushions near the fire; you'll be more comfortable.' Hardly had I spoken the words when the utter absurdity of such a possibility stared me in the face, and I could hardly repress a smile. Strangely enough, my uncouth companion did not seem to consider matters in the same light, for, uttering an exclamation which was something between a groan and a curse, he sank wearily on the proffered seat. I glanced at the clock and saw that it was about to strike the half after four. I was aware that at five o'clock the grooms would get up to attend to their duties in the neighboring stables, and that then I would have a chance of calling them to my assistance. But the comparatively short period of time which separated me from this blissful moment seemed like an eternity, and I felt the blood tingling in my veins with impatience and anger at the woful silliness of my situation and at the idiotic arrangement of a house where the servants' quarters were not in communication with the main apartments. It was difficult under the circumstances to continue the conversation which I had so aimlessly begun with my unbidden guest, but anything was better than an enervating silence, which was fast becoming an almost tangible thing.

"Just as I was on the point, out of sheer desperation, of addressing myself once more to him, the oft-heard, rasping sound of the stable portals met my ear, and I raised such a shout that the slender baccarat glass at my bedside vibrated as if I had struck it. The man started to his feet and took one step towards me, but, with renewed force and strength of purpose, I once more levelled my revolver in the direction of his head, and, in tones which were neither courteous nor soft this time, I exclaimed, 'Keep still, or you are a dead man!' A moment later the door flew open under the hand of my head groom, who was followed by two or three of his underlings, and I dropped my weapon from my tired and nerveless hand.

"My nocturnal visitor was at once securely bound and removed to an outhouse, where some of my men stood guard over him until he was handed to the local authorities. Poor fool, his presence of mind had so utterly forsaken him that during his long stay in my apartment he had not even thought of emptying his pockets, and it was the captain of *gendarmerie* who, with his own hands, recovered from his rags my rubies, diamonds, and pearls.

"During the period which preceded the trial, and during the trial itself, I regretted many a time that I had not allowed him to escape, for I am sorry to say that, being ridiculously tender-hearted, I felt continual remorse at the idea that that poor wretch was suffering a long series of mental and bodily discomforts, which I might have spared him by a little more leniency. I may as well add that I tried several times to withdraw my complaint and to obtain his liberty, but the laws are strict, and in spite of all the powerful influence which I set to work in the matter, I was, to my great disgust, completely unsuccessful. All that I could obtain was that, instead of being condemned to twenty-one years' penal servitude, he was let off with two years' hard labor."

"You foolish woman!" cried the Count, as I was concluding my recital, "why do you not tell them that you visit him regularly in his prison, that you tip his jailers so that they may treat him with especial kindness, and that you have sworn never once to wear the jewels which he tried to appropriate in so free-handed a way during his term of imprisonment!"

"That's Muzzi all over," replied Rudi; "oh, you silly girl, you silly girl! But here at last we are at home," he added, as we rattled into the yard of the castle.

I must conclude this chapter by stating that four years later I happened to be one of a hunting-party in the mountains of Tyrol. One morning we started at five o'clock to reach the summit of a peak where the chamois were plentiful, and after a few hours of excellent sport we repaired to a tiny châlet perched on a rock, in order to ask for a drink of milk and a piece of bread and cheese—the habitual mountaineer's fare. What was my surprise, not to say amazement, when, casting my eyes on the stalwart *Yäger* who opened the door for us, I recognized the features—so well graven in my mind—of my old friend the burglar! He also knew me in an instant, and his tanned complexion assumed the dusky red of a well-baked brick.

"Why, my friend," said I, "how do you come here?"

For a moment he twisted the rim of his soft felt hat between his hands, and then, with a smile that suddenly transfigured his heavy, lowering features into something almost winsome, he said, resolutely:

"I ought to thank you for having been the cause of this change in my circumstances. Had you let me escape that night as I implored you to do, I should have certainly pursued my career of theft and of crime, but your courage and your ultimate kindness to me, little as I deserved them, showed me what confronted me should I fall into the hands of people less good-hearted than yourself, in case of my reassuming my previous mode of life. So I turned my back on my old haunts, and by dint of hard work and perseverance I succeeded in earning enough money to travel to this place, and to establish myself as an innkeeper on these mountains, buying the châlet with that money which you gave me when I left jail."

All's well that ends well, and I went away that afternoon feeling as if somebody had lifted a heavy weight off my mind. I hope, however, that this little incident of my past life will not fall under the eyes of any gentleman belonging to the "*profession.*" For it is seldom, indeed, that a burglar is regenerated by being thus caught in the act, and I should very much dislike to encourage any of these gentry to try their hand at a similar experiment.

CHAPTER XIII

"Schweigend in des Abends Stille
Blickt des Mondes Silberlicht;
Wie es dort mit üpp'ger Fülle
Durch die dunkeln Blätter bricht!

"Wolken zieh'n auf luft'gen Spuren
Tanzend um den Silberschein,
Und es wiegen sich die Fluren
Sanft zum süssen Schlummer ein."

THE tiny wavelets of the Mediterranean, with a laughing, rippling sound, washed against the marble sea-wall of the villa. The night was perfect; flooded with moonlight and peace; redolent with the fragrance of myriads of orange and lemon blossoms, which starred the luxuriant groves on the hilly shore behind the vast gardens. Among the branches of a magnolia, nearby a couple of nightingales were warbling as if their little throats would burst in the very ecstasy of their rapture. Occasionally the splash of an oar or the voice of a sailor was wafted towards us on the night breeze.

So brilliant was the light of the moon that every detail of the wonderful land and sea scapes could be distinguished with absolute clearness. The flowers which filled the parterres, the tall palms raising their proud plumelike heads towards heaven, the snow-white buildings, backed by dense verdure, and the marble terraces where Cape jessamines and Virginia creepers ran riot, were, like the far-stretching waters, suffused by silvery rays which rendered the scene entrancingly beautiful.

> "Bring consolation unto me,
>   Ye stars that shine so bright;
> So shall I feel that mercy reigns
>   Above this realm of light!"

I murmured *sotto voce*.

"What a perfect night! It is like a foretaste of Paradise, and would almost make one satisfied with life," said my husband, who fortunately had not heard my romantic citation, shielding his eyes with his hand and looking seawards.

Reclining on a cane rocking-chair, I gazed abstractedly at the beautiful panorama which stretched before me, one of my hands nervously twirling the big pearls at my throat, the other toying with an Oriental cigarette from which I now and again drew little clouds of smoke, my feet resting on the back of a gigantic Russian bloodhound who was lying asleep on the mosaic flooring of the terrace.

Leaning my head back on the cushions of my chair, I shook the ashes from my cigarette and turned my eyes, from the surface of the waves which I had been contemplating, upon the stalwart figure of my lord and master, who stood lazily leaning over the wide balustrade. There was no use denying it, Karl was a magnificent specimen of humanity, over six feet two in height, broad-shouldered and slender-waisted, his blue eyes, fair hair, blond mustache, and especially his eminently aristocratic, well-modelled features, making him an object of undisguised feminine admiration wherever he went. Moreover, his age sat very lightly upon him, for he looked as if he were but barely twenty-eight.

"I am afraid you are sleepy, Karl," I said with a sudden attempt at cheerfulness; "you are astonishingly silent to-night."

"No, I am not sleepy, but I was thinking of a man whom I met to-day as I was walking home before dinner, a man who craves the favor of being introduced to you, and whom you will like, I believe, so I have asked him to come to luncheon to-morrow."

"A man whom I will like! He must be quite a paragon, then, for you know that, if I dislike women, I do not particularly like men either, except when they recommend themselves by really extraordinary personal value. May I ask who this *rara avis* of yours is?"

"Certainly; he is a young Scotchman of good family and excellent breeding, intelligent, witty, talented, and a very decent sportsman to boot—in short, your old playmate, Freddie."

"Why, I thought he had gone for a tour round the world, at least that is what I was told. How does he come to be here?"

"Well, you see, his health gave way after his last year in the Far East, and his physicians suggested the trip you mention, but his diplomatic ambition would not let him make up his mind to be away so long, and he is trying what a few weeks will do for him here on this well-named Côte d'Azur."

"Is he a confirmed invalid, then?"

"No, not at all. He was once threatened with consumption, I believe, but now his nervous system has simply been overstrained by hard work and tropical climates. There are also some family troubles, of which you have no doubt heard. They have upset his equanimity. He is a queer character, but somehow I like him—after a fashion."

"I hope I will, too, for I know you well enough to realize that you are about to enter upon one of your unquestioning enthusiasms, and that I shall be satiated with the presence of this highly interesting personage whom I lost sight of when he was nineteen and I fourteen years of age."

"What nonsense, Muzzi! Of course, if he is disagreeable to you, you need not ask him here again, but you may as well see him once to please me without picking him to pieces beforehand."

"I certainly will do that with pleasure. But, my dear Karl, if you have quite finished your rhapsodies about Fred, let us go indoors. It is getting positively chilly, and I am sure that it must be dreadfully late."

Karl picked up my fan and cigarette-box, my smelling-salts and a cluster of wood violets which I had allowed to drop in a confused tangle from my lap as I· rose, and followed me into the dimly lighted, spacious hall where a fire of cedar logs was burning brightly on the big hearth of carved porphyry. It was early in March, and the nights were still very cold. Tea and fruit and cold bouillon were brought to us, and we sat chatting almost amicably until the great clock chimed out the hour of twelve, and then we went up-stairs.

"I really wonder what kind of a person Fred has become," I mused, while trotting about in my dressing-room next morning. "I hope he will not be a bore; it would be too bad should Karl insist on my receiving him often if he does not amuse me. Men should be amusing or else very superior."

I always frankly admit to myself, and to others as well, that I do not like women, for I have no patience with their small vanities, their lack of physical courage, their continual efforts to please, their petty affectations, and their delinquencies where loyalty and truthfulness are concerned. The strong-minded woman, when I happen to come across her, only arouses my most withering scorn, and I sincerely think that viragoes ought to be put to death as a disgrace to their sex. Men I do not like very much either, excepting, as I had told my husband, when they distinguish themselves by extraordinary talents or qualities. I despise flirtations —a practice which I condemn as degrading—and to this day I cannot cure myself of indulging in rather merciless sarcasms, which overtake every one guilty of pose, a defect which I particularly abhor.

Just as my chief-woman Johanna was putting the finishing touches to my toilet, Karl knocked at the door of my dressing-room. He always observed with me, I am bound to confess, the forms of the most minute courtesy, treating me with that chivalrous deference which a subject shows to his sovereign. He held in his hand a large bunch of violets, and as he came towards me he placed them on a table and then kissed my hand in token of greeting.

"Your ponies have been waiting quite half an hour, my dear," he said, with a smile, "and your groom begs to know whether you intend to drive out before luncheon."

"Of course I will; the ponies have not been out for three days, and they will be sufficiently on their mettle to satisfy even me."

Riding was still the exercise which pleased me best, but I prided myself a little on my four-in-hand driving. The western wind blew straight into my face as I drove off over the sandy, tree-shadowed road along the shore. The ponies pulled a good deal, but I enjoyed this, my mastery being absolute over the four thoroughbred creatures, whose glossy necks shone in the morning sun like molten gold.

When I returned I found that the expected guest had not arrived yet, so that I had ample time to exchange my driving-suit for a gown of azure cloth, edged with blue marabout tips, and I was in the best of humors when I descended the broad, flower-laden staircase.

Guided by the sound of my husband's voice, I entered the smallest of the three drawing-rooms on the ground floor, and advanced with outstretched hand towards the young man, who precipitately rose from his seat as I appeared, and whom Karl now reintroduced to me.

One glance sufficed to show me that Fred had improved greatly, and would perchance find grace before me after all. Very tall, slender, and somewhat delicate-looking, he was eminently *distingué* and aristocratic in his bearing. Perchance there was a little shyness of manner, but this was far from displeasing to me, for self-assertion is to my mind a downright abomination. The pleasing features, olive complexion, and dark hair of the young man would have misled anybody with regard to his nationality, and it was difficult to imagine that he belonged to the proverbially fair-haired and blue-eyed Anglo-Saxon race. His eyes were his best point; they were very changeable in expression, the eyelashes were long and thick, and this gave the regard a languor and a charm very seldom seen in a man.

"A good, loyal, frank, soft-hearted boy," was the involuntary comment which I made inwardly, as I welcomed my visitor with more warmth than was my wont, for a feeling of sympathy, slightly tinged with pity, stole upon me as I noticed the thin cheeks and the wavering color which overspread his face as I spoke to him.

"This room is insufferably warm," I exclaimed, walking out, through one of the double glass doors, on to the marble terrace where I had sat with my husband on the preceding evening. Several cushioned lounging-chairs surrounded a little Cairene bench, where cigars, cigarettes, and a tiny cellaret were placed, among bowers of tall azaleas and mimosas in full bloom, growing in tubs of bronze.

The air was warm outside, also, but the striped awnings which shaded the terrace preserved us from being annoyed by the refraction of the noonday sun, and the view was nearly as lovely as it had been at night when seen by the light of the moon.

"The Riviera would have a far greater charm for me," I said to my guest, "if it did not look more and more, as time goes on, like a picture on the top of some satin bonbon box. They have spoiled the landscape by dotting it with too many villas, just as they have destroyed nature all around by creating public parks, and gardens which are planned in imitation of Egyptian, Indian, and South American scenery. I am never perfectly satisfied here; there is too much sweetness, too many perfumes, too much glare and too little simplicity. Now in Brittany I am absolutely content and wholly pleased; our place down there is my ideal of what a country residence should be. It is very ancient, and it has descended to us from an ancestor who lived many centuries ago. Of course it contains all modern improvements, as the prospectuses from real-estate agents term it, but still it has preserved its cachet of antiquity, the boisterous, gray-green waves of the Atlantic dash freely against its outer bastions, and its solitude is priceless."

"But, surely, you have not become a misanthrope?" exclaimed Fred, with ill-concealed astonishment.

"No, I trust that I am not anything bearing so ugly a name, but yet I assure you that my happiest moments have been spent in Brittany—or else in Russia or the Tyrol. I hope that you will some day see our dear old Breton vulture's nest, so that you may judge for yourself whether my enthusiasm in that respect is not fully justified."

"Invites you to come to Brittany?" laughed Karl, stretching himself in his chair and lighting a cigarette. "Well, that is an unusual honor. I am glad to see that you are rapidly reassuming your old place in her regard, Freddie."

At that moment Karl's valet brought him a card. He glanced hastily at it, and then, turning to me, he said: "Excuse me if I leave you to entertain our friend for a few moments without my assistance. Henger has come over to bring me his yearly accounts of the estates, and I am going to tell him to postpone business until after luncheon." Whereupon he re-entered the house, calling to Fred as he went: "I will not stay away longer than I can help, but I do not pity you much for remaining *en tête-à-tête* with Muzzi."

"What a delightful surname, and how well it suits you," exclaimed Fred; "it is quaint, unique, original, and charming, like yourself."

"What you say is very pretty, but I do not like compliments, especially when they are made by intelligent people. They can be forgiven to the usual run of men, as being the small change with which they repay our hospitality or our politeness. Do not think me rude if I say this, but, as I hope to see you often under my roof, wherever that roof may be, it is well that you should be at once made acquainted with my fancies and whims."

"How different you are from the child I remember playing croquet with under the beautiful shade of your aunt's celebrated trees," he said, wistfully, bending forward to look at me intently.

"There is nothing strange in that," I replied, laughing. "I am quite a matron now; besides, as you know, I have not been brought up like other girls. My greatest pleasures are to live in the open air, to ride, to drive, to shoot, swim, row, read, paint, or at times to throw myself headlong into music, violently and whole-soul-edly, as I do everything else, alas!"

"You do not mean to tell me that you do not like the world and all its glamour?" he interrupted, with a dubious smile. "You, who are created to shine there, and whose position makes you one of the queens of the *grand monde.*"

"There you are again! Oh! you are incorrigible; you will insist upon throwing paving-stones at my head. I like the world after a fashion—yes; I adore a good waltz, a play acted by first-class '*stars*'; I enjoy the gorgeous pageant of court-life, in a measure, but I am not a *mondaine;* no, ten thousand times no—not in the general sense attached to the word. The world expects one to wear continually a *camisole de force.* If one of its idols presumes to act independently, without anxiety about what it will think, that one is quarantined, or used as a target to be shot at by the classes and the masses, especially by one's best friends—for these aim well, and hit the bull's-eye every time."

"Good Lord, you do not look at life with rosy-hued spectacles."

"No; I look at it as it is, which is not saying much in its favor. But still I must confess that some clever people know how to manage. *Le monde! — le grand monde bien entendu,* I mean. Worldliness is like all other fine arts; it should be treated scientifically, and the secret of such a science is to *savoir se reprendre,* even if one occasionally gives one's self up to it for a while."

"You are spiritually and intellectually an epicure, I see, but it is difficult, when hearing you talk thus, to realize how very young you are."

"Oh! my education has—been liberally completed. I have ceased to gather daisies, *voilà tout !* My illusions have fled, *cher ami*, which is perhaps to my advantage, for reason never underlies any illusion, be it of whatsoever a kind."

He laughed a little sadly. "You are right, probably; but it is, nevertheless, a rooted custom with humanity never to quite exclude a hope of better things to come."

"Or a dread of worse ones," I retorted, impatiently, rising abruptly, for Karl was beckoning to us from one of the numerous glass doors leading from the house to the terrace, and the dull boom of the Chinese gong announcing lunch was calling us to that least interesting of meals.

I noticed very easily during the course of that afternoon that Fred was at once amused and pained by my frequent little acid satires and ironies, and the puzzled look in his soft, affectionate eyes seemed to contain at times a certain reproach and regret. I felt tempted to repeat to him some favorite lines of mine:

> "J'ai vu le temps où ma jeunesse
> Sur mes lèvres était sans cesse
> Mais j'ai souffert un dûr martyre,
> Et le moins que j'en pourrais dire,
> Si je l'essayais sur ma lyre
> La briserait comme un roseau."

His visits were frequent to us after that day, and when we left the South for the North he promised Karl and myself to join us during the following hunting season. Many months were, however, to elapse, and many great events to take place before we saw each other again.

That Karl was speedily wearying of my coldness, and I fear of my ill-disguised repulsion, was not a cause of sorrow to me, but of sincere relief. His conduct was such as to wound and insult any wife, but I felt neither wounded nor insulted thereby. By his more and more glaring infidelities he plainly showed that it was his nature to be unfaithful, and I only longed for an opportunity to loosen completely the sagging chains which still bound him to me. This opportunity came sooner than I expected, and came indeed in a rather nasty fashion, too, but I am thankful to say that by some extraordinary miracle my pride was saved, and I was able to avoid giving my friends and acquaintances, as well as my enemies, the chance of having a hearty laugh at my expense, or even of knowing what supreme disgrace had befallen me. Their contemptuous derision would have been hard to bear.

I one day promised, shortly after our return from the Riviera, to go and dine with Princess T., who was residing for a few weeks at a charming château which she owned, some five miles outside the city limits, and, as was my custom on such occasions, I sent my dinner dress there in the morning, proposing to ride over the short distance accompanied by a groom later on.

Having advised Karl of my intentions, I was just leaving my house when a telegram was handed to me. The Princess had been taken suddenly ill, and the dinner was postponed, but as the weather was very tempting, I decided not to forego a gallop in the open country, and, thrusting the despatch in my pocket, I rode off at a swinging trot, on the tan-bark *allée* reserved for equestrians, in the direction of the river.

So magnificent was the day that I prolonged my tour far beyond my first intention. In fact, it was almost night when I dismounted at my own door-steps, and, followed by the groom who carried my covert-coat, I walked slowly up-stairs. It was the servant's supper hour, so that the halls were deserted, especially as I had given no counter orders about the evening, and was not expected home. Softly and noiselessly we trod the

P 225

carpets, as thick as moss. The lamps in the gallery leading to my rooms were burning low, and we passed on silently to where the door of Karl's bedchamber, standing half open, cast a stronger ray of light at my feet. Surprised at this illumination of a presumably untenanted room—for he had told me that he would dine at his club—I paused on the threshold, and then recoiled with the surprise of what I saw almost into the arms of the petrified groom who had also seen what I had seen myself over my shoulder.

Unheard and unnoticed we hurried on. I was trembling with rage from head to foot, but this was no time for the indulgence of any personal feelings. *L'honneur du nom*, that had to be saved, and swiftly I entered my private library, drawing the English lad in after me and shutting the door carefully.

"Bob," I said, as calmly as I could, "I am not going to offer you hush-money about this—this incident—I think I can rely upon your discretion without resorting to such means. Promise me that not a word will pass your lips, and that I can appeal to your honor in this matter as to that of a gentleman."

I had struck the right chord. The youth straightened himself up to his full height—which was something below five feet—looked me full in the face with his bonny blue British eyes, and, in a voice which shook very much, declared that he would "rather be struck dead" than betray my confidence.

"That is right, Bob; I believe you;" and then I held out my hand to him and shook his with a sense of genuine gladness at his honesty and *quasi*-childlike but, withal, manly earnestness. That boy was, I knew, as white as white could be. God bless him for it!

Once alone, I hastily determined to have a final, conclusive, and immediate explanation with Karl. I rang the bell and told my maid, who was amazed to find me there, to request my husband's confidential valet—a great rogue and a traitor if ever there was one—to advise his master that I should like to speak to him at once.

A few moments later Karl entered. His face was singularly pale, and his eyes avoided mine.

"How do you come to be here?" he asked, a little breathlessly. "I thought that you were dining out?"

"I know you did," I replied, meaningly, although I spoke firmly, in a low voice, and without a trace of violence.

"Why do you say that in such a tone?" he said, arrogantly, vainly attempting to regain his usual self-confidence.

"I think that you know why," I said, in the same cold, ironical manner. "I have now all my rights to leave you if I choose—*infidélité sous le toit conjugal et tutti quanti*—and what an infidelity!—with a serving-maid, '*monseigneur,*'" I added, looking at him as if he had been a leper, for my patience was beginning to give way; "but I loathe scandal, and my wrongs will not be spread by me before the world. I will not fall into such helpless folly; I care for my honor, and for yours, too, in an odd way. No, do not interrupt me; it is useless; I must speak at last, and let you know what our future will henceforth be. Good Heavens, how little you know me! Do you think that I was not aware of the ignominy of your conduct? What fools men are, and what dolts! But now you have overstepped all bounds, you have passed the barriers which no gentleman should ever pass, you have behaved like a brute, and I am not inclined to condone such an offence, such an insult! Hear me out, *if* you please. From this moment you and I are strangers; we will continue to live together in order to blind the world to the true state of our affairs.

But never dare to approach me again when I am alone, or, God forgive me, I will kill you."

An exceeding faintness came over me, and I staggered slightly. He seized his opportunity, and, in the utter weakness of the domination which I had momentarily obtained over him, he began to plead his own cause, humbly enough—nay, cravenly and, in my opinion, revoltingly. But my blood was on fire. I came from a race who had never lightly brooked insult or pitied cowardice, and his lame and paltry excuses acted as a revivifying tonic upon me. By a great effort I restrained the bitter rage and the boundless scorn I felt for him, and I let the torrent of his words pass unheeded.

At last, when he came to a close, I merely said: "Now that I have heard you, I can tell you that my resolve is by no means changed. Be good enough to go; leave me to myself; it will be best so."

"Good Heavens, madame," he almost shouted, "do you think that I am going to submit to your rule? Do you, for one instant, imagine that I will give you up, that I will cease to be your husband in everything but in name. Do you really believe that I will run the risk of seeing my union with you remain barren on account of your whims?"

This was too much. I burst into uncontrollable laughter, a veritable *fou-rire*, which shook me as a hurricane might a plant.

"Your insolence is wellnigh inconceivable," I exclaimed, as soon as I could speak. "Oh! you madman, are you trying to persuade me that you love me, or that family ties and joys are of value to you? No! No! I see more clearly than you think. You merely fear ridicule, because you presume that the odium of your ways will become public property. You need not fear.

I know how to keep silent, and silence in this instance means as much to me, and more, than it does to you."

He stared at me with gloomy amaze, but I pursued, unheeding: "It is difficult for you to believe in silence and in discretion, because you possess none of these small virtues—you whom society has nicknamed ' William Tell'."

"That is false. None but a cur ever speaks—of certain things."

"Possibly; draw your own conclusions about society's verdict, then. And as to the barrenness of our union, it may serve to make you pass for a very learned and intellectual man, for if it be ever mentioned to you, you can quote Shakespeare, and say of us—

"Leaving no posterity—
'Twas not their infirmity,
It was married chastity."

"Excuse my levity; it is out of place, possibly; but, to tell you the truth, if I am erring now in taste and wisdom, it is thanks to the relief which the prospect of being rid of my wifely obligations towards you gives me. I have long ached to free myself from the incubus of your so-called love. I have wondered, wondered, wondered, why men like you should exist at all, and why fate should have been so cruel to me. My heart has grown sick with apprehension and aversion whenever I heard the sound of your step outside my door. Are you satisfied now that I have told you this? I have tried to bear calmly the horrible disgrace which such a love was to me. You thought that I did not feel; you were mistaken. I have suffered—oh! God of Heaven, how I have suffered! You found me cold, perchance stupid, and I was glad when you did so, because I did not care to let you see the disdain, the disgust I have for you. My silence arose from a mistaken sense of duty and from pride as well. If I had dragged what you are pleased to facetiously call your honor through the filthiest mire of Europe, it would have been no more than you deserved, but I have other ideas on such matters, and I hold my dignity high aloft, whatever you may please to do with your own. For the last time I repeat it now, go! I cannot bear the sight of you. Later we will meet in public as if nothing had happened, but for the present spare me the insult of your presence."

With sullen, scowling, irresistible subjection, he went, and I, shuddering and unnerved, remained face to face with the beginning of a new life—a life which I could make pure at last and cleanse from all the miseries of my union with such a man.

The *modus vivendi* which I forced Karl to accept— not without several instances of violent protest on his part, for his vanity was intensely hurt and he cruelly resented having been cornered—finally became an established institution; our intercourse was reduced to a mere courteous armed truce, and I avoided with scrupulous care ever seeing him alone. We filled our houses with guests, went out together often, and continued to be cited as a model couple, which was a mercy indeed, and of an intense but amusing irony. But apart from that, we could not have been more disconnected if we had been barely bowing acquaintances crossing the ocean on the same steamer. In fact, although no one ever, save one or two people, entertained any doubt about our perfect accord, the truth is that we managed to keep two distinctly separate establishments under the same roof-tree, which was what I had desired and achieved.

Soon, however, war and noises of war filled the land, and our own personal troubles were absorbed and merged into those of thousands of human beings struggling on bloody battle-fields.

Two great powers came to blows, and some smaller ones became hot-headed and rebellious. Fanaticism, misgovernment, misappropriation, were stated as valid excuses for all the horrors that came to pass, and then another great country—my adopted one—interfered, and marched many troops beyond the boundary-line of the empire. During the months that followed there was some terrible assumption of international responsibility, brave men fought and brave men died, reckless commanders played an uphill game, and won it, too! Ill-disciplined, half-savage, but well-armed hordes did much havoc, and bands of hill-robbers pot-shotted our soldiers most grewsomely.

The rapid march of events fired me with enthusiasm for the courage displayed everywhere, and filled me with pity for all the misery so nobly endured; and when Karl. was ordered to join the conflicting armies and to take up a command there, I decided to go too, in spite of great opposition. I not only succeeded in gaining my piont, but two of my friends, Princess T. and Princess W., filled with a spirit of emulation, joined me in this rash venture, and we set off to do some army nursing and some sort of soldiering as well, adorned with the insignia of the Red Cross on our campaigning, semi-military, and very serviceable garments.

The restless feverishness of warfare was upon me; I was full of dash and energy, and I had sometimes to pinch myself in order to realize that I was not dreaming, that I was not in reality a soldier, but merely a tiny bit of a woman, so bent on combat did I feel.

It seems anomalous to say it, but those long weeks spent among wounded, sick, disabled, and festering humanity count among the happiest of my whole existence. Heedless of the roar of artillery, the call of the bugles, the groans of the dying, I pursued my self-imposed task with strange cheerfulness, braced by the delicious feeling that for once I was being of some use.

I quickly grew accustomed to the stench and turmoil of the *champ de bataille*. The humming of bullets—which I at first mistook for the buzzing of bees—was not unpleasing to my ears, and it would seem as if the old proverb, which says, *"Bon sang ne peut mentir,"* had some truth in it, for my pulses beat all the quicker when the conflict was at its worst. I was never tired, and no hardships seemed to touch me, for I rode indefatigably over field and furrow, hill and dale, mountain and plain, collecting prostrate bodies and limbs, and caring for the wounded, who were, alas, frequently left to rot in their own blood, so great was the slaughter. I must, in justice to myself, state that there was no bravado in any of my actions, and confess, at the risk of passing for a heartless wretch, that I liked it all. So here goes another proverb—*"Bon chien chasse de race."* It may explain much—for instance, the fact that a soldiering spirit makes it possible to live happily in the close proximity of death. I saw sights that were simply hellish, overshadowed by the smoke of rifles and of cannons; my ears were deafened by the awful and perpetual growl of heavy firing, and yet I liked it. A great throb of my heart occasionally choked me, but again I would shout incoherently like a youthful demon for which *haut-fait* I experienced momentary pangs of shame, and my soul would melt within me with sorrowful regret for so many victims of their own heroism, lying prostrate under the glowing sky, which looked as if it had caught the reflection of the gore-soaked earth.

THE TRIBULATIONS OF A PRINCESS

After so many years I wake now sometimes in the darkness of the night and long for the excitement and the fiery enthusiasm of those days:

> " I dream of dead and gory days;
> Could I but hear, could I but hear,
> The trumpets blare, to carnage calling,
>   Then to the saddle would I spring,
> My mettled steed with joy bestriding,
>   I'd haste to join the noble ring
> Of soldiers who to fight are riding."

CHAPTER XV

" Vater, ich rufe Dich,
Brüllend umwölkt mich der Dampf der Geschütze,
Sprühend umzucken mich rasselnde Blitze;
Lenker der Schlachten, ich rufe Dich!
Vater, du führe mich!

" Gott, Dir ergeb' ich mich,
Wenn mich die Donner des Todes begrüssen,
Wenn meine Adern geöffnet fliessen;
Dir, mein Gott, Dir ergeb' ich mich!
Vater, ich rufe Dich!"

"ONE, two, three, four," counted the major as the wounded were brought in and tenderly deposited upon the bundles of straw which were to serve as couches until the moment came for the poor wretches to be operated upon. The wind blew fiercely, and shook the canvas sides of the large tent, under the folds of which rows upon rows of uncomfortable little truckle-beds were literally packed, while heavy showers of rain sounded like hail above our heads.

It was by no means an easy or a pleasant task to take care of all these poor mangled soldiers under such unfavorable circumstances, but I hated to acknowledge even to myself that I had undertaken a very heavy burden with regard to this bloody campaign, where we had to fight as best we could against the numerous and almost insurmountable difficulties placed in the way of conscientious sick-nurses, who have to dispense with all the conveniences and even the necessities of an ordinary hospital. We were often left without chloroform, without ice, of course, without beef-tea, or even, for the matter of that, without any nourishing food at all for our patients. Blankets were a luxury, and, as to lint and linen bandages, we had to exercise the utmost ingenuity to procure the best possible substitutes therefor.

"Five, six, seven, eight," continued the major, in a stentorian voice, which was nevertheless almost drowned by the sullen booming of the cannon echoing from the hills on our left.

"It is to be hoped that they are not going to kill our sick and wounded under the very shadow of the Red Cross flag," he snarled furiously, for the cannonading and fusillade rose louder and louder as it closed in upon us from all sides.

The situation was serious. The battle which had lasted since early in the morning had as yet by no means abated, although it was now half past four in the afternoon. Moreover, on this bleak plateau, where our ambulance tents were pitched, we were not properly protected, and in case of a defeat we had but little mercy to expect from the savage enemy, who, it was reported, were destroying everything wearing our uniform, whether prisoners, disabled combatants, or even corpses. Sorrowfully I stood watching the orderlies as they lifted the wounded from the ambulance-cart and sheltered them quickly from the downpouring rain. So absorbed was I in this pitiful spectacle that I started violently upon hearing my name called loudly by the major.

"What is the matter?" I cried, running towards him.

"Matter?" he growled; "why, everything is the matter. Here I am without assistants, and obliged to perform goodness knows how many operations single-handed. And, what is worse, I'll be hanged if I know whether the chloroform will go round."

235

This was certainly an ugly state of affairs, and I did not wonder at the major's moody face and brusqueness of speech. Brusque he always was more or less, this excellent doctor—or *major*, as all military physicians and surgeons are called in Europe, because this rank belongs to them by right—but still I had never seen so forbidding an expression nor so sombre a look on his much weather-beaten countenance. Greatly concerned, I caught his arm, and, looking up in his perturbed face, which towered so high in the air above me—the major prided himself on being the tallest medical man in the army—I said on the impulse of the moment:

"Let me help you with the operating part of it; you know that I have gained some little experience since I have been here, and—I am not nervous and never get tired."

A smile broke upon his lips, displaying two rows of dazzling white teeth, and he answered, more gently: "That's very true, but do you know what the physical fatigue of such an undertaking means? I have often seen men, hale and strong, give in on such occasions; and you—poor, little, delicate, slender creature—want to help me in my ghastly butcher's work?"

I laughed, so comical was the earnestness of his protest. "Have you anything better to suggest?" I said, impatiently. "We have now here only two Sisters of Mercy, who have more than they can attend to with the soldiers already operated upon. Princess W. and Princess T. have been sent for to assist in nursing the patients down in the valley, and the orderlies do not possess sufficient intelligence to be of any efficient use to you, so you see that my offer is not so silly, after all."

For a few moments he gazed at me with undisguised astonishment. Then he said, with a shrug of his heavy shoulders: "We might try it; I'm infernally sorry to be forced to accept this new sacrifice from you, but I really don't see what else I can do. It will be a rough experience for so young a hand, but you can get ready if you will be so kind; take one of my aprons, for there will be lots of dirty work, and look out that you don't faint. I have no time to spare in reviving you."

I shuddered slightly, for his words implied that, however hardened I believed myself to be, I was on the point of a new experience. Of course, I had seen many serious operations since the beginning of the campaign, and I had dressed many repulsive wounds, but I began to realize that my attempt at practical surgery was likely to be fraught with quite another kind of hardship than what I had already gone through. Notwithstanding, I set my teeth, and ran to get ready, according to the major's advice, and a pretty sight I looked with his gigantic apron tucked up under my chin and my sleeves rolled almost to the shoulder, for all the world as if I were about to undertake some difficult culinary operation instead of a great many grewsome surgical ones.

When I re-entered the main tent I must confess that I felt uncommonly like running away again, without so much as giving the odious place another look. By means of some sail-cloth, or canvas, or whatever it may have been, the upper portion thereof had been partitioned, and a long table, covered with rubber sheeting of questionable cleanliness, had been placed in the middle of this miniature amphitheatre. Near by on a stand were laid out in disordered array every sort of surgical instrument from a saw to some vicious-looking pincers, together with sponges and a provision of lint and absorbent cotton.

On the table lay a poor devil, whose face, as white as linen, bore an expression of the most terrified apprehension, while the doctor was saturating a small cloth with chloroform. Nerving myself to stand whatever would follow, I modestly approached, and, in a voice which I endeavored to steady, I reported in all due form that I was ready for work.

The major, without lifting his head, said in the most matter-of-fact manner possible: "Do you know how to administer chloroform?"

I gazed helplessly at him, and then shamefacedly admitted that my hand was as yet untried at so ticklish a job, although I had, to be sure, often seen it done. In a few short words he explained to me what I was to do, and although I trembled in a way that disgusted me, I set to work to carry out his instructions to the best of my ability.

In spite of the attention which I was giving to my task, I could not help casting an occasional glance at the horrors surrounding us upon all sides. The aspect of the whole place had become really terrible. Unceasingly the wounded were being carried in, and as there had long since been no more room on the hastily arranged beds, a couple of orderlies were scattering more bundles of straw on the floor to lay the groaning, miserable remnants of humanity upon as they arrived from the battle-field in a continual procession.

Moans of heartrending anguish filled the air, and in a corner a very young soldier, fair-haired and delicately built, kept up a soft, pleading murmur of entreaty, inexpressibly painful to hear, calling upon his mother, poor fellow, to come and take his pain away. Wounds which had been too summarily dressed by inexperienced ambulance-men had come undone, and nothing can give an idea of the aspect presented by the poor sufferers, torn and bleeding, their uniforms all covered with mud, and their faces so drawn, pinched, and haggard in the dim afternoon light of this stormy day, yet displaying still the thrilling enthusiasm of ardent fighters.

The patient on the table having in the meanwhile succumbed to the vapors of the chloroform, and the major being quite ready, we began the risky operation which is known to men of science under the name of "*disarticulation of the shoulder by the method of Lisfranc.*" It is what surgeons are pleased to call a "*neat and clean operation*" or "*quick and dainty*" as they have it, for a good operator can accomplish it in forty-five seconds. It may be that I was not scientific enough to appreciate its beauties, however, for I saw nothing "*dainty*" in the butchering of the wretched man whose livid head was pillowed upon my arm. I tried vainly to look another way, but wherever my eyes fell there was nothing but misery and distress of the worst description to be seen, and I could not help gazing with a kind of unaccountable fascination on "*my patient,*" who was now propped up in a sitting posture, by the orders of the major, and held fast between myself and a burly *ambulancier.* This assistant fortunately knew more about the work than I did, for when the major seized the deltoid muscle, transpierced the arm with his long, narrow-bladed knife, and detached the joint —all that in three masterly movements—the assistant needed no prompting to close the severed arteries with his thumbs, while the anxious surgeon was fixing the ligatures.

"Ah!" cried the major, "that is all right! I venture to bet that it didn't take me over forty seconds to do." I said nothing, for if the truth be known, I was feeling extremely sick, but pride came to my aid, and I even made a pretence of admiring the swift and business-like fashion in which he drew down and secured the "*flap,*" like a flat epaulette, although it was, to me at least, by no means a welcome spectacle.

"Do you know, madame," the major continued, "that there is always an immediate danger of death when one places a patient under the influence of chloroform in a sitting posture, and that, if proper care be not taken, all the blood can run out of the body in four minutes through the humoral artery."

No, I did not know all these interesting details, and although much obliged to the major for disclosing them to me, I did not lend him my undivided attention, for the patient was regaining consciousness, and I felt too deep a sympathy for him to be able to listen to technicalities. For a moment he cast a bewildered look upon the objects around him; then, catching sight of his severed arm, which still lay upon the operating-table, he glanced at his mutilated shoulder, and, to my intense dismay, he burst into a passion of tears.

"Halloo, my man," cried the doctor, "don't take on so; you are all right now." But the poor devil refused to be consoled, and it was pitiful to hear him murmur in a feeble, broken voice: "What do you want me to do now? How can I work to keep my wife and child from starving?"

I confess that I was nearly overcome, and even the major knit his brows and looked as glum as an owl. But we had no time to waste on talk, for on all sides agonized voices were imploring the doctor to "*please come*" and attend to their injuries.

The hours had fled, and now it was so dark that, in spite of the few oil-lamps which had been procured with difficulty, we hardly saw what we were about.

"Confound this hellish gloom," exclaimed the major, who rarely swore, and I understood his irritation, feeling that but for a little more I would be reduced to imitate his force and picturesqueness of language. By the aid of two ambulance lamps we succeeded, however, in obtaining sufficient light to continue the operations.

One after the other, legs, arms, fingers, toes, were amputated. Horrible scalp wounds, caused by the broad-bladed swords of our formidable opponents, were stitched up, and still we saw no end to our task.

I was so tired that I did not feel my limbs any longer, and a thirst, such as I had never experienced, parched my throat and mouth. I honestly believe that by this time the major had entirely forgotten who and what I was, for he ordered me about as he would any of his ordinary dressers.

Fortunately I have always been able to adapt myself quickly to circumstances, so that I had rapidly become acquainted with the services required of me. I now made no mistakes while handing him the instruments he required, nor when helping him in every other sort of way. How he could go on slicing, cutting, sawing, and stitching, in the manner he did, is to this day a mystery to me, and I am sure that he must have been made of iron, for the strain was something awful!

Towards midnight, all at once, he looked up from a frightfully mangled arm he was excising, and, noticing my face—a very pale one I presume—he said something to an orderly. The latter rushed off and soon returned carrying a pannikin filled with spirits, and water and a couple of biscuits.

"Take that," said my old friend, peremptorily, "you'll faint by-and-by if you don't."

I thanked him and tried to munch a tiny bit of the biscuit, but could not manage to swallow a single morsel. The brandy-and-water, strange as it seemed to me to drink it, did me infinite good; it put new life into me and gave me strength to continue my exertions.

The rain had ceased, and outside the stars were shining above the solemnly still world. The silence was doubly solemn after the deafening cannonading of the day. I stretched myself wearily, and prepared everything for a new operation, for the orderlies had just brought us a young cavalry officer, whose blood-soaked dolman and nerveless attitude told their own tale. His eyes were closed, and his features were covered with powder, blood, and mud. I began to rub the grime away with a wet towel, when, to my horror, I recognized in this maimed and crushed human being, who had wellnigh lost all semblance of human appearance, young Count C., the darling of a doting, widowed mother, a boy whom I had known all my life.

"Major," I called out, "see who this is! Just think of his poor mother!"

"So it is, so it is," replied he, shaking his big head sadly, for he, too, knew the brave and dashing young officer well.

"Why was he not brought here as soon as he arrived?" he grumbled. "How can I do anything for him now, after so many hours? Why, the boy is almost gone from mere loss of blood."

The wound—at least the principal one—was below the knee, and the major cried to the orderly to cut the trousers and underclothes as quickly as possible. When this was done the leg appeared in all its horror. The bones had been, so to speak, pulverized, and there was above the ankle a great gaping hole from which the muscle emerged like pulp. The young Count, by this time, had recovered consciousness, and, glancing from the major to me—without showing further astonishment at seeing us there—said, smiling feebly: "They have done for me nicely, have they not? I am afraid there will be no more dancing for me now, Muzzi."

No, indeed, poor fellow! His dancing days were over. In fact, I saw by the major's anxious expression and knitted brow that he considered him as good as dead already. The latter felt the injured limb, and, finding it ice-cold and pulseless, gave vent to a low whistle which boded trouble. The patient, in spite of his exhausted condition, noticed all this, too, and murmured, listlessly:

"A bad case, eh, major? Better slice it off at once and have done with it."

Slice it off—cripple this handsome youth for life, even if he managed to pull through the ghastly operation! What a frightful thing war is! I shuddered as I moistened the parched lips and wiped the cold sweat from his pallid face.

"I was going to propose the amputation to you, sir, and I am happy to see that you have resigned yourself to it," the surgeon said, very gently, all his brusqueness gone before so much quiet courage. "The sooner the better, you know; so if you have no objection we will proceed at once with the necessary evil."

"Oh yes, go ahead," replied the boy; "but may I ask a favor?"

"Anything you ask will be done. What is it you wish?"

"Simply that you should stay by me to the end." This was said to me with such a look of almost diffident entreaty that I was quite overcome and could hardly steady my voice sufficiently to answer: "Stay with you? Yes, of course I will stay with you, my poor dear. You know that I will, and save you, too, if devoted nursing can accomplish it."

The preparations did not take long. Already I had seized the chloroform while the surgeon turned to his tableful of instruments. I went through my share of the horrible affair like one in a dream, as though it

243

were the last drop which was likely to make my cup of fatigue and nervous exhaustion overflow. But I was obliged to rally my sinking strength, for at the very moment when the operation was over and the orderly was bearing off the severed leg, the Count opened his eyes, and, in order to avoid his witnessing this last act of the tragedy, I began to talk to him with all the animation and volubility I could summon up.

Shortly afterwards I found myself in the farthest corner of the ambulance tent, watching beside the bed where he had been laid. Operating was over, at least for that night, and I was trying to redeem my promise, although the condition of the patient gave me but little hope of being able to pull him through, as I had assured him that I would. The major had begged me hard to sleep for a few hours at least, undertaking to relieve me of all care during that time, but I felt that it would be impossible for me to attempt anything of the kind after all the excitement of the day; the unusual fatigue and the terrible anxiety weighed me down, on account of the precious life intrusted to my care, and my care alone —as I thought, at least—for was not the poor fellow a dear friend of all time?

My patient had dropped into an uneasy doze, troubled only too often by the moans of all the suffering humanity about us. Suddenly his eyes opened wide, for an instant he cast a glance of terror about him, then, in a voice of shocking agony, he said, despairingly:

"I think I am going to die—come to me—let me hold your hand."

I knelt beside his rude little couch, fondling him as if he had been a baby, and calling him by those endearing names which mothers use to their sick children in order to soothe their pain. At that moment I truly forgot that he was a stalwart cavalry officer, with a pair of fair mustaches which had worked havoc in many a feminine heart, and remembered him only as the companion with whom I had played in former days. His large blue eyes, so soft, heavy, and languid, were fixed on me with the regret of the life that he was about to lose clearly printed in their fast-glazing orbs.

"I am cold—cold," he muttered.

I threw my arms about him with the vague instinct that I could help him. He shut his eyes only to quickly open them again in the same startled manner as before.

"Say a prayer," he gasped, and almost mechanically I repeated the sublime words of our Catholic last blessing for the dying: "*Per sacrosancta humana repartionis mysteria remittat tibi omnipotens. Deus omnes.*" The words left my lips incoherently, for I was watching the last struggle of the departing soul with its earthly envelope. Gradually the features relaxed, the fair head fell back against my arm, and, with a sort of sob, the spirit took its flight.

I think that after this last shock I must have lost consciousness for a few minutes. The next thing I remember was lying half across the miserable little hospital bed. I rose to my feet, reverently closed the eyes of the dead boy, and then stood irresolute, not knowing what to do next.

The long, low, canvas-roofed ambulance, lighted only by a few smoky lamps, looked dismal indeed, while the heavy breathing of the slumbering wounded sounded from the deep shadows. I knew that there was no use in arousing my friend the major from his valiantly earned sleep to acquaint him with dismal news which it would be quite time enough to tell him in the morning. So I drew the coarse sheet over Count C.'s face, and, dazed and dizzy, I sank down upon the floor between his bed and that of a corporal of an infantry regiment who had been brought in earlier in the evening with a bullet-hole through his lungs and other injuries yet more serious. One of our Sisters of Mercy had come every hour to moisten his lips and to look at the dressing of his wounds, but now she was busy elsewhere, and he himself seemed to have fallen into a deep sleep.

Supporting my back against my dead playmate's little bed, and with my hands listlessly crossed in my lap, I let my eyes wander from one scene of misery to another. In the midst of my gloomy observations I was overpowered by all I had gone through, and, in spite of sorrow and of aching bones, I dropped into a stupefied slumber.

I dreamed all manner of confused things. I was fighting, struggling with scores of enemies; then a huge rock seemed to fall upon me from the top of a mountain, and I was vainly attempting to disengage myself from under its killing weight. I screamed, but the cry was strangled in my throat. Again I raised my voice loudly, and the sound of it awoke me. Was all this a dream? Was I really being crushed by some awful mass? My cry aroused two orderlies, and the major himself, who came rushing towards me. I vaguely remember their discussing my mishap. I felt them removing the weight from my breast, and then I sank again into confused visions and dreams.

Later I was told what had happened, and a shiver runs through my veins to this day when I think of it. When resistless sleep had conquered me, the wounded corporal, striving, in the throes of his last terrible agony, to free himself from that unconquerable grip which takes hold of us all alike when our time has come, had fallen from his bed upon me.

      *   *   *   *   *   *   *

It was during that campaign that I began to find out

that to help others in their trouble is the best way to lighten one's own burdens, and I was sincerely glad that we had gained permission to go with the troops to the field of war. Protected by the Red Cross badge of the "*Convention de Genève*," we seldom ran the risk of any actual danger, and, so far as privations were concerned, we did not mind them at all. This extraordinary declaration, coming from us who had been brought up in the lap of luxury, and who had not the faintest idea of what privations really meant, caused our friends to smile at our simplicity at the time it was uttered. But we were all three in perfect health, and firmly resolved to succeed; so we had finally succeeded. "*Ce que femme veut, Dieu le veut*," is a French proverb which has more than once proved only too true.

Our first weeks of campaigning were devoted to nursing the sick and tending the wounded. In spite of all that may be said to the contrary by idealists, it is not a pleasant task, and many a time have I quaked at the sight of some strong young soldier crippled for life by the bullets of the enemy or killed outright like my friend Count C. Habit, however, is a great master, and with time and several such experiences as the one above related, I became so well used to life in camp ambulances that I ended by really considering myself to be as cool and collected in the accomplishment of my self-imposed duties as any hardened army surgeon among us, and enjoyed them, if I am again to tell the naked truth!

No country on the face of our unfortunate planet has been more ravaged, no land more often soaked with the blood of its inhabitants, than that portion of Europe which our troops were occupying. Everything around us had been desolated by fire and bloodshed as severely as during the first invasion of the barbarians, hundreds of years before. Very grand, but very dreary and sad, was the landscape with its wonderful defiles and its high mountains enclosing rushing streams. The sandstone rocks, worn by erosion into fantastic forms worthy of Gustave Doré's pencil, took in the twilight, and at early dawn, the shape of huge dragons, lions, or other equally startling-looking objects. Then came great deserted plains, with here and there cottages built of clay on foundations of dry, loose stones covered with pieces of wood, little forsaken dwellings from which the inhabitants had fled in terror. It was difficult to procure food for the army, for the culture is always poor in this wild land, and everything available had been pillaged.

For the first time in my life I knew what hunger meant. An experience of that kind is liable to make one forever afterwards feel very charitably inclined towards the unfortunates who claim one's mercy on the plea of starvation.

Strange as it may appear, however, I had never felt better than during these months of privation and fatigue. Many a time, after being the whole day in the saddle, I slept on the bare ground, with nothing to protect me from the sharp night air excepting a rough military cloak, or else curled up against my reclining horse, and slept far better than under the velvet and lace canopy of my soft bed at home.

Just in the same manner did I relish a crust of soldier's hard bread, and a mess of more than questionable soup, eaten beside the bivouac fires with a ravenous hunger as an appetizer. Everybody was so courteous and considerate too. Those uneducated men of our army, although certainly roughened by the wild life of soldiers on active service, were always ready to give up their own scant comforts in order to add to mine, had I been disposed to allow them to do so. As it was, I had many a hard fight with my patients, so anxious were they to share with me the thin beef-tea or sup of wine which it was so difficult to procure for them. But enough of this, or my reminiscences will carry me so far as to weary my readers.

Shortly after the defeat of the enemy by our forces, at the most important and hotly contested point, our brigade was camping at the foot of some high and precipitous cliffs, one regiment being separated from the army corps by a superb defile of steep rocks. It was the most romantic site imaginable, plentifully wooded with oaks, beeches, and elms, but the excessively narrow road winding between the cliffs was strangely grewsome in its loneliness and awe-inspiring grandeur.

One afternoon I had ridden over from our camp, a distance of ten miles or so, to the other side of the defile, where Princess T. was doing her share of nursing. It was nearly dusk when I ordered my horse to be brought round, intending to ride back to camp before night. I refused the escort which the general in command most kindly and urgently pressed me to accept, for I knew that I would be far safer alone than when accompanied by soldiers wearing the hated uniform of the army of occupation. Besides, as I have, I fear, betrayed long ere this, I was absurdly romantic in those days, and I considered it more chivalrous on my part not to expose my fellow-creatures to the bullets and yatagans of the dreaded foe who were known to be always in ambush in the mountain passes.

After having succeeded in persuading the general of my perfect safety, I mounted my black charger "Dare-Devil," and was about to start off at a brisk canter, when the dear old general, putting his hand on the pommel of my saddle and coming close to me, whispered: "Take care, my dear child. It would never do for you to be caught carrying despatches." I laughed gayly, to reassure him, still I knew full well how true his words were. It would very likely mean nothing short of death to me. The fact was that, seeing me determined to ride back to camp alone, the commander, who thought that a woman protected by the brassard of the Red Cross stood a better chance of passing unharmed through the defile than any member of his staff, had intrusted to me a despatch of the utmost importance. It was written in cipher on a tiny scrap of flimsy paper, and, rolling it tightly, I had inserted it in the woodcock quill which was so jauntily stuck on the band of my military cap.

As I rode along in the gathering gloom I glanced once or twice at the two little revolvers in my holsters with a feeling of confidence and satisfaction, for I was, all boasting apart, a neat shot, and I believed that I was perfectly capable of defending myself if attacked. The trouble, however, was that those terrible mountaineers lay in hiding behind the jutting rocks, and that their mode of attack consisted in shooting the unsuspecting travellers who ventured through the mountain passes like so many rabbits in a warren, or sometimes in swiftly pouncing upon them from their places of concealment and making them prisoners before they had time to defend themselves.

The road was frightfully rough and uneven, for it was but the dried-up bed of a mountain torrent, full of sharp stones and bits of yellow quartz. I picked my way carefully in the fast-fading evening light, much to the disgust of my fretful young horse, who passaged from side to side in an uncomfortable manner. Fortunately, as I reached the beginning of the defile, the moon, like a huge golden lamp, rose from behind the mountains, lighting up the path with dazzling brilliancy, but leaving the steep rock-walls and densely wooded, precipitous slopes on both sides in inky darkness. This made matters less difficult for me, but still I could not take great advantage of this favorable circumstance or give my impatient mount his head, for I realized that should any sharp-shooters be lying in wait behind these dark ramparts, anything like flight on my part would surely hasten my fate.

Never before had I observed how loud a noise is produced by the hoofs of a horse on hard ground. It seemed to me as if all the mountain echoes had been awakened by "Dare-Devil's" really elastic step. Again and again I peered first on one side, and then on the other, imagining that this unearthly "*ra-ta-ta*" would at every moment bring something peculiarly disagreeable and undesirable about my ears. I cannot say that I was exactly frightened, as I was never much of a coward, but I felt a certain tightening about the region of the heart which I scorned, and which made me very angry with myself.

I had reached the middle of the pass, which was very narrow at that point, and was beginning to think that nothing was likely to happen to me after all, when, without the slightest warning, four gigantic figures rushed upon me, two from each side of the pass, and before I could even dream of seizing my revolvers, "Dare-Devil" was brought to a sudden standstill by an iron grip, and both my hands were being dexterously tied behind my back. This was shame, indeed, for so brave a little soldier in petticoats as I fondly imagined myself to be, and at the consciousness of the indignity to which I was being subjected all my courage revived. Luckily I spoke half a dozen dialects of that part of the world well enough to make myself understood.

"What do you mean by making a woman prisoner?" I cried. Then, as it flashed upon me that my address was hardly of a conciliatory nature, I added more gently,

"Since when have you sunk so low as to go to war with girls?" The moon shone so brightly that I could see a smile flicker on the superbly handsome bronzed features of the huge fellow who was holding "Dare-Devil's" bridle with no ordinary strength.

"We do not wish to harm you," he replied, very softly, "provided you mean no tricks."

"Tricks!" exclaimed I, indignantly. "Fine tricks I am able to play when you have begun by putting me *hors de combat!* Shame on you! Don't you see the Red Cross on my arm? I am"—here I slightly hesitated —"I am a sort of Sister of Mercy, an army nurse—do you understand? And many are the men of your race whom I have nursed devotedly during the last months."

"We know this well, and also who you are, madame. Do not think us ungrateful for what you have done, and if you are only willing to swear that you are carrying no despatches, we will take your word for it, and let you go free. Otherwise," continued the young man, who seemed, judging by his gorgeous costume, to be a chief, "we will make you prisoner in good earnest, and"— he finished his sentence with a gesture by no means reassuring.

This was a pretty mess, forsooth! I collected my wits as best I could, and, glaring ferociously at him, I exclaimed, drawing myself up as far as my pinioned arms would allow me to do: "I refuse to answer your impudent question. If you think that I am a likely object to be intrusted with despatches, execute your threats, make me a prisoner. It will be an easy job and a glorious victory"—this with a derisive laugh. "Search me, if so be your pleasure; it will only add a finish to your exquisite courtesy. But pray put an end to this distasteful scene, which has lasted long enough. I may be an *estafette*, after all, you know!"

A queer little creature I must have looked on my struggling steed, with my short, kilt-like riding-skirt, spurred boots, white dolman, and dashing military cap, through which the ominous woodcock's quill seemed to burn a hole into the very depths of my thick, tightly braided hair. My captors looked at me for a moment, then at each other. They were a long time making up their minds, at least it appeared so to me. Finally, at a sign from my interlocutor, one of them untied my hands.

"You are right, madame, we do not fight women," said he, baring his head, "and especially when they are brave like you. Go in peace. Had you been afraid of us, things would have turned out differently, but we admire a virtue which, above all others, we pride ourselves in possessing. This pass is not safe, as you have had reason to find out to your cost, and we shall accompany you until you are within hearing of your sentries. But be warned—do not tempt Providence thus again."

As he said this the handsome chief let go of "Dare-Devil's" bridle, a circumstance which this well-named animal immediately availed himself of by bolting with lightning rapidity. It was no easy task to rein him in, but I did so, not wishing to look as if I meant to run away. In silence we proceeded on our road, my stalwart body-guards keeping pace with me faithfully, until, at the end of the pass, which we reached some twenty minutes later the camp-fires became discernible, glittering like enormous glow-worms on the dark plain. I stopped my horse, and, beckoning to the chief, I said, not without some slight emotion:

"You have been very generous. I shall not forget it. Pray accept this as a small token of my gratitude," and I handed him my two revolvers, which were jewels of their kind. With a bow worthy a throne-room, the young man thrust them in his broad,,silken belt, which bristled already with weapons of the most formidable aspect; then, pressing most deferentially to his lips the hand I extended to him, he turned on his heel, and, followed by his imperturbable subordinates, he vanished, as he had come, in the inky blackness of the night.

In a few minutes I had answered the sentry's challenge and rode at a spanking gallop into camp. I could not easily have analyzed my very mingled feelings, but until the end of the campaign I repaid the chief's chivalrous conduct by tending the wounded mountaineers who fell into our hands with extra care and devotion. He had proved to me to be a friend indeed, as well as a friend in need, and I did not forget it.

CHAPTER XV

"O glorious land, O happy days and sweet;
But hush! he hears his prison-keeper's feet."

IT was bitterly cold, snow had fallen all day long, and now a violent wind had arisen and was shaking the icicles from the denuded trees on the streets and boulevards and chasing the inky clouds across the yet darker heavens. As I stood by the library window watching the storm raging over the beautiful town I loved, I felt unaccountably sad. Nothing had occurred since my return from the seat of war to make me more than usually discontented, and, in the eyes of the world at least, I had everything to make life enjoyable.

Moreover, on that particular night a kind of presentiment of coming evil seemed to weigh upon me, and I shivered in that warm, balmy room, brightened by a huge log fire and perfumed by the scent of many exotics, just as if the frozen atmosphere of the outer world had penetrated to my very heart. The noise of the opening door made me turn my head from the dark window-panes towards the softly illumined apartment. My groom of the chambers was standing before me with a letter.

"The bearer of this note entreats to be granted an audience to-night," the man said, with as much annoyance in his tone as he dared to display. "I have tried to impress upon her how unlikely it is that she should be received at this hour, but she seems in great distress, and refuses to go away."

Somewhat surprised, I took the note, which I at first believed to be a begging letter, but a glance at the few

255

passionate words of entreaty hastily scrawled on the paper showed me that I had been mistaken, and I gave orders that the late visitor should be brought to me at once. As I did so I glanced at the little clock on my writing-table; it was half-past eleven already—truly an unusual hour to receive a stranger whose errand with me seemed, to say the least, extremely mysterious. But the appeal was so full of agonized supplication that I had not the heart to resist it.

Once more the door opened, and a girl wrapped in a long cloak entered the room. The first glance showed me that she was not only very lovely, but also unmistakably a lady. Her features were drawn, her face singularly bloodless, and she was trembling from head to foot as she advanced towards me.

"What is the matter? What can I do for you?" said I, motioning her to a seat. With a low moan she sank down at my feet, and in a broken way, which was unpleasant to hear, she exclaimed:

"Oh, madame, how can I ever thank you for having received me—you who alone can save me!"

Forcing her to sit down, I urged her to confide to me the trouble which had led her to seek my assistance. It was a very sad story, which she related amid her sobs, and I felt more moved while listening to her, I think, than I had ever been before.

"My name is Nadèje Z., or rather, Nadèje B.," added she, blushing violently. "I am eighteen, and, although a Russian by birth, I have been brought up here, where my widowed father, who was exiled twelve years ago, for political reasons, from the Czar's dominions, has resided ever since. My father is a severe and embittered man, and, as he considers that his fate has been an unjust one, he hates Russia and everything Russian deeply. Two years ago I met at the house of one of my friends a young Russian officer, who is distantly related to them. We loved each other almost immediately. Of course I did not dare to tell my father anything about our attachment, for I well knew that the fact of Fédor being a Russian officer would be a more than sufficient reason for consent to our marriage being refused. My *fiancé*, however, did not believe this, and waited on him to ask for my hand. There is no use in my describing all I suffered in consequence. Sufficient be it for me to say that, infuriated by the discovery of our engagement, I was commanded to break it off, and forbidden to hold any further communication with Fédor. At first I struggled between my love and filial obedience, but at last, conquered by Fédor's supplications, I consented to marry him secretly. Shortly afterwards he was called to St. Petersburg, and I prevailed upon him to let me remain at home, for a few months at least, as I had as yet not the courage to disclose my secret marriage. Moreover, I hoped to succeed in mollifying my father, and, little by little, to reach a point where it would be easier to confess the irretrievable step which I had taken. In this I was mistaken, and I soon found out that the mere mention of Fédor's name only served to render my case more hopeless. To make matters worse, the time soon came when it was impossible for me to conceal my marriage any longer. Driven to desperation, I confided in the friends at whose house I had met my husband. Great was their perturbation, for, knowing my parent as they did, they realized how impossible it would be to ever obtain his forgiveness. They dissuaded me from telling him the truth, and agreed to help me temporarily in my great trouble. Consequently, they invited me to spend the summer with them at their villa on the Adriatic coast. There my little boy was born, and there, with a breaking heart, I was forced

R 257

to leave him in the care of an old retainer of my friend's family, when, in November, I was recalled home.

"During all this time Fédor had been unable to obtain leave of absence, and I therefore determined to allow matters to rest as they were until he came back to me. A month ago he wrote that he would be here shortly, when he would appeal to my father, and, with or without his consent, would take the child and myself back with him to Russia. Yesterday I received news from him to the effect that, having been unjustly incriminated in a Nihilistic conspiracy, together with three other officers of his regiment, he is being sent to Siberia, after a more than summary judgment. He swears that he is innocent, and that he has always been loyal to the Czar, that his only sin is to have incurred his colonel's disfavor, and that his condemnation is a mere act of revenge on the latter's part! What was I to do in this frightful emergency? I thought at first of starting for St. Petersburg and of appealing to the Czar, but what chance has my father's daughter of obtaining an audience from his Majesty? Then suddenly I remembered having heard that you have great influence at the court of St. Petersburg, and, as I knew you to be good and merciful, I ventured to come and cry out my misery to you, and to implore you to help me to save my love from this cruel iniquity."

With these last words the wretched girl cast herself once more before me, and, grasping my dress in her hands, pressed it to her lips. I had some difficulty in soothing her into something like composure, but when she grew quieter I began, as is my wont when much perplexed, to pace up and down the room, trying to collect my thoughts and to make up my mind how best I could rescue the doomed man. I fully realized what a wellnigh impossible task I had before me. In spite of my mother's influence at the Russian court, and of the fact that I was somewhat of a favorite there, I knew well that the ever-increasing atrocities committed by the Nihilists, and the great severity displayed by the Russian authorities towards anybody suspected of revolutionary tendencies, rendered my prospects of obtaining a free pardon for the young officer at this, the eleventh hour, exceedingly slight. Nevertheless, I decided that, come what may, I would do my best to save him.

Turning towards the girl, who was piteously sobbing, I said: "I shall start for St. Petersburg in the morning, and I will leave no stone unturned to restore your husband to you. Go back to your father's house, and trust me implicitly. This is a very serious matter, and no one must know of it for the present. I do not intend to communicate with you until I have either succeeded or failed. Promise me to keep calm and to worry as little as possible, and under no circumstances tell any one that you have seen me to-night or that I have promised to help you."

It is useless to enter here into the scene which followed. The poor girl was very grateful. But as I am not effusive by nature, I do not like to see others fall into emotional demonstrations. And I was very glad when I finally managed to send her home hopeful and comforted.

By this time it was almost morning. The first glimmer of dawn began to light up the deep layer of snow on the balconies outside, and shimmered through the feathery flakes that still fell noiselessly. But I did not feel tired, and walked up and down from the monumental fireplace to the doors of the winter-garden adjoining the library for more than an hour, thinking over my plan of campaign, and arranging in my mind the details of the coming journey.

At seven o'clock I went to my room and summoned Johanna, who was greatly shocked when she found I had not gone to bed at all. Her astonishment was not lessened by the instructions I gave her to be ready to start with me for St. Petersburg in three hours. When I ended by asking whether my husband was at home or not, her astonishment was complete. After having made due inquiries from the valet on duty in his master's antechamber, she informed me that the latter had just returned from his club, and was now drinking a cup of tea in his dressing-room. As was my custom now, when I had something of importance to communicate to him—a rare incident, it is true—I wrote a line to acquaint him of my departure by the morning express for Russia, stating that private family matters required my immediate presence in St. Petersburg. I received in return a courteous note, in which he expressed many amiable regrets that a previous engagement prevented him from seeing me off. Having thus discharged what I considered to be a mere matter of form, I began to prepare for my long trip.

At ten o'clock I drove to the station, where I found my maid, my courier, and a confidential "*valet de chambre*" awaiting me near my private car. As I entered it, I was somewhat astonished to find, on the small table before the divan, a superb basket of Russian violets fringed with lilies-of-the-valley. No one save my husband knew of my departure, and this fragrant message certainly could not have come from him.

"Who brought those flowers, Yégor?" I asked my courier, who was arranging everything for my comfort · in the little salon adjacent to my sleeping-room.

"They were handed to me a few minutes ago by a closely veiled lady," he replied, bowing low. Then he added, "There is a letter among the flowers."

In an envelope I found a card on which the word "*Merci*" was written, evidently by the same hand which had penned the note I had received the night before. Touched by this attention, I leaned out of the window, watching the snow-covered streets as we steamed slowly out of the station, and speculated on the possible results of my unexpected visit to the land of the Czars.

Gradually the motion of the train became more and more rapid. Soon we were going at full speed through the pine woods which lie like an ever-green belt around the city. Very dark and sad did the sombre firs appear against the background of snow in which everything was enveloped, and very narrow the horizon looked, veiled by the thickly falling flakes. So dreary was the outlook that I soon retreated from the window, still dwelling on the thought of the strange errand which I had undertaken. In spite of the horrible weather, I did not stop at Warsaw, but went straight on to St. Petersburg, where I arrived at length, rather worn out, but in a comparatively hopeful state of mind.

I drove from the station to the Hôtel de l'Europe, where a suite of apartments looking out on the Newski Prospekt had been ordered by telegraph for me by Yégor. I was heartily glad to have reached my destination, and I fully enjoyed the rest I stood in so great a need of after my hurried rush across the frozen plain of three countries.

Never had St. Petersburg seemed so beautiful to me as when I looked out upon it next morning. Snow lay on the domes and steeples, and swathed everything in its fleecy folds. The whole landscape was white and frozen, as if carved out of the purest alabaster. The fiery orb of the Northern sun burned in the clear blue sky, and the air was as intoxicating as a draught of champagne. The great city lying above the frozen waters of the Neva looked dream-like, embedded in its pure setting of snow, which dazzled the eye as if the whole land was covered with diamond-dust.

Before breakfast I sent a short note to Prince Alexander D., telling him of my arrival, and requesting him to obtain for me an audience from the Emperor during the course of the day. "Sandy," as Prince D. is called by his acquaintances, was an old friend of mine, and he nobly rose to the occasion by promising me the desired interview. I therefore set off for Gatchina shortly after twelve o'clock, and, on arriving there, found an imperial sleigh waiting at the station to convey me to the palace. The little town of Gatchina, nestling coquettishly on two shores of the white lake—a name which seemed singularly befitting this winter season—looked to me like an oasis in the still and solemn landscape I had just traversed.

The fine-looking gendarmes, in blue uniforms and tall patent-leather boots, awoke many memories of previous visits in my mind, and not even their forbidding countenances could abate the flow of good-temper and high spirits which had taken possession of me since the moment I had set foot once more on Russian soil. There was even something exhilarating in the thought that these conscientious and well-drilled officials would be truly deeply horrified could they guess that I was here to attempt the rescue of a Nihilist convict from the clutches of the Czar's police. While the sleigh skimmed along on the road to the palace, behind three splendid black horses from the Ukraine, I could not help laughing outright as this thought once more crossed my mind.

On we flew, passing the villa of Prince G., whose greatest title to everlasting fame is his having been permitted one day to take a plunge in the bath-tub which his Majesty had just vacated, to secure which inestimable favor he presented the Czar's valet with two thousand rubles. If this is not loyalty, what ought it to be called, although, myself, I have always thought it rather a revolting kind of loyalty, and I highly approve of the Emperor's remark to Prince G., when his Majesty heard of this piece touching of hero-worship.

"You are a good fellow," said the monarch, laughing heartily, "but what a fool !"

I was still thinking of this ridiculous episode, when we glided through the gates of the magnificent park which surrounds the castle. Every tree, every branch were encased in a sheet of glittering ice, like some enchanted legendary forest, and the groups of Siberian arolla and giant pines standing on both sides of the building sparkled like huge emeralds in a setting of silver.

As the sleigh drew up before the steps of the palace, two chevalier-guards, with their white uniforms and eagle-crested helmets shining gloriously in the sun, advanced to meet me, followed by the Emperor's aide-de-camp, Count O. A few minutes later I was in the august presence of the Great White Czar himself.

After the usual preliminary compliments on both sides, I launched into a vivid recital of the dramatic story which had brought me all this distance. We were alone in the great library, which was his Majesty's favorite apartment, and I spoke in all confidence and ease to the sovereign who had known me since childhood.

All the eloquence I could summon was exercised by me in pleading the cause of Fédor and of his poor young wife, but I observed that, as I went on, the Emperor's face gradually grew grave and stern. When at last I stopped, out of sheer exhaustion, Alexander said, coldly:

"You ask an almost impossible thing, Muzzi. I remember the affair perfectly well. Twelve years ago that girl's father was implicated in a very serious Nihilistic conspiracy, and the young man for whom you plead so warmly has, I am certain, not been condemned unjustly. Any one but you, my dear child," continued the Emperor, in a softened tone, "coming to me on such an errand would meet, I am afraid, with a curt and definite refusal."

Quite undaunted by this discouraging beginning, I jumped up from the big chair on which I had been sitting, exclaiming:

"Sire, you cannot refuse to investigate this matter personally, at my earnest request. The man swears that he is innocent, and I may add that certainly he would not be the first who has suffered an unjust condemnation at the hands of the police authorities here or elsewhere."

"These are big words, and not very seemly in the mouth of a lady who is half a Russian herself. I do not think that I can do anything for your protégé."

"But you must do something, Sire," cried I, now quite beside myself.

"*Must?*" said the autocrat, drawing himself up and gazing at me with rising anger.

For a moment we looked at each other unflinchingly. I was angry, and scarcely cared whether the Emperor noticed it or not, but suddenly I was struck by the ludicrousness of my thus laying down the law to the omnipotent ruler of "All the Russias," before whom millions of human creatures trembled, and I burst out laughing. This was too much for my imperial host, and he could not repress a smile.

"I am but a poor diplomat," said I, when I had recovered sufficient composure to speak, "and not at all accustomed to asking favors." Then, stepping towards the Czar and putting my hand on his arm, I looked up in his kindly face, and added, pleadingly: "I am very anxious to save that man, and I have always been treated so kindly by your Majesty that I have no fear of my entreaties being absolutely repulsed."

Again the Emperor smiled, and taking my hand in his own, he raised it to his lips. "That's better," said he, affectionately. "Alas! I am only too soft-hearted myself, and always anxious, I hope, to do what is right. I shall inquire into the matter at once; you have gained your point so far, and if the man's innocence can be proved I promise you that justice will be done to him."

I breathed a sigh of relief.

"However," continued the Emperor, "I will do this, solely and uniquely, because it is you who ask it. I have no pity for those who are tainted, be it ever so slightly, with Nihilistic tendencies. Russia is becoming more and more honeycombed every day with Nihilism; revolutionary principles are spreading in the army and in the navy, and must be stopped. Remember, I am not talking now as Czar, but as a simple Russian citizen. Nihilism may originally have sprung from a desire to put an end to autocracy in Russia, but to-day it has become a mere levelling theory, such as that which inspired the atrocities of the Paris Commune."

"Nihilists ought to be weary of their unceasing and vain efforts," said I, "for their plots and plans have met until now with but indifferent success."

"Indifferent, eh?" he replied, with a bitter smile. "In more than one case they might be satisfied with the harm they have done. The liberal principles about which there is so much talk now are only a purely euphonic appellation for anarchy, communism, or some such other empty Utopian ideal. Read the *Samow-*

praveline Organ Sotsialistoff Revolutsioneroff [Self-Government Organ of the Social Revolutionists], and you will see whether what I am saying is true."

"It is so sad," I could not help saying, "that severity to the culprits should entail so much suffering to innocent beings. I abhor Nihilists, and yet what other Utopia has ever begotten such unwavering and heroic sacrifice, such uncomplaining surrender of youth, wealth, power, enjoyment of life, to a lost cause, to a mere empty idea? What might be accomplished if all this enormous force, this senseless heroism, were directed in the right channel, instead of being wasted in rolling the rock of revolution up a steep hill, whence it must ever roll back, crushing those who futilely attempt to plant it on the summit of our modern civilization?"

"Believe me," murmured Alexander, wearily, "nothing will avail but to persistently crush every head of the hydra, every tentacle of the all-devouring octopus which is destroying the country. Leniency will not answer; in severity lies the only salvation."

The Czar had risen from the seat which he had occupied before his writing-desk during the latter part of our conversation, and was now striding up and down the long room, with knitted brows and compressed lips. I felt that once more my protégé's cause was hanging in the balance, and, anxious to create a diversion in order to change the course of the Emperor's thoughts, I bent forward to caress a gigantic bloodhound lying at full length on the ermine rug before the writing-table. With the mobility of mood which characterized him, the Czar wheeled round, and, gazing almost tenderly at this formidable-looking pet, murmured:

"Ah, yes! I agree with the clever statesman who said that what he preferred in mankind was the dog; there at least we find loyalty and fidelity without the planning and plotting you were talking about just now. But enough of this. I will keep my word to you, and in a few days I may be able to put before you all the circumstances of what you call an arbitrary condemnation. In the meanwhile, I hope that you will consent to be my guest and the Empress's at Gatchina. We cannot allow you to remain at the Hôtel de l'Europe, and you will surely not refuse us the all-too-rare pleasure of your presence."

To this, of course, I could answer only with profuse thanks. I felt intensely grateful to the Emperor for his kindness. I told him so, and was glad to see the heavy cloud which had hung about his brow pass off and to notice that he was smiling cheerfully again when I left him to occupy the suite of apartments which had been mine during previous sojourns in Gatchina.

The next few days consisted of a series of pleasures, among which was a great ball at the Winter Palace. I have always loved the Winter Palace *fêtes*. They seem to be more imposing in their magnificence than those given at any other European court. The entire suite of state apartments had been thrown open for the occasion, and were decorated with banks and mounds of violets, which filled even these enormous rooms with exquisite fragrance. As I danced in the *Quadrille d'Honneur* with the Czar, he whispered to me:

"Do not get impatient, Muzzi; I have set General G." (the chief of police) "at work for you, and we shall soon be able to tell you whether your protégé deserved his fate or not, or if there is any loop-hole of escape for him."

The ever-changing figures of the quadrille prevented me from answering in words, but I gave the Czar a look and a smile of gratitude. Later in the evening I met General G. face to face. I was walking through St.

George's Hall, towards the Winter Garden, with Grand-Duke V., and I smiled as bewitchingly as possible on the great man, who flattened himself against the wall with true military precision and deference as we approached.

"Ah, general," laughed the Grand-Duke; "active as usual? I see you grow younger with every passing year. I wish it were the same with me."

"Your Imperial Highness has no cause for complaint," replied the delighted official. "But as for me," he continued, with an ominous shake of the head, "I have cause to be watchful and active. Heaven knows I have." Resolved on winning his heart, I said, sweetly:

"Like Atlas's, your burden is heavy, general; but, like this strong and worthy personage, you carry it securely and nobly."

Was it reproach which I saw glimmering in the general's eyes? It may be that only my conscience pricked me for having made the said burden rather heavier than usual by my inroads on his domain, yet, as we passed on, I thought that I heard him sigh wearily, as if he were a very tired Atlas, indeed, on that particular night. Poor General G., worthy man as he undoubtedly was, I could have shaken him for not expediting matters more swiftly. I thought unceasingly of the broken-hearted girl who was so anxiously awaiting tidings of her young husband, and also of the miserable convict who, foot-sore and desparing, was even now being hustled towards the semi-arctic and desolate wilds of Siberia, while here all was light and joy, comfort and lavish luxury. I almost felt angry with myself for the careless, happy life I was leading, when I compared it with their agony, and yet more so for my unjust vexation at the delay which was so unavoidable in the investigation of so intricate a case.

Another week went by, and still I obtained no certainty as to Fédor's chances. I could do nothing to hasten the proceedings, for I feared by a word to spoil my case or to worry the Czar, who was in one of his periodical blue moods.

At last, one morning, as I was just leaving my apartments, Aide-de-Camp Baron E. brought me a message, requesting my presence in the sovereign's study. Preceded by the young officer, I made my way through the long suite of rooms leading to Alexander's private chancellerie. Here I found the Emperor seated before a table covered with papers. He was in earnest conversation with the chief of police, whose careworn features wore an expression of deep concern.

As I entered, both men rose to their feet, and the Czar, taking me affectionately by the hand, led me to an ottoman beside his desk:

"My dear child," said he, in a voice which I noticed was slightly shaking, "we have carefully sifted the affair which has brought you here, and I have come to the conclusion that the man has been treated unfairly, unjustly." Here he glanced at the chief of police, who literally shrank before his gaze. "It would take too long to enter into the details of this disgraceful business," continued the sovereign, impatiently; "suffice it to state that there has been foul play, that, even had the man been guilty, the condemnation ought not to have been so hurriedly pronounced, and that, as he was able to give, and gave absolute proof of his innocence, the sentence passed upon him was an iniquity for which the responsible persons therein implicated will suffer."

So exasperated did the Emperor appear to be, that I did not venture to speak a word in reply. The unfortunate chief of police, who was visibly shaking in his boots, and who was very pale under his tanned skin, was unable to contain himself any longer, and exclaimed, hoarsely:

"Your Majesty does not, I hope, hold me responsible for a crime committed by a person or persons entirely removed from my jurisdiction. I have—"

"There ought to be nothing beyond your jurisdiction within the boundaries of the empire, general," interrupted the Emperor. "However, I do not hold you responsible for the disgraceful state of things which renders it possible for a colonel to take so brutal and merciless a revenge on an innocent man, because the latter happens to be under his orders and to have aroused his jealousy. The chief occupation and desire of my *entourage* is, I see, to throw dust in my eyes, so as to blind me to the arbitrary doings of wretches like Colonel X. But this has been a good lesson, and I shall be ever grateful to you," he added, turning to me, "for having been the means of throwing light on the abuses perpetrated in my name. All this must and will change."

The silence which followed was broken only by the monotonous ticking of the great malachite clock on the high mantel-piece. The general stood motionless, biting his heavy mustache, and I mechanically pulled to pieces the knot of crimson roses fastened among the laces of my breakfast-gown. Alexander had sunk into the great arm-chair before his writing-table, and his light-blue eyes were fixed in deep reverie on the full-length picture of his murdered father hanging above it. Conscious that the position, to say the least, was becoming remarkably awkward, I plucked up spirit, and, softly gliding to Alexander's side, I half knelt beside him, saying, with much emotion:

"I am grateful to you, Sire—I can never say how grateful—for all the trouble you have taken on my behalf. But I am also deeply pained to have added to your Majesty's many cares."

I am not ashamed to say that the expression of suffering which lingered in the Czar's eyes brought tears to my own. It seemed so sad that this just and good man, whose power was practically unlimited, should find out how powerless he really was to prevent injustice and to carry out his noble designs. With a somewhat mournful but very kind smile, which softened his entire countenance, he pushed back the tangle of curls from my forehead, and, gazing into my eyes he murmured:

"Do not be sorry, my child; you have done a very noble deed, and it is I who am grateful to you for the pluck you have shown. General G. will see that the necessary papers are prepared at once, and that the man whom you have saved from so iniquitous a fate receives a free pardon. Later I will look to it personally that he is indemnified and rehabilitated, if such a thing be possible, for all that he has so unjustly suffered."

The general, at a sign of dismissal from his imperial master, backed towards the door, and, with a military salute of punctilious correctness, disappeared beyond the *portières* of the adjoining hall.

Left alone with the Czar, I once more attempted to express my heartfelt thanks to him, but he silenced me at once, and we fell to discussing the means of bringing Fédor back to St. Petersburg without unnecessary delay. Over two hours' conversation brought me to the conclusion that this would not be such an easy matter as I at first had believed it to be.

I knew without being told so that all Russian officials thoroughly loyal to the crown have so great and natural a horror for Nihilists that whoever would be intrusted with the task of pursuing the convoy of prisoners, among which was Nadèje's husband, would display but little enthusiasm and ardor in this fatiguing, not to say dangerous, undertaking.

To cross part of Siberia in mid-winter is never a pleasant or an easy thing, and to do so in order to rescue one of the abhorred Nihilists would be particularly painful and distasteful. It was unlikely that much credence would be placed in the man's innocence, and was it not more probable that his pardon would be regarded as an act of favoritism, due to a powerful intercession with the Czar. The convoy of prisoners had by this time certainly reached the plains, which precede the chain of the Ural Mountains, its destination being some mining district far beyond Ekaterinburg, and it would take both time and numberless hardships to overtake it in this season. I begged his Majesty to allow my courier, Yégor Nikolaïtch, an intelligent man, in the service of my family for many years, to be intrusted with this confidential mission, and this request was immediately granted.

Before I left the Czar, however, I had thoroughly decided to go myself. Of course I did not mention this hare-brained scheme to the Emperor, who would never have allowed it. But during the entire day I turned over in my head the means of leaving St. Petersburg for Siberia without my plans being discovered.

The spirit of adventure was strong in me in those days. Moreover, I had an intuition that, left to the mercy of officialdom, Fédor would not be rescued for a long time to come, if he were ever rescued at all.

Red-tapeism is more prevalent in Russia than anywhere else, and if the free pardon I had obtained for the young officer was sent officially and transmitted by officials, it would be a crawling business at best, whereas I, once in possession of the papers granting him his liberty and of a safe-conduct signed by the Emperor, could—money being no object to me—reach him in a comparatively short time. That night I summoned Yégor, and made a clean breast of my project to the faithful fellow.

He was at first absolutely horrified, and entreated me to abandon the idea of attempting so difficult and fatiguing a journey at such a time of the year; but, having known me from a child, he soon saw that nothing would shake my determination, and, good fellow that he was, he immediately began to discuss with me the best manner of putting my plans into immediate execution.

"Listen to me, Yégor," said I, "this is what I am going to do: I shall announce to-morrow to their Majesties that I intend to leave St. Petersburg on the next day but one. And I shall do so—I'll have to, you see, for I shall certainly be taken in great pomp to the station— worse luck! At Iuga you and I will leave the train, letting the maid and valet pursue their way home alone, while we shall return here and from thence proceed to Moscow, Kazan, Perin, and then to Ekaterinburg without a moment's delay. I am going to leave letters for the Emperor and Empress to be delivered to them two days after my departure, explaining my reasons for going to Siberia. By that time I shall be so far out of reach that matters will have to be allowed to take their course."

Here Yégor interrupted me respectfully but firmly: "The Emperor will never forgive this," said he, mournfully.

"Yes, he will. Of course he will be angry at first, but ultimately he will understand my motives, and he is too noble-hearted not to sympathize with my reasons for doing this. Besides, there is nothing so very formidable in what I am going to do. The greater part

S 273

of the trip will be made by train, and it is only when we have ascertained the exact route taken by the convoy that we shall be forced to take to a *kibitka* [half-covered sledge] in order to overtake it."

"May I venture to point out the difficulties and dangers of a journey in a *kibitka* on the frozen plains of Siberia?" suggested Yégor, much distressed.

"You may, if it please you," I said, laughingly, "but I do not wish to hear any croaking; I am perfectly healthy and strong, well used to out-door exposure, afraid of nothing, and, what's more, I am absolutely resolved, and nothing you can say will alter my decision. So enough of all this. To-morrow you can buy for me and for yourself all the fur-lined garments, cordials, medicines, rugs, arms, and even surgical instruments your forethought may suggest. See to it that all we need is packed up and left at the Hôtel de France, in the Bolshàyá Morskàyá Street, under your own name, for it is there that we shall come on our return to St. Petersburg, and from thence that we shall start for the North. And now, good-night, Yégor; pleasant dreams to you," I concluded, with another burst of unconquerable merriment, for the poor fellow's woe-begone countenance was irresistibly funny to me.

When he had gone, I sat down by the fire and fell into one of my customary deep reveries, which was, however, rather disagreeably interrupted by my suddenly noticing that the long train of my white velvet court-dress, which had, unheeded by me, lain in too close a contact with the smouldering embers, was slowly beginning to burn. Crushing it beneath my foot, I said to myself, gayly, that this was a good omen, for had I worn on that particular occasion a frock of lighter texture there would surely have been a sudden and most unwelcome end to all my philanthropic dreams and to myself as well.

CHAPTER XVI

"We freeze, we starve, we feel
    The anguish in our breast,
Hard is our lot, but yet
    With freedom we are blest!"

SUCCESS crowned my departure from St. Petersburg, as I knew that it would, and I started on my Siberian trip with a light heart and a hopeful mind. The papers which I carried not only included all the documents concerning the delivery of my convict—as I began to call him—into the hands of one Yégor Nikolaïtch Fúlòw, but also a safe-conduct for the said Yégor and party, charging all authorities to protect and aid them on their journey.

Of the railway portion of our voyage little need be said. It was what all such journeys are, rendered more trying at that season by the extreme severity of the weather and by the hurry with which we had to proceed. I must, however, admit that this precipitation had its advantages, as it spared us any lengthy stay in the filthy inns which are the only substitutes to be found on the Siberian road for hotels. Most towns on the way from Moscow to Perin have a desolate appearance, the streets are narrow and absolutely innocent of any kind of pavement, the wooden houses look dingy, dreary, dismantled, with a general air of neglect and hopelessness about them very depressing to witness, while the flatness of the landscape, broken here and there by clumps of dwarf willows, showing like inky marks against the blinding whiteness of the snow-covered steppe, is most bewildering to the unaccustomed eye.

Yégor worked wonders for me, and managed to spare me many petty annoyances and also many of the privations unavoidable under such unpropitious circumstances. But all his care could not make those railways anything but atrocious, uncomfortable, and strange jolts, and the mysterious noises with which their onward progress was accompanied is not easily forgotten when once experienced. By a judicious mention of my " lofty rank," of my intimacy with the imperial family, and by a well-advised exhibition of passports, my diplomatic courier secured for me the most distinguished consideration and respect from the authorities wherever we went—a fact which greatly contributed to make my lot a comparatively pleasant one. Moreover, employés and chiefs alike soon found out, too, that gold glided easily through my fingers, and that it was to their interest to be obliging. So that I had no reason to complain of any want of *empressement*. The three Cossacks who had been appointed as Yégor's escort were useful, and in spite of their forbidding aspect showed so much good temper that during the first part of our journey they were invaluable to me. I christened them Og, Gog, and Magog, for they were the tallest Cossacks I have ever seen, and their bearded and grim countenances reminded me vividly of Cruikshank's portraits of the three heroes of the Tower of London.

As we neared the Ural the temperature became almost unbearable, the cold was piercing, and the softly descending, feathery snow-flakes froze as they fell. A *tourmente* during the crossing of the mountains was all we needed to make things unendurably lively, and we got it with a vengeance! The roaring wind blew the snow in whistling clouds, and the heavens seemed to open to give passage to so dense a downpour that we felt as if we were being buried alive under icy winding-sheets.

When we reached Ekaterinburg, it seemed to me as if I had been travelling for years, and I was glad to stop there in order to make inquiries about the convoy of convicts we were pursuing.

We put up at the Hôtel Plotinkof. Now, guide-books go quite out of their way to prove to the guileless traveller that this is a very good hostelry, provided with every modern improvement, and it may be owing to my exaggerated fastidiousness that I was so disappointed with it. I must add, however, that the most conscientious among these guide-books mention that insect-powder is a necessary armament for the guests of the Plotinkof! So I should think; for the fleet-footed inmates of the bedrooms there, whose generic names I should blush to record, are the most bloodthirsty parasites which it has ever been my unhappy luck to encounter. Woe be to the thin-skinned traveller in these regions, for his peace of mind and body stands but an unfair chance against the manslaughtering exploits of a sportive army which overwhelms him with its indelicate attentions, and pesters him with a zeal and energy quite beyond all praise or description.

On the night of my arrival I hit upon a Machiavellian plan in order to obtain a little rest. Piling my fur rugs on the floor in front of the ponderous stove which heated the room, I placed four lighted candles at the four corners of this improvised couch. It appears that—well, that those many-legged gentry I was just talking about are afraid of a bright light and dislike strong perfumes. This being given, with the help of a pint or so of extract of verbena, I succeeded in sleeping undisturbed for several hours. The burning candles gave my installation a dismal resemblance to a catafalque, a resemblance which was not diminished by the sombre blue-black furs on which I reclined, and which might have alarmed and painfully impressed a person of nervous temperament. I, however, preserved my equanimity and slept very soundly.

When, the next morning, the waiter came in with the breakfast-tray, and saw that I had not slept in the crimson-curtained bed, so elaborately prepared for me, his ill-concealed indignation was more than human gravity could bear. He informed me that this was the "*Imperial suite,*" and even volunteered a long explanation from which I gathered that the sheets were changed *almost* after every traveller! Awed by so luxurious a precaution, I looked helplessly at the man, who strode majestically out of the room, sustained by the integrity of his conscience.

This one instance of Siberian hotel life will suffice to give a general idea of what those Northern inns were at the time when I honored them with my patronage. The Plotinkof was one of the best, and there were many worse. They are, as a rule, one-storied log-buildings, presenting nothing that is particularly interesting or nice to the eye, and very uncomfortable withal. The food is coarse and bad in all cases, and tea is about the only decent thing one may obtain in those distant latitudes.

The time had now come for us to resort to *kibitkas* in order to proceed on our journey, if we wished to catch up with the marching party of two hundred and fifty convicts, among which I hoped to find my protégé. I foresaw that we would have to rough it, even more than I had expected, for the weather had become decidedly worse than ever. The sky was dark, almost purple, and when the sun condescended to put in an appearance it afforded us absolutely no heat, and its cold rays paled before the dazzling whiteness of the snow which covered the limitless plains.

I shall never forget the morning when we bade good-bye to all apparent vestiges of civilization. Yégor and I climbed into our *kibitka*, and set out with a *troika* of strong and enduring post-horses towards an unknown destination. It was not without decided misgivings that I contemplated what lay before us, and yet, having now gone so far, I was anxious to proceed as soon as possible. Yégor, who until then had forborne from admonishing me on what, to judge by his looks, he lamented inwardly as my unpardonable recklessness, shook his head ominously as the horses, rattling the numerous bells on their arched collars, started on their way, and even Og, Gog, and Magog contemplated me with a severe and quite withering expression of blame.

I might as well acknowledge that, as I began to taste the bitterness of the icy air of the steppe, I could not wonder at this, and I drew my thick furs about me with an unwonted feeling of anxiety. The temperature was something awful—forty-eight degrees below zero—the horses were almost hidden from our view by the thick steam which rose from their bodies, and a cloud of frozen moisture filled the atmosphere. All my usual buoyancy could not prevent me from suffering from the cold, but I was far too stubborn to acknowledge it; and when we stopped at the post-stations to change horses, I assumed a cheerful mien, with the fallacious hopes of misleading the watchful eye of poor Yégor. Even the burning-hot tea swallowed on these occasions did not warm us up, and as hour followed hour our tortures steadily increased.

One of the most unbearable sensations we went through was the terrible shaking and jolting of the *kibitka*. Our road was cut up with deep furrows, little hills and little valleys of hardened snow, and the sledge, as it crossed over them, bobbed up and down like a ship in a gale of wind, with the distressing result of something very much akin to sea-sickness. A horrible sensation of faintness often came over me; the air would become pregnant with millions of blue stars, the cold grasped me in the region of the heart, and once or twice I completely lost consciousness. The process of resuscitation through which I was put was always extremely painful, and although I was grateful enough to be aroused from a condition which in this intense frost is often fatal, still it was with great difficulty that I restrained myself from scolding my rescuers for their apparent heartlessness and roughness.

After leaving Ekaterinburg, our Cossack escort evidently imbibed a considerable quantity of alcohol in order to combat the effects of the arctic temperature we were undergoing, and I regret to say that they were by no means what can truthfully be described as pleasant when in their cups. Fortunately they seemed to look upon me as if I had been endowed with some supernatural power, and I was usually able to conquer their frequent fits of ill-temper. Yégor, who, like all Russians, could handle with amazing rapidity the vituperations in which his native tongue is so singularly rich, swore at them elaborately upon the least provocation, but his words never had any practical result, and in the end I was always forced to interfere in order to restore something like peace in the breasts of my bodyguards. Perceiving that at any moment words might lead to something far more deadly, I endeavored to control my rough escort as best I could, but I knew how slight was my hold on these semi-savages, and this thought gave me many a qualm for our subsequent safety. Things, indeed, looked very black for us in more ways than one. We had as yet been unable to overtake the convoy, and the very elements seemed to conspire against the success of our foolhardy expedition.

This portion of our journey remains engraved on my mind like a frightful nightmare. How long it lasted I could not tell; looking back upon it now, I should say it must have been months, and dreary, desolate months at that. Hour after hour there was no break in the wide, white track we were following, save at some wretched post-house where the tired horses were changed. The snow fell ceaselessly, the icy wind howled about us, during the short days and the long steely-hued nights. Often we could plainly hear the baying of the wolves in the thickets of misshapen pine-trees which we passed on the road. Verst upon verst of that fearful plain was covered, and in spite of all my efforts to keep the three giants and the driver in good humor by showering presents upon them, my escort grumbled aloud now. They claimed, with some reason, I own, that without having committed any crime to deserve such punishment, they were subjected to the same fatigues and privations as are Siberian convicts, and I saw that the moment was approaching when they would refuse to go farther. How this was to be prevented I could not possibly imagine.

One night, about eleven o'clock, the climax came. We had been travelling fast and furiously in the teeth of a violent storm of snow and wind, for I had hopes of obtaining certain information about the chain of convicts at the next post-station. The sledge was driven along through drifts and hurricanes on a road where all tracks were obliterated and amid a darkness rendered livid by the refraction of the snow. It was a night when death hovered everywhere, and we realized only too vividly the many dangers with which we were so fiercely struggling. At length the glimmer of distant lights became dully discernible, and soon the panting horses were pulled up half dead before a cluster of miserable Isbas.

The postmaster, wrapped in sheepskins up to his very eyes, came out with a lantern and helped us to alight. The house was poor and looked more repulsive than any place I had yet seen. But there was a large stove in the corner, and I was glad, indeed, to stretch my tired limbs on the big bear-skin brought from the sledge, in front of the glowing fire, and to sip a cup of scalding tea. We were to rest here for three or four hours, and to start again at dawn. I lay watching languidly the three Cossacks, the driver, and the postmaster, as they sat down at a clumsy table with their favorite meal of brown bread, raw onions, *kwass*, and spirits before them. The postmaster was also a Cossack, of Herculean proportions, with a heavy head, enormous mustaches, and a peculiarly sinister cast of countenance. He was talking in a low, growling voice to Og, Gog, and Magog, and his frequent glances towards me clearly indicated that I was the subject under discussion. When he had seen to my comfort, Yégor approached this repulsive-looking group, and I heard him ask the postmaster to tell him at what time the horses would be ready to start. The latter thrust his gigantic fists deep into the pocket of his *touloupe*, raised his bullet-shaped head, and, gazing defiantly at Yégor, answered, laconically:

"I have no horses to give you."

"What do you mean by that?" exclaimed my courier, angrily. "Show me the book on which the departure of your last horses is inscribed, so that I may see whether you lie or not."

"I have no book to show you," was the stolid reply.

"This is nonsense," cried Yégor, now thoroughly roused. "If this be as you say, you have committed a punishable offence, for the law demands that you should keep a post-book. You must find us horses before dawn; my mistress is travelling with a safe-conduct signed by the 'Little Father' (the Czar) himself, and any impertinence on your part will be cruelly visited upon you."

The big man shrugged his shoulders contemptuously, and, pointing to my escort, said, quite unmoved: "Your companions here claim that they are being badly treated, and are weary of this endless journey through storm and snow, and as they belong to my people, I mean to see them righted."

The scene which ensued is impossible to describe. The wordy warfare grew loud and discordant, and threatened to end in a hand-to-hand fight. Half dazed by cold and fatigue, I did not succeed in rousing myself sufficiently to interfere, and continued to watch the proceedings as if they were only part of a dream, instead of a very stern reality.

Suddenly a small side door opened, and a woman came in, with an uncertain, wavering step. Her face was strangely white, and her red-rimmed eyes had a vacant stare in them which made her look like a maniac or an inveterate drunkard. She was trembling from head to foot, and her general appearance was one of low debauchery. She addressed her husband in a hoarse voice—"*Une voix de rogomme*"—requesting him to be still, as the noise was hurting "*the boy.*" Through the door she had left open I could plainly hear, in the silence which followed her entrance, a succession of pitiful moans proceeding from the next room. So lamentable was this sound that it awakened me at once from my half-slumbering condition, and, impelled by some power that conquered my weariness, I rose and unceremoniously walked into the dimly lighted chamber. The spectacle which met my eyes was degraded and nauseating beyond words, and in spite of my agitation I noted every detail thereof with lightning rapidity. The place was repulsively dirty, the floor of beaten earth was covered with rotting straw, and the only furniture consisted of a long, wooden bench, a rickety deal table, on which a tallow candle guttered in an iron candlestick, and a shelf attached to the wall supporting an Icone (religious image enamelled on metal), in front of which a little hanging oil-lamp was lighted. In the corner to the right of the door was a large, low stove, on the top of which was what the Russians call a *palati*, and which serves as a bed for the family during the winter months.

On this strange couch lay a boy of fourteen or fifteen years old, whose features bore an expression of such terrible suffering that for a moment I recoiled in dismay. The mother had followed me into the room, and, turning towards her, I asked what was the matter with the lad. From her loud and disconnected lamentations I at last gathered with some difficulty that " *Yvan*," who had always been delicate, had three days previously run a long splinter deeply under his nail, and that since then he had been suffering from violent convulsions. One look at the patient told me that he was threatened with a most horrible death by lockjaw if the cause of the trouble was not at once removed, and I hinted as much to the mother, who thereupon broke forth in violent curses against everything and everybody, including a country where no surgeons could be found, for, as she said, in Siberia people ought to be always in good health, as in case of illness it is necessary to do without medical assistance. While we were thus employed, she in pouring forth dreadful invectives and I in trying to calm her, the boy suddenly gave an inarticulate cry and fell into a fit of hideous tetanic convulsions. His thin, emaciated body became contracted by spasms which drew him backward in so frightful a fashion that his head and heels almost touched each other, forming a rigid arch, while his neck and throat stiffened to bursting. I called to the mother to help me hold him down, but she was either too drunk or too frightened to heed my words, and, before I could prevent him from doing so, the patient had fallen from his miserable couch, rolled to the floor, and, upsetting the table and the candle, plunged us into total darkness. I seized hold of him so as to prevent, if possible, his doing himself any further injury, and called loudly for help. My cries brought Yégor tearing into the room, followed by the postmaster, who was carrying a lamp. The table was soon set on its legs again, the light placed upon it, and the men, having lifted the writhing lad from the floor, held him down on the bench according to my directions, until the spasm ceased. Having learned from the postmaster that no medical man could be reached in the whole district, and that there was not even a *Feldsher* (old soldier or military orderly who dresses wounds and administers physic in Russian villages) to be found far or near, I told the father, who was casting wild looks about him, that his son was lost if a simple operation were not at once performed. I had, of course, by now some slight knowledge of plain surgery, and I asked him whether he would like me to try what I could do to save the boy.

Glancing at poor little Yvan, who was visibly in the last stages of exhaustion now that the acute attack had subsided, his father replied, with a growl: "Try if you like, but if you don't relieve him, I'll kill you and your beast of a servant with you!" With which encouraging speech—one that Yégor would have resented had I not pacified him with a peremptory look— the Cossack giant seized a sharp axe lying on the floor, and, placing it between his knees, squatted down on an overturned box, and waited there in order to put undoubtedly his amiable threats to instant execution. I shrugged my shoulders, knowing well what braggarts the Russian peasants are, and bade Yégor bring me my travelling-chest of medicines, which contained also a few unpretentious surgical instruments. The scene was dismal beyond words, for what between the howls of the storm raging outside and the dirt and squalor of the room in which we were assembled, there was enough, without the singularly dramatic condition of affairs, to shake the nerves of the coolest of human beings. The three Cossacks of my escort were snoring in the adjoining room, where they had cast themselves down before the stove to sleep the heavy sleep of drunkenness. The mother, crouching on the ground beside her husband, shed maudlin tears, and the husband himself was watching me savagely as I selected a small pair of forceps and a bistoury from my little surgical case.

I will not enter here into any details of the operation, which was a singularly long and painful one, thanks to the condition of my patient and to my own nervousness. I did the best I could under the circumstances; that is all I can say for myself; and when I got through I had the gratification of seeing young Yvan drop into a deep and peaceful sleep under the influence of thirty drops of laudanum which I had administered to him, and also to receive the somewhat shamefaced thanks of the father, who relinquished his formidable weapon and left the room muttering words of regret for his past violence. He spoke to the other Cossacks, and soon brought them round to a better frame of mind; for an hour later everything was ready for our departure, and the contrite and sobered postmaster went so far as to give us cheering indications as to the route followed by the chain of convicts, so that we ended by starting under altogether altered and favorable auspices.

We travelled without rest for two days and nights, enduring more torments than I care to describe; but our perseverance was rewarded at last, for at eight o'clock in the morning, just fifty hours after leaving the post-station where we had met with so startling and un-gracious a reception, we reached a long, straggling village consisting of a double line of miserable-looking log-cabins, with a post-house painted a bright blue standing a little back from the road. In front of this building were several hundred convicts surrounded by a cordon of soldiers armed to the teeth. Crowds of children and peasant women were distributing to them loaves of coarse black bread and little round cheeses, which the poor wretches fell to devouring greedily as soon as they received them.

The jingling of the chains and the muttering voices of the exiles made a most dismal and ghastly concert, and as my *kibitka* forced its way through the throng, tears of sympathy for these melancholy travellers rose to my eyes. The air was so thick with drifting snow-flakes that we could hardly distinguish anything, but the little we did see was enough to hurt one's very soul. Many disabled and tired-out convicts were lying down in the freshly fallen snow, unable to take another step, and an officer of Cossacks was inspecting the irons of some pallid-faced wretches who were being marched past him.

The convicts stared at us with great curiosity, as we

got out of our sleigh and entered the station-house, and a few of them even removed their tattered woollen caps in respectful salutation. I made up my mind, as I gazed upon them, to inform the Czar of all this condemnable harshness, and I mentally registered a vow to enlighten him on the subject if I ever reached St. Petersburg once more. I may add that this vow was religiously kept later on, although it was no easy task to impress the Emperor with the horror of the spectacle presented by these haggard men walking backward and forward on the snow, attempting by violent exercise to keep themselves from freezing alive, nor to describe to him the livid countenances caused by the stiff and aching limbs, the countless privations, and want of proper food and clothing endured by the condemned offenders I saw before me.

Indeed, it was with a heavy heart that I entered the low-ceiled room where several officers and guards were warming themselves around the stove.

I at once inquired for the officer in command of the convoy, and after some delay he presented himself before me. He was a tall, broad-shouldered man, clean shaven but for a long reddish mustache; his hair was closely cropped, and his forehead and bushy eyebrows protruded forbiddingly over his light-colored, piercing eyes. Taken altogether, his appearance gave one the impression of his being a nasty customer to deal with. He stood bolt upright a few steps from me in the attitude which in military language is designated as "*at attention*," and saluted me with the grace of an automaton.

"You have among your prisoners a man of the name of Fédor Andreitch, I believe," I said to him.

He pretended for a moment to consult his memory, and then answered, in a loud, metallic voice: "Yes, your nobility, there is an unruly fellow of that name in our chain of convicts. He is called now, however, number 179."

As soon as the words were pronounced his mouth closed spasmodically, and his head, which he had turned towards me while speaking, reverted with a jerk to its former position of "*attention.*"

"Then here are some papers which will show you that by the order of his Majesty the Czar, this convict is to be set free and delivered into my hands," I continued, handing him the documents in question.

He carefully perused them from beginning to end, then looked puzzled and stared at me vacantly. At last he said, in the same monotonous fashion he had used before:

"This paper bears the name of one Yégor Nikolaïtch Fúlòw: that is not your nobility?"

I readily perceived that I had adopted an utterly false method, and therefore hastened to repair my mistake by explaining matters to him as glibly as I could.

When I ceased speaking he knit his brow, scratched the back of his head, and then, wheeling to the right about, he took three paces in the direction of the door. Suddenly, however, he hesitated, turned on his heel, and, once more approaching me, said, shortly:

"I cannot give up the prisoner without the sanction of the governor of the province."

I tapped my foot impatiently on the floor and asked him whether an order from the Emperor needed, in his eyes, sanction from anybody. To this he made no answer, but stood motionless in a manner which would have tried the patience of an ancient Stoic, and, sad to relate, nothing that either Yégor or I could say seemed to produce the slightest effect upon him.

Things were looking their blackest, and I had almost

despaired of ever coming to any satisfactory understanding with this man, when they took the most unexpected turn, and, as in a novel, a *deus ex machina*, appeared miraculously on the scene at our worst hour of need.

The crack of a whip and the shrill jingle of sleighbells were heard. The door was thrown open, and a gentleman wearing a general's uniform marched into the room. I learned later that he was the military governor of the district, and that he was accidentally passing through the village, where he had stopped to change horses. Curiously enough, the worthy creature seemed to know me well by sight, and when he discovered me in the filthy post-house of this far-Siberian settlement, the extremity of his amazement was most amusing to witness. There are snobs on every rung of the social ladder in Russia, as well as in every other country of the world, and this explains the enthusiasm with which this high official greeted me.

"Is it possible," he exclaimed, "that I should behold so lofty a personage in this dismal place? And if my eyes do not mislead me, can I be of any service?"

Much surprised at this grandiloquent tirade, for, unless the general had seen me at some court reception in St. Petersburg or Moscow, I certainly had not the faintest recollection of ever having met him before; I nevertheless explained my dilemma to him with the greatest possible despatch.

His rage when I told him that the officer in charge of the convicts refused to obey my injunction was a delightful relief to me and most ludicrous to behold. He raved and swore till I thought that an apoplectic seizure would be the reward of his overweening energy.

"Do you know, sir, whom you have the honor of seeing before you?" he yelled to his unfortunate subordinate; and, pointing towards me, he began to enumerate my titles and dignities at such a length and with so much eloquence that sheer modesty forbids me to transcribe his words here. The captain of Cossacks, who seemed ready to sink through the floor, muttered some obsequious excuses.

"Don't speak to me; you are a disgrace to the country which you have the altogether undeserved privilege of serving!" roared the general, crossing his arms on his fat chest and glaring furiously at the crestfallen officer. "Go and fetch this gentleman whom this noble lady has come so far to rescue from your clutches, and show him proper respect, I beg of you."

Proper respect to a convict, whom the general governor designated as "a gentleman." The nonplussed officer looked as if he might have dropped with surprise.

His intelligence was not sufficiently great to show him that his superior cared very little whether thousands of exiles were left to rot under the Siberian ice every year, but that he cared very much to obtain the good graces of his Majesty the Czar by serving him in this instance. At any rate he obeyed with remarkable alacrity, and a few minutes later re-entered the room, followed by a young man wearing the *tolu-shuba*, or long coat of sheepskin, with the tanned side out, which is the garment of marching convicts; dark-blue woollen trousers, long, loose boots, big leather mittens, and a worsted cap drawn over the ears, his heavy leg-fetters being held together by a long, clanking chain attached to a broad leather belt, and a tattered crimson handkerchief bound around his throat.

The face and figure of this man were in glaring contrast with his infamous garb. He was tall, fair, and athletic, with a high-bred look on his remarkably beautiful aquiline features, but exposure and fatigue had

worn his splendid frame and emaciated his handsome face. I had risen, and as he came near I held
out my hand to him in welcome, saying, with some
emotion: "I am very happy to have found you at last,
Fédor Andreitch, and to be able to hand you the Emperor's free pardon." As I spoke his eloquent and
feverish eyes sought mine with an agony of doubt and
anguish, for the officer had evidently not told him what
awaited him. A shiver shook him and a sob rose in
his throat.

"Is it true?" he said, in a dreamy, hesitating voice.

"It is; I have come to fetch you, and to bring you back
to those you love."

"Are you an angel come down from heaven to save
me?" he said, passionately, his white lips pronouncing
the words so low that they hardly stirred the air. Then,
with a sudden motion of his tall figure, he knelt down
on the beaten earth before me, and, burying his face in
the folds of my cloak, he broke into those heartrending
sobs which shake strong men in their agony.

We were alone now. The general, with a tact for
which I would not have given him credit, had ordered
every one out of the room and had taken himself off for
the time being. I bent over the kneeling man, softly
touching his bowed head, as I would have done that of a
troubled child, and whispered words of comfort and of
hope. Gradually the paroxysm subsided; he lifted his
eyes to mine and gazed on me with an expression of
grateful adoration and joy which went far towards re-
warding me for the hardships I had lately undergone
on his behalf. When he grew quieter I related to him
briefly the events which had brought me to Siberia, and
asked him whether he felt strong enough to start that
same day for St. Petersburg. I could not help noticing,
in spite of his efforts to conceal the fact, how much he

had suffered from his terrible experiences on the Siberian road, for a hard, dry cough shook him intermittently, and there were hectic spots on his thin cheeks. He would, however, hear of no delay, and implored me to start as soon as possible.

His agitation was something terrible to behold, and for more than an hour he paced the length of the dingy room to and fro, overcome by feelings which he could not master. In vain I urged him to lie down for a few hours. The shock had been too great; the moral resurrection through which he had gone had brought on a high fever which nothing seemed to soothe. In the meanwhile, with the help of the kindly general, who went to no end of trouble on this memorable occasion, I procured some clothes for Fédor, and that afternoon we set off on our return journey. The general-governor had begged us to come and stay for a few days at his residence, which was only fifty versts off, and I must say that I was so anxious to see my patient—as I now considered him to be—take the repose he so much needed, that I pleaded my own fatigue as a reason for accepting this invitation for twenty-four hours.

The government-house was a stout, shambling building made of logs, like all houses in Siberia, sheltered, after a fashion, from the sweeping wind by clumps of remarkably well-grown pine-trees. We arrived there about six o'clock in the evening, and were most cordially and affectionately received by the general's wife, a fat, motherly, middle-aged lady, with a fresh, healthy complexion, who wore a remarkable structure of lace and ribbons upon her head, and a stiff purple silk gown, which rustled like strong paper when she walked.

Dishes of cold meat, tea, eggs, boiled dried fruit, and cheese composed the meal, but, simple as was this fare, it was such a comfort to sit once more at a table, in a clean, warm room, and to eat off china and silver, that I do not think I ever enjoyed a repast as I did this one. Both my host and hostess treated me with so much elaborate ceremony, however, that my pleasure was somewhat marred thereby, and I was relieved when, some little time after supper, I was at last conducted to my rooms. There were no chests of drawers, wardrobes, or cupboards in my apartment, but I found an immense sofa, some large arm-chairs, and a long ottoman, which left but little space to move about in. I noticed also regretfully that there was no bath, but I remedied this by means of my rubber travelling-tub. In the morning I had the pleasure of discovering that there was a bath-room in the house, and a very large and comfortable one, too.

Nothing could exceed the kindness of my entertainers. When I rose I found my hostess in the large bath-room mentioned, getting it ready for me with her own hands, carefully seeing that the temperature was correct, and on my return to my own rooms discovered that a huge open fire had been lit in spite of the big one roaring in the porcelain stove in case of a chill after my warm plunge.

My hostess had three children, and was evidently very much devoted to them, but I observed that she never kissed them even to say good-night, a pat on the head being the only sign of affection that she ever gave them. On my speaking of this to her, she answered, "But I give them my hand to kiss," and added, "I think you foreigners kiss your children too much. It is not good for them." I smiled at this, but I must say that her boys were robust, like young bear cubs, which they somewhat resembled, for they had real Tartar faces; they were, it is true, somewhat heavy and stupid, but their doting father never tired of relating their many exploits and their many deeds of courage when they accompanied him wolf-hunting.

In this atmosphere of sympathy and peace Fédor Andreitch seemed to revive with every passing hour. His bearing and manners were those of a refined and cultured gentleman. It was inevitable that his recent sufferings should have left indelible traces on his countenance, and he still looked fatigued, but there was something so winning about him that he became at once a general favorite. We were genuinely sorry to have to say good-bye to our new friends and to their hospitable house, yet, now that we were thoroughly rested, we felt that every moment of delay was fraught with needless cruelty to Nadèje. We started, accompanied by the good wishes of the general and his family, who, in spite of the faling snow and the extreme severity of the temperature, stood on the door-steps waving adieus to us until we disappeared from view.

On the third day of our return trip we witnessed the most magnificent spectacle which it is possible to conceive. The snow had ceased to fall early in the morning, and towards mid-day the sun, which had not shone upon me since our departure from St. Petersburg, suddenly broke through the dense gray layers of clouds, its golden rays transforming the gloomy landscape like the wand of a magician. No pen can describe the dazzling splendor of the endless frozen plains shimmering like waves of molten silver to where the horizon melted in a faint blue line against the yet paler blue of the sky. Every branch of the bushes, every blade and tuft of the frozen reeds sheathed in transparent ice reflected the light in rainbow hues, and as the wind lifted some of the loose snow far up into the air it seemed to us as if we were surrounded by a slight veil of crystals wonderfully spun by the hands of a genie.

THE TRIBULATIONS OF A PRINCESS

We gazed at this beautiful scene, speechless with awe and admiration. Even our Cossacks, who generally looked as interested in our surroundings as bears awakened before they had done hibernating, actually gave vent to a series of enthusiastic if rather discordant hurrahs. The horses seemed to catch the infection, and, bounding like deers, they flew over the snow with the fleetness of zephyrs. Unfortunately this delicious state of things did not last very long, and after an intensely cold, starlit night the weather relapsed into storm and falling snow which followed the faint red of a sullen winter's dawn.

On that day I came upon a flower which at that time was completely unknown outside of Russia's greatest and most arid province, but which since then, I believe, has found its place in the herbarium of many a distinguished botanist. My Cossacks told me that this blossom was called the " *luck star* " or the " *snow flower,* " and, for all I know to the contrary, it may still bear these names in the far Northern lands where it has its home. It grows only where snow covers the ground for many months, and raises its wonderful head from the frozen, glittering surface of the steppe. It begins to bloom at the beginning of January, opens in a day, and, at the end of the third day succeeding its glorious birth, fades and dies. It has five petals, each being four inches in diameter, covered with what looks like crystallized snow. The petals are exquisitely formed in the shape of a large star, and at the end of each sparkles an octagonal point like a diamond or a huge petrified dewdrop. These are the seed-pods of this marvellous plant. It is claimed that whenever the wearied traveller meets on his road this heavenly-looking blossom it brings hope and good-luck to him, and thus it is revered—nay, almost worshipped—on the grim plains of Siberia.

Driving on and on, never pausing save to change horses and to take a hurried meal at a post-house, we went through the same tedious routine I had already experienced; but at last we reached Ekaterinburg, and put up at the *palatial* Plotinkof. Arrived there, I sent a despatch to Nadèje, telling her of Fédor's safety. The latter, as we came nearer to our destination, puzzled me by his gradually sinking energy. He often slept for hours together during the end of our trip in the *kibitka*, and when awake his mind seemed absorbed and full of dull, feverish day-dreams. At first he had talked almost unceasingly of Nadèje and of their child, but now he never mentioned their names. Once I asked him to tell me what ailed him, and, fixing his dark-blue eyes on me very sadly, he said, simply:

"The ineffaceable past lies heavily upon me, and is like a ghost tracking my steps. I did wrong when I induced Nadèje to marry me secretly, and this thought hangs like a millstone about my neck. My punishment has been hard already, but never so hard as now, when I have seen what you, madame, have undergone to save me."

"Do not say that!" I exclaimed, much annoyed. 'You have no need to regret anything so far as I am concerned. This trip has been to me a pleasant novelty in a monotonous round of self-indulgence, and also a great pleasure, I assure you."

He shook his head and murmured wistfully: "You say so, and I wish I could believe you, but it does not lessen my debt of gratitude, a debt which I can never repay."

"Nonsense!" I rejoined, impatiently; "when I see you living happily with your Nadèje I will be more than repaid for a little trouble and fatigue." But as I said the words a curious feeling of doubt assailed me, and I wondered what of happiness or sorrow lay in the future for the young couple in whom I had taken so great an interest, although our acquaintance was, comparatively speaking, so short.

We stayed two days at Ekaterinburg, and then went on to Moscow and thence home, where we arrived at last, one evening, much exhausted, but greatly pleased to see the end of our exhausting journey. I left Fédor at the door of the Imperial Hôtel, promising to communicate with him as soon as I had seen Nadèje and had prepared her for the joy of their reunion.

A storm of reproaches awaited me at home. My husband, who had by this time learned my reasons for going to Russia, was in a towering rage. He received me with a very magnificent speech which, if it did not impress me much, had at any rate the merit of coming straight from the heart. The position was a trying one for him, I readily acknowledge, for although he liked publicity himself, he hated anybody else to attract it, and the news of my Siberian undertaking had, through some indiscretion on the part of my servants, become universally known, so that, to his great chagrin, I had created a genuine sensation. As I declined to receive his admonitions in a tame spirit, he soon cooled down, and the subject was dropped for the nonce.

The next morning I drove to the address given to me by Nadèje as that of the house where she lived with her father. It was in an old quarter of the town, somewhere near the river, and the place looked dark and dismal on this blustering, rainy forenoon to inspire one with positive ideas of suicide. I sent my footman to inquire whether I could see the mistress of the house, and was surprised and distressed to hear that she had been from home for a week, but that *der gnädige Herr* was in! I immediately decided to see the old gentleman, and to find out, without, of course, betraying his daughter's secret, where I could find her. With some difficulty, I obtained admittance, and was ushered by an aged man-servant, clothed in funereal black, into a melancholy salon looking out on to a narrow, gloomy street.

Everything in that room was singularly depressing: the sombre hangings and ebony furniture, stiffly arranged on the oaken floor, which was waxed and polished to a dangerous extent, and had an uninhabited appearance. The large coal fire burning in the grate did not succeed in brightening this preternaturally unfriendly apartment.

I waited so long that I was on the point of ringing the bell to remind the household of my presence, when the door opened and a man, who must have been sixty years of age at least, if not more, though still erect and unbending, entered. His black eyes flashed with sullen fires, and his thin-lipped mouth had something cruel about it which I thought very repellent. He bowed low before me, and asked in excellent German to what he was indebted for the honor of a call from me.

"I came with the hope of meeting your daughter," I said to him, "but your man informs me that she is not here. Would you oblige me by letting me know where I may write to her?"

He shot a look of deep aversion at me, then, controlling himself with evident effort, he said, in a strange, hollow voice:

"I have no longer a daughter. She forfeited all claim to my affection when she debased herself by a secret marriage with a man whom I had forbidden her to ever so much as speak to."

"Do not say such words," I said, sternly; "your daughter has sacrificed her happiness for your sake, and the secrecy of her marriage was only the result of your unjust prejudice."

He listened to me with bitter scorn depicted on his sharp, pale features.

"I do not wish to lack in courtesy towards a lady of your exalted rank, madame, and yet I must decline to discuss this matter any further with you. Ever since I discovered my daughter's treachery she has been dead to me, and nothing will make me reconsider my decision so far as she is concerned."

His voice was cold and resolute, and I saw that, as he said himself, nothing could move him in his resolve.

"Will you at least tell me what has become of her?" I exclaimed, forgetting in the intensity of my eagerness to resent this strange personage's extraordinary manner.

He hesitated a moment, then reluctantly replied: "She was summoned to R—— a week ago. That is all I know; ask me no more."

She has gone to her child, I thought to myself, with a pang of pity for the poor young mother, as I listened with anger rising in my heart. But I knew now what I had come to learn, and, with a slight inclination of the head, I walked across the room, too provoked to trust myself to speak. When I reached the threshold I turned and involuntarily looked back. He was still standing by the mantel-piece, his face motionless and as bloodless as that of a corpse, and the expression of his eyes was so relentless and fierce that I could not help exclaiming:

"You will yet live to regret what you have done!" Then I walked rapidly down-stairs, deeply concerned at the unexpected turn which this sad affair was taking.

On my way to the hotel I vainly puzzled my brain, wondering how this awful old gentleman had come upon his daughter's secret. But even with the help of Fédor—who was intensely distressed by what I told him

—I could not imagine how it had happened. The poor fellow looked so wretched that I became seriously anxious about him: We decided that he had better start for R—— without further delay, and I made him promise to let me know at once how he found Nadèje and her baby, and also not to hesitate to call me should he need my help. We knew where Nadèje was, that was all, and we were thankful for that, but, unfortunately, her only friends, who were also Fédor's relatives, were wintering in Egypt, and so we were unable to ascertain what had occurred during my absence. The young husband was almost beside himself with grief at the thought of the misery which the hapless girl he had married must have endured for his sake, and a heavy sense of guilt lay upon him. Indeed, I was amazed by the ravages these emotions were working upon him, and I began to wonder how long his strength would last if this state of affairs did not change for the better very soon.

Three days went by without bringing me any news. I had once more resumed the ceaseless gayeties of my hollow mundane existence. The *Fasching* was particularly brilliant that year, and I was immediately caught in a regular whirlpool of dinners, balls, and receptions, until my Siberian tour seemed but a dream of my fancy.

On the night of the third day I had just come home from a ball at the English Embassy, and was sitting in my dressing-room, when my chief woman-in-waiting brought me a telegraphic message. I tore open the envelope and read the following words with a start of horror:

"She is dying, and is asking for you. Can you come to us?
"FÉDOR."

I gazed vacantly for a moment at the pink silk hangings on the walls, at the great mirrors which reflected the light of the lamps, and I unconsciously pushed from me a bowl of lilies which stood on a table near me, for their perfume suddenly sickened me. The news was so unexpected that I felt dazed and stunned. Dying—this poor girl to whom I had restored her beloved husband! It seemed cruel enough to be true, although I could hardly realize it! I decided to start by the first train I could catch, and I was glad of the bustle of preparation attending my hurried departure, for it kept me from thinking, and drove away, in a measure, my anxiety. One cannot devote many weeks of one's life to the service of friends without becoming proportionately attached to them, and the young couple had gradually crept into my affections.

I took the early train south, and went straight on to the coast. I knew the exact situation of the villa where Nadèje's baby had been born, and therefore, on alighting from the train, I drove at once to the small seaport of R——.

This lovely part of the world is but little known to the ordinary globe-trotter, a fact which has always surprised me, for the scenery is beautiful, and possesses a savage grandeur seldom to be met with in more civilized countries. The shore is perilously abrupt, and the great red cliffs, crowned with cacti and olive-trees, press around and seem to shut in on every side a series of semi-landlocked lakes where the great waves of the sea have hollowed out deep caverns and crevices.

The villa Rodoïtza nestled in a nook of the bay where aloes and mimosa grew thickly, and was reached by a winding flower-lined path which led up to it along a steep incline cut out of the live rock.

The weather was perfect, and as I proceeded rapidly towards my destination I could not help admiring the sublimity of the landscape which appeared to me all the more delightful after the bleakness of the northern regions which I had so recently left behind me. The sea was buoyant, but not rough, and the long, curling waves of the Adriatic beat rhythmically on the sands far below the road I was following. Flocks of white-winged gulls flew above the water, dipping occasionally in the hollow of the surge, while a wall of rock rose in many ridges towards the road, where it ended in a thick hedge of prickly-pear-trees and arbutus.

The villa was excessively pretty, and looked like a miniature paradise, surrounded as it was by thickets of tall rose-laurels and backed by huge palms. It was a low, white house, built of Ferrara marble, with a long terrace studded at intervals with blue majolica vases filled with blossoming plants. Blue-and-white awnings protected the windows from the glare of the Southern sun, and the entire place was so full of life, color, and gayety that I could not imagine how so beautiful a place could harbor death and sorrow.

The door was opened for me by an old woman wearing the picturesque garb of the peasants of that region. Her wrinkled face was very pale, and her eyes red and swollen from weeping. Without saying a word, she preceded me into a small but very pretty room with panelled walls and old-rose hangings, and left me standing there in no enviable frame of mind. In a moment more the heavy curtains of the doorway were quickly drawn apart, and Fédor stood before me with the light of the bright, joyful day shining on him and showing me a face so white, so troubled, so drawn, that I rushed towards him with outstretched hands, exclaiming:

"My poor boy, what has happened?"

Silently and quite feebly, as if all strength had gone from him, he sank into a chair and looked at me dumbly with the expression of an animal wounded unto death.

Then, in a broken, stupefied fashion, while his eyes gazed aimlessly through the open terrace windows, he told me the sad story of the past few days.

I gathered therefrom that the baby had sickened from diphtheria, and that the distracted foster-mother had written to Nadèje, imploring her to come at once. By some fatality the letter had fallen into the hands of the girl's father, who, oblivious of his daughter's despair, had turned her from his house. She, broken-hearted and almost mad with pain and anxiety, started at once for R——, where she arrived only in time to see her little one die. Weakened by fatigue and sorrow, she had caught the dreadful disease, and that very morning, at dawn, had breathed her last.

I listened to all this, sorrowfully and mutely, for I was unable to find words of consolation adequate to so great a trial, and when Fédor asked me whether I would care to see her again, I followed him wearily up-stairs to a pretty pink-and-white room, where the young mother lay on a bed with the fair head of her baby pillowed on her breast. Armfuls of flowers had been thrown across the coverlet and dropped on to the floor; in the cold hands of the dead girl a cluster of white roses had been placed, and the cushions on which her charming head was reposing were covered with snowy violets. As I knelt beside this fragrant couch of blossoms and verdure, I thought of the many useless lives which are spared while hers had been taken in all its beauty and strength just when her dreams and hopes were about to be fulfilled.

Fédor had implored me to remain with him for the funeral, which was to take place on the morrow. I will say nothing of those long hours which he and I spent in the sunny villa over which death had spread its gloom. We hardly ventured to speak to each other, for fear of breaking down, and I cannot remember having ever before or since lived through such pathetic, tragic moments.

The slow, melancholy day wore on. The clock ticked tediously in the room where we sat together. Outside the waves sparkled in the rays of the setting sun. The fragrant air blowing over the gardens carried to us the perfumes of flowers and of the sea. ·They brought us food, but we could not take it.

At last, night came down, and the darkness was a relief. Worn out in body, I slumbered where I sat, awakening in the early morning with that heavy, stunned feeling of anguish which follows a sudden sorrow. When I opened my eyes I was alone, and with surprise I heard the howling of the wind and the beating of heavy rain against the casements. During my short sleep one of those terrible storms so common in those parts had swept down from the mountains, and it seemed to me now as if nature itself were weeping for the dead. The scene had entirely changed. Boisterous gusts drove the waves in frothy masses against the foot of the cliffs. A thick veil of mist shrouded the bay, and the heavens were overcast with greenish-gray clouds.

I cannot, even now, remember that morning without shuddering. It was so dreary and so very sad, this funeral of mother and babe, carried to their last resting-place in this chilly, misty, stormy day. The moaning wind scattered the flowers on the white-draped coffin, and the ceaseless rain drenched the reddish mould of the little cemetery.

I see yet the tiny church, half hidden by dripping ilex-trees, the wet grass on which we stood, while the humble village priest sprinkled the grave with Holy Water. I hear the piteous cry of agony wrung

U   305

from Fédor's lips as the first spadeful of earth rattled on the coffin! With a gesture of agonized supplication, of heart-breaking pain, he stretched his arms out despairingly and then fell forward senseless on the sodden ground.

For many hours he did not recover consciousness, and when at length he did so the village doctor, whom I had called in, was evidently at his wits' ends to find a name for his malady. I summoned the best medical men from the nearest city, and they confirmed my fears. Fédor was dying of meningitis.

The next four days were anxious and terrible. The unfortunate man lay motionless in an almost continual state of coma, never looking up or speaking, but often holding my hand in his with the clinging tenacity of a sick child. I hardly left him day or night, for as soon as I withdrew my fingers, were it ever so gently, he became restless and delirious. He slept little, and when he awoke from occasional snatches of rest he fell into comatose apathy again—apathy from which nothing could rouse him. I knew that there was no chance of recovery, and yet I hoped still against hope, and the physicians and myself did all in our power to save him.

At last the end came. On the fifth day after Nadèje's funeral, still lying in that dreadful silence, he said, suddenly, in a scarcely audible voice:

"It will soon be over now, and you will be released from all this worry."

I stooped over him and answered, softly:

"Do not say that; you may get well yet."

The pallor of his face grew greater still as he feebly pressed my fingers.

"It is better so," he murmured, "better that I should go now, while your hand is holding mine." Then he added, with a childlike appeal in his quavering, breath-less utterance: "Promise me not to leave me."

My eyes swam with tears as I heard him. "No, I will not leave you, not for a moment, while you need me. Have you so little faith in me that you doubt it?"

"I have caused you nothing but pain and trouble," he said, so faintly that I could hardly catch the words. Then, with a sudden and surprising energy in one so weak, he raised himself on his pillows and looked at the glory of the rising sun which streamed through the open windows and over the bed, a beautiful smile beamed over his thin, emaciated, but still handsome face, a deep sigh struggled from his breast and es-caped his white lips, and he fell gently back into my arms.

I closed the dark-fringed eyelids, gazed for a moment at the countenance so peaceful in death, then, laying my head down on the bed, I knelt beside him. How long I remained there I never knew. I was aroused by the physicians coming for their morning inspection, and I let them lead me into the next room. Then for many hours all grew dark about me.

The past months of fatigue and anxiety and over-strain of mind had done their work, and, now that my task was accomplished, I succumbed to an overwhelm-ing lassitude and weariness.

Thanks to the strength of my constitution, I recov-ered very quickly, and as soon as Fédor's funeral was over I sailed for Madeira, where I was to rejoin my Empress. The idea of returning at once to the world was noxious to me, for I needed calm and peace, and especially her presence, which to me was always the best of panaceas, and it was only at the beginning of the next winter that I returned home.

CHAPTER XVII

"On some his vigorous judgments light,
In that dread pause 'twixt day and night—
Life's closing twilight hour;
Round some, ere yet they meet their doom,
Is shed the silence of the tomb,
The eternal shadows lower."

THE Emperor and Empress had just retired, but many members of the court were still scattered about here and there in the dazzlingly lighted rooms of the palace, discussing the various events of the court ball, while the strains of the last waltz of the *Hof-Kapelle* floated on the perfumed air.

As we stood for a moment in the crowded throne-room — Karl, Frederick, and myself — we appeared to attract an unusual amount of attention. Fred, who had arrived a few days before, was arrayed in the full dress of a Scottish laird—with kilt, claymore, and tartan—which might have accounted for the unwonted curiosity displayed, while Karl, whose embroidered dolman was covered with decorations, looked, it is true, handsomer, and of yet more commanding presence than was his wont. Still, all this very marked if courteously repressed attention puzzled me. My husband's features bore a marked expression of haughtiness and a *blasé* look which, coupled with the strange shiftiness of his blue eyes, made his face more than ever unattractive to me. A glance at him always sufficed to convince that he was a man who could not be trusted, and who might become a very ugly customer on the slightest provocation—as those who served under his orders had bitter occasion to know. I was aware, of course, that I was looking my best, always a pleasant feeling, even to the least vain of women. My court-mantle, which was attached to my shoulders by diamond *fleur-de-lys*, was of rose-leaf velvet, edged with a thick garland of natural white lilac. The skirt and corsage were of old Venetian point, strewn with clusters of lilac, and my neck and arms were blazing with diamonds, pink pearls, and rubies. I turned to speak to Karl's greatest friend and confidant, Count Paul, a tall, slight, dark-eyed lieutenant in the guards, who for the last year or two had been my husband's constant companion and crony, besides being his favorite aide-de-camp.

"I wish we were well out of this," I exclaimed, drawing my train aside to allow a score of officers to pass; "only it is too early yet to go to bed."

"Why don't we go and have some supper," said Fred; smiling. "The buffet here is not what I admire most."

"All right," replied Karl, "that's what I call a sensible proposal. You had better drive with Muzzi in her carriage, Fred; I will follow in yours, with Paul, and we shall be there almost as soon as you will."

"I had rather you would come with us, Karl," I interposed, hastily.

"What for?" he replied, peevishly. "Can't Fred take care of you? Please do as I ask you, and don't regret our presence too much, for your train would be ruthlessly crushed."

I shrugged my shoulders as we turned to go, and we rapidly passed through the long suite of salons, the white walls of which were illuminated by myriads of wax candles, in rock-crystal sconces and candelabra. Groups of pink and white blossoms backed by tall, feathery palms and fragrant mimosa, filled every corner, and were tastefully arranged in front of the countless mirrors which stood between the long rows of windows.

Reaching the palace hall at last, we stopped a moment to talk to Count K., who wore a blue-velvet, fur-bordered Attila thickly covered with jewels, as were the hilt of his damascened sword, the aigrette on his *kalpàk*, and the heavy gold belt which encircled his yet slender waist. He looked every inch what he was, a soldier as well as a great statesman, and it seemed but just and fair that he should hold as he did one of the highest positions in the land. Looking up at him with a smile, I asked him if he were not very glad that the ball was over.

"You must feel so warm in all your splendor," I added, touching the fur-lined dolman which hung by golden cords from his left shoulder with the tips of my fingers.

"Indeed I do; but don't let us talk about so uninteresting a subject as myself. Allow me to congratulate you on your appearance. You are the very personification of youth and loveliness."

"Fie, Excellency! What a flatterer you are! I am afraid that I shall have to avoid you in future."

"You know that I mean what I say, always," murmured the old courtier, as he offered me his arm to lead me to my carriage, which had just been announced.

"I must believe you then," I rejoined, laughingly, as I entered my brougham, followed by Fred. While the equipage was moving off at a sharp trot, I thrust my head out of the window, and with the freedom of an already long acquaintance I kissed my hand to the Count, who was still standing bareheaded on the marble steps of the portico.

The lights from the carriage lamps and the street gas were strong enough to let Fred see my features perfectly and I was vexed with myself to observe that he noticed how all my gayety and animation dropped like a mask, and that I lay back in the carriage with a deep and weary sigh.

"What is the matter, Muzzi?" he asked, taking in his own my hand, which lay idly in my lap, and bending his handsome head to look into my face. "Are you tired? Has something pained you?"

His voice was not very steady, and his eyes betrayed a depth of tenderness which disagreeably startled me. I unconsciously drew myself up, and, turning away my head, I replied in a quiet tone, the effect of which I fear was spoiled by the involuntary flutter of my hand as I withdrew it from his clasp:

"Yes, I suppose I am tired. This evening has been dreadfully long, and court balls are always a bore."

He evidently understood that I did not choose to mention the true cause of my listlessness, and for the remainder of our short drive he remained mute.

On alighting at S.'s famous restaurant, Fred at once asked for a private salon, and we were ushered into a small but eminently comfortable room, which was thrown open with a flourish by the head-waiter. As the door closed upon us I unwound the lace scarf which protected my head and threw off my long wrap. I was just approaching the mirror to arrange the curls on my forehead, which had been slightly ruffled by the weight of my tiara, when there was an audible scuffle in the passage outside the door, and the voice of the *Ober-Kellner* was heard to exclaim:

"You must not enter; this room is occupied. I respectfully beg pardon, but I cannot let any one pass."

We looked at each other perfectly amazed, for it was my husband who replied, in angry tones:

"Don't talk such trash. It's my wife who is in there,

Robert." At this moment Fred, hastily opening the door, interposed himself between three or four waiters and my husband, saying with intense astonishment:

"Good Heavens! my dear fellow, what is all this about?"

"Only that these good people here imagine that I will be *de trop* between you and my wife," replied Karl, with a sneer, rudely brushing past Fred and entering the room.

He was evidently much annoyed, and for once not quite without cause; but seeing the frown on the young Scotchman's brow, he deemed it more politic to turn the whole thing into a joke, and, flinging himself down on a sofa, he added, with a cynical laugh:

"Oh! our waiters are well trained here, and it would be a wellnigh hopeless task for a man, whoever he might be, to attempt following his wife too closely—that is, if husbands cared to go to so much trouble nowadays."

This last remark fell rather flat. I had taken up an evening paper, which I pretended to be reading with absorbing interest. Fred had left the room to order the supper, and Count Paul was looking out of the window, making a great show in his embarrassment of admiring the file of equipages leaving the Grand Opera-House on the other side of the broad thoroughfare.

A few minutes later we sat down to a dainty supper, at a small square table decked with mousseline glasses, Dresden china, and shallow bowls of Russian violets and narcissi. There was apparently no trace left of the painful impression caused by the waiter's unfortunate blunder, and the conversation soon became animated, and even pleasant.

"What a quantity of charming women there were to-night at the palace!" said I. "Did you notice Lady

L., Fred? I think she is the loveliest Englishwoman that I ever met."

"She is certainly very fine-looking," replied Fred, "but I do not admire her greatly. I never fancy those Juno-like women."

"You don't admire her, eh? Well, we all know that your ideal woman is of a very different type," snarled Karl, with a quick glance of scarcely veiled impertinence at me. But I took care to give no sign of applying his remark to myself.

"Lady L. is an admirable creature in every sense of the word," continued my husband; "besides which she is one of the best-dressed and most graceful women in our English colony."

"I think one can hardly say that," I could not help replying. "For instance, her gown to-night was quite unsuited to the occasion. It would have been well enough for an ordinary ball, but it was neither worthy of a court reception nor of the splendid jewels she saw fit to wear with it."

"You are very critical, Muzzi, and very unjustly so. I must say that I admire the comparative simplicity and modesty of that gown extremely. It is quite refreshing to meet a woman for once in a way who does not appear in public in the super-*chic* garb so fashionable now," he added, glancing significantly at my laces and lilacs.

His intention of teasing me was so patent that Count Paul attempted to change the conversation. Karl was determined, however, to make me pay for the ridicule with which he had been covered at the moment of his ludicrously sensational arrival at the restaurant, and, unceremoniously interrupting his friend, he exclaimed:

"You women of the world ought to be told the truth

sometimes. One blushes for you when one sees you wearing dresses that would be considered overdone even for a queen of the comic opera, and flirting nineteen to the dozen. How singular it is that you should, all of you, insist upon imitating the ways and customs of the most notorious and most extravagant of characters!"

I raised my eyes from my plate and looked my husband steadily in the face. I felt myself becoming a shade paler, but, fortunately, my voice was perfectly calm, although I could not help there being a ring of contempt in it as I said:

"Spare your blushes, my dear Karl; they are few and far between, and therefore of untold value. If there really are women, worthy of the name, who debase themselves by imitating the ladies you refer to with so much good taste, they probably do so with a view of pleasing men like you, who are, as is well known, very fervent admirers of the genus you mentioned just now."

There was a burst of laughter at his expense, while he gnawed his fair mustache viciously. He would, I know, have turned upon me with a few more of his sarcasms had it not been for the fact that the head-waiter, approaching on tiptoe, presented to him a card with some lines in pencil scribbled across it.

"Of course, of course!" he exclaimed, and, jumping to his feet, he hastily whispered to me that Grand-Duke A., who was supping in the neighboring salon with the Muscovite ambassador, requested permission to join us. A few minutes later the two Russians had taken their places at our table. Fred relinquished his seat on my right-hand to the Grand-Duke, and Count Paul vacated the chair on my left for the benefit of his Excellency, Count von M.

Almost at once the Grand-Duke began to complain, in his melodious, high-bred voice, of the terrible cold which had set in since morning.

"Really, if this continues, I am afraid that we shall have but a poor time to-morrow," he said, plaintively, alluding to an imperial hunt which was to be given in his honor on the next day. "Our systems cannot stand such severe weather. Do you mean to tell me, Muzzi, that you will muster courage to accompany us under such uninviting circumstances?"

"Oh yes," I replied, "I am very fond of hunting, both a-horse and a-foot; it breaks the monotony of one's existence."

Karl, who seemed to have fallen into one of his moodiest fits, looked up from the ortolan he was delicately dismembering and exclaimed, impatiently:

"Women are utterly out of place in that kind of sport, and are apt to bring men into peril, for no man can possibly take care of himself while he has the safety of a woman to attend to."

With which enunciation of doctrine he helped himself to a glass of kümmel from the square bottle at his elbow.

"Oh, I know," he continued, "there are people who believe in the possibility of sport and flirtation hunting in couples, but I do not. In my humble opinion, women who take up that line of thing are unpardonable; they soon become as horsy as ourselves, and I call it more than silly to attempt to shoot big game while dressed up like figures from the carnival, and to follow us in the furrows with a walk that is an absurd cross between a swing and a strut!"

"How very ungallant you are!" said the Grand-Duke, "and how very erroneous in your ideas! Why do you not scold him, Muzzi?"

"*Que voulez-vous il-y-tient!* A few minutes ago he

attacked our costumes and our ways, with quite unnecessary fervor. I am beginning to think that he has mistaken his vocation; he should have been a *couturier* or a moralist! Moreover, his last sentence is already known to me, for I heard it this very afternoon from the august lips of the aged Archduchess, whom we irreverently call '*Madame Minerve*' at court. Karl is a good and dutiful Telemachus, eagerly absorbing and repeating the maxims of this sage petticoated mentor!"

There was another laugh, and Karl, completely routed, relapsed into a sulky silence. I, however, was beginning to feel the effects of his singularly ill-timed bad humor and of his unjustifiable behavior, and my temper—always difficult to control, as I have confessed before several times—was getting slowly the better of all my good resolutions.

With a totally mirthless laugh, I therefore could not resist the temptation of picking up the gauntlet which he had so imprudently cast down at my feet, and, nervously twisting my rings around my fingers, I continued, coolly:

"Let me give you the tenor of the delightful conversation which I had with '*Madame Minerve*' this very afternoon. Her *entrée en matière* was worthy a great tactician, for she went straight to the point, I can assure you!

"'There is nothing so hateful or so disgusting as an unsexed woman!' she declared to me with a suddenness which was amusing, ominously glowering at me through the glasses which she had planted upon her haughty nose.

"'May I venture to inquire whether your Imperial Highness intends this remark for me?' I replied, meekly, and with a heroic effort to control my merriment, for a tall pier-glass, which stood directly opposite me, revealed my image to perfection, and my small stature and youth did not appear to me at that instant to look much like the typical virago.

"'Yes, my remark is intended for you, and I cannot but regret to see that you are adopting a decidedly horsy and sportive demeanor. Your love for the hunt and the chase will end by changing you into one of the beings I was just thinking of. Ah! dear me, to think of you, young and dainty as you are now, and then to realize that you will soon be transformed into one of those women who use the slang of the stables and of the race-course whenever they open their mouths, who delight in bruising their tender flesh with the recoil of a gun, who swear and smoke, and walk in a shocking way which is an unhappy mixture of a swing and a strut.'

. . . I beg to attract your attention to the fact, *messeigneurs*, that the '*swing and strut*' are her own expression, not Karl's; I am also sorry to confess that at this juncture I burst into a peal of laughter which was as irreverent as it was uncontrollable. Extremely offended, the Archduchess rose from her chair and advanced towards me as if she were on the point of annihilating me.

"'Laugh, my good child,' she said, with withering scorn, 'but remember that I have warned you. Upon my word, I do not know what has come to women lately. If I were your husband, I would lock you up in a room and keep you there until you mended your manners.' And with a thoroughly dramatic gesture of horror she swept out of the room, leaving me to digest her tirade as best I might. I do not like the Archduchess, of course, for she is, without a shadow of a doubt, the most overbearing, narrow-minded, sarcastic, and unkind old woman whom it has ever been my unhappy luck to encounter, and I am forced to add that she dislikes me just as much as I do her. I also have a temper of my own, as you all know, and I most imprudently have displayed it on more than one occasion in her presence, with the result that she believes me to be, I think, some kind of an untamed little animal in need of an occasional lash of the whip. That I do not take very kindly to these periodical remonstrances goes without saying, and, moreover, her disapproval of any of my actions makes me all the more eager to persevere in the very course condemned by her. I may, therefore, declare most solemnly and truthfully here that my enthusiasm for sports of all description, my love for breakneck rides, four-in-hand driving, shooting big game, swimming, fencing, *et tutti quanti*, is, if not begotten—for, alas! alack! it was born in me—at least fostered and strengthened by her opposition and by her scathing criticisms. I do not wish to deny that the Archduchess is a *maîtresse femme*, with spirit enough for a hundred cavalry soldiers. Cabinet ministers are as babes in her hands, and the entire court-circle is at her beck and call. She looms large and imposing on the horizon of the whole empire, and almost everybody bows before her edicts, for, although she is not loved, her extreme cleverness and marked superiority of intellect make it easy for her to rule her entourage with an unflinching sceptre. Moreover, she shares beyond doubt Sganarelle's opinion to the effect that '*cinq ou six coups de bâtons ne font que ragaillardir l'affection.*' But, with lamentable short - sightedness, I decline to share her views in the matter, and I set up my back defiantly, notwithstanding the fact that my lord and master here present chances to be one of her favorites and is as malleable as wax in her hands."

"*C'est bien fait pour toi,*" murmured the Grand-Duke

to Karl, who was staring at me in positive amazement this time, for I had seldom before accorded sufficient importance to his words to answer him in kind.

Soon afterwards the party broke up, and I drove home alone, closely followed by Fred's brougham, in which he and Karl were probably sitting side by side in utter silence, for there was storm in the air, and certainly neither of them would dream of unbending sufficiently for small-talk.

The abrupt stopping of the carriage roused me from my waking dreams, and I ran swiftly up-stairs to my private suite, forgetting in my hurry to close the door of the ante-chamber leading thereto.

When I had dismissed my women and re-entered my bedroom, wrapped in a loose batiste gown, I stood at the door petrified with surprise, for there, facing me, stood my husband, his broad shoulder leaning against the high mantel, and his head held defiantly up. There was a faint smile on his lips.

"May I inquire," I said, quietly, "to what I am indebted for so flattering a *tête-à-tête?* This is a strange time of night to transact business—the only existing tie between us now."

"You must excuse my intrusion," he replied, with a sudden courtesy to which my attitude compelled him, "but I am vexed and disgusted beyond description, and I think that it will be wise if I let you know my reasons for being, as I am, thrown out of my habitual calmness and self-possession."

"You do me much honor in making me your confidante, but, as I remarked before, the time is ill chosen."

"Never mind the time. I want you to explain to me why you try to make my position unbearable at court by your caprice and your repellent behavior towards a personage of so exalted a rank that any other woman's head would be turned by his admiration."

I glided into a low chair with an apparent docility which, under the circumstances, both pleased and surprised me, and, leaning my head upon my clasped hands, I looked inquiringly at him.

"You must forgive me," I said, slowly, "if I fail to understand your meaning. I dare say I am dull to-night. What are you alluding to?"

"Simply to this. You are a clever and thorough-paced woman of the world, a great lady, and you are surely sufficiently well versed in social tactics to know how to keep a man's love at burning-point, without any surrender on your part. But, instead of doing this, you are, as usual, cold and brusque, allowing no possible loop-hole in your attitude for a ray of hope which would serve to lead on—well, we will mention no names—and yet you know that my entire future, my whole ambitions, depend upon the favor of this all-powerful person whom you choose to repulse so unwarrantably."

"What would you have me do?"

"Good heavens, Muzzi, what a question to ask! You must be purposely trying to misunderstand me."

"I am afraid that I do understand you now," I replied, rising to my feet and confronting my husband. "Do you mean to insinuate that I ought to encourage such attentions? Is this your advice to your wife?"

"Pray do not jump at conclusions. You are not a *petite bourgeoise*, and, moreover, you should not talk so crudely."

"Indeed!" was all I said; but I trust that the scorn in my eyes intimated the rest. My contempt pierced Karl's intense vanity and made him wince and smart.

"Yes, certainly, your words are unnecessarily crude," he repeated, sullenly scowling at me. "I do not need to take lessons from you; the name I bear has a lustre which has until now been among the greatest and most undimmed in history."

"Very likely," I replied, trying to control my anger, "but your extraordinarily azure blood does not prevent you from asking me in so many words to sacrifice my own feelings, not to mention my own conception of honor, to your boundless ambition."

A fearful rage held him speechless for a moment; then he uttered a very ugly oath, which was an entirely new departure from his usual courtesy, and exclaimed, with a positively ferocious look:

"Be silent, if you cannot keep your words within ·bounds."

"Do you suppose for an instant that you can frighten me?" I said, very quietly. "We had better not begin to measure insults; my account against you is pretty heavy, and can never be balanced on that score."

The quietness of my words lashed him to a worse fury.

"By God! I will be your master yet!" he cried, savagely, jumping up and attempting to seize me by the wrist. "You shall learn to obey me, madame."

"Take care what you say," I replied, without even raising my voice, and shaking myself free from his grasp. "Do not try my patience too far, or you may live to regret it. You have always preferred the lowest kind of company to mine. You know how I abhor the very sight of you. Go back to those who will welcome such advice as you would give me, I say, and in future spare me scenes of this kind. If we are to continue to live under the same roof, the less we see of each other in private the better."

He was silent, and in a measure subdued. He knew well that his violence had been cowardly, and that by his covert advice he had disgraced both his name and his rank. For one fleeting moment he looked as if he felt ashamed of his unmanly behavior.

"Muzzi," he muttered, in lower tones, "I would prefer *you* as a companion if we could understand each other better."

A shudder of intense repulsion shook me from head to foot, and a feeling of absolute horror swept over me.

"Spare me such overtures at least! How dare you? How dare you?" I continued, shaking all over with indignation. "Now that you have offered me the worst insult that a man can pass upon the woman who bears his name, rest satisfied and leave me."

I put out my hand and pointed peremptorily to the door. There was so much suppressed passion in the action that he was momentarily cowed, and muttered, sullenly:

"Do not be so melodramatic; you misunderstand me."

"Misunderstand you? No, indeed, I do not. I know you too well for that. But, thank God, I am getting accustomed to the knowledge of your sins and vices, and they are not the measure of my duty. Did you think that it was for your sake that I am outwardly indifferent to the life you lead? Were it so, I should long ago have fled from you. But how can I expect you to understand me? You, to whom honor and self-respect are mere empty words?"

"You talk very confidently of your merits, madame. You forget that women are changeable. Wait until you have been really tempted before you boast of your many virtues. They will last so long, and no longer!"

I really staggered, and I bit my lips in order to once more master myself; then I said, in a voice hoarse with rage:

"You are a coward, and beneath all contempt. Go, or I shall truly become irresponsible for my actions!"

Beside himself with frenzy, my husband forgot that he was a gentleman, and, advancing towards me, he raised his arm as if to strike. Before he could touch me, however, with a swift bound I reached the bell-rope, and, grasping it, exclaimed:

"Leave this room at once, or I shall summon my household, and never you dare to enter my presence unbidden again, or you will have plenty of cause to regret it."

Afraid that this delightful matrimonial scene should, indeed, become public, he recovered himself, bowed low, and walked towards the door, but, as he was about to close it behind him, he said, viciously:

"I'll make you far more sorry yet for what you have said and done to-night, my fair lady, mark my words!"

When the noise of his footsteps had died away in the distance, I dropped on my knees before the same dusky wooden statue of the Madonna which had comforted my childish sorrows, and which now hung, as of old, above the praying-stool at the side of my bed, and gave way to a fit of agonized weeping—a rare occurrence with me under any circumstances. Never had I felt so utterly forsaken and alone as I now did, but after a few moments of exhaustive grief I rose, crossed the room, and, sitting down on a pile of cushions in front of the fire, I looked aimlessly into the leaping flames.

My years of wedded life, and such a life, had left their mark upon me, and I greatly dreaded the hour when my courage would forsake me, at last and for good and all. Pride had hitherto come to my aid, but, like metal slowly but deeply bitten into by a powerful acid, that also, I feared, would soon give way and leave me without strength to endure.

The even ticking of the clock jarred on my nerves, and the perfume of a basketful of strongly scented exotics on a table near by made me faint and ill.

*   *   *   *   *   *   *

When I woke up from a troubled sleep some hours later it was snowing heavily. Snow lay on all the streets, and the broad river was freezing fast. There was to be that night a gala representation at the grand opera in honor of some foreign royalties, and, moreover, it was the day of the bear-hunt.

I lay drowsily on my pillows, my eyes lingering with a sense of pleasure on the objects which surrounded me. My bedroom was of my own designing, and I was very proud of it, for I considered it to be a great success. The walls and ceiling were covered with a heavy, dead white silken stuff, embroidered with garlands of violets and heather; above the alabaster mantel-piece hung a large mirror framed by a *ronde* of cupids holding up a drapery. The dressing-table, covered with point-lace over pale violet velvet, was littered with platinum-stoppered bottles and platinum-backed brushes studded with amethysts. A thick white carpet covered the floor, and huge white bear-skins were scattered around. Upon one of them my faithful Ulmer dog lay at full length in possession—monarch of all he surveyed. On the tables and cabinets there was a profusion of flowers in iridescent vases and bowls, and through the open doors of the room beyond a sweet smell of violets was wafted in, proceeding from the swimming-bath, which was always in readiness for me. My maid moved noiselessly about, drawing back the curtains, so that from my low bed I could catch glimpses of the plants in the winter-garden. Without it was a dark, bleak winter's day, but within it was as warm as summer, and mellow with soft color.

I stretched my arms above my head and yawned slightly.

"Johanna," I said to my Abigail, "I do wish I was not obliged to get up; there's something unpleasant in the air to-day."

The woman looked up with a slightly surprised expression on her good-natured face. I knew she had often wondered at the comparative patience with which I bore my husband's neglect and cruelty. Therefore she, who was devoted to me, hated him, and would have heartily rejoiced in any misadventure that might have befallen him.

Her glance made me smile, and, having partly recovered my usual mental elasticity, I shook myself together and performed my toilet with unusual speed.

After donning a fur-lined shooting-suit I swallowed a hasty breakfast and drove to the station where the general rendezvous had been appointed by the Emperor's *grand veneur* to join the hunting-party.

Before noon we reached the thickly wooded, high hills where many great brown bears, made ferocious by the severity of the weather, had their lairs. The hunters were scattered under the deep shadows of the pines, cedars, and firs; the day was still and intensely cold, with no gleam of sunshine. A promise of more snow lay hidden in the leaden-hued clouds, a true sportsman's day, in fact. Followed at some distance by my husband and by Count Paul, I advanced silently, waiting and reserving my fire for any large beasts the *Yägers* might start and drive towards us from the heights above. We were speedily joined by the head huntsman, who whispered to Karl that he would post me at the most favorable spot, and finally left me under the dusky half-light made by the snow-covered boughs.

It was the beginning of the winter, just before the

325

bears commence to hibernate, and when, on the look-out for a last good feed, they are especially eager for their quarry.

Karl, Count Paul, and I paused at a place where four narrow paths met, waiting and watching in absolute silence.

We had been standing almost immovable for some time, when down one of the dark drives, above which the heavy branches met like a black canopy, there came rolling and swinging towards us a huge, shaggy beast, which probably would have gone by without scenting us, as we were under the wind, had not Count Paul, carried away by the irresistible impulse of all true children of Ishmael, fired twice at it as it reached a spot scarcely within gunshot.

Neither bullet had entered a vital part, and the animal, rendered frantic by pain, reared on its ungainly hind-legs and advanced towards him, bent on serious combat, as was testified by its great, grinning, foaming fangs.

Instantly I fired, and this time the shot struck nearer home, for, with a tremendous crash, the brute fell on the snow, with blood pouring from its jaws and writhing in agony.

With a singularly cruel light shining in his eyes, and hunting-knife in hand, Count Paul ran towards the prostrate animal.

"Take care!" yelled Karl. "It is dangerous to touch a wounded bear."

But Paul heeded not the words. He stooped to plunge his broad blade into the bear's heart. At that moment the dying brute gathered all its oozing strength together, and, leaping upon him, dashed him to the ground, mauling him terribly with tooth and claw. In a second both Karl and I had sprung towards the struggling mass formed by the hunter and the hunted, and the bear received his *coup de grâce*. Then, with much difficulty, we disengaged the young Count's tall form from beneath the huge carcass of his dead enemy, and laid him down gently upon some fallen pine-needles which formed a kind of natural couch on the side of the path. The wretched lad was deluged with blood, and his face had assumed a grayish pallor which made him look like a corpse.

"He is dead!" murmured Karl, shudderingly.

"Nonsense!" I retorted, hastily, and, leaning over the wounded man, I quickly cut away his shooting-jacket, his fur waistcoat, and soft silk shirt, stripping him to the waist in order to judge how serious were his injuries.

They were both numerous and severe, and I realized at once that if we did not obtain assistance without delay his chances of recovery were indeed slender. While I was trying to stanch the blood as best I could with my handkerchief and begging my husband to run for help, Count Paul's eyes opened suddenly and fixed themselves with a vacant stare upon mine.

I placed my hand upon his heart. Its beatings were weak and irregular, and an intensely cold wind which had arisen was turning his bare body to ice.

All was still around us, with that awful and impressive stillness of the great woods. Karl had run off swiftly for help, and nothing was in sight save the gigantic dead bear, which lay on the blood-soaked snow.

If aid did not come in a few short moments, the labored breathing would stop, and nothing could avert the end. I shuddered and sank on one knee beside Paul.

Soon the wintry day would come to a close, leaving a dusky, sultry gloom to brood over the loss of this strong young life. I was overcome by a vague and sudden

327

awe, for the large, dark eyes of the dying man had softened with a pity that did not seem to be caused by his own terrible plight.

"Forgive—the share—which I have had—in your—your unhappiness—" he gasped. The dark-red blood, slowly welling out and staining the bluish snow, formed a little pool where I knelt, in spite of the temporary dressing which I had improvised by tearing Paul's shirt into strips. My short fur coat, thrown over him to protect him a little from the biting wind, was turned in places to the same ghastly hue.

"Hush!" I murmured. "I know, and I forgive—for your sin was chiefly one of heedless short-sightedness, and without premeditation. I forgive you fully, all that has already passed—all that may yet be to come."

A wan smile of something like derision hovered about his ashen lips. "Give me your hand," he whispered. "It is getting dark here—dark forever—" He gazed upward and looked at the dim green boughs above us with a wild, delirious, appealing pain, and the white, drawn mouth moved in a gasping prayer. One last breath shivered like a deep-drawn sigh through his entire frame, a convulsive shudder shook the rigid limbs, although life seemed still to flicker faintly, as though loath to leave forever this handsome being in the strength of his youth—and then he died.

When, a little later, the huntsmen who had been beating the woods above arrived upon the scene, led by Karl, they found the Count stretched dead upon the pine-needle-strewn snow. Standing erect before them, though I was trembling from head to foot with cold and emotion, I said, in a hoarse voice, which sounded to me as if it were not my own:

"You have come too late to save him!"

CHAPTER XVIII

"Frisch auf, frisch auf mit raschem Flug!
Frei vor dir liegt die Welt;
Wie auch des Feindes List und Trug
Uns rings umgattert helt!"

Two days later I met Fred at a dinner-party given by Archduchess M. At eight o'clock I went up the stairs of the archducal palace, thinking as I went that really life was not worth living. I was sad and tired, and still much shaken by the incidents attending Count Paul's death. As I entered the anteroom and laid aside my furs, the Flemish tapestries which hung over the door leading to the inner apartments were pushed aside and the Archduchess advanced to meet me. She was clad in sweeping black laces, with a collar of rubies at her throat, and her slender figure looked wonderfully attractive under the brilliant light of the chandelier, while a smile of genuine welcome displayed her dazzlingly white teeth.

"How good you are to come in spite of this fearful weather," she exclaimed, leading me into an adjoining salon, and drawing me down on a low ottoman in front of the blazing hearth. "Warm yourself, my dear; you must be nearly frozen. Where is your husband? Is he not coming?"

"I suppose he will be here soon," I answered, lightly. "I have not seen him to-day."

At that moment my host came in somewhat precipitately, and looked about him as if he feared to find the room already full of people.

329

"Always late, you incorrigible man!" exclaimed the Archduchess, playfully, shaking her finger at her husband. He was about to reply when Nicky E. was announced. The other guests soon arrived in rapid succession. They were Archduke A., the English ambassador, Prince G., Lord P., and, lastly, my husband and Fred, who had met him at the door.

The dinner was quiet and unpretentious, though the cooking was remarkable. Our hosts were both *gourmets*, and the wines were perfect. A wealth of tea-roses and lilies-of-the-valley, arranged in low Labrador *jardinières*, adorned the table, where egg-shell china, *mousseline* glasses, and pyramids of superb fruit were tastefully grouped.

I did not speak to Fred after the first words of greeting, but several times our eyes met. Indeed, I said little to anybody, and, as often my moods were very silent, this attitude of mine attracted no remark. The conversation began by a general complaint about the continued severity of the temperature.

"If only we could get away before the beginning of the *Fasching*," said the Archduchess; "there is nothing I would enjoy more than to run down to Nice or Cannes. How very nice it would be if we could make up a party and all go there together for a fortnight or so! Don't you think it is a good idea, and would you not like it?" she added, turning to me.

"Very much indeed," I said, quietly, and without enthusiasm, "were it not that I am starting for Petersburg in a few days to spend a week there. Then I go on to Brittany, where my mother has been royally pleased to invite me."

There was a general murmur of regret around the table, every one being, or appearing to be, heartily sorry to hear so lamentable a piece of news. Karl coolly stared at me, and said:

"This is a sudden decision."

"Yes," I replied, decisively, "it is; I only made up my mind on the subject lately."

"I do not approve of your travelling alone with your servants," continued Karl, perversely; "you had better postpone this trip, or ask Fred, there, who I know intends starting for Berlin soon, to accompany you at least to the frontier."

"I am afraid that, however happy it would make me to accept so tempting an offer," retorted Fred, "I will be unable to do so, as I am called to England on important business."

"Fie! how ungallant you are!" laughed the Archduchess, flashing a look from her bright eyes upon him.

"Not at all, *Kaiserliche Hoheit;* please don't be so uncharitable. My denial is my misfortune, not my choice."

Karl smiled a curious, half-mocking smile, and the subject was dropped for the time being, thanks to Fred's *présence d'esprit.*

Dinner over, we sauntered into one of the prettiest salons of the palace, called the Turkish room. Delightfully comfortable couches ran along three sides of this charming *buen-retiro,* and on the walls hung some singularly fine specimens of Oriental arms. The Archduchess, throwing herself on a pile of cushions, opened a small cigarette-box and expressed a hope that everybody would smoke there, instead of running away to the smoking-room.

I lit a Russian cigarette and turned to speak to Prince G., who was standing near me.

"Would it very greatly displease you," he whispered, "if I were to express my admiration for your exquisite

331

symphony in yellow?" (I was wearing a lemon-hued gauze gown, bordered with natural yellow jessamine and some "*canary*" diamonds.)

"No; I would merely thank you in the name of my tailor," I answered, with a smile. "I cannot accept a compliment which he alone deserves."

"Now you are wrong for once, my dear; all depends on the way a toilette is worn. Many women spend fortunes at the immortal Worth's, for instance, but that does not prevent them from looking often more or less like scarecrows."

"You are very severe. Some women cannot answer for a want of taste probably inherent to their nature. Worth, if he clothes them, is much more to blame in this matter than they are. He is always a little *outré*, and in my opinion his style best suits actresses and other creatures of the same kind."

"Actresses and other creatures of the same kind!" laughed the Prince. "That was well said; it is what I call an excellent definition as regards the *Napoléon de la couture*. Truly, Muzzi, you possess considerable ability for presenting our most cherished heroes' little weaknesses to the public in a very brilliant but exceedingly uncharitable way."

"Never was such a compliment paid to my powers of discrimination, although your criticism is a little harsh in what regards the weakness and lowliness of my spirit," I laughed, and was about to make a further remark, when the Prince hastily rose, murmuring under his breath: "Goodness, here comes your dear husband; excuse me, Muzzi, but to-night, somehow or other, he is a trifle too much for me."

So funny was the expression of terror depicted on the great statesman's face that I could hardly control my features as I saw him literally scuttle away and seek refuge behind a heavy table covered with books and albums at the other end of the room. Karl, whose spirits were evidently depressed, bore down upon me, and took the place vacated by my old friend. He threw one knee irritably over the other, leaned back on the cushions of the divan, and said, shortly:

"Well, what new freak is this about going to Russia? Were you discussing your projects with G.? I saw him laughing and flirting to his heart's content, the old sinner! He always pounces on the choicest morsel or the best-looking woman, and in his idiotic and senile way makes violent love to you."

"Nothing of the kind, I assure you," I replied, much amused. "The Prince knows too well what he owes you to flirt with me."

"Tut, tut! I am not quite so blind as you may think; indeed, my eyes are very wide open. That old *coureur* is trying to pump state secrets out of you under cover of his antiquated devotion. You need not think from what I am saying, however, that I am jealous, for it is not G.'s admiration I grudge you; no, indeed, only please beware of him. You are singularly clever and wide awake, and a power in political circles as well as in others, but I want you to understand that I infinitely dislike your turning your attentions to such matters."

"Really," I said, coldly; "may I inquire to what I am indebted for so flattering and sudden an interest on your part?"

"Certainly you treat all I tell you with a silent contempt which is very galling, but I have a right to question you if I please. Why, then, do you confide in the Prince, make such a fuss about him, and why, especially, are you going to Russia?"

"Your curiosity in the matter is very gratifying to me," I interrupted, somewhat impatiently, for I could see now what Karl was driving at, and I was beginning to be annoyed.

"Wait a minute; I'm not through," continued my irrepressible spouse. "Do you know what exasperates me about you? You keep your own counsel too well, and justify too completely your nickname of '*The Icicle.*'"

"Thank you so much; I take this as a great compliment, do you know?" I said, laughingly, for my vexation was overruled by a keen sense of the unconscious humor of this speech.

"Don't mention it. That doesn't mean that I may not be brought round to a better understanding of your extraordinarily complex nature if you will do me the honor of explaining some things to me."

"You overwhelm me, indeed," I said, somewhat bitterly. "Are you really dense to the point, my dear Karl, to imagine that I am not thoroughly aware of your reasons for desiring to prevent my trip to Petersburg? You object to my turning my attentions to political questions, as you say, but I would annoy you less if my timely interference in certain directions did not coincide with the doings of a high and mighty lady—whom we will forbear from mentioning by name—but who basks in the light of your protection, and enjoys your help and sympathy. My counter-mines have not the fortune of your approval. *C'est dommage.* Pity, too, that I should know so much, and that G., who has been my friend, and, after a fashion, my mentor since I was a child, should be the wonderfully keen-sighted man he is, instead of the senile imbecile you are trying to make him out to be."

Karl winced. This was a tender subject I had touched upon, for the favorite of the moment had, I happened to know, lofty ambitions, and was using my lord as a mere cat's-paw, which was more than I cared to countenance. His countless infidelities were of no importance to me, but I was afraid to see him compromise himself, politically speaking, while in the hands of so dangerous an *intriguante*. I considered rightly that the honor of his name, which was mine as well, and the safety of his country, which I loved as my own, must not be endangered by this cold-blooded, designing woman and the insanely vain, weak-minded man whom she fooled, so I felt obliged to protect him in sheer self-defence from his overwhelming *suffisance* and wholly silly infatuation.

"I am unable to comprehend your allusion," he said, wrathfully, biting his mustache and moving his admirably shod foot nervously. "You are very mysterious to-night. Perhaps your flirtation with handsome Fred is making you melodramatic."

"My good friend," I replied, calmly, "I am afraid that your dulness is becoming chronic. I will not stoop to refute your delicate allusion to Fred, although it might give me a chance of giving you some neat little hints, not only about the eminently shrewd person who remains nameless between you and me, but also about Mademoiselle Bécat, the delicious soubrette who serves you as a screen to shelter the stainless virtue of that very person. It is not my intention to interfere with your—love affairs; they are quite outside my province, thanks be to a merciful Providence, but I am glad to have the chance of warning you that you are just now treading on very thin ice. There is a husband not far from here who resents your—reverence for his wife, and, singularly enough, he is in many respects so much in sympathy with you that his jealousy extends to the delicious soubrette above mentioned. Poachers are liable to feel at times inclined to get rid of each other when they meet on the same ground. Beware!"

"You know a damned sight too much, madame. Your spies are well informed, but so are mine, and I repeat it, you love Fred!"

"Don't talk nonsense," I said, with a little laugh. "Such weapons as you are trying to use are very pointless and misdirected. I will end by thinking that you are purposely aggressive. At any rate, let us drop the subject for the present, for we are in danger of being mistaken for a pair of genuine turtle-doves if we get into the habit of secluding ourselves in corners like lovers."

He swore under his breath; but, without seemingly noticing this breach of good manners, I rose and left him to digest my oration as best he might. In my own mind, however, I cursed the fatuous and perilous conceit of the man whose wife I had the misfortune of being. As to Fred, I made up my mind instantly to let him know, without the possibility of a doubt, that his presence near me was causing comment. I dreaded to give him pain, for he was easily hurt, and I never put in question the depth of his affection, although he had never said a word about it to me. Women possess a fifth sense which makes it easy for them to detect such things a long while before the man himself is aware of his own feelings. Moreover, Fred's state of health was extremely precarious. Years before he had been consumptive, and although the lung trouble had disappeared, yet his sojourns in the far East as a diplomat had enfeebled his constitution, and he often looked pathetically frail, in spite of his tall stature and usually merry and cheerful mood.

Before taking leave of the Archduke and Archduchess I asked him to lunch with me on the morrow, and to drive afterwards to the Castle of S——, which was at that season deserted. There we could talk in peace while walking in the immense park and grounds. He gratefully accepted, and I left him and Karl talking most amicably together, apparently, having to go home to change my dress for a ball at the Turkish Embassy, where I had promised to put in an appearance.

At that very ball, by-the-bye, a peculiar incident occurred. Shortly after my arrival in the salons of the embassy, a tall and remarkably handsome Oriental made his entrance into the so-called Throne-room. Where had I seen this splendid specimen of manhood? —those great, dark-blue eyes, fringed with abnormally long lashes? that firmly chiselled chin? that beautifully curved mouth, shaded by a long, silky mustache? Suddenly I remembered my captor of the C—— Pass. On the impulse of the moment I started to my feet, and, much to the amazement of all onlookers, I rushed up to the hero of my adventure, and, extending both hands to him, I exclaimed:

"How happy I am to see you again!"

His extremely puzzled expression urged me to add, stupidly enough:

"Surely you cannot have forgotten me?"

"No, I have not," said he, while a distinct blush overspread his sunburned skin, "but you must remember, madame, that when I last saw you you were a little soldier, while now—" His sentence remained unfinished, much to my satisfaction. There was a slightly awkward pause, and then, pointing to the silken, pearl-embroidered belt which encircled his slim waist, he showed me my two little jewelled revolvers.

"I have worn them ever since," said he, softly.

    *   *   *   *   *   *   *

At two o'clock on the next afternoon Fred and I set off for our proposed drive in my brougham. The weather was fine, and we soon reached the imperial castle, which was completely deserted at this time of the year, as I have said already. There was not a cloud to veil the brightness of the sun, the broad beams of which slanted among the massive trunks of the leafless trees and fell like arrows of gold on the frozen turf. We walked silently through the park, where the ice-bound lake gleamed beautifully. We had hardly spoken a word during the drive, and our lunch had been both hurried and silent. Even now it seemed as if we were both afraid to break a spell by talking. We bent our steps towards a knoll where some deer stood looking at us from a distance, and stopped to admire the beautiful, shy creatures. And then our eyes met! Fred bent his tall figure towards me, and, taking my hand, pressed it to his lips. His self-possession was evidently forsaking him, and he looked as if the snow-covered ground and the sunny blue sky above were whirling around him

"My friend," I said, gently, "this is dangerous play. You must go away before it is too late." I paused! It was very hard for me to say what I knew I must tell him, and we stood for a moment in an uncomfortable silence.

"It is too late already, at least for me," he murmured at last, sadly, turning his head away.

Tears welled up in my eyes, and I stretched out both hands towards him with a gesture of entreaty.

"Will you promise me one thing?" I said, very softly.

"I promise you all things. What is this one?"

I looked unflinchingly at him with what courage I could muster.

"You love me. You need not say so—I know it. I am—you have certainly guessed it—occupying a difficult and a sometimes singularly painful position. Promise me, therefore, that you will not add to its' difficulties, and that you will go away, at least for a while, until the sky is clearer."

Twice his lips opened to speak without any sound coming from them. At last he said, brokenly, and with touching obedience and tenderness:

"My dearest and best, I will do as you wish. I will be what you would have me be—a friend, and a friend only, faithful until death, and devoted in all things to you and you alone whether I be far or near. But remember that if you need me I will come at your bidding, from wherever I may be."

I looked up at him through a mist of unshed tears, and said:

"Thank you; I know that I can trust you. It is safer and better for you to go now. I do not wish the breath of scandal to touch either you or me, or to furnish society with fuel for its ceaseless desire to condemn innocents. I am very, very fond of you, my dear boy, and it hurts me to send you away, and especially to give you pain; but you do understand, do you not, the motive which urges me to do so?"

"I do, I do; but it is hard, indeed, to see you leading this miserable life. How can I ever endure your pain? What need, what use is there for this sacrifice? You know that I shall keep my word to you, that I shall obey you in all things, but why should you not try to alleviate the miseries of your present position? My whole existence is yours, to use or throw away as you choose. But do not, for Heaven's sake, allow yourself to be insulted, to be trampled upon, as you do. Your marriage was an error, a cruel mistake. You are throwing away your every chance of happiness in this world for the sake of a guilty, thankless man, who finds his only pleasure in shame and in sin. Will you never insist upon your rights?"

339

"I know that I have every right to leave my husband if I cared to do so," I said, impatiently. "But I cannot countenance the scandal and shame of it all, not so much for my own sake, but for the sake of the name I once bore, and also for the sake of the one I bear now. Do not offend me by asking me to do what for years I have been eager to avoid. On the contrary, encourage me if you can to patience and to endurance, for thus you will serve me best."

He saw probably the conflict that was going on within me, and, taking my hand once more in his own, he exclaimed:

"Hear me, Muzzi. Had I seen you living a serene, though a loveless, life, I would never have spoken to you of my adoration for you; but I saw you outraged, injured, forsaken for rivals who are so base that to talk of them before you is to degrade you. Can you ask me to look on patiently, to remain mute? Remember how I love you, and think of my despair."

While he spoke we had been pacing up and down under the trees in the bright sunset glow. We had nearly reached the gates of the palace, where my horses were waiting. I stopped short, and, turning my face towards him, I said, resolutely:

"Listen, Fred. Once and for all, I tell you that I will not become the talk of Europe. I hate to pain you as I know that I am now doing, but although I am ready to put your happiness before my own in every other respect, I cannot tamper with what I consider to be the only honorable course I can adopt. What I am going to tell you may seem dictated by pride, if not by conceit and self-complacency, but, were I an ordinary woman, my brilliant life as a leader of fashion and a petted personage at court would be fully sufficient to satisfy me; were I less rigid in my ideas, in spite of my perpetual and misleading banter, I would doubtless have allowed myself to be entangled long ere this in some *affaire de coeur*, if only to fill up the void of my life. But I am not built that way; and, although I often turn in revolt against the injustice which I must confess has been done me, I will never swerve from the path I have laid out for myself, and I will pursue it, weary, alone, and unaided, without even so much as allowing myself to think of what might have been, were I made on different lines. I owe this to the memory of my father, and to my love, gratitude, and tenderness towards the Empress."

"My dear, my dear," he murmured, "I know that you are right, but how can I live out my life without you?"

"Am I then to accept this tenderness which you offer me, am I to fall to the level of other women who seek consolation in unlawful affections? No, a thousand times no! Anything is better than that! My present sufferings, at least, are not of my own making, and I feel that disgrace in my own eyes is the one thing I could never endure." I clasped my hands together until my rings cut into the flesh, praying from the bottom of my heart for strength to persuade, convince, and comfort this poor boy, whose ashen face and mournful eyes were to me a sort of unbearable reproach.

He noticed my agitation, and in a simple, manly way, which went to my heart, he drew my arm through his, and, resolutely walking towards the carriage, said, in a voice which trembled with emotion:

"God send that I am never again tempted to bring sorrow into your already overburdened life. Forgive me, dearest, for having spoken as I have done. The future is in better hands than mine, fortunately. Let matters stand as they are now for the present. I cannot help loving you as long as my life endures, but I can

341

help giving you additional anxiety and worry. I did not intend to leave you, although last night I pretended to have been recalled home with a view of stopping your husband's further teasing, but in two days from now I will go, and stay away, too, until you call me back. I am yours forever; of that rest assured."

I nodded. To save my life I could not have uttered a word, and I was glad that my servants and carriage were by this time near enough to make it impossible for me to answer.

That night there was a gala representation at the opera, and, *nolens volens*, I had to be present. When I entered my box at nine o'clock the house was hushed, the music thrilled through the stillness, and on the stage stood Faust and Marguerite. I sat down in my accustomed seat, and, leaning my cheek upon my hand, I fell into a fit of melancholy musing. I was very tired and sad, my temples throbbed, and my head swam. The dazzling light, the brilliant scene, had no charm for me. Near me was my husband in his brilliant, gold-laced uniform, but I was hardly conscious of his presence.

Many men entered my box, between the acts, but somehow I seemed to have lost all my usual elasticity, and conversation was an effort. Fred bowed low to me from his place in the box of the British ambassadress, but did not come near me.

The violins wailed softly, the atmosphere was scented with hot-house blooms, and the loveliest women in the world sat in their *loges*, displaying their beauty and their jewels. The glittering uniforms and the gorgeous costumes of the magnates made a blaze of color and magnificence not easily forgotten. But I was heedless of it all. I only thought as I watched Karl, with the light falling upon his sullen, dissatisfied face, of all the peace which might have been mine had he only been like Fred.

I forced such thoughts back fiercely and pulled myself together. It was, I thought, high time to cease bemoaning my lot, for I have always detested plaintive people. To shoulder one's burden, whether it be light or heavy, is the only thing for the brave to do, and I was sincerely ashamed of my momentary weakness.

> "You have heard the beat of the off-shore wind
>   And the thresh of the deep-sea rain,
> You have heard the song—how long, how long?—
>   Pull out on the trail again."

That is the size of it! "*Pull out on the trail again*" —and pull well!

I left the opera as soon as I could and drove straight home, for I wanted a little time in which to shoulder this increased burden of mine anew.

Karl, when handing me into my carriage, excused himself, with his customary courtliness when we were on parade, from accompanying me, as he had, so he said, an important appointment at one of his numerous clubs. I smiled, for I knew only too well what those pressing appointments meant.

I awoke next morning from a troubled and restless sleep with a bad headache. The sun had hardly risen, but I felt that a sharp gallop in the first crisp cold of the rising day would do me good, and half an hour later I was off and away, breathing in deep draughts the icy air, clear as crystal and invigorating beyond compare.

My horse, a thoroughbred of exceptional beauty of form, was mettlesome enough to occupy my entire attention, a welcome circumstance, and it was only when I got him beyond the central *allée* of the park and upon the turf that I had leisure to look about me. White frost was turning every blade of grass into a prismatic brilliancy exquisite to behold, and overhead the sky was of

343

a luminous blue, glazed with the gold and rose of sunrise, which dazzled and fascinated the eye. My spirits rose, and soon I even caught myself humming snatches of an old popular Breton *Gwerz*, which I used to sing when I was still light-hearted Pierrot.

> " Et ar mevel emez ann ti,
> Vit gout petra z——oa gand ar c'hi,
> Talc he Kement da randoni !"

(The slave has left the house to find out wherefore the dog continuously made a row), I muttered. The harsh syllables rolled off my tongue mechanically, and then I laughed outright, for my own slave, who took the form of a severely accoutred English groom, as dignified and correct as a diplomat, was precisely engaged in discovering what my dear old dog Czar, the pride of my soul, was barking at so furiously in a dense thicket. The turmoil turned out to be caused by Czar's discovery of a large-sized hedgehog benumbed by the cold, whose mysterious and dangerously cuirassed personality exasperated the gigantic silver-coated Dane. At last the magnificent creature was persuaded to relinquish his awkward prey, and came bounding towards me joyfully, although a curious uncertainty in the faithful eyes seemed to denote anxiety concerning the fashion in which I would take his escapade. Dear, majestic Czar, an imperial dog, indeed, and an imperial gift, presented to me when yet quite a puppy by his august namesake, the Emperor of All the Russias, and who was my constant companion day and night, a loyal, strong, reliable comrade, upon whom I could always depend, come what may. I have always owned dogs, good and handsome, also faithful and true, but none did I ever possess who could in any way bear comparison to that one!

344

When I reached home I was feeling almost entirely myself again, and as I ascended the steps leading to the main hall I turned to call out to my groom that I would want the four bays put in the phaeton at eleven. To be out-of-doors seemed to be the most potent remedy for my troubles, and a double dose of this agreeable tonic appeared none too much to help settle my nerves. Just as I was about to walk up-stairs, Karl's aide-de-camp came running down, and, at the sight of me, stood stock-still, pale to the lips and trembling from head to foot.

With instantaneous and almost supernatural penetration I divined what had happened when his eyes met mine.

"What is it?" I whispered, grasping his gold-laced sleeve. "Has Karl been wounded?"

The young man hesitated. His lips were as white as his face. He answered hoarsely, almost unintelligibly:

"There was a quarrel at the club last night—they fought this morning—he is—dying."

"Here?" I queried, horror-stricken.

He nodded, and pointed to the upper hall, where the steps of several men were distinctly audible. "The doctors!" he said, shuddering.

I waited for no more, but swiftly ran to my husband's apartments. On the broad, low bed lay Karl, surrounded by several physicians, who made way for me at once.

The sword of his adversary had entered his left side and passed out through the lung beneath the shoulder-blade. One look sufficed to show me that he was as good as dead already. Indeed, it seemed almost incredible that they should have been able to transport him to his home.

"Send for a priest," I said, quickly, to the young aide-de-camp, who had followed me and was still trembling like an aspen-leaf. Then I knelt on the floor and took Karl's nerveless hand in mine.

For one moment he opened his eyes, and his lips moved.

"You will forgive," he muttered. "Too late; it is too late, too late!" he repeated, breathlessly, with a sort of shuddering, choking sigh, and with that sigh his soul passed away to meet its Maker.

What did I feel at that supreme moment? I could not myself have told, so conflicting were my emotions. Fortunately the dumb Breton obstinacy of my race made it possible for me to appear outwardly calm and to retain my self-control, so that none of those present were able to know whether I was broken-hearted or totally indifferent. All the world knew that he had died for the sake of another woman and under peculiarly unsavory circumstances, but good taste and good breeding forbade me to let it be known that I was aware of this.

Immediately after the pompous and gorgeous funeral I withdrew to an old castle in the mountains, which was my own property, having been left to me by my godfather two years before. There I remained alone with my household and my own thoughts, refusing to see anybody.

CHAPTER XIX

" The storm is stilled, the ocean's face
    Is smooth to see, and calm once more;
The rising moon's bright rosy beam
    Its placid surface glideth o'er.

" The minstrel's fresh green laurel wreath
    Floats on the water buoyantly,
The regal circlet of the queen
    Lies at the bottom of the sea !''

MY mother kindly suggested that I should come to Brittany, or else let her join me in my mountain fastness. It would, so she argued, look more seemly were she to do so. I respectfully pointed out to her that I did not care a jot about what looked seemly, and that I needed a little time to pull myself together in solitude. I did not add that the absolute freedom from a union which I had loathed was not to be tampered with just then. Nobody save the Empress had ever heard a word of complaint from me during the five years of my married life, and I was far from inclined to indulge in *postmortem* revelations about a man who could offend no more. It was impossible for any one to discover whether I was relieved or sorry, for there were none there to watch me, Heaven be praised! I never uttered a syllable nor wrote a word which could enlighten my friends, or even my attendants, as to the state of my feelings. The only person who sent me no message of condolence throughout the length and breadth of Europe was Fred, and I understood his silence, which was in keeping with the loyalty and truthfulness of his whole attitude,

Why should he condole with me? Why, indeed? And how could he communicate with me without doing so? His was the quintessence of eloquent silence, indeed, and I appreciated it.

This wonderful peace, so soothing and so complete, was not destined, however, to last. I could not forever seclude myself from the world, and after three long, blissful months of contemplative existence I left my poetical retreat, much to my regret, called away by a passing indisposition of my mother, which she purposely magnified with a view of forcing me out of my voluntary imprisonment.

I started off at noon and travelled straight to Paris. I had gloomy forebodings, and felt for some reason or other intensely miserable. It was late when I reached the railway station. The express was on the point of departure, and I hurriedly boarded my special car. Then I stood motionless, looking out upon the little woodland terminus. Soon the train rushed out of the station through the heavy, gray darkness; the lamp swinging above me shone upon my face, on which I knew well that there must surely be a piteous expression of sorrow. Suddenly I threw myself on my knees beside the cloth-covered seat of the compartment, and, burying my head in the cushions, I sobbed convulsively for a few moments. There was no sound but that caused by the oscillating of the train swinging at headlong speed over its iron sleepers. The weather was cold. I rose feeling better for those tears—an unusual luxury with me—and, wrapping my cloak around me, I sat motionless, thinking of the past and of the future very mournfully.

Every time when the train stopped, my courier and confidential servant, Ferdinand, came to inquire if I wanted anything, and the solicitude of this old soldier,

" MILADI !"

whom I could trust blindly, was very welcome. Ferdinand was intensely devoted to me, in whose service he had been ever since my marriage. Many were the little kindnesses I had been able to show him, and, strange to state, he was not ungrateful. He often said himself that there was nothing that he would not do for my sake. He was then a man of forty-five, who, with his smooth-shaved countenance and singularly refined manner, had nothing smacking of the flunkey about him.

I remained but a short time in Paris, the brilliant city which has long since become distasteful to people like myself who are monarchial to the backbone. Princess Pauline M. had asked me to spend a few weeks at her delightful castle of P—— *en petit comité*, and I gratefully accepted the invitation. Life at P—— was charming. Everybody enjoyed perfect freedom, for neither the Prince nor the Princess considered it a duty to bore themselves and their guests by forcing upon them a prearranged succession of so-called amusements in a regular line of order. The only cast-iron rule was the demand made upon all guests to appear at meal-times with truly military punctuality. An early breakfast, consisting of fragrant chocolate and toast, was generally sent to one's bedside, but at the eleven-o'clock *déjeûner à la fourchette* everybody was expected to be present, and the dinner at eight found us all assembled under the hand-coffered and gorgeously painted ceiling of the banqueting-hall.

Princess Pauline, when in the country, rose with the lark. She was one of those women who could dance all night and then stroll out into the garden to watch the awakening of day as though she had retired at eight on the previous evening. She used to tell us that she delighted in these early rambles, for, as she put it, in her quaint manner of speech, "Nature looks as if God washed it clean every morning, and at noon it is already quite crumpled-up by contact with humanity." Beneath her apparent *insouciance* there was a great deal of feeling and even of poetical instinct in the Princess's composition; and, although this may appear paradoxical on her part, I have heard this *mondaine à outrance* bitterly complain of the conventionality of society, and regret her being forced to endure a life made up of everlasting spectacles, excitements, and revelry, instead of being allowed to "plant her cabbages in peace." The "*cabbages*" of the Princess, I may add, were an unparalleled collection of orchids, for which she entertained an inordinate passion.

In spite of all that may have been said to the contrary, the Prince and Princess lived together on excellent terms. When he married his wife—whose hare-brained follies had been the talk of all Europe since she reached her teens—Prince Richard knew that he was not taking to himself a lackadaisical maiden who would "sit and spin the silken threads of matrimonial love forever," or whom marriage would turn into an easy-going *Hausfrau*. With praiseworthy tact the husband made every allowance for his consort's somewhat trying superabundance of vitality. She has been accused of many peculiar eccentricities, but "one lends to the rich," and in her case there has been much more smoke than fire. Anyhow, the world liked her none the less for all that, and, moreover, *grande dame* to the tips of her almond-shaped finger-nails as she was, she managed to render acceptable deeds and words which from any other woman would have seemed reprehensible, as mere peccadilloes. I never met any one else who possessed in so eminent a degree what the French call *du charme et de la séduction*. Always in a good humor, her voice shrill and sweet like a silver whistle, her large black eyes sparkling with mirth and malice, there was about her a contagion of wit and cheerfulness which no one could resist.

On one subject more than on any other did the princely *ménage* agree, and that was in so far as the improvement of the peasants living on their estates was concerned. They founded schools for children, unlike any other institutions of the kind, in which only the rudiments of education were imparted to the little ones. Very autocratic, and an aristocrat to the core, Pauline asserted that elaborate education of the lower classes begot a multitude of theorists, and was the root of nihilism, anarchy, socialism, and revolution.

A consummate musician, Prince Richard spent long hours at the piano, playing with a perfection of skill only equalled by the exquisite tenderness of his interpretation. I have heard Liszt many a time summoning the spirit of music to his masterly call in the concert-room of P—— and elsewhere, but even this grand and inimitable artist often declared that none could succeed in touching one's sense of harmony as did the Prince when he dreamily wandered over the keys of his perfect Pleyel, touching them lightly and softly while evoking memories of every land and epoch in a quaint succession of Magyar czárdàs, German reveries, French berçeuses, Spanish fandangos, voluptuous Viennese waltzes, and weird songs from the Ukraine.

Every year during the hunting season, royal and imperial guests assembled at P——, and the whole place became filled with animated and brilliant life. Great hunting-parties made the country ring for miles around with the sound of horn and rifle; the *bijou* theatre echoed every night with the laughter aroused by the performances of Princess Pauline, one of the most peerless actresses in the amateur world, and the ballroom was the scene of superb cotillions.

Passionately fond of all kinds of sports, the Prince and Princess shot, rode, swam, and even played billiards together, like two good comrades who thoroughly enjoyed each other's company. Although the abnormal intellectual powers and numerous accomplishments of his wife seemed sometimes to oppress the Prince with a vague sense of inferiority, yet in his humble measurement of himself he was ever ready to yield to what he called her *"superior comprehension of life."* And thus everything went as merrily as marriage bells with them.

Their kindness to me during this, my last, visit to them was intelligent, unobtrusive, complete. They forbore from filling their house with many people, but selected a few choice spirits, among whom was Prince Alex S., the handsomest youth in our army, and who, according to Pauline, was fated to become my second husband.

I cannot conceal the fact that I was fond of Alex, and I would have been blind indeed had I neglected to see that this fondness was more than mutual. He was then about twenty-five years old, with delicate, exquisitely modelled features, great sapphire-blue eyes fringed with long, curly lashes, a slight blond mustache, just a couple of shades lighter than his wavy, short-cropped hair, and an expression at once gentle and cold. His height was great, and his bearing not only that of a soldier, but of a typical *grand seigneur*. His life was one of the most envied in Europe, for he possessed practically limitless wealth to uphold one of the oldest and most glorious names in the universe.

We had been friends ever since my marriage, and I, with my incorrigibly analytical mind, could perfectly

352

appraise his feelings. He was not in love with me; he loved me I was not quite so sure, however, of what I myself felt for him; admiration in a way, sympathy, comradeship, and that fondness which I have mentioned just now, but which was quite untinged with any tenderer sentiment. He was evidently the magnetized, not the magnetizer. The ice of my temperament, which dated from my wedding-day, was not of a kind to melt under even the most volcanic of atmospheres. Love to me was indeed an absolutely empty word, and I often used to hum to myself the ironical lines which sound so melodious and soft as they have been written:

"Dari mana datang linta?
Dari gounoung touroung di kali.
Dari mana datang tchinta?
Dari mata touroung di ati. . . ."

(Whence cometh the leech?
From the mountain it descends to the river.
Whence cometh love?
From the eyes it descends to the heart. . . .)

It had never descended to my heart, although my eyes had certainly rested on many an attractive countenance, but I had until then invariably succeeded in changing my admirers into the friends I wanted them to be, and I certainly gave no thought to a second marriage at present.

"You believe neither in love nor in sorrow," Alex said one day, abruptly, to me, à propos de rien.

"Why should you say so, Alex?" I replied, somewhat nettled. "You know that I have reason to be aware of the fact that sorrow exists."

"And what about love?" he continued.

"How stupid, how intensely stupid you are, my poor boy! What do you mean by putting such ill-timed questions to me?" I exclaimed, thoroughly provoked.

z   353

"I mean this, Muzzi. You cannot make any pretence of regretting Karl. I knew him, and I know you, so I may make bold to state that all conventionality can be laid aside even at this early hour between us. My words are previous, that is true, but I love you too dearly to run the chance of losing you, for I fear that there is somebody else looming up on your horizon. I have been wretchedly unhappy about you, my snow-flower; I thought that I had conquered my folly, but now the gods have played into my hands, and I would be ten times a fool to leave anything to chance. Will you marry me, Muzzi, as soon as your official period of mourning comes to an end?"

He spoke with animation. His cheeks were slightly flushed. His eyes were full of light, and there was a restrained masterfulness about him to which I was not accustomed.

"Permit me to question your taste—which is invariably so perfect—in speaking as you do," I said, coldly. "Your tirade reminds me of the celebrated crumpled rose-leaf. You are, my dear boy, crying for the moon, like any other spoiled child, and trying to make me mistake you for a martyr, which you emphatically are not. Domitian and the cabbage-garden all over again. You are witty when you care to be so, but if you are going to become *élégiaque*, it will not suit your style."

"I regret, Muzzi, that you should ridicule me in this way," he retorted, much annoyed. "Men, I think, are more romantic than women. Your merciless little laugh often haunts me, I assure you; it conceals so much that I would give my life to read. I have been dreaming of awakening you from the torpor in which you have allowed your heart to fall. You belong to the epoch which is known as *le temps où la Reine*

Berthe filait, and yet you pretend to be as indifferent to every human emotion as if you were made of stone."

"You are talking great nonsense, Alex," I replied; "and as to awakening my heart, as you so graciously put it—*excusez du peu, mon ami!*—it would take pity, for instance, or some other such soul-stirring sensation, to accomplish so dark a deed. Now, conscientiously, my good fellow, are you an object for pity, or for sympathy even, *dites la vérité?*"

"Excess always carries its own retribution, Muzzi. You are overdoing your part. I cannot understand you, especially lately."

I walked through one of the doorways into the open air, anxious to put an end to this conversation, which by no means pleased me.

"Don't be sententious," I called back to him over my shoulder. "*C'est agaçant;* give me time to think your proposal over. Truly, your haste is indecent."

"That is a very shocking speech," he said, wrathfully, marching after me on to the greensward.

"Pray excuse me, Alex, dear; you are paved with good intentions, but I cannot just now stay to hear you explain them to me. The dinner-bell will ring in half an hour, and, in spite of my '*crapy*' condition, I cannot appear before our hosts in the costume I wear now."

His face grew cold. A deep displeasure darkened his eyes. He drew back, and then stood stock-still, watching me. Remorse immediately overcame me, and swiftly I turned and came close to him.

"My dear old chap," I said, repentantly; "do not take my words amiss. I am awfully fond of you, dear, but you know that I cannot make up my mind about so grave a question on the spur of the moment. We have always been such friends, please do not disturb

355

what exists that is really beautiful between us by your rashness."

"But I love you, Muzzi," he pleaded, softened, and looking very boyish and earnest.

"Of course you do, you goose! Where is the harm? I am not scolding you for that, am I? But do not be melodramatic : it is so absurd and so tiresome."

"All right," he said, with an effort. "I'll wait, dear girl. But still I wish you would give me your word; I know that you will keep it."

I shrugged my shoulders and fairly ran across the lawn to the conservatories, where I gathered some gardenias, intending to fasten them in my dinner-dress of black gauze.

That very night, as we sat in the music-room listening to some of Prince Richard's exquisite melodies, a letter brought by special messenger was handed to me. It was from Fred—a long, rambling, rather involved epistle, incomprehensible, indeed, excepting to the initiated. I read between the lines and found out that he had been very ill, that he was lonely, wretched, miserable! Some blundering ass of a doctor—I beg his honorable pardon, for he was, indeed, a great and celebrated specialist—had bluntly told him that he could not live six months, and the poor fellow had, this being given, refrained from uttering a single word of love or tenderness, although his feelings oozed through every sentence of his curious epistolary effusion. My eyes grew moist as I read this unconscious appeal, and Alex, who was sitting within a couple of feet of me, bent suddenly forward and asked, irritably :

"What is the matter now, Muzzi? Any bad news? You are as pale as a ghost. Who has been bothering you?"

"Nobody, my dear," I replied, with some impatience.

356

"If you are so curious, I may tell you that this letter is merely from a friend of mine who is seriously ill."

"Oh, indeed!" he exclaimed. "A very dear friend, then, I presume?"

"Very," I said, shortly, nettled by his tone, and, rising from my chair, I swept out of the room. Jealousy is a feeling I despise. It lowers the object thereof as much as the person who inflicts it, and I never could tolerate it. Alex was, therefore, in disgrace, and I seized the first possible opportunity to bring my visit to a close, leaving him apparently very disconsolate, but deservedly so, in my humble opinion.

Upon my arrival in town I was requested by the Empress to precede her to the south of France, where she intended to spend a few weeks. While there I met Fred, lounging under the palm-trees, gazing with evidently incurable melancholy upon the thickets of high rose-laurel, the hedges of cactus and aloes, and the oily blue waves which are the greatest characteristic of this region, *de l'éternel printemps.*

He did not look, when we so unexpectedly met, as if "granted wishes were self-sown curses." His thin face lighted up extraordinarily, and he was so visibly enraptured that I felt deeply touched.

Admirable feminine logic! Enviable faculty of caring for persons in proportion to the need they have of one!

I do not know whether other women are like myself in this respect; the man who begs you to lean upon his strength and to take shelter under the almighty wings of his protection has never appealed to me! My life has been one long resistance to the insufferable conceit of the "*stronger sex*" with all its attending paraphernalia of superiority, and yet I hate a "new woman"—more than that, I despise those of my sisters who claim equality with their mankind. This seems to be an insolvable puzzle and paradox, and an aphorism as well, and so I must not linger over it. The tender, soft-hearted male being, who is manly with everybody but myself, is what I like and admire, because perchance a man's weakness, his tears even, his clinging love, are the subtlest of all flatteries when such feelings are displayed to me alone. Otherwise I would certainly call them contemptible. *Hercule filant aux pieds d'Omphale*—that's the billet, evidently, but Omphale must be myself, that goes without saying—*on est égoïste à ses heures!*

With the sea at our feet and the mountains at our back, we spun out a very pretty idyl during those golden days on the Côte d'Azur. He loved me. He was ill and helpless and reliant upon me, poor, dear old boy, and finally I promised to marry him. A quiet life for a little while is very wholesome, but very impractical. I lost sight of the fact that a tremendous commotion would be created by such a decision on my part. I did not realize that, when once we are of the world worldly, we cannot easily get rid of the world and of its bitterly uncharitable way of judging situations. I was serenely indifferent. Once I had married to please my mother, and once was enough, I fancied. That is just what I thought. Of late years I had always done what I chose, I had always been obeyed when I spoke, why should I not persevere?

I began to think seriously that the thing was feasible. The difference of race, of nationality, of religion, and others, were, I knew, tallish obstacles, but I relied on my influence and on my Breton stubbornness to get over them with flying colors. Alas! poor colors, how often they were made to dip before the storm!

There is something of the savage in all of us; at

times we get tired of the trumpery and folly of the world, and we deem it pleasant to lose it, for we are then especially conscious of its shallowness, of its sheer imbecilities, its cruelties, and its insincerity. I hate notoriety of all kinds, for it hurts my pride, and I look upon it with ineffable contempt and disdain, but notoriety is one of the finest products of our civilization, carried to a fine point, indeed, and is enviable to many. As Fred's wife I could once and for all *" plant my cabbages in peace "*— as Pauline would have said—of that I felt certain, which shows that one must never be sure of anything.

> " Les délicats sont malheureux ;
> Rien ne saurait les satisfaire."

Festina-lente, Pazienza ! The world can take its revenge, and does so, as a rule, pretty thoroughly upon those who at heart despise it, and who dare to show that they do. Ah! even now, I, who pride myself, unduly perhaps, on being somewhat of a stoic philosopher, turn pale and shiver with a vague and intangible terror when I think of all the misery we went through. Fortunately my will was iron to endure, therefore I trained myself to give no sign of distress, to show no inclination of yielding after the fight had begun, and the poor world, great spy though it be, how surely, how universally it can be chicaned! If the hidden canker ate in the heart of the rose, none were the wiser, nor dreamed that so many repeated blows had been felt through a well-tempered armor. Forced to watch the slow approaches of the pitiless flame, the prisoner chained to the stake finds joy in disregarding outwardly this gradual onward creeping, for to fool the world is a legitimate and delicious pastime when one's conscience is at rest and reproaches one nothing.

The first intimation of my resolve was met by a veritable hurricane of violent protest. Everybody made it his or her business to interfere, to entreat, to command, to intrigue, to attempt force even—which was the worst and most dangerous step which might have been taken, for it anchored me more firmly in my decision.

Morning, noon, and night, early and late, at all possible times and moments, I was attacked, implored, and threatened by turns. Nor was Fred spared, for his people were just as adverse to the whole thing as were mine. A religious warfare was the cover for many other causes of disagreement too long and too wearisome to describe. Fred's father stood my friend through it all. He was a trump, a bona-fide stand-by, and as fine a gentleman as ever drew breath. Poor dear, he went through his share of sorrow on our behalf, and we brought into his life a sense of stormier emotion than we cared to raise. He became passionately attached to me, and I to him; and every blow directed at me and which struck him maddened me with rage.

Here again I pause before the inadequacy of words, the impotency of such tools as pen and ink, to evoke before the mind of a reader the bitter-sweetness or sweet-bitterness of situations one has lived through, but is powerless to recount. The beautiful loyalty and steadfastness of Fred, the risks we ran, the dangers we marvellously escaped, the anguish we often felt, all these terrible sensations belong to the vast number of indescribable things. Fiction treats such chapters in a hero's or a heroine's life much better and much more ably than truth, for truth clips the wings of the would-be writer, and with a weary sigh the poor, troubled scribe allows a sense of the impossibility of such a task to weigh down pinions fluttering with a desire to soar. *Et voilà comme on écrit l'histoire.* Great sorrows, great sacrifices, great loves, great joys are best left to the imagination. So are great hatreds, for dissection suits them ill, and yet—

" Je suis si bien guérie de cette maladie,
  Que j'en doute parfois lorsque j'y veux songer ;
Et quand je pense aux lieux où j'ai risqué ma vie,
  J'y crois voir à ma place un visage étranger !
Muse, sois donc sans crainte, au souffle qui t'inspire,
  Nous pouvons sans péril tous deux nous confier
Il est doux de pleurer, il est doux de sourire
  Au souvenir des maux qu'on pourrait oublier."

CHAPTER XX AND LAST

"I landed on the shore, my sails I furled,
A dreadful tempest bravely I withstood;
Past Scylla and Charybdis dangers dread—
My brow did sweat.

"I yet have vineyards and far-reaching fields
Of golden grain, while love and liberty
Dwell in my house; and from my gracious God
Shall I ask more?"

Upon leaving the Côte d'Azur I went straight north and reached my home on a Monday, followed by Fred at two days' interval. At seven o'clock on the following Saturday I drove to the railway station in order to take the Paris express. It was not so cold as on the preceding days, although it was still snowing slightly, but the dark sky and slushy streets looked dismal, and deepened my depression. Notwithstanding the early hour and the inclemency of the weather, several of my intimate friends who had stuck to me through thick and thin came to the station to bid me good-bye, and, as my brougham stopped in front of the large terminus, Fred ran down the steps and offered me his arm to lead me towards my saloon carriage. It wanted but a few minutes of the hour of departure, and they were fully occupied by leave-takings and wishes for a speedy return.

I laughed and talked feverishly, shielding my eyes with a bunch of violets I carried, for I dreaded that they might tell their own tale. As I was about to enter the train, I approached Fred and extended my hand to him;

362

he raised it to his lips with a look of unutterable tenderness and said, in a low voice, "*Que Dieu vous garde et vous assiste.*"

I drew myself up, and there was a confident and trustful smile on my lips as I looked him full in the face. I felt that the corners of my mouth quivered a little, but I did not reply, and, turning to my courier, I gave him my instructions about our trip. I then took my place, the little knot of friends said their last God-speed, and the train began slowly to move upon its way. Once more I fixed my eyes upon Fred's pale, drawn face, with the same intention of cheering confidence. As I sank back in my seat the express passed out of the station, rolled on faster, and in a moment had left the dear city I loved so well far behind.

The snow lay deep on the country. The train rushed onward through pine forests, with their sombre masses of fir and Siberian arolla looking dusky in the grayness of the day. Everywhere there was frozen water, and in the dim distance the snowy ranges of the mountains were barely discernible through the mist.

For a long time I sat silently watching the blurred landscape, thinking of Fred and of the mysterious future I was going to enter upon for his sake. It was soothing to feel that I was his only care, and it was with rising hope that I gazed on the brightening panorama that met my vision on every side.

The track ran between two forest roadways, overshadowed by grand old trees; on the right a mighty torrent rushed through heavy bowlders, white with perpetual foam. Near the horizon there was the gray sheen of glaciers, glittering behind the naked branches of the denuded timber. Where any of it had been cleared, wide tracts of frozen heather and of broom stretched forth like patches of brown velvet, and as the train went swiftly onward I noticed here and there some abandoned woodman's hut, under the drooping boughs of the pines. The solemn stillness of winter had overtaken the little chattering mountain streams and confined them in their icy beds, which appeared now and again among the dead grasses like fine traceries of silver. ˙

The day wore on. When the sun began to sink behind the mountains the whole landscape was for a moment illuminated by a pink-and-golden light of exquisite brilliancy. Far behind, where my starting-point lay, a huge bank of black and threatening clouds had gathered, but ahead of the rushing train there was a sky of purest azure, in which the crescent of the new moon was beginning to show its silver sickle.

"This is a good omen," I thought, gazing at the strange contrast. "May my new life be as pure and bright as the picture which stretches now in front of me. Life cannot be unhappy for me with Fred," I said to myself, half aloud. "Soon I shall be his wife, and then all this struggle will be at an end."

Again I sat quite still, facing the grand amphitheatre of ice and snow that flashed in the sunset and glowed like molten gems. The wintry moon rose higher in the heavens. The descending night threw its shadowy veil over hill and dale, and in the far distance the lights of a great city began to glimmer. There the express stopped for half an hour, and then pursued its hurried flight through the increasing darkness and cold. Nestling in the soft furs of my couch, I dreamed the bright dreams of youth, oblivious of coming evil.

Twenty-four hours later I arrived, with my attendants, at the Hôtel Continental. The noise, the movement, the brilliantly lighted streets of Paris fatigued and wearied me. I stood at the window and thought again of Fred, who would in all probability reach the French capital almost immediately.

At noon I drove to my mother's residence. I had given no notice of my arrival, and was therefore not expected. My Lady Mother was alone when I was announced, and seemed very much astonished at my sudden advent. I told her the whole truth, without resorting to either subterfuge or reticence, and her anger was terrible. In her mind, a marriage with Fred was a hideous offence against all the rules of worldly wisdom which she fondly imagined I had by now assimilated, and she had not as yet taken my plans on the subject into serious consideration.

"I wonder how you dare come to me, your mother, with so absurd a proposal. All sense of the fitness of things must be dead within you when you venture to speak to me as you have just done. Has that man bewitched you? Is he your lover?" she exclaimed, wrathfully.

"You know that what you say is untrue, mother. Fred is not my lover, and you should think twice before you use such words to me."

"I know nothing of the kind, and I believe you to be capable of almost anything, after what you have had the inconceivable effrontery to tell me."

"Should I have come to you if I had fallen so low?"

"Perhaps. You are clever enough to have planned your visit to me in order to blind the eyes of society to your escapade."

"You think very ill of me, mother."

"I do. And now listen. You must choose between this man and me. If you persist in your resolution I will banish you forever from my heart and home. Good God! what can such a union do for you? Can it destroy the past? Why lose all that is worth having?

What you have just told me is known only to us both, to the Empress, and to one or two other persons. It must remain so. The world need never find out your error if you yourself do not become its informant by acquainting it of your insane idea with regard to so unbefitting a second marriage."

"Permit me to repeat that there has been no—error, and never will be," I interrupted, as gently as I could.

"I say that there is!" exclaimed my mother, violently. "With me the intention goes for the fact. But let us end this. Will you, or will you not, obey my commands? If you consent to write to-night to this wretched fellow, telling him that in accordance with your mother's wishes you will abandon all idea of marrying him, I will try and forget what has passed. Should you refuse to do so, I will consider myself entirely justified in closing my doors upon you. Speak now. What will you do?"

"Mother," I exclaimed, "I entreat you to think well before you act. Remember that my first marriage was entirely and solely your work. I was a guileless and innocent child, and knew not what I was doing. It is not for you to turn against me now if I care to marry an honest gentleman who loves and honors me. How can I, at your bidding, break my promise to him who trusts me, and all that for the sake of the world's opinion. You do not know what I have suffered during all the years of my wedded life with Karl, else you would not be so pitiless."

"Suffered! Why, you had, and still have, everything a woman can wish for—rank, position, youth, beauty, fortune; what more did you want?"

"Simply happiness, and a husband whom I could love and esteem instead of a *débauché* who was both cruel and faithless to me."

"If you were a Christian, you would know that a wife must bear with her husband's faults and charitably overlook his mistakes."

"Faults, mistakes!" I cried, bitterly. "Were you to say crimes, you would be nearer the point. He practised vices so low that I would not defile myself by even hinting at them. I implore you, mother, reconsider what you have said. Let me come and live with you till I have married Fred. Public opinion, which you fear so much, will then be satisfied about my choice, even if it be at first taken by surprise."

"Never!" she exclaimed, sternly. "Never will I consent to sanction your folly. If you persist in your purpose, you must do so on your own responsibility and at your own risk."

For a few seconds, which seemed hours to me, silence reigned supreme between us.

"Is this your last word, mother?" I said, finally.

"It is. Choose now the path you want to follow," she answered, with a cruel sneer.

"My choice is made, then," I replied, hotly. "I cannot change my mind for you, who love me so ill that you are ready to sacrifice my life once more for the sake of society and society's verdict. I will marry Fred—but remember one thing, if there is scandal it will be your doing, not mine. For with your help it might have been avoided. You are committing an unpardonable injustice. I have done no wrong, and I swear that I will do nothing that even you could blame. One day you will regret your harshness, but it will be too late."

She rose from her seat and stood erect, one hand resting on the carved work of her high oak chair. She looked cold, stately, and disdainful, with the sweeping folds of her black velvet dress falling to her feet like a queen's robes.

"You have made your choice. Now go!" she said, mercilessly.

Under that last and intolerable insult I staggered, then, mastering myself with a sudden effort, I bowed low, and without a word, without a look, I left my mother's presence, blindly groping my way along the stately corridors, hardly knowing whither I went, and left her house with a burning pain at my heart.

While this painful scene was going on at my mother's residence, Fred had arrived in Paris and sat waiting in a private salon at his hotel. The weary day dragged on its course, and still he remained without news. When night came on his anxiety grew unbearable, and when at last I arrived he was looking ghastly. I advanced towards him, throwing my furs from me as I moved, and said, in a sort of lifeless way:

"It is I—I have no one left but you in this world. I came to tell you this—and also that I kept my word to you in full."

Fred's face became paler yet, and the tears stood in his eyes.

"Muzzi, my poor little Muzzi," he whispered. Then he threw his arms about me and pillowed my head on his breast, adding softly: "What has happened, my dearest, to hurt you like this? What new pain has been laid upon you?"

"My mother has dismissed me from her house, like the meanest of her attendants," I answered, with a dry, choking sob. Then, springing from the shelter of his arms, I began to pace violently to and fro, my chest rising and falling with my labored breathing. In a few words I told him how I had been repulsed, how shamefully my confidence had been derided.

"Oh, Fred," I said, wringing my hands, "you did not know what you did or what you asked when you first told me of your love. Terrible obstacles will be thrown in our way; you cannot realize all that will be attempted when it is found out that my mother disowns me. She has warned me that she will turn my entire family against me, and if I claim my rights now I will be simply laughed at and cast away."

"Don't talk so, my dearest," interposed Fred, drawing me once more towards him. "What would life be to me without you?. Do not be faint-hearted now; you are my promised wife, the woman I would have chosen from a thousand as the purest and best, the noblest and bravest that ever lived. Let me see you smile again, and hear you promise never to despair. It is not like you to do so, and I cannot bear it."

I looked up at him with eyes in which tears were still swimming.

"Forgive me, Fred," I said, much ashamed. "I have been odiously weak, more so than I ever was before. Have no fear; I will never let you see tears again, whatever may happen. Now tell me what you want me to do; it is for you to decide."

"God bless you, Muzzi," he murmured, "I will try to justify the confidence you place in me. You must leave Paris as soon as you have put your affairs in the hands of able and intelligent lawyers. I think that Italy will be the best spot for you to go to at present. I will follow you there after a few days, for we must be careful not to give the world food for gossip, and I will live near you in order to be always within reach of your call. We will then be married quietly and travel until the whole thing is forgotten."

"All right," I exclaimed. "*Ils l'ont voulu*, and let us hope for the best. Should there be sorrows and disappointments in store for us, let us be prepared to face them courageously; I cannot imagine what made me

lose my sand like this. I am disgusted with myself;"
and so, indeed, I was.

We left the hotel and drove in my carriage to the Continental, where we arrived in a more cheerful frame of
mind than was to be expected of us under the circumstances. I was deeply moved by the tenderness which
poor Fred displayed. How could I ever do enough for
the dear lad who loved and trusted me so boundlessly,
and yet I felt my present awful predicament deeply.
I did not mind so much abandoning position, distinc-
tions, family ties, but I knew well that, however guilt-
less I might ever remain, slander would surely reach
me now, when it became known that I had left all to
wed him.

I certainly did not lack courage, but I abhorred scandal of every kind, and I was very proud of the undimmed glory of my name. Yet I felt capable of braving
calumny and slander—yes, capable of incurring false
censure if encountered in the path of justice and of what
I considered now as being my duty to Fred. This feeling made sacrifice easy to me, and I felt certain that he
would always be worthy of my devotion and self-forgetfulness; but still I fretted in spite of my resolutions.

During the few days I was forced to tarry in Paris,
while definitely arranging all my affairs, I had occasion to notice that already the serpents of calumny
were at work. Many who had been my devoted friends
until then, although well aware of my presence, forbore
to call upon me. A few days before my departure for
Italy, as my carriage was bearing me through the Avenue
des Champs Élysées, on the way from my lawyer's
house, I passed the equipage of the Russian ambassadress, who for many years had been numbered among
my valued friends. Now the large, melting, black
eyes of the Muscovite great lady met mine with the

calm, cold stare of a stranger, and there was no recognition in their vacant gaze as she slowly drove on. This direct cut smote me to the very soul, for it was the first time in my career of perpetual social triumph that I had been thus treated. A few minutes later Archduchess S., who was staying in Paris at the time, passed me, and the same blow was repeated, but in a much more unmerciful fashion, for there was an insulting smile on the thin lips of the acrid-minded Princess. I knew that she was glad to be able at last to humiliate me— as she thought. I did not allow a single flash of anger from my eyes to betray my feelings; I negligently leaned back on the cushions of my victoria and smiled, a slow, amused smile. As soon, however, as her carriage had disappeared from view, I ordered my coachman to drive home as fast as possible.

Perchance her joy would have been more complete could she have known what a tempest she had raised in my heart. When I reached the hotel I shut myself in my rooms, anxious only to be alone, and to hide from all eyes the ungovernable rage which made me tremble from head to foot.

For the first time I had tasted the ashes of humiliation, and I felt the experience bitterly.

I sat motionless, with my back turned to the light of the windows, my hands clenched, my teeth set tight, struggling with the throes of abdication. I had worn my diadem long and proudly, and, in spite of all available pluck, I suffered terribly. I felt that I, who for years had been the pampered darling of the great world, had just been treated as if I had, after a fashion, lost caste.

Unfortunately for me, my mother and her family at once took sides squarely against me, and I had to fight my battle alone and unsupported. Not one of my former friends, except the Empress and Rudi, whom I entreated not to move in the matter, stood by me in this hour of need, and, of course, Fred could not take up the cudgels on my behalf without compromising me, a thing I dreaded beyond everything else.

The anxiety and pain which I endured were nevertheless telling severely upon me, and I very unwillingly lingered in Paris, kept there by important business. I longed for the calm and tranquillity of the country, and also for the end of this long and wearisome period of tantalizing misery which was becoming unendurable.

One morning, as I was sitting alone looking over some important papers which had been sent me to sign, Fred entered the room. He looked pale and tired, and I saw at a glance that something had gone wrong. But I refrained from questioning him and greeted him as unconcernedly as if I had noticed nothing.

"Have you heard lately from the '*Great Powers*'?" said he, throwing himself on an ottoman near the window. "I am very anxious about all this."

"Yes, I had a letter this morning, but what is the good of worrying? We cannot hurry matters, and so we must try to bear the delay patiently."

Fred sighed wearily, and leaned his head upon his hand. His face grew paler still, and his lips quivered slightly.

"We must try to bear the delay patiently, must we? You do not seem to realize how miserable this very delay makes me, Muzzi."

I passed my hand over his forehead with a soothing gesture, but said nothing.

"Look here," he continued, "I would not have spoken thus had it been possible to keep still, but I have heard to-day that your mother and others have used their influence with the French government to such good purpose that a decree of expulsion has been granted by the authorities, and that you are on the point of being ordered to leave this country, for political reasons!"

I started to my feet, and with a gesture of terrible anger I exclaimed:

"But what is their idea in doing this? Do they suppose that persecution will induce me to yield to their wishes?"

"I do not know," he muttered, wearily; "they seem to love intrigue and persecution beyond all things, and are trying to tire us out; to force us into our last intrenchments. Believe me, they will leave no stone unturned—I can see it now—before they have ruined you forever."

"What is to be done, then? What do you wish me to do?"

He looked at me with grave tenderness, then he said, slowly: "It makes me very unhappy to think of the fate which I have brought upon you."

"Fate? There is no fate except that which we carve for ourselves in this world," I answered, looking at him with fearless eyes. "Don't be downhearted, Fred; this is no time for losing courage; we must act, and act wisely."

"You are right, dearest. I will prove to you that you have done well to trust me after all, and yet I cannot bear to see you suffer all this for my sake."

"I am not suffering. I do not complain. Have enough faith in me, Fred, I beg of you, to believe that no trial, no pain, will ever exhaust my stock of endurance. My affection for you would be of little avail if it did not inspire me at least with common courage."

"Courage like yours is a gift more rare than you think, Muzzi;" and as he spoke he stooped towards me, and, taking my hand, he pressed it tenderly in his own.

"Look here, Fred," I continued, "you must worry no longer about what is past and done. We should now think only of the present and of the future. Every moment is precious. We know where our enemies lie, and how best we can baffle them, for they will not spare us if we let them close around us. I will leave Paris at once; the important thing is to do so without attracting attention, and there lies the difficulty. However, Heaven helps those who help themselves—is it not so?" I added, with a smile, for I noticed how dejected he looked, and resolved to rouse him at any cost from his despondency and to dispel his gloomy thoughts.

When I found myself alone once more that night all the extent of my troubles came back to me. I had promised Fred to think matters over and to tell him in the morning what course I would adopt. Although I was barely twenty-one, I had lived a life which had taught me some harsh lessons, and given me much insight into the failings of humanity in general. I well knew that Fred's position was growing daily more difficult, more painful, and I realized that the time might soon come when his self-control would be tried beyond endurance. He was a man of high principles, but he was also a man of warmer feelings and tenderer heart than most, and I was sincerely and deeply sorry for him. Far into the night I sat in my dressing-room, reclining in the cosey depths of a large arm-chair, thinking despondently of the troubled seas I was navigating, and of Fred's sorrow and precarious state of health. Great tears gathered in my eyes, but I angrily brushed them off, for I needed strength and could not afford to give way.

When the light of dawn began to glimmer through the curtains of my room, I rose from my chair with a sigh, and, walking towards the window, threw it open, in order to cool my hot face in the fresh morning breeze. My struggle was ended, my mind was made up, and I felt as if that long night's vigil had worked a great change in me.

When Fred appeared a few hours later I greeted him with the following words, spoken cheerily:

"Fred, I have thought over what is best for us to do, and I think that I have at last come to a wise decision."

"Where do you propose to go?" he asked.

"To Italy, as I have intended all along, but I shall start at once, to-day; and I am, what is more, going to marry you, my dear, without any further hesitation. I have written to the Empress, advising her of my final decision. Now let worse come to worst. As your wife, at any rate, I will be an English subject, and will escape the jurisdiction of all other governments. I should have thought of this sooner. For your sake I tried to save as much of the past as I could, and thought that a little diplomacy would achieve this end; but enough of this nonsense. I am in the mood to fight, and fight I will—*tant pis pour les écrasés!* Patience is not my forte; so *avanti*, and may God be with us! Let the responsibility of the future rest on the heads of those who have willed it so."

While I spoke he had raised his head, and was now looking at me with an adoration passing all words. Silently he threw his arms around me, and, drawing my face close to his, for the first time he pressed his lips to mine in a long kiss.

*   *   *   *   *   *   *

The sun was shining brightly on the summit of the Sabine Mountains, and shedding its golden light over the undulating plains of the Campagna. Far away, near the horizon, there was a glancing line that showed where the sea was beating on the sands near Ostia, while the cross of St. Peter's, clearly defined in the distance against the azure of the sky, rose proudly above immortal Rome.

The spring had come, and both earth and sky were wrapped in the glory of this season of youth and of love.

In the stately, melancholy rooms of a spacious villa which stood on a rising slope outside the gates of Rome, Fred and I were arranging pictures, tapestries, statues, old bronzes, and old brocades, which lay in a picturesque and artistic litter on the tessellated floor. Outside in the shady gardens birds warbled their morning song among the camellias, and gayly hued butterflies hovered over the flower-filled lawns.

This was the place which we had rented soon after our arrival in the City of the Popes, and we spent many hours of each day under the palm and ilex trees in the lonely, balmy gardens. The abode was well chosen, and delighted me with its moss-grown terraces, where ivy flourished, its walls of flowering rose-trees, and its dusky, bronze-hued masses of cedar and magnolia. Here at last I felt a perfect sense of repose, of peace, and of security. I had left far behind me the buzz and noise of the world, and I now enjoyed in all its fulness a complete rest of body and soul which I had never known till then.

Our work completed, we went out into the cool April air and sat on the marble steps of the terrace. We were happy in spite of the knowledge that everybody blamed us, were ready to tear us to pieces and to crush us beneath their virtuous indignation. Little did we care about society's censure, so long as we knew in our hearts how undeserved that censure was. My second marriage had created an enormous sensation. None knew whither we had gone to spend our honeymoon, and the mystery which surrounded my disappearance from social circles added, no doubt, great piquancy to the numerous stories told about me under the shelter of jewelled fans, in aristocratic salons, or in smoking-rooms after the ladies had retired.

"I wonder sometimes," Fred said to me, "that I could have ever lived without you. My past existence seems to me like an utter blank." Sitting at my feet on the terrace, he kissed my hands with a lover's first ardor.

The only stranger who ever came to the villa was a dear old priest who lived near by, a remarkable man, much beloved by all who knew him. He became greatly attached to us, and, although a simple-hearted person, he proved a great acquisition to such exiles as we were, in our new, strange home.

The poor people of the neighborhood asked no questions and showed no undue curiosity, and we really enjoyed our isolation and solitude. All the stir and blaze and noise in which we had dwelt for years were gone as though they had never existed. A great and solemn silence was always around us; we heard nothing excepting the murmur of the breeze in the trees, the distant shouts of the vine-growers, or the soft, silvery notes of the nightingales in the dusky park. Never had we felt so perfectly free. We went out together in all weathers — when gray floods of rain drifted noiselessly over the Campagna, and when the wind rose in its wrath and raised columns of shimmering dust about us. We often returned home drenched to the skin, but it never seemed to hurt us. My sole anxiety was lest Fred should tire of this quiet, uneventful life.

"Tell me, dear," I said one day to him, "are you certain that you regret nothing?"

He looked at me. We were walking in a long, shadowy *allée*. It was a beautiful day; the air was warm and fragrant, and it gave a color to his cheeks which made him look unusually well.

"Regret?" he exclaimed, impatiently. "Why will you always say that? How can I regret anything when I am near you? Do you not see that my love for you is growing every day more intense and more passionate?"

I slipped my hand through his arm and looked in his eyes, my face uplifted to his.

No, he certainly did not look as if he regretted any-thing. Men are strange animals, very whole-souled sometimes, and very true.

And now I will stop for a while. I have tried my reader's patience sorely, no doubt, by once more indulging in the luxury of setting down on paper a true state-ment of facts, with all their lights and shadows, their painful and their fewer happy sides. There is more to tell, for these facts took place long ago, and I fear that I am becoming a hardened offender, and thus I close now; but it is with a suspicion that I shall yield later to the temptation of recounting, perchance in the same familiar way, what further befell us.

FINIS

www.ingramcontent.com/pod-product-compliance
Lightning Source LLC
Chambersburg PA
CBHW020835030726
47496CB00001B/242